ALBERT

CH01424675

BY

FRED CRAMPTON

Copyright © 2007 Frederick A. Crampton

SECOND EDITION

First Published 2009

ISBN: 978-1-909424-20-3

All rights reserved.
No part of this publication may be reproduced,
stored in a retrieval system, or transmitted in any form or by
any means without the prior written permission of both the
copyright owner and the publisher, nor be otherwise
circulated in any form of binding or cover other than that in
which it is published and without a similar condition being
imposed on the subsequent purchaser.

Printed and bound in Great Britain by;

www.direct-pod.com

ALBERT'S ARK

Contents

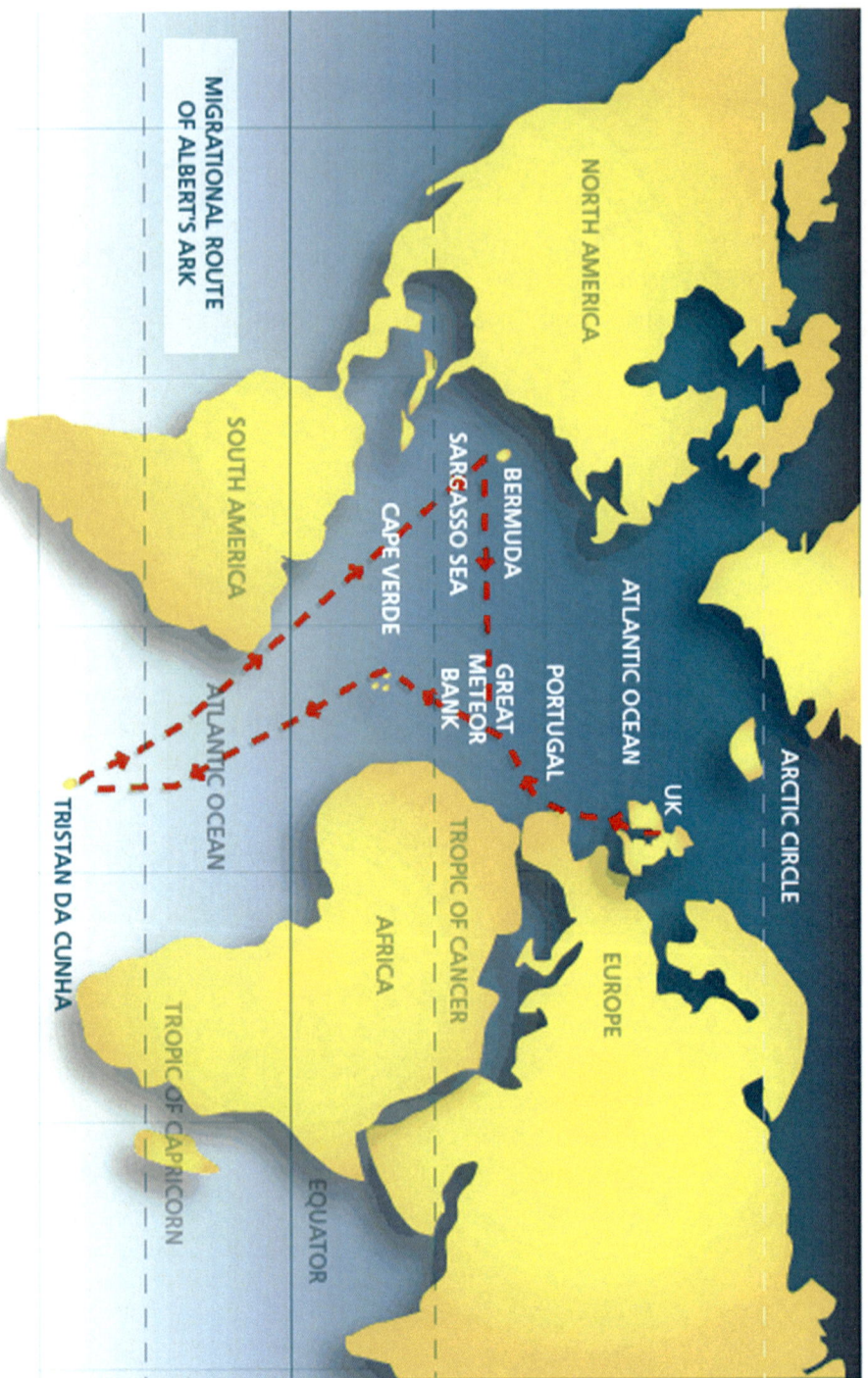

MIGRATIONAL ROUTE
OF ALBERT'S ARK

NORTH AMERICA

SOUTH AMERICA

BERMUDA

SARGASSO SEA

CAPE VERDE

GREAT
METEOR
BANK

ATLANTIC OCEAN

PORTUGAL

UK

ARCTIC CIRCLE

ATLANTIC OCEAN

TROPIC OF CANCER

AFRICA

EUROPE

TRISTAN DA CUNHA

TROPIC OF CAPRICORN

EQUATOR

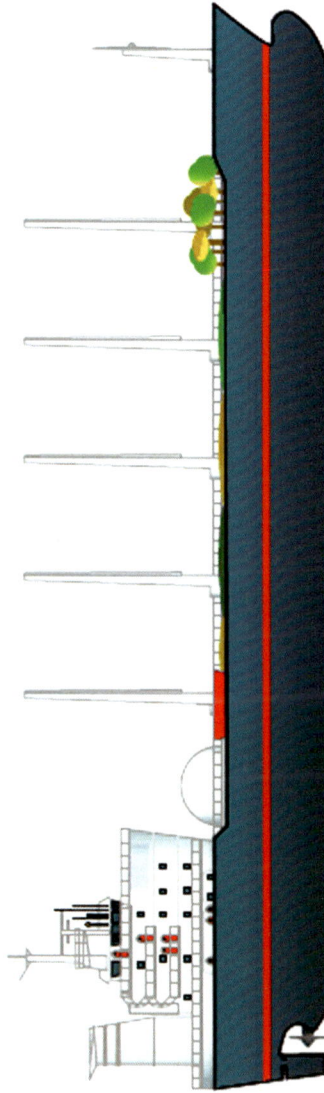

ALBERT'S ARK

LIVING QUARTERS

BIODOME | DESALINATION PLANT

FIELDS AND CROPS | MECHANICAL SAILS

ORCHARD | HERB AND VEGETABLE GARDENS

WIND TURBINE

SOIL STRATA ONBOARD

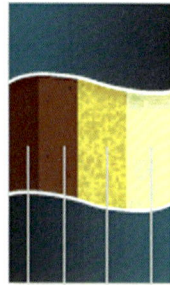

TOPSOIL

SUBSOIL

SAND MIX

SANDSTONE

1. IN THE BEGINNING

Albert strolled through the lanes of his picturesque village on a balmy, sunny late summer evening. While he meandered along the path, for a rare moment, he felt settled and content, very at home in his little part of the world. He shut out everything beyond it. He had supped his pint in the local pub and was now on his way to pick up a meal from Sonny Patel's takeaway in the village centre. It was not too far, only half a mile and he could soon smell and taste the herbs and spices of his favourite dish, which he was looking forward to collecting and taking back home to enjoy with Amy. She would be warming the plates, preparing a salad and getting the smooth, cold *Cobra* beer from the fridge; a perfect Friday night.

He was so glad he did not have to deal with the aggro, queuing up with the riff raff in the takeaways in town. Turning the corner he could see the front of Patel's ahead. His mood changed as he arrived; the happiness and peace he felt suddenly disappeared. He saw the backs of three men in current thug's uniform: beanies, baggy jeans and dark quilted shirts. They were shouting abuse at the staff, threatening and menacing customers with muscle and aggression, standing over them, causing aggravation. Albert waited outside and watched, weighing up the situation. Then he saw one of them pull a knife and threaten Sonny Patel, demanding money.
'NOW!' the heavy growled loudly through his teeth at Mr Patel, thumping his clenched fists hard onto the counter which separated them.

Moving slowly forward Albert walked up to the door quietly and then stormed in.
'Come here you little bastard and take *my* money!' he raged. The startled yobs turned to look at the intruder, surprised to see a middle aged man stood in the doorway challenging them. They laughed; in their eyes, he was past it and no match for one of them, let alone three! The ringleader lurched towards Albert wielding the knife, egged on by his accomplices' jeering and swearing. He thrust forwards and Albert grabbed his wrist, turning the blade away, forcing his arm behind his back. The stench of stale alcohol made Albert hold his breath. As the knife dropped clear, he pushed the youth's face into the window. The plate glass did not break but shuddered with the impact of his weight. A sickly, painful thud and crunch, then blood splattered in several directions across the crystal surface. The few remaining seated customers panicked and scrambled out of the way.

1

Jeers from the other two had stopped suddenly; they looked at each other and then at Albert, waiting for their brain cells to operate. Eventually, something must have clicked in the larger of the two: he was on a mission, lunging head on towards Albert. Albert looked straight into a pair of small, black dot pupils in sunken, drug glazed eyes as he grabbed his attacker's shirt with both hands and brought him down by rolling backwards to the floor, using the thrust of the thug's body and his own feet to flip him over his head. This sent him careering through the air to land on top of his mate, who was still sat on the floor by the window groaning, nursing his smashed face. The third lad scuttled to escape through the door, jostling together with the disappearing customers.

'Have you got any cable ties or string Mr Patel? Let's stop these two from going anywhere until the police get here.'

'Yes I have Albert, I will get them. Wait there,' he replied as he headed into the kitchen.

When he returned he handed Albert some rope. Kicking the last victim in the groin, encouraging him to lay face down, Albert tied his hands behind his back. The other was still holding his bloody nose and he quickly bound him too. Seeing the knife and thinking it was sloppy to leave it there, Albert kicked it across the terracotta floor where Mr Patel bent down to pick it up.

'No!' shouted Albert. 'Leave it where it is; let the police deal with it. Two out of three's not bad,' he congratulated himself, dusting his hands down as if to brush away contact with the ruffians from his palms.

'Thank you so much. My wife has called the police, and they will be here in one hour.'

'One hour; where are they coming from Mars?' Albert added, annoyed. 'And look, all the customers have deserted us: our witnesses. Typical!'

Albert composed himself and approached the counter.

'Can I pick up my food order now please?'

'Yes certainly; thank you Mr Albert sir. It is on the house'

As Albert walked home he churned over the evening's events in his mind and thought this was the last straw. Violence had come to his own village, his haven: one last place of calm and tranquillity! After all the government promises, things were no better than ten years ago, in fact worse. Gun and knife culture, drink and drug related crime was rife. Politicians were advised by advisers who have their own advisers and they still can't get it right! Albert was growing more agitated with each step as he thought about his pet frustration: the New Europe systems of education, police, health and social welfare organised by Brussels Eurocrats at their all expense paid lavish banquets, lunches and dinners.

'What a load of tossers!' he muttered as he touched the entry pad to let him indoors.

*****

In September 2014, Albert Crowther was heading for his mid fifties, and too rapidly in his opinion. He still had the mind of a man of thirty. He was six foot tall and had always been physically fit. His face was a cheesy grin on the rare occasions he managed to smile, but he did have a broad, deep sense of humour. This man was a walking library of life history, heaped with knowledge and experience. He kept his hair short to hide his ageing. Once a bright ginger biscuit colour, it had faded to sandy, with white at the sides, thin on top and he was very conscious of it. He was defiantly not ready to accept old age yet.

The son of a farmer from the Midlands and the youngest of six boys, he was the last one to flee the nest after he lost his mother to cancer. He went off, leaving his father on his own, never to see him again and this bugged his conscience throughout the rest of his life. As Albert drifted through his early years, he often wondered why his older brothers had left their parents so soon to seek out their fortunes at such an early age, only rarely returning to the household, to be a temporary family unit. What had gone wrong? Was he too young to understand at the time? Perhaps that was so and he had just missed all the family politics; memory is a strange thing.

In Albert's youth, his father taught him how to work the land to produce good quality food by keeping the soil fertile with organic matter, and the benefits of crop rotation. Although he did not realise at the time, this understanding would be of significant use to him later in his life.

At sixteen, he went to live with one of his brothers in the south of England. He found a job as a trainee mechanic, which he enjoyed, and took to it as second nature, becoming confident in the workings of many different types of machinery. Then his brother moved on, leaving him behind at just seventeen, a little bemused and lonely, but then he began to realise that he wasn't much different than anybody else that he knew.

All he thought he would have to do was work hard, meet the right girl, settle down, make a family that stayed together to create a unit that would grow from his and his wife's children, to grandchildren and so forth. He wanted a solid, loving family that met on regular occasions, and the job would be done. Simple! This was his new aim in life and he got on with it, but he didn't find the right girl to settle down with straight away.

Within two years, he started to become bored and wanted to see more of the world. He got a job as a labourer for a short period, travelling to contracts throughout the UK for a large Civil Engineering company. This work soon dried up and he decided to apply to Her Majesty's Forces. He passed the physical and admission tests and joined the Royal Marines. This took him all over the world to many diverse situations. Some were very hostile, and he changed from an eighteen year old novice to a professional soldier.

He met Amy when he was twenty five. She was just nineteen years old, from Winchester, and they soon married. Despite several attempts at IVF treatment, they never had children. They continued to try without medical intervention with hopeful hearts, but nothing came of their efforts. Albert's long absences on tours of duty didn't help and Amy sometimes wondered if the worry factor played a part in their failure to conceive.

At the age of twenty nine, he found himself on active service in Kuwait and Iraq during the conflict in the early ninety's. Sergeant Albert Crowther and his squad had arrived at Dhahran airport in Saudi Arabia just as the first gulf war kicked off. They were billeted at the airport where the aircraft transport C130 Hercules had delivered them with their specialist equipment. They settled for the night, ready for the next day's move nearer to the operation area. At shortly after 0300 hours, they were jumping from their makeshift beds as a huge explosion, less than three hundred metres away, shook the ground with its shockwaves. The first scud missile had made its impact, and landed very close to Albert and his squad. They were quickly outside to see the extent of the damage and if there were any causalities. The destruction was minor; it hit a clear area just making a small crater.

Later that day, they prepared to move towards Kuwait. Albert's squad was made up of hardened men with extensive active combat service under their belts. Their experiences included long stints in Northern Ireland to the many skirmishes in Africa. After what seemed like endless, tense waiting about, the order was given to move forward through Kuwait to the Iraqi border by the Euphrates, from where they made raids deeper into Iraq using assault boats, moving up the river to areas where they did as much damage as possible, and captured Iraqi Officers, bringing them back for questioning. They were very successful in these abductions and were party to the interrogations that were crude but effective. Albert saw it as a necessary job to be done, as screams from the prisoners echoed around the cell before the information was extracted. He was emotionless, his conscience unaffected by the torture. The war was short and over in a few months, when the politicians decided to stop short of conquering the country and pull out of Iraq once Kuwait was liberated, leaving Saddam, the Iraqi dictator, to stand and fight another day.

Returning home to Amy, his doting wife, he promised to consider leaving the service after his next tour of duty. She pleaded with him to try home life instead. His next home visit came all too quickly and he had to face the same pleas again, so he said he would apply to end his time as a proud Royal Marine with honours for bravery under fire from the enemy and friendly fire.

At thirty one, he was pensioned off from the Royal Marines at the rank of Staff Sergeant and sent on a retraining programme to prepare him for Civvy Street. On finishing the course, he applied for many jobs but they all seemed very boring and he looked at security posts, which was quite a common option for ex-military personnel who had combat experience. Amy thought he had something fairly domestic in mind, like a night watchman or a bank cash guard. His problem was to explain to her why he was considering going to Angola to give advice on government security. The money was very attractive and his time away was half that of when he was in the Marines. Albert was persistently persuasive, so eventually he won the day. What he did not disclose to Amy was that it wasn't just advice he was giving, but he would be a paid mercenary, operating on the northern border with the Congo, quelling political unrest. He made several trips and then he and his very close friend, Chopsy Finnon, fell into an ambush. It was obvious to Albert that information of exactly where they would be had leaked out and the result was the loss of Chopsy. He never forgave his employers for what happened and finishing his contract, did not ask to renew it.

He realised he had made a mistake in doing what he did for adventure. It gave him a buzz when the action made his adrenaline rise, making him feel like some fictitious cult hero, going to battle and not knowing the real reason why. He was using his professional, military skills to kill and destroy the opposition, and if it had been the opposition paying him, he would still be doing the same, irregardless of moral or ethical issues. It wasn't until he lost Chopsy that he thought that it was time to stop, before his own luck ran out.

So he gave up his security work, not telling Amy the real reason why, other than he would like a change and give Civvy Street a try. He went back to his old trade of engineering and, after a refresher course, applied for work in the construction industry. He had no problem getting employment locally, as there was a shortage of skilled people throughout the country. Initially, he accepted the new way of life, settling down to, as Amy put it, '*a normal married life*'. They bought a house in the idyllic Hampshire village of Kingsbourne Tarrant, which had half an acre of land. Albert soon knocked it into shape, converting the land around it from an overgrown field to a beautiful, fully cultivated garden. As a joint effort, they produced an abundance of fruit and vegetables, using the knowledge and skills Albert's father had taught him, all those years ago. They also enjoyed superb homemade wine and preserves. He devised mechanical irrigation systems and heated the greenhouses using solar and wind turbine energy. He loved creating things and was very environmentally conscious. This continued for several comfortable years. Albert became a popular character in the local community, which revolved around the Coach and Horses, bridge nights in the village hall and the Patels' local post office, open all hours shop and adjoining curry house for Albert's favourite chicken tikka masala.

But Albert felt that real life was passing him by and was forever criticizing the European and world political arena. Over a period of time, he became increasingly disgruntled with things that were happening in the UK, the New Europe, and with the USA wanting international domination. He started to realise what was going on in the world. He felt very angry that government leaders were making themselves extremely rich, at the cost of the environment and ordinary people. While he was being very conscious about environmental problems and working hard, like millions of others doing their best, people were being brainwashed by the media, who were indirectly controlled by the government of the day. Some politicians were making obscene amounts of money whilst in office and continued to expand their coffers when out of office, especially if they had connections to the mineral extraction, arms and construction industries. Weapons were being sold to countries which had valuable assets, either raw materials to be exploited, or buildings and infrastructure. The latter was often destroyed by the arms sold to their neighbours by profiteers and then rebuilt by the international construction magnates, also making vast profits from them. And all this was going on amidst widespread death and misery for those unfortunates in the way. Albert was conscious of his earlier naivety and of his own contribution to the acts that were carried out under the cloak of farcical government foreign policies. He was sick and tired of this New Europe that taxed everyone to the hilt on everything they earned and spent, no matter who was in power. The masses had no way out of this vicious circle. The oil fields were now drying up and the lives and money that had been spent to control them for power seemed a futile waste.

After his experience at Sonny Patel's that night, Albert decided he must do something about his world. He'd had enough of what he called 'those political and business fat cat crooked bastards'; the crime and violence that was filtering into everyone's lives and the loss of individual freedom. He had been milling over an idea one day while enjoying his teatime few pints of bitter. That was his thinking time. But he would not be able to change the situation on his own.

His vision was a floating ecological self-sufficient and self-propelled island: a modern day Ark! He gradually thought it through and, after several more planning sessions in his local pub, he went home and put his ideas on paper. He knew that, because there was an abundance of obsolete oil tankers, it should be feasible to obtain and convert one of these massive ships into a floating island, his ecological dream. But how could this be financed? It would take a good few million euros. Undaunted, he decided to advertise his idea on the internet, just to test it out, to see if it would generate any interest. He set the website in the name *Letsgetoffthisplanet.me.uk* and was thrilled with the result. Also other research which revealed the large number of multi-millionaires in France and the UK amazed him; surely one of them would fund and support his project?

Albert put forward the idea to Amy, showing her the overwhelming response to his website. Although slightly sceptical, she went along with the next stage, which was to advertise for a serious financier and the various types of inhabitants required and Albert enthusiastically set about compiling pages of notes for the advert.

2. THE ADVERT

Albert had to create an advert that would attract the right kind of people: those who wanted to be isolated from rest of the world; have no financial, political or religious pressures; and be part of a community working together both for themselves and each other. This would be on a floating, ecological, self-sufficient and self propelled, converted oil tanker, with the cargo holds filled with rock, sand and soil to represent the earth's strata. It could then be used like a small farm growing the necessary produce, and rearing animals to live on. Albert thought it sounded idealistic yet feasible. He did not want to alert the authorities to his plans so he omitted direct references to the oil tanker.

This was the basic outline of his idea in an internet advert, which detailed the categories of people required to make the project work. It read:

WOULD YOU LIKE TO BE PART OF AN ECOLOGICAL PROJECT ON AN ISLAND GROWING ORGANIC PRODUCE?
If you fit into the categories listed below and want to live the good life, then reply by email, giving your full CV and present situation to this web site address.
THIS ECOLOGICAL PROJECT REQUIRES:
One Multimillionaire (Self made) and Opposite sex Partner.
One Mechanical Engineer (Genius), with opposite sex Partner and Young Family.
One Qualified Practitioner in Herbal Healing Remedies, Being Handy with a Scalpel would be an Advantage, with Opposite sex Partner and Young Family.
One Maritime Navigator with Large Ocean Going Vessel Experience with Opposite sex Partner and Young Family.
One Agricultural and Horticultural Operative with hands on Experience in Farming with Opposite sex Partner and Young Family.
One Merchant Seaman with General Ship Handling Experience With Opposite sex partner and Young Family.

The advert went on the internet with Albert very worried about the so called 'political correctness' and bias of the wording. He needed people to be heterosexual to maximise breeding the next generation. And he thought it necessary to exclude some groups that may cause problems. This was based on certain categories that had caused him trouble in the past, especially bank managers, insurance salespeople etc. He also had a real dislike for politicians and those with extreme religious beliefs so he added in at the foot the following:

PEOPLE THAT NEED NOT APPLY
Bank Managers, Tax or VAT inspectors.
Criminals, Convicted or Not,
Rapists or Potential Rapists and any other Type of Sex Offenders.
Game Show Hosts and Gays or Potential Gays.
Insurance Sales Persons, Male or Female.
Perverts, Politicians or any body with Extreme Religious Beliefs
YOU WILL BE SCRUTANISED
Interviews will be held in the UK. Once selected for this once in a life time opportunity, a full and total commitment will be required.

The response to the advert was huge. The problem that Albert had now was to sift through the replies and pick the ones he thought were genuine and arrange the interviews. It wasn't until Amy had seen the response and started to read through the replies, that she thought perhaps Albert wasn't so mad after all. So she decided to help him pick and choose the possibilities. Out of the several hundred that had replied, they whittled it down to twenty people that fitted the criteria. Albert replied to each one and arranged to interview them over four days. He hired his local village hall for the meeting place, setting a time for each one individually, not wanting them to congregate together prior to, or after the interviews.

The priority was to select and get the one hundred percent commitment of a benefactor. Without this, the project would be dead in the water. Out of the three people that were interviewed for this post, there was only one who produced his bank statement and his investment accounts that showed he had the cash, and it was available. He was the right age and guaranteed that if he was selected, he would have a female partner to accompany him. Because he would not divulge any information about his partner, Albert thought she may be a celebrity or even royalty, you never know these days with the high flyers of the capital cities, they all socialise together. Albert respected his keeping her identity secret, just simply out of respect for the cash he had available.

The applicant's name was Miles Overstrand and he managed casinos and other gambling houses for a large international concern. He said he had made his money at the gambling tables himself and invested his winnings as the statements he produced showed. He had been working the casinos for several years and now had more money than he ever imagined and just wanted to settle down to a quiet and peaceful life and think about a family. He insisted he was looking forward to the adventure side of the project though. Miles was aged thirty five, about five feet ten, of medium build with a good-living paunch. Very smartly turned out, he appeared in a standard pin-striped suit and he wore Oxford brogues and looked a typical man from the city. To Albert he seemed very boring and he could not imagine him digging up potatoes or helping mucking out the pigs, but you never know, even if he could not lend himself to do that sort of work, there would be plenty of other tasks to do onboard. Miles came across as mild mannered and very well spoken, as one would expect of a high flyer.

Amy insisted on sitting in on the interviews, which turned out to be very helpful when it came to choosing the right people. She was able to sense when people were false and she made notes on the characters. She had always enjoyed people watching. Whenever she sat in a public place for example a pub, a restaurant, at a bus stop or even a doctors' surgery, normally with Albert or her mother, she would make discreet critical comments. In Miles' case she found him genuine enough but something was amiss. Albert overruled, saying she was being too pernickety, he was obviously influenced by the bank statements. Amy agreed that out of the three potential benefactors he was the best, but was slightly concerned because he perspired so much during the interview. Amy had always had faith in her husband because he was one of life's survivors, so she went along with Albert's wishes and they decided that Miles would be the chosen one to spend his money.

Miles was notified by letter from Albert saying it had been a very difficult choice, because of the amount of people wanting 'to get off the planet', so to say. Miles was relieved and delighted thank Christ for that, now we have a target to aim for to get out of this mess, he thought to himself. He telephoned Albert to thank him and wanted to have the details of an account to transfer one million euros there and then, as goodwill. Amy was concerned about this.

'It's too good to be true! There must be something wrong'.

'No. He's just like you and me, so fed up with the shit we have to put up with to survive in the injustice of living today,' explained Albert.

So Albert had his way and Miles Overstrand it was. He accepted the money into his account. He knew that the authorities could track this transaction immediately and be knocking on his door, wanting to know all the details. Sure enough, this happened within a few days. The Customs and Excise were hounding him. Albert explained that his colleague had forwarded the money for Albert to purchase a sailing vessel, because they wanted to take to the sea. This he hoped would stall them enough he thought, until they were far away at sea, not wanting to explain to them what was going on.

Amy became more positive and enthusiastic. She could see it was probably the best option she had to be close to Albert for the rest of their lives. Albert immediately put their house on the market and it was sold within a few weeks. He and Amy paid the proceeds, together with his Armed Forces pension into a trust fund that could only be touched if he returned within twenty five years. After that, the total sum would go to a children's charity. They both took the plunge and decided to take up the offer and stay with Amy's mother, Albert knew this would be a risk for him, but then he weighed up the pros and cons. He had been under enemy fire before, although not as heavy as the prospect of this. Now that the funds were in position, Albert was keen to move on to the other candidates.

The next person selected to be interviewed was German, Gunter Keller, age thirty five from Dortmund. Amy had sympathy with him, from reading his CV, and persuaded Albert to give him a chance. He was at least six feet two, slim-built with a wiry physique. He had long arms with huge hands dangling on the ends like shovels, his sharp facial features, long blond hair swept back over his rectangular head and curled up at the base of his neck. With a body built like that, you would think he was a man from Connemara, a big strong Paddy: hardworking, proud and the salt of the earth, Albert thought. He was positive he had some Irish in him; certainly a man who stood out in a crowd.

Gunter applied for the navigator's post having qualified in this field at one time. His CV showed that he had been out of the profession for a couple of years, due to a navigational error he made whilst working for a very well known North Sea Ferry company. During one of the many repetitive crossings under his control, the ferry just happened to hit an oil tanker!

Albert thought, at least now he knows what one looks like but then with not so many oil tankers about and hardly any today in the Atlantic Ocean, hopefully we should be reasonably safe in our new home. The damage Gunter caused was embarrassing to the ferry company and expensive for the insurance underwriters. He was obviously fired and found it impossible to find a job in the only profession that he knew. Gunter said that he could retrain and try something else, but he loved the sea so much and the ferry crossings meant he was home with his family regularly. The press had persecuted him and given him the knick name 'Gunter the Shunter' that went with him whatever he tried to do.

'My wife is called Greta,' Gunter continued. 'She is very supportive, especially under the circumstances we find ourselves in. She is an infant schoolteacher, for up to six year olds. We have a daughter, three year old Stella. I am very sorry she could not come here today. She is working and has to collect Stella from kindergarten. I have a family photo of us here, please take a look... We have discussed the project in great depth, including Stella's future and would like to increase the size of our family. It would be perfect for us and we would certainly be reliable and give full commitment.' Albert was convinced.

Another successful interviewee was Frederick Preswick, thirty years old from Hull. ('Somebody has to come from there!' Albert said to Amy when they saw his CV) He told them he was the son of a merchant seaman, he thought, because that is what his mother told him. Five feet six short, medium build and quite muscular, he was totally bald via a regular shave to cover up his partial baldness. Albert wanted to know about the breakdown of his earlier marriage.

'I first got married at the age of eighteen. It didn't last long. While I was away at sea, my wife preferred to be with other male company, I found this out the usual way, from my best mate. I'd finally had enough and divorced her at twenty one, when I joined The Royal Navy. I have a knick-name, *Ched*, which I answer to, as I've been called it for so long.

'How did that come about?' Albert asked. Frederick replied that from when he was in his nappy days he stunk like mouldy *Cheddar* cheese. This was shortened to 'Ched'.

From leaving school and then to college to the present day, he had been working in the shipping industry: fishing in trawlers; a merchant seaman; a short period in the Royal Navy (before the 'Royal' was dropped and changed to 'Euro'). Then he decided he wanted to be out of the forces when he met Millie, who is now his wife. They have a two year old daughter called Vicky.

'My present occupation of working as a shipyard welder is very boring. Millie has recently completed three years at Agricultural College near York and loves working on farms, especially with animals.'

'That is interesting.' Albert replied. 'You both have obviously discussed this project and I think Millie might be of great value in the agricultural aspect of things. When can we meet her?'

'She is here wandering around the village and quite possibly in somebody's farmyard. If you like I'll call her on her mobile to come here now?'

'That would be a good idea. Don't you think so Amy?'

'Yes, of course.'

Ched left the building to make the call to Millie who arrived about ten minutes later, slightly out of breath. She had been running and was excited about being interviewed. Millie apologised for not having prepared a CV, but she did have her certificate from the agricultural college in her handbag, which showed the areas of farming she was qualified in. When Albert read it, he realised she should be well able to run all aspects of an eight acre smallholding floating about on the Atlantic. Millie was twenty eight, an attractive, slim woman of medium height. Her face was slightly weathered from working out in the elements all the time and she obviously had not looked after her skin. Her medium length hair was tied back in a pony tail and when she smiled it lit up her face with warmth. She apologised again, for her appearance and for not being dressed for the occasion.

'It's better because we can see the real you,' Albert answered.

Amy wanted to ask Millie about her child.

'Excuse me Albert... Now, Millie, how do you think your daughter will cope being brought up in a community that has cut itself off from the rest of the world?'

'I assume and would expect, that there will be other families with small children in the same circumstances and that the project would have qualified child carers with a nursery and school, allowing parents to do their daily tasks knowing that their children are totally safe and well cared for'.

'That didn't quite answer my question,' Amy replied, 'but you are right in your assumption. The children will be well catered for. What I meant was, your daughter is only two years old, and her character is still developing. Is Vicky strong enough to cope with the upheaval?'

'Yes', replied Millie, 'I'm sure she will cope.' Albert thanked them both for attending the interview and shook their hands warmly.

'We will be in touch with you as soon as all the interviews have been completed, with an answer one way or the other.'

Next on the selection list was the herbalist, Montgomery Percy Ackroyd. Albert greeted him.

'That's a good Yorkshire name', and then he introduced him to Amy. Born in Leeds, Monty, as he said he preferred being called, was the son of a wealthy bed manufacturer. Most of his early education was in private schools and he managed to get a degree in Chemistry at university, but had lost his documents. After that, he took an interest in herbalism which he said became his passion in life, and he never looked back. Albert thought to himself that by the look of him: probably more time on his back looking up than not looking back! He said he had been practising herbal healing for about thirteen years and had been growing and processing cannabis for pain relief for a friend who had MS (multiple sclerosis). But he was fed up with the police raiding his flat and just wanted to be free to use his skills as he pleased.

Monty was thirty five years old, but to look at him he could be fifty five. An ex eco-warrior from Todmordon in West Yorkshire, *'The Valley of the Weed'*, he said he was a campaigner around the year 2000 to *'Free the Weed'*. He looked as if he could do with a good hot dinner; he was just a bag of bones without an ounce of fat on his body. If he stood up straight he would be six feet tall. He had been a hippy from his university days and had no interest in changing for anyone. His long grey straggling hair was partly in a pony tail and the sides hung down plaited with coloured beads around his ears. When he entered the room he removed his brown leather trilby type hat which revealed a bald crown. It was difficult to describe his features, other than big baggy eyes and sagging skin on his face, like well used leather. At a first impression, Albert thought he'd write him off, but the way Monty introduced himself with his Etonian style speech and manners of a gentleman, he impressed both Amy and Albert.

15

Amy had done some research on herbal medicines and asked him questions on the sort of herbs he would use for various ailments, just as a quick test.

'What would you use for pain such as toothache?'

'Clove - that's *Syzygium aromaticum*, or Red Pepper - *Capsicum*, various species,' he quickly replied.

'What about morning sickness?'

'Ginger tea is probably the best remedy.'

Amy said she was impressed by his answers and asked one last question.

'How would you treat a burn?

'*Aloe Vera*; it has been used since ancient times for first and second degree burns and other wounds.' Then Albert joined in.

'Would you be able to provide a comprehensive list of herbs and plants that would grow on a floating smallholding in Mediterranean temperatures all year round if you were selected?' Monty gave a positive 'yes'.

'There is one other question. Can you tell us about your partner?' Albert asked.

'Oh, err, I have a... err, a number to choose from.' His reply was unsteady, 'I haven't decided on which one yet.'

'Well,' said Albert, 'she will need to be fit and healthy, and be able to have children, so you will need proof of this from a medical practitioner, stamped and signed and it will be followed up to check its authenticity.' After several more questions and answers on both sides, Albert thanked him for attending the interview.

'We will be in touch and inform you of our decision, one way or the other.' Monty left.

'What do you think Amy? With your nursing experience, could you work with him?'

'Yes. I think so; should be very interesting but he has a strange odour.

After a string of several unsuitable candidates, Amy and Albert met Glaswegian, Magnus James McNulty aged thirty nine; married with a teenage daughter. Magnus had a degree in mechanical engineering and renewable energy, which had made it easy for Albert to put him on the list. Since leaving Glasgow University, he had worked for various companies as Magnus put it, that just dabbled in renewable energy.

'Whichever company I worked for, there was never a big enough budget to develop alternative energy systems. The governments of the day promise lots to keep in power, but once in, there is always something else to spend the money on.' Magnus then explained to Albert some of the systems he

16

could engineer for propulsion of the ship. He described his ideas to supply the ship with electricity, without burning fossil fuels: from wind and wave power; photosynthesis; solar collector cells and a methane gas collector from the animal and vegetable waste. Albert was impressed with his technical knowledge and eco-practicability. Plus he had such enthusiasm. Magnus was obviously a very frustrated man who had a mission to release his knowledge into something worthwhile and on seeing this project could not wait to be part of it.

'What about your family?' Albert asked. 'It may seem ideal for you, but how will they take the isolation from the outside world?'
The reply was unexpected.
'It will be a total shock! At the moment I'm frightened to let my daughter, Melanie, out of the house at any time of the day or night even to go to the shop for a message. Oh, sorry, I mean 'to run an errand', in English. The drug culture is everywhere, even in the school she attends. Kids are expelled on a regular basis for involvement in drugs. I just want to be in a place where I can expect a reasonable quality of life for Melanie and, ma hen....'
'Oh. Do you keep chickens?' Amy interrupted. Albert cut in again.
'Amy, it's a colloquial expression. You're talking about your wife aren't you Magnus?'
'I'll be honest with yea, she hasn't a clue what's going on. Patricia's a couch potato. All she does all day long is watch daytime and night-time TV and stuffs herself with chocolates and crisps, guzzling cheap lager while she's watching these mindless programmes. No wonder Scotland has the highest rate of mortality in alcoholism and obesity! I want to be able to take my family away from this terrible situation. If I don't do something soon, anything could kill them at an early age.' There was a silence from Albert and Amy. They were momentarily dumbstruck. Albert, normally unmoved by emotions, actually felt for him. He had to shrug these feelings off and try to remain impartial.
'Right Magnus, thank you for attending this interview. We will confirm to you whether you have been successful or not when our interviews are complete.'

Magnus left, thinking he had blown it, because he had explained about his wife.

'They probably think that she would want to lie on deck next to a swimming pool all day long and be fed with a fish supper every time she commanded, well at least I tried for them,' he muttered to himself as he went away feeling he'd failed.

After much deliberation between Albert and Amy, sometimes going on well into the night, they finally agreed on the line up of interviewees that were most suitable, in their minds, for the project. A letter was put together, written by Albert, to each family selected, with a time schedule for replying and a programme of events.

Gunter was at home when the post came, he had been waiting every day since returning from the interview for the letter he hoped would change their lives. Forever being the optimist that the news would be good, he rushed to the post box to collect the mail, excitedly thumbing through the letters. 'Wunderbar' he shouted, even before opening the letter, dropping the other boring looking envelopes to the ground he quickly ripped it open and pulled out the contents. The news was just what he wanted. 'Fantastic, ich muss telefon Greta' leaving the other letters he rushed to the telephone to tell his wife of the acceptance.

Millie was first home with Vicky from nursery in the Preswick household. Not expecting such a speedy response, she was shocked into sudden excitement when she read the letter, grabbing Vicky, lifting her into the air twirling round and round shouting to her.
'We've done it! we have done it! I can't wait to tell Daddy, he'll be so pleased Vicky.'

Monty's post, when he had some, arrived early, long before he was out of his pit. When his eyes finally saw the light of day, he was surprised to see a letter on the floor, thinking the postman has got the wrong address. He picked it up to look at the addressee; it had his name on it. Rubbing his eyes to clear his vision, he read his name again.
'I suppose I'd better open it,' he mumbled to himself and was even more surprised with the contents.
'Bloody hell, I've been chosen!' he said aloud. His thoughts started to gain momentum: now I've got to find a woman! Why is everything difficult in life, man? I just want to chill out on my own; that's not much to ask, is it?

'Now let me think. What female owes me a favour that I can call in?' He began to focus hard to come up with a suitable victim.

Magnus arrived home from work as usual, let himself in to find Patricia on the sofa, watching TV with a line of empty lager cans by her side.
'Hi hen, where's Melanie?'
'She's in her room, there's a strange letter addressed to you came today.'
Strange because all letters normally are addressed to Patricia.
'I thought it must have been a mistake and nearly threw it in the bin, but you had better have a look first.'
'Where is it?' he snapped at her.
'On the kitchen table,'
He rushed through to the kitchen, grabbed the letter and quickly opened and read it.

Dear Mr McNulty.
Amy and I have great pleasure in asking you and your family, if you would join us on this adventure with the opportunity to use your skills on this project and develop the well being of your wife and daughter.
A benefactor has been chosen and the necessary funding is available. However, due to the delicate nature of this venture, please do not give out any information, especially to the media and the authorities. We look forward to an early reply confirming in writing of your availability, after which further instruction will be sent to you.

Yours faithfully.
Albert and Amy Crowther.

Magnus was flabbergasted and he felt a lump form in his throat. But how was he to tackle Patricia and Melanie on the subject and to convince them to come? I know, he thought, I'll leave it to the last minute. Then I'll tell them I've accepted a new job that will mean the whole family travelling together on a large ocean-going vessel, living at sea for some time. It's the truth. I'm sure they'll agree to it, he convinced himself.

3. THE SHIP'S PURCHASE

Miles set to work and located one of many oil tankers that he had enquired about that were waiting to be scrapped. It was still afloat and anchored near Pembroke Dock, Milford Haven in South Wales. Arrangements were made to go and view it. Miles, Albert, Ched and Gunter left London after meeting Miles at his apartment. Under the new Act of Parliament, Miles was the only one of them that was permitted a car. Cars were mainly for business use now, or the very wealthy, politicians of course and a few other very restricted users. Albert, Ched and Gunter did not fall into any of those categories. They had met at his home in Knightsbridge, a moderately sized apartment, worth several million euros. The others were impressed by Miles' nice new BMW, which was now made in China along with nearly every other European brand of vehicle.

They travelled out of London through the many different congestion charging points. Each time a computerised voice was heard inside the car.
'You have just passed through sector five and will be charged one hundred euros from your debit card.' This happened several times until the car entered the access to the M4 motorway.
'You will be charged automatically on the motorway exit you choose,' the voice chipped in again.
'Bloody hell Miles this will cost a fortune,' said Albert. 'Now we've gone from pounds to euros everything seems to have increased in price. It's like when we converted to decimal currency in 1971.' Miles just smiled and then there were several minutes silence before Miles started up the conversation again.
'I was surprised at the number of oil tankers available, not so many in the UK though. The widest choice was in Rotterdam, which would make any logistics for us difficult, besides their asking prices are a lot higher.'
'What sort of price were they asking?' Ched inquired.
'Between two or three million euros whereas the one we will be looking at today will be considerably cheaper.'
'It should be quite a big lump of metal weighing in at nearly half a million tonnes,' Albert commented. Gunter kept quiet, just trying to take it all in. The rest of the journey was quite tedious because of speed restrictions and motorway maintenance programmes.

Eventually, they arrived at the dock and were met by the tanker owner's representative. He handed his business card to Miles.

'I'm Mr Howard; pleased to meet you. The MD of the waste metal recycling company has asked me to show you around. The ship was acquired from a defunct American oil giant.' They walked across to some steps on the quay which led down to a small tug, boarded and cast off.

As they came closer, Mr Howard pointed out the tanker to them. It was between two smaller vessels. There was an air of excitement amongst the hopeful purchasers. Its huge bulk stood out in the bright light of that fresh April morning in 2015. Albert asked if they could have two circuits around the ship: clockwise and anticlockwise. On passing around the bow, they could see the ship's name: The Atlantis Liberty.

'More like Atlantis *Liability*,' muttered Albert as he thought about the massive amount of oil she carried and the pollution it must have caused over her past life. He took the first of many photographs while Gunter started to make a digital recording.

The tug pulled to and made fast at the bottom of a flight of metal steps fixed to the tanker's side. Mr Howard stayed on the tug saying he didn't like heights and Miles told him they would be back in a couple of hours. Albert was the first up and he eagerly climbed the forty feet or so to the access door. Ched, Miles and Gunter quickly followed. Once onboard, they made their way to the bridge. All four stood inside it looking forward to the bow.

'You could fit about three football pitches on here. Jesus this is a big bitch!' Ched piped up.

'Now, now,' Albert cautioned, 'don't go saying anything derogatory about her. She may be listening.'

'It's just the biggest ship I've ever been on, how about you Albert?'

'Yes me too.'

'It's certainly the biggest for me,' Gunter added, 'but I've been very, very close to one similar, at very close quarters indeed!' Remembering how Gunter got his knick-name *Gunter the Shunter*, they all laughed.

'It's the first time I have been on a ship of any size; I've always preferred to fly everywhere!' Miles said. This comment dulled the excitement somewhat.

They discussed how best to inspect the ship and decided to split up into three. Gunter and Miles would look at the living accommodation and all the facilities connected with the upper decks. Ched would inspect the engines, turbines, generators etc. leaving Albert to view the length and breadth of the ship, its structure and suitability for them. The crude oil storage tanks had already been cleaned for safety reasons to prevent a build up of volatile gases from the secretion of crude oil deposits in the tanks. Albert wanted this survey to give him some information on how the ship's inner structure could be redesigned to convert it to an ecological floating island, and make his grand idea a reality.

They agreed to meet back on the bridge in two hours. Albert walked around the ship taking more photos and making notes. His main concerns were how to convert the hold to take the mechanical sails, and the area in between the sail housings for the earth's strata, with drainage and recycling of water. He decided on a suitable place for the animals at the bow of the ship. This would be close to the methane gas collector which would come from the manure and compost waste. He was gradually getting a better picture in his mind, and, at this point, he rested himself on a capstan winch near the bow, to continue with his notes and make some sketches.

They all met back at the bridge within the two hours, saying it wasn't really enough time to do it justice. They could hardly believe they'd been inspecting that long and agreed they needed to spend more time surveying, so they continued. Another hour later, Albert was briefed by Ched and Gunter on what they had found and their points of view. Everything they had seen was up to standard. The ship had been well maintained.
'How good is it?' was Miles first question.
'It's perfect,' Albert replied. 'One of the good things about the ship is that it was designed to operate with a minimum crew, so control from the bridge to the engine room was auto. I just hope you have enough money to buy it and convert it Miles.'
'Don't you worry about that, my friend I will sort that part out.'

They left the bridge and made their way back down the metal steps to the tug, where a frustrated and cold ship owner's representative was impatiently waiting.
'That took you long enough. Its freezing stood here. It's only a lump of scrap you know!' He was annoyed having to wait so long.

'Yes', replied Miles, 'It certainly is a lump of scrap and not worth anything at that.'

'Oh?' replied the man, 'I wouldn't say that.'

'Well let's talk to the owner and not the bellboy.' This shut Mr Howard up completely; the return journey to the quay was in silence.

They arrived back to their cars and Miles followed Mr Howard to the ship owner's offices. On arrival they were greeted by Alyn Jones who pompously stated he was the Managing Director of Taff Recycling and Steel Holdings.

'Do you think they realise that abbreviates to T R A S H?' Albert whispered to Miles. Miles grinned.

'We are the owners. We acquired the ship when the oil company went bust. Welcome to my office. Can I get anyone drinks?' Alyn's offer was declined by the visitors.

'Let's get straight down to business,' Miles said to him. 'We will take it off your hands for one euro plus you will have the cost of moving it to a dry dock.'

'Come, come now Mr Overstrand. That's hardly a reasonable offer.' Miles turned to Albert and the others.

'Would you gentlemen mind waiting outside while Mr Jones and I have a serious discussion?'

'Of course,' Albert shrugged, 'Let's go chaps... Come on Mr Howard that includes you!'

They made their exit and decided to wait in the cars.

'That's strange.' Albert remarked to the others. 'I thought it would be better for negotiations if we were all together. Well, best leave that sort of thing to him. He knows what he's doing. That's how he made his millions, by being shrewd, I suppose.' After only ten minutes, Miles and Alyn Jones came out shaking hands.

'Thank you and good bye.' Mr Jones did not look a happy man. Miles turned away from him quickly to conceal a grin, got in the car and tried to keep a straight face.

'Right gentlemen the ship is ours for a peppercorn price of one euro, but we will have to pay to move it!'

'One euro!' spluttered Gunter. 'I cannot believe that. How ?' Miles quickly started the car and sped off.

'Well that didn't take long,' commented Ched. Miles turned to them all and started laughing quietly which grew into collective, boisterous and triumphant laughter.

The group gradually calmed. They were not looking forward to the arduous return journey. Gunter, still disturbed by the deal Miles had sealed, spoke up again.

'How is it possible to buy a ship worth millions of euros, for just one euro? Please explain Miles.'

'You have to realise what is happening in the world's commodity markets. At the moment, scrap steel is worth nothing because it costs so much to dispose of it. Tell me Gunter, when was the last oil tanker built? When was the last major euro railway line built? When was the last time anything was built in steel in Europe?'

'I don't know,' a confused Gunter replied.

'You see China has taken on the world's manufacturing centres, mainly through making things cheaper. The Chinese bought up every iron ore mine and steel plant that they could, in the world a few years ago, so they make almost all steel products and now no country can compete with them. In fact, China makes virtually every other manufactured good that the rest of the world requires. But now, like other countries before them, China has become a victim of its own success. It produces such good quality goods that last and nobody at present can improve on them so there are less new orders. As for oil tankers, that's simple: with the vast oil pipelines that have been established to transport oil when and where required and the fact that oilfields are drying up worldwide, if there's very little oil to move, what are you going to do with oil tankers? They're obsolete. Perhaps our ship will set a trend and the Atlantic Ocean will end up like some mid England barging community on a larger scale.' The others did not know what to say, so they all kept quiet.

Nothing was said until they were nearing the services at the Newbury turn off on the M4.

'That part of the journey seemed to take forever.' grumbled Albert, 'Why is it so slow?'

'It was the same time as going there,' Miles replied. 'What do you expect? The M4 has an electronic distancing device with an inbuilt speed control of 90 km per hour. It was introduced by our new Prime Minister to log car users' movements. Your ID is on the screen of your car and you have to be

24

a registered driver for it. It's "Big Brother" that has gone mad! The system was also designed to manipulate traffic to move over, to let ministers' cars move past everybody at high speeds to get to important meetings, or perhaps, more likely, their mistresses, in reality!'

'That's enough of the current affairs lesson. Let's have some coffee,' Albert said. 'I must have a pee first though, I'm bursting!'

Miles got the coffees and they sat around a table to drink them from dreadful recyclable cups.

'The ship is registered in Panama.' Miles told them. 'We'll have to reregister it in a company name, and I think the classification is better left as an oil tanker. I'll sort that out. You, Albert, need to come up with a design so that drawings can be put to shipbuilders and fabricators to price the modifications we require.'

'Ok, but I'll need to make another visit or two to make my final specifications. I'll also need the help of Magnus, our engineer.'

'Fine, make sure Magnus gets adequate funds and just keep a record of what you spend. Please continue.'

'Thank you. Ched and Gunter, you are off on a crash course, although not so much in your case Gunter. Ched you're on a Captain's certificate and Gunter navigation. So let's finish our coffee and get a move on.' Miles was extremely enthusiastic all of a sudden!

When they arrived back in London, he dropped them off at Waterloo Station for them to return to their various homes.

'You all know what to do, just get it done,' Miles said. 'And Albert, when you require any funds, please let me know, although the million euros in your account should keep you covered for a while! We'll meet again in two weeks to discuss a timetable and put the ideas to a marine architect.' Good God, he's become a bossy so and so! Albert thought, but he let it go. Miles was providing the funds after all. They each went their separate ways with heads full of ideas and enthusiasm.

Albert contacted Magnus to discuss the project with the information he had so far. He wanted his input on the energy side and also to get him to look over the ship. This would enable them to make outline drawings on the alterations required to convert it into a self sufficient, self-powered vessel. Albert had fixed a date to meet Miles in London within a fortnight. He brought Magnus with him. Miles had arranged for them all to see a marine architect. A design was finally agreed. This was put together using the original computerised blueprints of the ship, then Albert's data was entered into the architect's laptop, and in minutes, detailed drawings were being printed. Each had a set: Albert and Magnus to ponder over and Miles to put to shipbuilding contractors.

They left the architect and went back to Miles' place to discuss a timetable for the rest of the project. They agreed to have all the alterations completed and ready to float by the end of that year, 2015. That gave the contractors approximately seven months to complete. It would then take three months to construct the infrastructure of the land mass and to stock it with the required crops, plants, trees and animals ready for the start of the growing season in the northern hemisphere. Then the ship would be boarded by its permanent occupants for its first six months or so at sea off the coast of Wales. This would be the old oil tanker's new life as 'THE ARK' or as it came to be named 'ALBERT'S ARK'. When the trial period was complete, they would set sail to the southern hemisphere to spend the winter months somewhere in the South Atlantic, just below the Tropic of Capricorn.

Miles had agreed the alterations with a contractor and their first task was to get the ship into dry dock. Albert and Magnus set off on public transport to Pembroke Dock to oversee the work, but their journey was so slow, the ship had already been moved and was in place by the time they got there! The re-cleaning of the crude oil tanks was to start immediately. Albert and Magnus went off to find temporary accommodation until they sorted out the living quarters onboard. The next day, when Albert and Magnus arrived at the dock, they found themselves behind an army of Chinese workers passing through security.
'Where are they all going? Albert muttered 'There are an awful lot of them.' As they headed for the ship they realised where they were all heading to: their ship in dry dock.
'My god,' said Magnus, 'there's half of China here!' They were growing in numbers by the minute like an army of worker ants, overseen by a big fat man bellowing into a microphone, giving out the orders. Albert and Magnus went to the ship's living quarters to assess what was needed. After re-familiarising themselves, they could see there was very little to be done there. They went through everywhere else and compiled a list of alterations, including sealing any access doors at mid ships, so that the only way to board was to the deck.

The weeks passed by and these turned into months, with the Chinese contractors working seven days a week. By the end of November, things had really taken shape. The sails had been fabricated on the dock and were ready to be lifted by crane into their housings. This took just a week and they could now test how well they operated. Albert and Magnus were heavily involved with this, testing them over and over again. All that remained to do before the ship could be floated, was the painting of the hull and upper decks. The hull was coated in environmentally friendly epoxy paint the colour of aquamarine blue and the upper decks in sky blue. The specification was very high so it would not require recoating for many years. This was all completed by the 1st December, a significant day as it was Amy's birthday.

The ship was ready to be floated out of dry dock on its newly painted bottom. Tugs towed it to a berth so that the next stage of the project could take place: making up the earth's strata and drainage. The first material to be laid in the cargo holds was sandstone. This was covered with three metres of sand which was washed into the rocks below. Each of the holds had a stone built well that housed a submersible pump to automatically pump water out of the ship when the level got to a certain height. Subsoil covered the sand and land drainage pipe work was laid to drain into the wells before the topsoil covered it all. When this part of the operation was being carried out, the sky went dark as every seagull in the area descended on the freshly laid topsoil full of worms! Huge escalating conveyer belts lined up along the dock carried out each stage of filling the holds with the various sand and aggregates. Massive tipper trucks dispersed the loads into the foot of the conveyors to transport material up into the ship's hold. It was then spread and compacted by bulldozers that were craned into each hold. The process was continuous for the next three weeks; with shifts working twenty four seven until the level of soil was brought up to two metres from the top of the gunwales or sides of the ship. This gave the effect of a huge walled garden.

Now that the ship was moored at its berth and the conversion was well on target, they made preparations to go home for the Christmas and New Year holiday. Before Albert left, Miles left a message asking him to make sure he was happy with the work and, if so, to sign it off so payment could be made. Albert dealt with the snag list quickly and thoroughly, because he knew the contractors would not be able to rectify any faulty work once the Ark was at sea. Then he left for his temporary, penultimate home.

Albert was never one to celebrate Christmas, other than to be with his wife, but enjoyed seeing in the New Year in his local pub with a few old friends. Only this time, he had to tell them he was going away on a sea trip for a long time and it would be very unlikely that he would see them again. They didn't know whether to cry or celebrate when Albert announced his intentions, but they soon carried on seeing in the New Year, in the normal fashion.

It was January 3rd 2016. Albert and Amy had spent the last few days going through personal belongings deciding what to take. Albert found it very difficult to choose from the vast amount of treasures they had collected over the years. Many had only sentimental value but memories more important to them than if they had the crown jewels. They packed the maximum they could, including a photo of Amy's mother. The crates were sealed and labelled ready to be collected and taken to the spacious storage onboard the ship. Albert closed the suitcases full of their travelling luggage as they waited for the taxi to take them to the station.

Several hours later they were stepping into another taxi to take them to the ship. When they arrived, Albert organised someone to transfer the cases to their living quarters, which was the former Captain's cabin. Amy was surprised how spacious and well designed the accommodation was.

'Where's the kitchen?' she asked.

'Ah,' replied Albert, 'It's not here. We have a canteen where we all eat together or in rotas.'

'I'm not cooking for fifteen people three times a day. And who's going to wash up?'

'No, No, Amy, it's not going to be like that. It will be organised so that these types of duties will be done, not by one person, but a number, on a rota basis, until one particular person wants the job full time. Come on, I'll show you the canteen. It's complete with all the best cooking and dishwashing equipment. Everything's powered by sunlight through banks of solar collector cells which convert the light into DC electrical current through batteries.'

'Albert, please don't get all technical with me. You know I won't understand.'

They both entered the canteen which was laid out like a restaurant. At one side was a bar with beer pumps and optics, at the other side was the entrance to the kitchen. As they pushed through them, the swing doors revealed the immaculate, stainless steel, fully equipped kitchen. Amy was extremely impressed.

'Well, you have been busy. It looks great and easy to cook in and keep clean. For a while Albert, I doubted you, for all the time you spent away last year. I thought you might have found some Welsh lady, down here in the valleys!'

'Don't be silly dear they only have sheep in the valleys.' They both looked at each other and smiled with watery eyes followed by an immediate embrace.

'I love you Albert. I'm sorry for doubting you.'

It was late in the day and all the work had stopped. Albert thought that some of the other occupants might have arrived, but no, Albert and Amy were the first to occupy the Ark's living quarters. Amy decided to mark the special occasion.

'Lets have an early night Albert; it's been a long day and I'm tired.'

'Ok my dear. I won't be a moment.' Amy was already in bed and thought, wouldn't it be nice if we could christen the Ark by being the first couple of the community to make love here. It might even give the ship good luck. I'll have to work on him though. I know he's tired but I can usually stir him into action. Then Albert slipped under the sheets.

'Good night, my dear... Oh, that's nice. Oh, that's really nice. Oh Amy, please don't stop that's wonderful.... Oh.' Albert soon found that old cock of his was still in working order, as Amy gently rubbed his nipples sending a sensation through him. She lowered her hand to hold his erection and make it harder. Her head disappeared beneath the sheets to lubricate him slightly.

'Oh, Amy, that's nice, oh that's really nice.' She reappeared from down under and positioned herself across him so that he could slide gently into her. She raised herself up and down, very slowly, up and down, her breasts hanging down for him to fondle, caressing her nipples with immediate effect. She continued her steady movement, up and down. At last she could feel him throbbing inside her as he released his fluid into her, same as he had many, many times over the years they have been together. To them it was just as beautiful as ever. Amy collapsed on top of him holding and kissing him with the perfect tenderness that he thought only a loving woman can give a man. The Ark was christened!

Dawn seemed to arrive too quickly after a sound night's sleep, but the pair where soon up and about with an air of excitement with the thought of the arrivals that will form the Ark's community. The first that day, an excited Magnus appeared with his wife Patricia, who Amy thought was ridiculously obese. Magnus had originally described her as a couch potato. She resembled a beached whale, Albert thought; how sad it is that people let themselves get to that state! Following behind was their daughter, Melanie. Magnus introduced his wife to Albert and Amy.

'Pleased to meet *ya*', Patricia greeted them in a strong, Glaswegian accent. Her acrylic fur coat with matching hat and gloves made her look even bigger than she was. Magnus then prompted Melanie, their spotty faced fourteen year old, to say hello.

'Hi,' she spurted out, reluctant to stop chewing on a chocolate caramel bar. She was carrying a guitar case in her other hand and a rucksack on her back. Her mousey hair was long and straggly with strands caught up in her snack bar as her hand waved about to try to disconnect them.

'And what type of guitar music do you play?' Albert asked her.

'Classical and some Japanese stuff.'

'Very good' He replied.

Oh my god, Albert thought to himself, I hope they don't think there is going to be chocolate onboard or daytime television. We'll have our job cut out to do something about their physical condition. What a sight!

'Pleased to meet you both,' said Amy, taking charge of showing Patricia and Melanie to their quarters while Albert and Magnus got talking on technical issues as they followed on with very heavy suitcases and several carrier bags.

Next to arrive was Ched with his wife Millie and toddler Vicky. Albert and Magnus were way over at the bow of the ship debating the methane gas collector when they arrived and were unable to greet them at the time. So Ched and family made their own way to the living accommodation. Amy caught sight of them wandering around, not knowing which cabins were theirs. Millie was first to speak.

'Hello Amy, this is Vicky.'

'Hello there Vicky and how was your trip down here?' Vicky immediately burst into tears, huge, real tears streamed down her cheeks as she rubbed her eyes, catching her long blonde hair between her fingers.

'Sorry Albert's not here to greet you,' said Amy. 'He'll be back soon.'

'That's alright don't worry about it.' Ched lifted Vicky into his arms but she still sobbed uncontrollably, making such a noise that any further conversation was impossible. Fortunately, Albert had shown Amy where everyone's quarters were first thing that morning, so she was able to settle them in quickly and get away.

Amy had asked the ladies to meet her in the canteen as soon as they could. She wanted to get to know them and find out how they felt: to get the female angle on their new adventure on the Ark. While Amy waited in the canteen she started to feel very hungry. She thought to herself that with all that had been going on she'd forgotten to eat and Albert must be starving. She needed to go food shopping. Patricia arrived with Melanie and Vicky. Millie had persuaded Patricia to take care of Vicky while she checked out the animal holding area. So Amy explained what needed to be done and off they went shopping. They made it as far as the security gates, when who was coming into the dock: Gunter, Greta and little Stella, who was asleep in her buggy. They had just collected their entrance passes. Amy waited until they were through, welcomed them and then they all made their introductions.

'How do we find our quarters please?' Gunter asked. Amy thought he sounded *so* sexy, just like Arnold Schwarzenneger.

'Um....could you find your way to the canteen and wait there until we get back please. We need to buy some provisions. Oh Greta, would you like to help us?'

'Yes, sure,' she replied, leaving Gunter with several suitcases and a child.

'Greta, please take Stella,'

'Of course,' Greta took Stella who was still fast asleep in her buggy and totally oblivious to the situation. Gunter collected some of the suitcases with a sigh of relief and headed to the berth, explaining to security he would be back for the remainder shortly.

Later, Amy and company returned to the ship with everybody carrying supermarket jute carrier-bags full of food. They made it to the canteen to offload the purchased goods after their shopping expedition. Greta was expecting to see Gunter at least there waiting, but he wasn't there.

31

'Don't worry, he is obviously checking the stars or something,' commented Amy.

Greta looked puzzled. She didn't understand the joke. Amy carried on regardless,

'Well ladies, we are going to need feeding sometime today. I don't know how all these things work here, so let's get ourselves acquainted with the kitchen and organise a meal for everybody. We won't send out a search party for the others, we'll just cook something that smells good and fan it out of the windows, like those fast food shops do. They'll be here quickly enough.' The others gradually made their way back to the canteen from their various areas of interest of the ship. Some were enticed by the smell of cooking and some by sheer hunger. They all arrived at various times. Amy, with the aid of her new companions, had made a huge pot of Spaghetti Bolognese, which was a speciality of hers. It was all much appreciated.

As everybody was sitting and chatting after the meal, Albert asked Ched and Gunter how they got on with the training courses Miles had sent them on.

'We finished on time and gained our certificate, but wasn't it strange Gunter, how everybody else took a test but we didn't have to? Yet we got full marks?'

'Oh you do surprise me! There's more to Miles than meets the eye.' Albert grinned but before he could explain any further, a security guard appeared, asking for him.

'Excuse me sir, there's some old Hippie with a young girl and baby asking for you at the gate. They seem a bit strange sir. I didn't let them in.'

'That must be Montgomery. Thank you, I'll come and check them out or in whatever the case.'

Albert returned with the guard to the gates to identify the visitors. Sure enough, it was Monty and the partner he had promised to bring with him.

She was introduced as Marigold and baby Lucy, who was strapped to her chest by a swaddling cloth band which tied at her waist. Albert thought that Marigold had obviously been busy in her local jumble sale and charity shops the way she was dressed! She was wearing a long skirt almost touching the ground and a thick multi-coloured jumper that was far too big for her. She had bright green hair that had an odd number of plaits with occasional bows tied in them; a pale complexion and she was not looking healthy at all.

32

'Where is your luggage?' Albert asked Monty.
He pointed to a number of carrier bags at each side of him.
'Oh, travelling light then?' said Albert.
The reason security would not let them in was because they had no identity cards. Albert sorted this out by getting them a temporary pass. They were told they could not leave the country without an official Euro passport.
'Ok,' said Albert we'll sort that out later as well.'
'What's the use of a passport?' Monty asked.
Albert ignored him and, in exasperation, picked up the carrier bags and pushed Monty ahead of Marigold and child, away from security, before he got himself into any more bother. They slowly made their way to the ship's berth. Albert wanted to have words with Monty. He was so shocked to see his almost instant family. Marigold was lagging behind and couldn't hear Albert questioning Monty.
'Is the child yours?'
'Sure, she is,' came the reply.
'How on earth did you manage to convince that young girl to have a child sired by you and come on this floating community for the rest of her life?'
'I told her if we could make a baby together I would take her on a world cruise and visit sunny climates.'
'What for the rest of her life?'
'Well, I omitted that part of the information, just told her on a need to know basis!'
'And how old is the baby?'
'She was only born yesterday! It's been a bit of a rush, I can tell you.'
'What? She's only a day old?'
'You sound a bit agitated, Albert.'
'Agitated, I'm fucking flabbergasted and annoyed, poor girl!'
Nothing more was said.

They arrived at the canteen where everybody was still chatting away. As they entered there was a hush and looks of interest at the new arrivals. Amy was quickly there to greet and welcome them to the Ark, offering food. Introductions were exchanged and immediately Greta and Patricia made it straight to Marigold to look at the baby.
'What's the baby's name?' asked Patricia.
'Lucy.' Marigold replied.

'She's beautiful and so tiny.' As Patricia was making a fuss, Millie was not the least bit interested, she was more concerned with her own thoughts about the numbers of animals to stock; how to avoid too much inter-breeding; and does it really matter when they are for food anyway?

Everybody settled into their new home and set about organising themselves into the various tasks that they would have to do to make the ship function and create a good quality of life for their ecological experiment.

4. STOCKING THE SHIP

The stocking of the Ark had already started with the most important cargo: the human kind. This was made up of, Homo sapiens the species known as 'man' developed one hundred thousand years ago to bring us to what we are today. The arrival of this cargo went very smoothly although there were a couple who had not yet put in an appearance. Questions were asked on a regular basis as all were inquisitive to what they would be like. The rest of them soon made the Ark their home, sorting out their duties. The men, apart from Monty, were all busy making sure they were familiar with the mechanical systems and the controlling of the ship. When Albert was not organising that, he was setting up his brewery and distillery. Patricia, to the surprise of Albert adapted very quickly took on the running of the kitchen, along with Amy, and added the laundry to their repertoire. Marigold was still too frail, and with a newborn child, wasn't any help for the time being. Greta set up the nursery and school with the reluctant aid of Melanie. This caused concern with Greta seeing that the teenager had an attitude problem making everything a chore.

Millie set to work marking out where every tree, shrub and the crops would go. She had already designated an area for the garden to grow everyday vegetables and set out a herb area for Monty. This all had to be planned before she could start putting a list together of quantities and types of plants and seeds to order. She told Albert she would need a lot of help initially, to get everything planted in time for it to be established for the first growing season. She had almost eight acres of land to manage besides the livestock. Animal feed would have to be imported until they could produce their own. Her first shopping list was headed 'Well established Plants and Trees.' This consisted of eight apple trees: Bramley's and Coxes Orange Pippin, the good old traditional type. Two pear trees: Conference and Albert's favourite, the Portuguese Rocha; two plum trees: Victoria, a good all rounder for jams and wines; cherry trees: two of Marasca which makes a good liqueur and lovely bottled fruit; orange trees, just the Spanish and Portuguese varieties. Strangely enough, she remembered they're not indigenous to those countries, but originated in Asia. She included the Seville sweet orange and tangerine. Next, two lemon trees, rich in vitamin C, for the fruits' citric acid, for drinks, salad and fish dressings, general flavouring and as a cleansing agent. There was one type of tree to add that was very important for the production of oils: the Olive. Two mature trees would be planted of *Olea europaea* variety. Millie had consulted Albert for advice on the trees of the Mediterranean because of the knowledge he'd built up when travelling in that area.

The list of soft fruits was simple to compile: blackcurrants, very important for young children they love them, and so nutritious with the high vitamin content. Raspberries-Albert again insisted for they make good wine and preserves; Millie was worried about its prolific growth and the problems that can cause if not checked, but he persuaded her she could keep the growth in check by removing the plants entirely every couple of years and replanting. She added gooseberry, for its pectin, which helps the setting of preserves; blueberry, a request from Monty, for his healing potions and lastly the soft fruit that everybody usually likes: the strawberry. Again, she knew this can take over the land area very quickly but she would cut the runners back. A stock of seeds would have to be bought in initially and kept in a dry place. This was vital to get started, also as a safety net in case they didn't manage to save seeds from the produce they grew.

She was relieved when her list was finished but her mind still kept racing, thinking of other plants they would need, cotton, for instance, which would eventually be a necessity, to establish a crop for an alternative for toilet paper and sanitary requirements.

Millie was so hyped up thinking about the power and responsibility she had been given, that suddenly it overwhelmed her and she became worried that if her produce failed at any time, the rest of the crew would suffer and blame her. She went into a stalled mode, almost like a mini breakdown; unable to concentrate on anything for long before thinking she should be doing something else. She had to slow down; stop her workaholic activity and try to put it all into perspective.

Millie received the delivery several days later and was both nervous and excited at the same time. Contractors were paid to place the semi-mature trees where Millie had painstakingly decided they should be planted. They were young fit Welsh lads that smiled and winked at Millie. She lightened up and started to smile at some of the gestures they made to her and her smile turned into laughter. A rapport blossomed between her and these young men; she knew they found her attractive and it made her flirtatious for the day. She soon forgot her temporary depression and could not believe the weight that had been taken off her. She felt wanted and liked and these lads seemed to take delight in working with her. Ched is due for a rough time she thought and smiled as she imagined the two of them making love.

The contractors finished the planting and left. Now there was an orchard. Millie sat down amongst the trees and wondered if it would work? Her mind was jumping from one thing to another: I quite fancied those lads today, especially the one with the tight jeans. He didn't leave much to the imagination! I could have quite happily.......... Come on Millie, get back to reality. Bloody hell! I can't stop fantasising, what is it about this place?

The next few days Millie made herself concentrate on watering-in the trees. The weather was mild and it would help bed the roots in. Next the cereal crops needed ordering. Again she prepared a list and gave it to Albert to process along with the medicinal herb and plant list from Monty plus some culinary herbs and spice varieties from Amy. Millie also discussed with Albert the fact that no provision had been made for growing produce under glass. Even in warmer climates, some plants need protection and humidity. 'And are we having any bees?' Albert, without question, said he would organise it all straight away. They decided two well-stocked beehives would be sufficient, to be placed between the herb garden and the orchard. The experts they had consulted came onboard a few weeks later to install them, allowing the bees to settle. This was a delicate operation as bees normally do not like being disturbed. The specialists explained how the two colonies of honey bees would hopefully regenerate for years to come, and provide essential pollination for plants with a bonus of honey and beeswax as by-products.

Another delivery, of what could only be described as a large, clear polycarbonate golf ball, with a couple of chaps to erect it, caused a lot of excitement. Millie was delighted. She was asked where to put the new greenhouse and chose a place near the front of the upper decks, so that it would get some shade and protection. The last time she had seen anything similar was at the Eden Project, in Cornwall, to which she had been a regular visitor to the huge biomes, especially in the months prior to boarding the ship, that had become a huge inspiration to her.

The infrastructure of the Ark was gradually coming together. Magnus was working his socks off. He had help from Ched and sometimes Albert leant a hand. They were building the methane gas collector and installing gas storage tanks. They had completed work on the wind generators that were connected to the power system, along with the solar panel collector cells. Magnus had also designed and built a number of wave powered generators which had yet to be put to the test, but he was confident that they would work. The next project for Magnus to tackle was the desalination plant. He was using much the same principles that Albert was working on each day in distilling spirits, only using this method to remove salt from seawater. Water desalination and purification was going to be extremely important to them on the Ark because there would be no guarantee that if and when the rain would fall it would be enough to sustain the requirements of the crew, the animals, the trees and crops. Also the desalination process would supply an abundance of salt, again vital, for preserving meat and fish as reserves. Millie's most pressing concern now was she needed the mini tractor and its implements, the Rotavator the furrowing and harrowing attachments. She got onto Albert to chase them and get a firm delivery time.

It was March 10th 2016 and the new equipment was on the quay: a small fishing boat with nets, lines and lobster/crab pots; an inflatable with outboard motor and the mini tractor with attachments. Millie saw this and it was like Father Christmas had been. She was so thrilled she leapt up to Albert, clasping her arms around his neck and her legs around his waist, well, as far round as she could get them anyway; kissing him on his unshaven cheeks. Albert thought to himself, Bloody hell! I could do with some more of that. Behave yourself you silly old fool! The awaiting cargo was soon craned onboard and Millie was off down the virgin fields, driving the tractor over the hint of grass already growing.

On the 17th March, St Patrick's Day, Millie, with Ched's help, had completed the first early seed potato planting. In future, this could be staggered all year round, after the initial season off the coast of Wales. Other crops had been sown: wheat for bread flour, for Albert's brewing, and as animal feed; a limited amount of corn, barley and oats mainly for livestock, poultry feed and again, for brewing. The vegetables that Millie had selected to plant as and when the time was correct, were all the basic cottage garden produce: carrots, peas, beans, radishes, turnips, beets, cabbage, broccoli and cauliflower, etc. Salads included lettuce, spinach and celery and in Millie's new greenhouse, tomatoes and cucumber. There was

38

a delivery of grapevines that Albert had added to the list, these he knew would take some time to establish.

'These are great!' Millie said to Albert when she unpacked them. 'I'll look forward to a nice glass of grape juice.'

'And I'm looking forward to a nice glass or two of *wine* from them.'

Amy was taking care of the herb planting and sowing, now that they had arrived. Monty gave Amy a hand in the planting out. It was obvious that Monty was not used to doing anything the remotest bit energetic, but as they worked, he explained the healing qualities of each plant to Amy. There was rhubarb to mix with apple juice, lemon peel and honey for constipation. Thyme has many healing properties, from adding to a hot bath for back pains, to infusing in hot water for an antiseptic gargle. Salvia and sage were for hair washing and to prevent hair loss. Rosemary and oregano, mixed with other antioxidant herbs, could be made into teas. Monty had asked Millie to grow red peppers of any variety to use for toothache and also they would be another rich source of antioxidants. There were one or two items that Monty did not divulge the uses of....... After a while, Amy began to tire. It had been a long day and she couldn't take it all in, so she left Monty labelling the herbs.

All the purchase orders and requests for extra cash that went to Miles via Albert, with Miles footing the bill, arrived without question or exception. Miles had certainly excelled himself in his guarantee to sponsor the Ark. But there was still no sign of either him or his partner. And still, not even Albert knew a thing about her. He just hoped that they would adapt to this new way of life.

Every day since Albert arrived onboard, he spent two to three hours on his pet project: building his small brewery and still, so that he could continue in one of his favourite pastimes: supping a couple of pints of bitter while having a game of darts, cards or even dominos occasionally. He wanted to create a pleasant social atmosphere in the community and took it for granted that the others would join in as part of their entertainment too.

Marigold had Lucy to look after, who was just a couple of months old and the tiniest thing you could imagine. She coped well, always being independent, was quiet and considerate. Since the birth, Marigold had become stronger and looked much healthier. She would help out whenever and wherever she could. Monty did not take part in the parental activity always being busy in his little laboratory or checking the herb garden on a daily basis.

Greta had told Gunter that she had missed a period, but thought it too early to be certain she was pregnant. It wasn't long before, they announced she was happily expecting again.

Every one was delighted. Gunter was ecstatic and proud and had the bonus thought of the firstborn on the Ark. Always busy in the school, Greta and her assistant Melanie, who had now lost her facial spots, probably due to the change, for the better, in her diet. There was Stella, Greta's own daughter who was now four and Vicky would be three in August, who were near school age. Melanie was gradually getting into the swing of things and being far more inquisitive about the whole system. This seemed to compensate for the further education she was missing. She practiced her guitar music with Greta, who could play piano, but lacked one, so a request was put in to Albert, with immediate response. Within a few days a piano was waiting to be shipped aboard. An old-fashioned upright found a new home in the canteen.

It was nearing the end of March and only a few days before the proposed sailing date. Whenever Albert asked Miles when he would be arriving, Miles was always vague.

'Don't worry; we'll be there,' he assured him. Apart from Miles and his partner, there was only the livestock missing. First to be delivered were the poultry. These were kept in a large netted area until they felt at home enough to be let out to free range. Then the pigs: three young sows, all with their first litters, and a lucky boar to look after them. Millie had chosen Berkshires, Yorkshires and Chester Whites, hopefully to benefit from future cross breeding to make good hybrids. Again, these were put in a penned area initially, to be let out into the orchard later.

Angora goats were selected for: additional dairy produce because their milk and cheese is more favourable in its nutritive value compared with cows; then meat and also pelts and hair for clothing etc. Merino sheep would provide fine wool for clothing and other textiles, plus lanolin oil, they would eventually require. The sheep and goats arrived together. Then Millie had great difficulty herding them into their pens; they just wanted to nibble at every thing in sight. Last, but not least, a cow christened Marina

40

with its calf, Mermaid, ambled into their fields and a little shaky after being sedated for the task of craning them aboard, gradually headed towards their shed. They were Holstein-Friesian, chosen for its high yield of milk. Millie had decided that would be sufficient to start with. She had organised to hold a sperm bank and use artificial insemination (AI). It would be easier than keeping a bull. (Noah would not have approved!).

There were only a few days to go and it would be April. Millie wanted to get everything in that could be planted in the open ground, leaving until later other plants that would be affected by frost, and seeds that would not germinate because of cold ground temperatures. She wanted to play safe to ensure success and there was not any rush: plants soon catch up in the right conditions. Because the animals were confined to their pens to get them used to their new homes, manure was building up inside. Millie wanted to clean out the pig pens. The grass in the orchard was growing very well and the ground seemed to have settled down quite solidly. So she put the pigs out into the orchard to forage and give her a chance to clean them out. She started by wheel-barrowing the heavy pig manure to the conveyor system which took it to the methane gas collector; then used a high pressure hose to flush the sties out into the livestock drainage system. It all seemed to be working well.

Meanwhile, Ched was on one of which was becoming an habitual walkabout, an excuse to be out of the way and started to wander about down towards the animal pens, where he saw his wife busy at work, hosing down. He stopped for a while and studied her coping with her jobs in her new domain. She was wearing a green boiler suit and matching Wellingtons, splattered with various types of shit. He just stood there looking at her rear, visualising her body underneath, knowing she had no bra and only a skimpy pair of lacy pants on. Her body was loose inside this slightly over-sized boiler suit, a body he knew so well, but still found exciting and fascinating. Millie hadn't realised he was there watching her, and now he started to fantasize about her. He looked around. No one was in sight. He crept up behind to surprise her and grabbed her, putting his arms around her tightly. She immediately let go of the hose which started to flick everywhere, drenching them both. She screamed, and then realising who it was, screeched at him.

'You stupid bastard, you frightened me to death. I thought I was going to be raped!'

'Oh. Don't be mad at me. You've really turned me on. I just fancied you, how about a quickie?'

'Oh, go on then.' she said, 'but be really quick.'

'Yea, that's what I thought, in case anybody else comes along. Being quick won't be a problem!' They kissed passionately with hands all over each other. Millie snatched at the zip at the front of her boiler suit and pulled it down, showing her breasts to Ched.

'Oh, shit I'd better get my pants off.' He fumbled, and in his excitement, ended up with his fly zip jammed. Millie was already out of her boiler suit and boots and found a clean area on top of some loosened hay bales. Ched looked at her naked body waiting for him.

'Come on. Hurry up she pleaded! The moment will be lost.' He felt so frustrated as he yanked down his trousers and headed towards her, only to trip up as his pants fell to his ankles.

'Bollocks!' was his only word as his head landed within a couple of inches from where Millie's two lovely legs met. She grabbed his head and pulled him the extra distance to where she wanted him, although this wasn't his original intention.

'That's thoughtful of you. It's not like you to think of me first. Give it some RTM Ched, Rapid Tongue Movement, lovely!' She held his head right into her. Ched tried to speak but was unable to answer.

'Remember what your mother said Ched, it's rude to speak with your mouth full,' as she held him to her, his tongue had finally found the place that he always had trouble finding. He knew he'd hit the target because she slowed him down and was squirming with pleasure. Thank Christ for that, he thought to himself. We might be able to get on with it, before I finish. Ched was desperate to put his cock inside his wife. She finally let him up because she was sinking too deep into the hay. He clambered on top of her and entered, to his relief, moving in and out as fast as he could …

'Hello, is there anybody home?' Albert appeared from behind the pigpens not expecting to see a bare arse bobbing up and down into a pile of hay. (By this time, Millie had disappeared into the soft hay again, out of sight.) It must have looked rather strange to him.

'Oh shit!' said Ched aloud.

'I hope that's Millie in there,' Albert replied as he walked away leaving them to their embarrassment.

42

Ched started to laugh and fell to Millie's side, as she blew hay from her mouth to get some words out.
'Who was that?'
'Albert.'
'Oh no, we'll be sacked!' she moaned, 'We're supposed to be working Ched.'
'That's just it, we are! A couple of seconds later it clicked with her. She realised he meant Albert would have been pleased with what they'd been up to: after all, he did want the Ark's population to increase! They both laughed and rolled about in the hay.

Miles finally informed Albert that they would be arriving on the morning of 1st April and to be ready to sail.
'He's giving me orders again,' grumbled Albert. 'He thinks he's in charge just because he's got all the brass.'

Tugs were organised to be ready to tow the ship to the exit channel. At last Miles arrived with his partner and, to Albert's and the other males' delight there was a stunningly attractive woman who Miles introduced as Jane. The line of people waited to greet them almost as you used to see people meeting royalty, but without the curtsies and bows. She was about five feet ten, twenty three years old, slim-built with a perfect female shape and long, natural brunette hair. Miles asked if it could be arranged for their luggage to be collected and brought aboard, saying it was a substantial amount.
'That won't be a problem.' said Albert as he showed them to their accommodation, which had been prepared to a very high standard, as with all the living areas, but theirs was a lot more spacious. Both Miles and Jane were jubilant with their new home.

Miles made his way to the bridge. When he got there, Albert, Ched and Gunter were waiting. Albert started to brief Miles on what they had achieved so far and invited him to a full inspection of the ship and its new contents. Magnus showed off his power systems then they walked to the bow, through the cultivated fields to the livestock area, where Miles was introduced to Millie and shown the methane gas collecting system. Then it was back to the upper decks to look at the rest of the facilities. Albert explained that stocks of foods and other requirements to last them for the next eighteen months or more, including methane gas and water, were all in place. He wanted to assure Miles that his money had been wisely spent. Miles asked about contact with the outside world.

'Will there be mobile phones or radio contact and is there a satellite navigation GPS (Global Positioning System) onboard?'

'We have radio contact, but no mobile phone network. As for GPS, Gunter has the equipment to use, if required, but we'll use charts, compass and a plotter to navigate our way around, the old fashioned way, so we really know what we're doing. We have radar, but this takes energy to operate and will only be used sparingly: in transit or poor visibility. So, it's manual lookout duties whenever we can, when there's clear daylight or good night vision.

A welcoming meal and get together had been organised for Miles, the Ark's VIP sponsor, the lovely Jane and the rest of the sixteen adults and children who made up the basis of the Ark's new community. They hoped it was to be the first of many such celebrations to be organised in the years to come. The mood at the first gathering was very relaxed and informal. The special buffet meal and drinks were all from the Ark's imported stock, which was purchased from the only source these days that of the supermarkets. The local butcher, baker, grocer, green/grocer had long gone, the control of food was by the mighty, the multinational chains giving so called value to the people. It would be some time before the produce growing onboard was established enough for consumption. Hopefully, within a few months their own-grown food, and whatever they managed to catch from the sea, would filter in to take the place of the bought-in items, because when at sea, they wouldn't be able to pop into a supermarket to purchase groceries and other goods anymore.

The meal was well under way, with an air of excitement as they drank and munched away. Amy and Albert looked at each other and then at their plate of food, then back with eyes meeting.

'This is tasteless crap, not a patch on the food we grew at home,' Albert said

'Yes, and we know we can change it. We have just to be patient, with all the work and dedication we will succeed, Albert.'

5. THE FIRST FIVE MONTHS

All the power and energy systems were now functional and Magnus was happy with the way that everything was working. The past few weeks had been very busy for everyone onboard. Magnus was worried that there would not be enough methane gas, collected from the animal waste during the seasonal stays, to power the gas turbines. Gas would be required in large quantities, to get them to their destination in stormy seas, when it was not possible to use mechanical sail power. He approached Albert with his dilemma and went through the calculations he had worked out for the amount of gas required. Albert paused before his reply.

'Well, it will be a question of balance: depending on how much produce we can grow in the periods that we stay in the seasonal areas. We will need to increase not only the number of animals, but also the number of humans and the quantity of produce we grow. Waste must be rigidly controlled, balancing food production to the number of livestock and ourselves.

'Yes,' said Magnus, none the wiser after Albert's waffling and he stifled a yawn as Albert was determined to continue.

'We need to continuously feed us all with fresh food. The idea of season hopping is to cheat the plants into thinking it's time to start growing again. This is only my theory and it's untried, but knowing nature, it will eventually adapt to the situation, providing we give it some help.'

'Yes,' said Magnus and he went away with his problem still unresolved.

Before the Ark could set off, official paperwork from Customs and Excise had to be signed and stamped; this was another task for Miles. When he returned from the customs office, he had a very serious look on his face.

'Because of the unusual cargo for an oil tanker,' but he could not resist his smile when announcing, 'WE ARE FREE TO GO!' This was April 2nd, 2016, the Ark's Independence Day! Tugs arrived to tow the Ark from its final berth at the old BP jetty to face west to make an exit via the West Channel in Milford Haven. The tugs released their tow lines with the Ark's bow pointing seaward. The Ark was ready to move under its own power. All the crew, bar Magnus who was busy in the engine room, congregated, children included, in and around the bridge. To them, it was the most important and historic moment of their lives. Ched moved the engine control for slow ahead. Gunter stated the first course to take them to the West Channel in a very nervous manner, then to steer 210° SW for four miles. The Ark slowly moved very smoothly towards the sea. Albert thought hopefully, that it would be many years, if ever, to dock or to set foot on terra firma again. Passing St. Ann's Head to their right, they would gradually turn to the north to a course of 335°, and then they would pass Skomer Island across Saint Brides Bay to Ramsey Island off Saint David's Head. The Ark steadied at four knots taking an hour to the next change of course.

As they headed out of the estuary the sea became choppier, but did not affect the smoothness and steadiness of the Ark. On the bridge, there was silence as everybody, now including Magnus, looked back at the exit to the port of Milford Haven but still in view of the land mass on their port (left) side. There was an intense feeling of relief that they had made it out of port successfully and, for most of the adults, a wonderful sense of freedom from the intense pressures of modern life: to earn more, to buy more, to pay more taxes and so on. The Ark and its passengers had only to keep afloat using their individual skills and talents to keep them alive; to live the good life, and pass on these skills to their offspring, for no other purpose than to have a contented life. Hopefully, to realise this aim, the Ark would achieve a balance of the sexes for generations to come. It was going to be a challenge.

The first destination for sea trials was Cardigan Bay, South of Lleyn Peninsular and about twenty-five miles southwest of Bardsey Island; Albert's reasons for choosing there being that it would be quiet and the only shipping around would be fishing boats and leisure craft. This would give them uninterrupted time for the first few months to get the food chain working and everybody familiar with the ship and each other and the environment. Gunter requested the change of course to 335° north for eighteen miles. This would take them to a position of 029° longitude and 053° latitude. At this point, Magnus returned to the engine room in anticipation of a mechanical breakdown. But he was relieved to find the automatic controls working perfectly. As they headed out of the Bristol Channel and into The Saint Georges Channel, Ched moved the control to increase speed. He wanted to achieve in excess of eight knots. The Ark steadily slid along the south west coast of Wales heading for Saint David's Head. Once past Ramsey Island, they were due to turn north into the Irish Sea. Control of the ship was left to Ched and Gunter. Everybody else gradually left the bridge and returned to his or her usual routines: be it in the laundry, in the canteen, or school, child minding, or animal care. On her

46

way back to the nursery Melanie mentioned that Millie had the easier job, compared with looking after the children, Ched overheard.

'Why not go and help her muck out the pigs.'

'I was only joking,' was her reply, as she increased her pace to the nursery. Miles stayed on the top deck and just stared at the mainland wondering if he had finally left his past behind him. Jane had left him to watch the view, as she was getting cold.

The Ark was nearing Ramsey Island, just a few miles off Saint David's Head. Albert raised the binoculars and tried to pick out Solva, a little fishing village on the mainland. He studied the coastline intently, from Solva to Ramsey Island. It was a good distance off and difficult to identify. Then he looked at the chart that Gunter was using. On it, he noticed that, to the port side of them, was an area of sea previously designated for the dumping of unwanted munitions.

'Whatever were the decision makers thinking about to desecrate the seabed with such unstable polluting waste, Gunter?'

Albert continued to study the coastline remembering that this coast was where he had his first sea experience, when he was just eighteen years old. He had a job with a large Civil Engineering company, as a labourer, on a contract to move building materials in an old ex navy landing craft, from Solva to the harbour at Ramsey Island, for the rebuilding of the harbour there. He recalled to himself the times when the craft was in choppy waters. It was tossed about on the sea and was difficult to handle, because of its flat bottom. Albert would sit between two V8 petrol engines at the stern (rear) and operate them from the pilot's orders, relayed from the helm at the bow (front) of the vessel to him in the engine room. The pilot would use a wheel to steer the boat via rudders. Every time a splash of water came over the hatch and landed on the engines, they would cut out. If he kept the hatch shut, Albert would bake in the heat created by the engines. How they managed to deliver troops to the Normandy beaches in such crafts as those, in the Second World War, was incredible, Albert pondered.

It was time to change course again, now that the Ark was well past Ramsey Island, and head north into the Irish Sea. Gunter gave Ched the course to steer of 017° N for fifty-one nautical miles. Slowly the Ark changed its course to the destination. Albert decided that if there were a reasonable south-westerly wind there, it would be a good opportunity to try out the sails. He called Magnus from the bridge.

'How are things down in the engine room?'

'Excellent Albert! It's a pity we don't have enough fuel to power the engines all the time.'

'Well, we must use alternative power whenever we can and now is that time so I need you up here to help me with the sails. Before shutting down the engines we'll raise the sails in turn, starting at the bow and pitch them at about 30°.' When Magnus arrived, they walked to the number one sail, which took about ten minutes; this was almost a third of a mile away! They started to operate the hydraulic motors that hoisted the sails up out of their respective slots in their holds. The design was crude but practical. On top of each mast was a wind indicator, which gave them some idea of the angle to pitch the sails. They raised each sail in turn until all five sails were up before returning to the bridge to see what speed they were making; this was fifteen knots with the engines still running.

'Let's try shutting down the engines now Ched.' Albert suggested. Eventually the Ark settled down to ten knots, with which they were quiet pleased.

'I believe we could achieve more speed from the sails alone, if we altered their pitch slightly, but we haven't got enough distance before the next change of course, to experiment. We'll have to think about slowing down miles before our destination point each time we need to come to an anchor point.'

When the last change of course was due, Gunter gave Ched a direction of 000°. Albert, Gunter and Magnus returned to the sails to adjust their angle to suit the new course. This would only be for a short time because they were close to their destination. The men stayed on deck, which was now mainly fields, checking the sails for excessive movement, ready to lower them at the given time. When the moment came, they dropped each sail in turn, back into the holds. The Ark continued with the momentum for a number of miles until almost stationery, when they dropped the anchor. The position was 005° Longitude and 040° Latitude, just twenty-seven miles south-west of Bardsey Island. Albert, Magnus, Ched and Gunter all shook hands, congratulating themselves. The bridge door opened, Miles and Jane entered the room with a tray of Champagne glasses and two bottles of bubbly, shortly followed by the other residents. Miles asked for hush before raising a toast.

'Please accept this drink as a toast from Jane and I, to you all, in appreciation of your hard work and dedication to achieve this memorable moment. I bought this Champagne with the last four hundred euros I had. I am now penniless, but in some ways, I've never felt richer, richer than I was when I had my millions. Here's to the Ark and a happy, adventurous future.'

It had been a long and arduous day. The glass of Champagne was most welcome to Albert but was not quite enough to replenish the parts of his body that had disappeared during the physical tasks of the day. As soon as the ceremonials were completed, he decided to go to the canteen and try his first pint of the bitter he had concocted. Ched and Gunter said they would risk it, but Miles and Magnus thought better of it, and went to their cabins instead. Albert pulled three pints. It was a little cloudy, but as they got the taste of it, it didn't take long before wanting another. The effect of the drink soon relaxed them and loosened their tongues.

Albert mentioned to his two companions about the operation of the sails. Although the control of the sails was by hydraulics via electric motors, it was the running between one sail to another that was quite a task. He wondered whether the number of physically strong males in the crew would be enough, especially if there was an illness amongst them.
'But it's a bit late now to think of that. Perhaps I could approach Miles to help?' Albert suggested.
'Phew!' Ched said, 'He won't want to get his hands dirty, will he?'
'He is going to have to find something to occupy himself,' commented Gunter, 'otherwise he'll wear himself away with that lovely young woman he's got in his cabin.'
'She'll have the same problem too. She can't lay on the bed all day long with her legs open.'
'Don't be so crude Ched!' responded Albert, 'But I know what you mean. They'll both have to muck in like the rest of us.... I suppose there are two ways we could tackle getting them to help us. One is to coax them into helping by asking, regularly, if they could give a hand with whatever any of us are doing here or there, so that they get the message. The others would have to be aware of this of course. The only drawback is that it would be underhand, but it should work. The other way, is to confront them and ask them outright. Tell them we would appreciate some help from them,

49

especially when we are in transit. The area most help is needed is with Millie on the farm.'

'I can't see them feeding the pigs or shifting manure,' chuckled Ched. They all laughed at the thought.

'So which of the options do you favour Ched?' Gunter asked.

'Option two; let's tell them straight.' Albert and Gunter thought the same.

'It's done and dusted that way,' Albert agreed. 'So it looks like we've got a delicate, diplomatic task on our hands.'

'It certainly looks that way. Rather you than me, though,' said Ched.

'Yes. It's definitely the job for you Albert.' Gunter confirmed.

'Oh, thanks a lot! I suppose I talked myself into that.' They supped up the last of their pints and left for their cabins.

A system was organised for a bell to ring when meals were ready to be served in the canteen. This was normally for everyday breakfasts and evening meals, for those who were not on watch shift or certain other duties. At other times, a cold buffet was always available to eat, whenever it suited people. The day they anchored for the first time, the evening meal was a little later than normal. The bell went at 1830 instead of 1800 hours, and there was soon a queue at the serving hatch waiting for their plates to be filled. The entire ship's crew and their offspring, except Millie, were there, looking forward to the dish of the day. They were soon tucking in and obviously enjoying the meal. Miles and Jane joined Albert and Amy. Albert commented on the quality of the meal and said that Patricia had come on in leaps and bounds in the catering department. He explained to Miles and Jane that he and Amy had insisted that all meals had got to be based on a balanced diet and not a stodgy and fatty mass. Even Patricia and daughter Melanie had adhered to the request, which had reduced Patricia's weight down to twenty stone, the fact of which she was very proud.

'She's still got a long way to go, Amy.' Miles commented.

'Yes but it's in the right direction, even Melanie has lost the spots from her face, that's because there isn't any chocolate to stuff herself with.'

'At this rate,' said Jane, 'we will all be fit as fiddles soon.'

'One would hope so,' added Amy.

Albert arranged to have a chat with Miles after the meal, on his own, to discuss the physical help that was required, while it was still fresh in his mind. He thought he'd better not offer him a pint of the ship's bitter after going on about a balanced healthy diet, so he invited him to look at the swimming pool. It was on the top of the upper decks and Miles hadn't been shown it in detail before, because it wouldn't be in use until the summer and in warmer climates. Amy managed to keep Jane chatting as Albert and Miles set off for the pool. When they got there, Albert switched on the lighting that shone into and around it. Miles was surprised at the size of the pool.

'It's ten metres by thirty,' said Albert, 'and it should help to keep us all fit. We have a good diet but exercise is important too, don't you think?'

'Yes. I'm impressed,' answered Miles. They walked to the front of the top railing to look at the view over the whole of the Ark's main deck, from the fields of crops and the gardens, orchard and livestock accommodation, to the bow. They could see Millie walking back along the illuminated walkway after a long day's toil. Albert took a deep breath; he was not normally hesitant in getting his words out.

'Er…, Miles, I realised today on the journey here, we were short of manpower in certain areas. Would you and Jane be able to help out generally with daily tasks so as not to put everybody else under too much strain?'

'Of course!' replied Miles, 'Jane and I have already discussed this prior to joining the ship. We wondered how we were going to occupy ourselves after our honeymoon period was over.'

'Thank fuck for… sorry, I mean thank heaven for that, Miles. We had the terrible thought that you would just want to sit back, like on a holiday.'

'No, no. We wouldn't dream of such a thing.'

'You said honeymoon, Miles. Have you two tied the knot then?'

'No, not in the eyes of the state; but on joining the ship for life, that is our marriage. I'm getting a bit chilly out here Albert. Can we go back in now that you have your question out of the way?' he smiled.

'Certainly Miles, thank you for understanding my predicament.'

'You will have to realise and also explain to the rest, that we are total novices at this way of life. We didn't even cook our own meals before. Like most people living in city or urban areas, we either dined out or had takeaways or delivered meals. So I hope we will be shown what to do and not just be expected to get on with it and be made fools of.'

Miles went back to the cabin, to Jane. He explained what Albert had said.

'Well, at least it's out in the open, and we'll just have to see what contribution we can make Miles.'

'I know, let's have an early night and sleep on it. Perhaps we'll come up with something tomorrow?' Jane thought that she'd rather he came up with something tonight! In no time at all, they were both completely naked and cuddled up together in bed. 'Oh Jane, you're gorgeous. I love you so much ....'

Albert had returned to the canteen to see if there were any stragglers, but mainly to have a pint of bitter. Ched and Gunter were seated at the bar so Albert went over to join them. They were just finishing their drinks.
'How about another?' asked Albert.
'We shouldn't.' Gunter replied. 'We are under orders, especially me. You know, with Greta's pregnancy.'
'Millie will be back soon and I haven't collected Vicky from Greta yet,' Ched added.
'Just have a half then, while I explain what happened when I approached Miles about helping out.'
'We wondered where you went after dinner, didn't we Ched?' Albert poured the drinks, took a good mouthful of his bitter and explained his conversation with Miles.
'So how are they going to help us?'
'Well, I've given it some thought. You'll have to tell me what you think. Initially, Jane could take shifts on lookout. I know it's not so important while we are at anchor, but she's got to be taught what to look out for, especially when we move to the south. We won't have radar on all of the time because of power conservation. She will need to know the different positions of lights that other vessels carry for identification, and so on.'
'And who is going to teach her that?' asked Gunter facetiously.
'Who else but you Gunter, you might like that?' said Ched.
'I might, but Greta won't... *Scheißer!*' he swore.
'Well you'll just have to be squeaky clean, and mean it. Besides, it takes two to tango and we don't want the problem of any complications between couples,' warned Albert.
'Ok, I can handle it, even if Jane might find me irresistible!' They all started laughing and Ched poked him in the ribs.
'You see Gunter; you Germans have got a sense of humour.'

'What plans have you for Miles?' asked Ched.
'I thought that's where you would come in Ched,' Albert replied straight away.

'What me? I don't need any help. I'm quite happy on my own thank you.'
'Now come on. That's not the point. He's got to be made to feel useful and I'm sure he will be.'
'What will he be doing to help me then?' Ched asked in an agitated way. 'Teach him the controls of the ship while we are at anchor and get him to understand the systems? That won't take all summer.'
'You'll be going out fishing tomorrow; he can go with you. Teach him to fish and help you,' Albert suggested.
'Oh shit! Why can't he help you Albert, in the brewing department?'
'No. That's far too specialised,' Albert grinned as he spoke.
'That just about sums it up,' said Ched. They all supped up and went off to their cabins.

Breakfast was finished and Ched had the job of asking Miles if he could help him with the fishing. Miles, being obliging, agreed.
'Yes, I've never been fishing before,' thinking he would be sitting peacefully on the Ark somewhere, with a fishing rod and a flask of coffee for the day. Meanwhile, Magnus was already busy getting the twenty foot fishing boat up from the hold, complete with nets and lobster pots, to be hoisted over the side. There was a light breeze and just small wavelets. Visibility was good, ideal for a first trip out, using the new equipment. Miles followed Ched with apprehension. He realised they may be going out in a boat.
'Are we going out in that?'
'Yes,' replied Ched, 'you'd better put this wet weather gear on, just in case...'
'In case of what' Ched paused for a moment and thought he was going to have some fun here.
'In case we get caught in the storm that's forecast.' Ched looked over to Magnus and winked.
'A storm' Miles gasped, panicking, 'In that small boat?'
'Yes, Come on! Let's get in then Miles. Magnus can lower us over the side. The sooner we get going the sooner we get back.'

They climbed in and Magnus hoisted the boat in its cradle over the side of the Ark. Miles turned pale. Ched looked at him as they were being lowered down.
'If you're going to throw up please do it over the side.' At that point, Miles fell to his knees and retched into the water. Ched smiled to himself, cruelly

53

thinking, mission accomplished! He released the cradle as the boat hit the water, started up the motor and powered the craft away from the side of the Ark as soon as he could. Miles was still hanging his head over and clinging to the side retching, not feeling too good. Ched ignored him and concentrated on aiming for an area he had seen on the chart.

At the time, Jane was on lookout under the helpful arms of Gunter showing her how to focus the binoculars and to try to pick things out at sea. The only activity they could focus on was Ched, with Miles, hanging over the side of the boat in an undignified manner.

'What's happening Gunter, is Miles looking for fish?' Gunter took the binoculars from Jane to see for himself.

'Yes Jane. He's probably looking for fish.' Gunter had to think of something else to show Jane to take her mind and vision away from Miles' suffering. He decided to try to explain the sea charts to her and took her off to the bridge. Gunter was struggling and very uncomfortable with his tuition task. He had not been as close to another very attractive woman since before he was married. When they arrived at the bridge, Jane was full of questions.

'Why do they call this a bridge?' Gunter explained that it came from the days of paddle steamers when the huge paddlewheel housings on either side of the ship blocked the Captain's view, so a bridge was built joining the housings together and the control of the ship was made from there.

Meanwhile, Ched and Miles were about three miles southwest of where the Ark was anchored. The chart showed some wrecks there and it wasn't deep. 'Fish like hanging around this sort of area,' he told Miles as they bobbed up and down over the small waves. Miles decided to stand up alongside Ched and started to breathe in and out deeply. Clinging to the front of the cockpit, he gradually came to. Ched looked at him and began to feel a bit sorry for him.

'You'll feel better now you've got that out of the way. Let me give you a few tips. Don't try to keep yourself still. Move with the boat and look to the horizon moving your head as much as you can. Try to keep up those deep breaths; you'll be fine.'

'Thank you,' replied Miles gratefully. He took the advice and started to get some colour back to his face. Looking around and back to the Ark, he was beginning to feel quite good compared to a few minutes ago.

Ched looked at his compass and log and guessed he would be near the chosen area. He slowed down leaving the motor ticking over.

'We'll get rid of the lobster and crab pots first Miles, and then we'll have a go with the net.' They dropped each pot over the side leaving a small marker buoy attached so they could be found on return, spacing them out about fifty metres apart. Moving away, Ched slowed the boat down again.

'Right Miles give me a hand putting the net over the rear of the boat and we'll try a bit of mini-trawling.' They neatly let the net out in a loop from one side of the boat to the other. The floats on the net kept the top afloat whereas the bottom had weights attached, keeping the net stretched out underwater. Once it was spread and clear from the rear of the boat, Ched slowly pulled the net behind the boat for about two miles, then he stopped the engine.

'I think we have something. I can feel it dragging, slowing us down. Now Miles, this is the hard bit. We've got to pull the net in evenly into the well of the boat. When it's in, I'll deal with the fish if you can hold the net. I'll be throwing back anything too small or not fit to eat and everything else goes into that bin.' Miles flinched.

'Ok, yes. I think I've got that,' he said sheepishly. Slowly, they pulled in the net. The nearer the net came to the boat the heavier it became, until they started rolling it into the well, gradually releasing the catch into the bottom.

'Wow! It's nearly all cod,' shouted Ched, 'and some lovely ones too.' He set to work sorting them out while Miles struggled to pull in the net, trying to close his ears to the dull thumps of Ched's club as he stunned the lively ones. Finally, the whole net and catch was in and Ched was very happy with their achievement.

'That's it Miles. Let's get back to the Ark.'

'But what about the lobster pots,'

'Bloody hell!' said Ched, 'It'll be a couple of days before they have anything in them.'

'Oh.' replied Miles,' almost disappointed.

They motored back. Magnus lowered the cradle over the side ready for Ched to connect it to the boat. It was soon on its way up the side of the Ark and onto the deck.

'Ched it looks like you missed that storm.'

'Yes, we certainly did Magnus,' replied Ched with a smile. Miles climbed out of the boat.

'Don't disappear; we haven't finished the job yet Miles. I'll need a hand with the catch. We have to gut and wash them.'
'Gut them? You mean cut out their insides?'
'Yes, of course!' Ched looked up to see Miles' face but he was already heading for the steps to retch over the side again.
'Oh dear, Magnus said, 'It looks like he won't be giving us a hand with the fish.' Ched gave a snigger.
'What a bloody wimp!'

After unloading, Ched and Magnus returned the fishing boat back into the hold, made it secure then gutted and cleaned the fish before taking them to the kitchen. Albert arrived at the scene as they were throwing the waste over the side for the gulls.
'Hey! Hold on a minute. I'm sure we should be able to recycle that. Seal it up into containers for now and I'll have a word with Millie later. Thanks lads..... By the way, how did it go Ched? And where's Miles?'
'I should think Miles is lying down on his bed. He wasn't feeling too well last time we saw him.'
'Was he seasick then?'
'He was at first, when we went out but soon got over it and seemed to be enjoying it out there. It wasn't until we got back onboard and I asked him to give us a hand to gut the fish he felt a bit sick and rushed off. We haven't seen him since.'
'I'd better go and see if he's alright.'

Miles and Jane gradually eased into the flow and spirit of things in their new way of life, and were enjoying the daily routines. Miles began to like going out fishing when it was calm but still could not bring himself to gut and clean the fish. Jane took an interest in things navigational, but soon became bored with the almost static scenery. When Miles was out fishing, and it was not Jane's shift on lookout, she would go and seek out Amy, to see if there was anything she could help with. Amy would usually find her something simple to do. When she tired of that, she often went to see what Albert was up to in his brewing and distillery area. She was fascinated by it and was quite helpful to Albert in the preparation and controls required. After only two weeks, with her attention to detail, the quality of the beer improved.

Millie was getting the help she wanted when she asked, even from Miles. The pattern of life onboard became moulded; the only things that were changing were the people themselves. Marigold and Melanie began to blossom. Marigold had lost some of her hippy-ness and turned out to be a natural blonde with a nice complexion. She gave everybody a lovely smile, even though her child bawled its head off all day long. Her only conversation was asking when the ship was going to start its world cruise. No one had the heart to tell her the truth and besides, that was Monty's problem. Melanie practiced her classical guitar with the help of Greta who had studied music herself. Greta's pregnancy was progressing, with the baby due in September. This was causing some anxiety for Gunter, the thought of having the child delivered without an experienced midwife, although there was enough females onboard with practical, first hand knowledge. Also, Monty would be at hand, if required, although Gunter didn't rate his professional skills very highly!

Patricia had lost another three stones and were now nearly seventeen stones, mainly due to the hot summer; working hard and sweating profusely in the kitchen.
'That's why the gravy has been so salty...' Ched had joked to everyone's disgust!

Monty was always very busy, when he was awake, making compounds and tending the herb garden. Amy also continued to take a deeper interest in the subject. One of the plants she was keen to have more information on was the Maca plant, especially after Monty told her the name, *Lepidium Peruvianchalon* or *Peruvian Ginseng* also known as *Peruvian Viagra*.
'When would it be ready to use?'
'Very soon; do you want to try it out, because it works for both men and women?'
'How is it administered?'
'It will be in tablet form.'
'I'll have the first batch, if that's ok?' Monty nodded a 'yes' and told her a bit more about its use.

On walking around the herb garden she noticed some poppies just coming into flower.
'They are pretty. Aren't they unusual? And what's the green spiky plant over there?'

57

'Oh that.' replied Monty, It's just a weed.'
'Shouldn't it be pulled up then?'
'Oh no! Don't do that! I'm sure it'll have some use. I'll look the variety up and see what.' Amy walked off, leaving Monty relieved that she didn't ask any more questions on the poppies and the hemp. (He was keen to preserve his secret opium and cannabis sources.) Monty's other problem with hemp was that he needed to cultivate it in a better environment; it needed more humidity. Amy's mind was full of *Peruvian Viagra*. She wondered how long it would take him to make the tablets and thought I'll need to feed Albert with them before he has something to eat to get the best effect, hmm, sounds exciting. I must ask Monty how it works the next time we are in the herb garden. It's strange that a plant related to the cabbage, could possibly have such an effect on the body!

ALBERT'S PRIVATE LOG   APRIL - AUGUST 2016

Off Bardsey Island - West coast of Wales UK

Well I thought I had better do some sort of a record of what has been going on during the time on the Ark: a log of things that have happened and my thoughts: a private log.

We finally put to sea and made it to our first anchorage unscathed and to think it's about eighteen months ago since we purchased the Ark. I just hope we can manage the maintenance and any repairs to the ship that may be required at sea. I'm amazed at how well the ship responds under its own power, getting out of port was a bit hairy though. I hope we never have to go back into port for a very, very long time, if ever.

The sails worked well on there first outing, although physically difficult to operate, making me realise we are definitely short of manpower.

Everything is taking shape on this floating island, and it's fantastic to look out from the bridge to see crops, animals and trees in the distance. When it starts to turn cold at the end of our summer here, we can lift anchor and take this beauty with us to a warmer climate for the winter.

Everybody seems to be settling into their new way of life, even Miles and Jane. I wonder how long it will be before she falls pregnant. I'm glad Jane has taken an interest in brewing; it's certainly the help I need. I must improve on my technique: the bitter is only just drinkable.

Millie is doing an excellent job with the farming and she is so dedicated; she puts Ched to shame in the working department. She is the salt of the earth we float on and the key person in food production. I must make sure she gets any help she may require; we don't want her stressed out and unable to function. I have seen this happen many times before through people working too hard!

Ched finally has got over the initial 'Miles hasn't got a clue' problem and has begun to respect him, probably for Miles' willingness to try almost everything he has been asked to do. He likes going fishing on calm days but cannot stand the sight of gutting fish.

Monty is a strange one; he hardly joins in the community thing. He may have talents, but will not gain respect here by being a loner. He doesn't seem to do much at all, but always has something else to excuse him when volunteers are called for. I feel sorry for poor Marigold; mostly he behaves as though he thinks she's not there. She has a full time job with her little Lucy and we do see more of her than at first but Amy has also sensed the problem and she will keep an eye on their wellbeing, as I will also.

Gunter handled things well on the move here and seems a very solid man. Everything he does is methodical and precise; a typical German. Makes me wonder how he could have possibly made an error to cause the damage in his previous job. He does seem quite relaxed in his new environment. And, we will soon have the first baby born on the Ark: Greta is due in September, at about the same time we move to the southern hemisphere for the winter. I hope the baby does not arrive while we lift anchor and are trying to get under way.

It's now coming to the end of the first five months' stay off the coast of Wales and completion of our successful trial. Each person on the Ark has played their part in some contribution to making a functional community, even Miles, who at first I had my doubts about of what practical help he could give. He even gave assistance to Melanie's further education, particularly her maths and trigonometry, without the aid of calculators and computers. I am surprised how well a young teenager has coped without modern technology to entertain her. I'm sure she must have been like other kids, relying on their mobile telephones. Television programmes, the internet, and music players etc. She's developing into such a lovely natured girl too.

Gunter taught Jane the basics of how to plot a course for the ship to follow and she is able to do a lookout shift as well. She was reluctant to do a late night to early morning stint, which was understandable for a *newlywed!*

Patricia has really surprised me, I thought she would want to sit around all day long, but working with Amy in the kitchen and laundry has changed her outlook on life and she's losing weight at the same time.

Magnus always keeps busy, making sure everything functions properly, even down to a door hinge. If it squeaks, it gets oiled. Personally, I would rather it squeaked as an early warning system, so I can hear someone is coming through. Also creaky stairs: I think it's better they creak when you are in bed, as a pre-warning. It's just the way I've got used to living over the years, being on my guard. I must admit, my mind is more relaxed living on the Ark, and I hope it stays that way.

So far so good, the next few months will be the real test with the journey to the Southern Atlantic.

6. WILL THEY EVER GET TO TRISTAN DE CUNHA?

There was an air of excitement, as the crew worked hard to get ready for the first journey to the southern hemisphere. Ripe crops were harvested. Blackcurrants, raspberries, gooseberries and even rhubarb had already been collected and made into preserves and wine. The grape vines that had been bought as mature plants bore very little fruit; they were obviously not as well established in their new environment, as the other soft fruits.

'We'll have to rely on the supplies we purchased that's left in storage, for the next eighteen months at least, so that may mean at worst, some rationing of food, to eek it out until we can produce enough.' Albert told them all. 'So we will have to keep a constant stock control to ensure we don't run out of essentials.'

Potatoes were lifted and stored and a second lot of seed put in the ground to grow in the southern hemisphere. The same applied to carrots. Wheat was harvested, straw bailed. The hay had been collected earlier in the season and stored for the animals. The grain was ground and made into flour and stored ready to make fresh bread on a daily basis. Harvest had been a progression, from the rapid growth of the grasses, which fed the cows, goats and the few sheep, to the salads, the first early potatoes and of course the brassicas such as broccoli, cabbage, and cauliflower. Monty and Amy's herbs were a tremendously successful display. Some of the Ark's own grown produce was being consumed within a couple of months of leaving Milford Haven. Most things grew well on the huge, walled small holding.

Last minute nerves were making people feel anxious and apprehensive. It was decided to make a special, social occasion of the day before lifting anchor and putting to sail. Albert hoped this would lighten up everybody's spirits, ready for the six thousand mile long journey of three to four weeks, to their winter anchorage. A banquet-style meal was arranged for everyone that evening using some of the produce they all had worked on, but mainly organised and toiled at by Millie. The only thing they were short of was meat; none of the animals were quite ready for slaughtering yet, but because of the special occasion, they decided to spit-roast one suckling pig, the rest were needed for more feeding up and for breeding. They had been living on imported meat held in the freezer during the first five months but this stock was getting very low and there was not a great deal of choice left.

They had had some success at fishing, mainly mackerel and cod. Ched and Gunter had been out in the fishing boat a few days ago and laid some lobster pots. They decided it was time to go out again, bring them in for the last time there, and see what else they could find. They were amazed at the amount of fish etc being pulled in: lobster, crab, shrimps, cod, mackerel, sea bream and squid. The fishing boat was lifted out of the water, complete with Ched, Gunter and catch and hoisted up over the side onto the deck. The crew onboard the Ark were all eagerly waiting to see the fish that had been caught, leaning over the side of the fishing boat, looking at the variety, pointing at the fish with interest. Once onboard, it was sorted and carted off to the kitchen. All hands were busy making the preparations for that evening.

Even Miles joined in. He'd had problems at times, in occupying himself in this first five months. He was lost initially, without his computer. He must have read every book in the ship's library; but he did spend time helping Melanie with her schooling, especially mathematics which she struggled with, and she was very appreciative.

Albert and Amy took charge of the fish preparation. Mackerel and sea bream were gutted ready for grilling. The cod was filleted, coated in batter and deep fried. Lobsters and crabs were put into the deep freeze for twenty minutes to stun them and then into pans of boiling water for twenty minutes. Shrimps were boiled and peeled. The squid was gently boiled, then refrigerated and served cold. The table was laid and the food spread decoratively; it completely covered the table with barely enough room for plates. There were salads, grown onboard, potatoes, goats cheese, the mackerel served with gooseberry sauce, shrimp cocktails, dressed crab and lobster, fresh fruit salad with goat yoghurt and of course the suckling pig, not complete without the apple sauce.

A procession started arriving at the canteen and there were big 'Wows!' as they gazed at the spread of food and at what some of the others were wearing. It was obvious that almost everyone had dug deep into wardrobes, (or suitcases, for those who hadn't fully unpacked yet!) Fashions ranged from Miles in a dinner jacket and Jane in a lovely sapphire, silk fitted evening dress, visibly, but tastefully without a bra, to Magnus, who was very casual in chinos and shirt accompanied by Patricia wearing a beige sack-like creation with Melanie in tight jeans and a cheap, cotton cropped top. Albert, Ched and Gunter were in smart suits with wives in long dinner or cocktail dresses. Monty turned up in a slightly grubby, cream, unpressed summer suit and finally Marigold was still wearing the same clothes she had on for the past two days: a multicoloured, long loose dress with a non-matching cardigan; clutching tiny Lucy.

It was a help yourself situation with the drinks; this first harvest feast had to rely on imported wines from the ship's store, but the next time Albert assured them it should be from the Ark's own fruit. The beer was brewed onboard. Albert still hadn't quite perfected it, despite Jane's help, but it had the desired effect. The spirits were under lock and key, to avoid anyone not feeling too good the next day, for the start of the long journey ahead. The evening went very well; there was an initial toast to the good life and then everybody tucked in.

After the meal, Melanie was encouraged, initially by Albert, then cheered on by the rest, to show her musical skills, by playing some of her now well-practiced work on her classical guitar, which was a pleasant surprise to all. She made a very nervous start to 'Cavatina' a classical piece that was used as a theme tune to the old film 'The Deer Hunter'. She soon became more confident. This was followed by 'Romance' a well known classic, probably made mostly popular by the Guitarist John Williams. There was a great deal of applause for her rendition. For the finale, she altered the tuning of the strings of her instrument to the bewildered audience. Melanie introduced it as 'Koto' music, which is for a thirteen stringed Japanese instrument and that it originated from Japanese court music of 1614-1685. No one there had heard it, or of it, before but was delighted in the outcome. A huge applause was well deserved with all thanking her for the wonderful entertainment.

Everybody was congratulating each other and wanted their success to continue. It was wonderful to feel the freedom from financial worries, no pressure from the dreaded tax man or anything else, other than to stay afloat and provide the food required to keep them healthy. The evening was drawing to an end and the children were packed off to bed. Tables were being cleared away and the remaining people congregated around the small bar to have a final drink together, before retiring for the evening. They were joined by Jane, Marigold and Melanie who had returned from putting the children to bed. Miles moved to behind the bar to get the three ladies'

63

drinks, then returned to join them all on the other side of the bar to give a final toast, thanking them yet again, for their hard work and kindness. At the end of this, he and Jane said their goodnights and left sharply to go to their quarters.

'I bet he's going to get his leg over tonight!' Ched commented. Melanie blushed.

'The lucky sods,' Marigold said, as she looked hopefully at Monty. I expect you'll be fast asleep as soon as your head hits the pillow.' Albert sensed a difficult conversation coming up.

'That's it folks,' He shouted out. 'The bar's closed. It's time for us all to go to bed. We've had a long day today and it's going to be a very long hard day tomorrow, so please drink up.' The request was soon acted on, with empty glasses placed on the bar and most of them left to go to their rooms.

Albert started clearing the glasses away to wash them.

'Oh, I'll give you a hand Albert,' Melanie said, turning to Magnus, saying, 'I'll be along shortly Dad. I'm just giving Albert a hand to wash up.'

'Ok, come in and say goodnight before you go to bed.'

'Yes Dad.' Magnus left the bar. She started to help by drying up the glasses that Albert washed, 'I'm still being treated like a little girl,' Melanie opened up to Albert. 'I'm nearly sixteen.'

'Well,' said Albert, 'they are just being protective.'

'Protecting me from what? There are no young men to meet, what am I going to do? I'm trapped on this ship and I'll be lonely for the rest of my life.' Albert paused before answering.

'Yes Melanie, I can understand your feelings on that score. You are a young lady now and you will have needs.'

'Albert I've got them already.'

'Please Melanie be patient, I can't control boy meets girl situation. We'll just have to wait and see how the next couple of seasons go; you never know what's around the corner, or in our case, what's over the horizon'.

They both finished the clearing up and said goodnight to each other. Amy was waiting up for Albert; he was glad she was still awake, because Melanie had pricked his conscience. He realised that, all of a sudden, she was a fully developed young women. Albert repeated the conversation he had with Melanie to Amy as he was preparing for bed, hoping she would say something that would ease his mind. Amy's reply was not very helpful.

'You can't supply what is not there Albert.'

'I know that, but when we started out I saw her as just a little schoolgirl without all these thoughts of love and romance in her head, and now, all of a sudden she's a young woman.'

'There's nothing you can do about it at the moment, so let's get to sleep. Goodnight Albert.'

'Goodnight, my love.'

Miles and Jane had not gone to bed yet. They were still quite lively and decided to have a nightcap of some brandy Miles had brought with him when he joined the ship. Jane was feeling good, bubbly, happy, and pleasantly inebriated. They were chatting and laughing. Jane was feeling amorous and decided to put a bit more zest into the evening and do a striptease for Miles. She stood, put down her empty glass and faced him. Posing provocatively, she slowly released the zip at the back of her dress, just enough to let the low-cut evening gown glide gently down over her beautifully formed breasts. Her pert nipples were pointing at Miles and she watched him gaze as her magnificent shape was revealed. She stepped out of the dress and kicked it along the floor, still in her high heeled shoes and a minute thong. Stretching her arms upwards she did a single twirl, to face Miles. She brought her hands down slowly to her breasts and started to caress them, tweaking her nipples. Miles' eyes got bigger and bigger. Jane moved closer to him putting her hands to his head, and brought his lips to each nipple in turn for him to suck. He was just enjoying the pleasure of them when she pulled away, still caressing her breasts as a tease. Dropping her hands to her thin waistline down to the top of her thong, she moved her body in a slow dance, side to side. She pulled the lacy thong down over her thighs until it was loose enough to drop to the floor but took one foot out, leaving it around the toe of her right shoe. She raised her foot into the air, kicking off the skimpy underwear straight into Miles' face.

He was completely stunned, by her beautiful, natural, naked body and erotic performance. He fell to his knees where his eyes met the top of her legs. Placing his hand on her buttocks, he pulled her to him, burying his face into her. Gently, he pulled her to the floor as she opened her legs for him to explore her with his tongue. He soon found the spot which made her judder and she gave a delighted moan. She held his head there, until she had reached a climax of pleasure.

65

Then she pulled him up on top of her, frantically tugging at his shirt buttons as he undid his trousers, pulling them down to his knees along with his boxers. He knelt between her splayed legs, displaying his now enormous penis. She sat up to hold it.

'My, my, Miles, that's the biggest I've ever seen you!' She lay back, pulling his erection to her. Miles crouched over her and she gave a pleased moan on his entry, which became louder and louder as his thrusts increased in speed. He became so excited he ejaculated with a massive throbbing pulsating sensation. He had never experienced such delight before. Suddenly, a sharp, unbearable pain shot across the top of his chest. He became light-headed and started seeing small bright blue spots of light in front of his eyes surrounded by white light at the circumference of his vision, the blue lights changed to zigzags, then it all faded to darkness.

'Miles what's wrong?' Jane asked as she rolled him over to her side. 'Miles, Miles, wake up!' she pleaded as she slapped his face, but to no avail. She realised something was seriously wrong, opened his mouth to give mouth to mouth resuscitation, but still no movement. With his eyes wide open with a constant stare, she realised he was gone. She closed his eyelids and burst into sobs, which went to a frantic crescendo as she raised him to her arms to hold him close.

'Oh Miles, why have you done this to me,' She got up and immediately put on a dressing gown, pulled up Miles' trousers with difficulty and fastened them. Then she tugged his shirt together and did up some of the buttons. Still sobbing, she went to the bedroom, took a sheet from the bed and covered him, then came a thumping on the door.

'What's up Jane? Are you alright? We heard you crying.' It was Gunter. He banged on the door again, 'Jane, Jane, are you alright?' Jane went to the door and opened it to Gunter and Greta.

'What's up Jane? Where's Miles?' They went in and she pointed to the sheet on the floor that covered the lifeless body. Jane continued sobbing. Gunter, followed by Greta, went over to Miles.

'You haven't killed him, have you?' Greta asked. Jane screamed hysterically.

'Oh Jane, I'm sorry.' Greta went to comfort Jane as Gunter knelt down, lifted the sheet to expose Miles' limp left arm and tried to find a pulse, but there was nothing.

'I'm sorry Jane, he's dead.'

66

'I know, I know; it's my fault.' Jane sobbed again in between gulps of breath. Greta gently took her arm.
'You had better come to our cabin.'

Gunter ran to get Albert, banging on the door several times. Albert had gone into a deep sleep. Gradually coming round, he realised something was up. Amy didn't stir.
'Bloody hell who on earth is that?' Putting on the bedside lamp, he slid into his slippers, pulled on his dressing gown and headed for the door.
'Alright, alright, I'm coming, I'm coming.' Albert opened the door to a distraught Gunter. 'What is it?'
'Please come and help, Albert. It's Miles. He is dead!'
'Dead, are you sure?'
'Yes Albert. I'm positive, he's *beendet,* finished. I've checked his pulse and there is nothing.
'How did it happen?'
'I don't know. I can only imagine that he might have had a massive heart attack.'
'What could have caused it?'
'You will have to ask Jane.'

They entered the cabin and went towards Miles.
'Where's Jane?' Albert asked.
'With Greta in our cabin,' Albert lifted the sheet covering Miles' ashen face then covered it up again.
'Poor Miles and poor Jane, she must be devastated.'
'Yes Albert,' agreed Gunter, 'she seems to be blaming herself.'
'We'll have to get him into a body-bag for now' Albert whispered. 'Would you fetch one from the stores, please? I'll stay here until you get back.'
'Of course Albert, I'll be as quick as I can.'

Gunter was back in ten minutes and stretched out the bag, unzipping it alongside Miles.
'The last time I used one of these was over twenty years ago in the Gulf, said Albert grimly. They rolled him in and zipped it up.
'Well there's nothing more we can do here at the moment, probably best if we can all get some sleep. They left the room with Albert locking the door behind them. Gunter and Albert returned to their cabins.
'Jane will be alright with us tonight.' Gunter assured him.

'Ok, thanks. Goodnight.' Albert entered his cabin to find Amy wide awake.
'Where have you been Albert?'
'It's Miles. It looks like he's had a heart attack. There's no easy way to say this Amy, but he's dead.'
'Oh my god, where's Jane?'
'She's with Greta and Gunter.'
'I must go and see the poor child.'
'For fuck's sake Amy, they're looking after her. Let's get back to sleep.'
'No Albert, you insensitive old sod, she needs our help now!'
'Oh shit!' exhaled Albert as Amy was through the door still putting on her dressing gown and, in no time at all, knocking on Gunter and Greta's door.

Gunter got up from the sofa, to where he'd been confined, and opened the door.
'Amy. They are in the bedroom. Greta is trying to calm Jane down. She has been hysterical, keeps blaming herself,'
'I must see her,' demanded Amy.
'Of course,' said Gunter, trying to be diplomatic, 'but Greta is doing her best with her.'
'Don't worry Gunter, this is a 'my generation' thing. The older you get, the more people you know who die. But this is tragic, he was far too young. I know nothing can bring him back; but it's the living that counts now. Jane is very young and looked to Miles for strength, and now she will feel lost. She'll need a lot of help Gunter.'
'*Ich verstehe*, I mean I think I understand Amy. Go to her as you wish.'

Amy tapped at the bedroom door where Greta was still comforting the bereft Jane. The sight of Amy made the sobbing increase. Jane lifted herself off the bed, pulling away from Greta and stumbled forwards to Amy. Both opened their arms ready to clasp each other. Amy grasped her.
'Oh my child, my dear child, you have suffered so much this evening but now you need to conserve your strength and try to get to sleep. Nothing can change what has happened. He was a loving man and he loved you.' This calmed Jane to some extent and she nodded her head in agreement. Jane gradually relaxed, the sobbing had ceased. Jane breathed in deeply as they held each other tightly.
'Thank you Amy,' she whispered.

68

'Come on now,' Greta said as she got up, 'let's all get some sleep and face the next day as it comes.' Amy and Jane released each other. Jane felt numb but she knew she had friends to go to that felt for her, and was comforted by that. Jane got into Greta's bed and Amy made her exit as Gunter pulled a blanket over his head on the sofa. Amy returned to Albert who was in bed snoring and totally out for the count.

'The useless bastard could have waited up for me!' she mumbled to herself, as she slid into bed alongside him and stretched her arm around his paunch, thinking that it was definitely getting bigger. Eventually, she fell asleep. The Ark was silent.

Albert was up very early the next day. He had to plan what to do. Later, he made a fruit juice drink and brought one in for Amy, who was just stirring.

'Good morning my dear, I feel as though I had a terrible nightmare last night but now I've come to, it was worse than a nightmare, it has happened, we've lost Miles!'

'What are we going to do with him?' asked Amy. 'We are still in UK waters and, by law, shouldn't he be taken to the mainland to be dealt with?'

'Technically, yes... but no Amy, we are not turning back, if we stay and transport him in the fishing boat to the mainland there will have to be an autopsy and an inquest, and the interrogation that goes with it. Then before we can finally put him to rest, there will be a funeral to organise. We'll lose the momentum of the whole project. It will be weeks before we leave to go south. We have to cope with death onboard as it happens. By going through this situation, it will condition them all for the ultimate and they'll know how to deal with it when the next time comes. We will give Miles a proper funeral. He will be buried in the orchard under the apple trees, as will all of us, when we go. It will give a new meaning to being buried at sea. But poor Jane, this will take some getting over.'

'She's young,' said Amy, 'and strong. It may take a little time but I'm sure she will get over it. The only problem is, when she does get over his death, she will probably want another partner. That's going to be the biggest problem.'

'Oh shit! Albert replied. That's double trouble, what with her and Melanie.'

'Well, enough of that, Albert, we have to tackle today first.'

'Could you look after Jane and explain the arrangements, Amy, while I tell everyone else what's happening?'

At breakfast time, as soon as the others had all arrived, Albert called for silence and made his sad announcement. He then told them of his plans to bury Miles at 1500 hours that day, in the orchard, if Jane agreed, and said he would get back to everyone to confirm. Before finishing breakfast he took Ched, Magnus and Gunter aside and asked them to meet him on the bridge at 0900 hours.

'I hope to have confirmation from Jane to go ahead with the funeral by then.' he said. 'We'll need to organise the digging of a grave because we can't have a dead body lying about, so the sooner he is buried the better. I will have to come up with some sort of a sermon if that's the right word, because none of us are really religious. It has to be done out of respect for Miles. We must give him a proper burial and send off.'

Shortly after the meeting, Albert discussed the situation again with Amy, not having Jane's consent yet on his burial plans, they both agreed to take the risk and go ahead with the preparations anyway, because his thinking was, if it was done rapidly then it would all be accepted and forgotten sooner.

He met the three others on the bridge and between them they planned the day. There was a grave to be dug and made safe, so that Miles could be buried without them all falling in on top of him. Magnus asked about a coffin and said he could make one, but Albert said that he would decompose better, just in the earth. Then, trying not to be too indelicate, he added that the body would improve the soil quicker that way.

'We have to remove Miles from where he is and prepare him for burial, but we also need to keep Jane out of the way while this is being done. I've got to think of a few words to say over him and then we should have a bit of a wake afterwards. So we had better get cracking.'

7. A FUNERAL

Shortly after meeting Albert, Ched and Gunter set off for the orchard. They walked to the bow of the Ark between the animal pens and the main fields that stretched all the way back to the upper decks and bridge. The orchard started at the starboard (right) side and went across to the port side with access at each edge to the animal pens. It measured about fifty metres across by thirty metres in depth. The trees were developing well and the apples, pears, plums and cherries were in fruit and some ready to pick. The olives, oranges and lemon trees were not established enough to produce anything but this should change after a year or so in a warmer climate.

Ched and Gunter met up with Millie and they looked around the apple trees for a suitable place to dig a grave for Miles. Millie picked a spot.
'Just here guys.' They were just about to put spade to earth when a female voice shouted at them.
'Wait!' It was Jane and about sixty metres behind her was Magnus carrying some lengths of timber. Ched and Gunter stopped work and waited for Jane to arrive.
'I'm sorry but I would like to pick the spot where Miles is to be buried.' Millie, Ched and Gunter looked at one another, shrugged their shoulders and all spoke at the same time.
'That's fine.' They were surprised to see her, thinking she would still be sobbing in the cabin, but it was obviously important to her where he was laid to rest. Jane looked about the trees, circling each one and studying them hard. As she was doing this, Magnus arrived, puffing and panting, heavily laden with wood and a saw.
'It's a long way to here.' he complained.
'Stop moaning, I do it several times a day.' Millie responded.
'But you're young and fit.' he replied.
'I can't do anything about your age Magnus, but if you did more walking on a daily basis, you might improve your fitness!'
'Point taken,' murmured Magnus, 'we will need some more timber to shore back the earth while the excavation is being dug. I'd better go and get some.'
'You could use the tractor-trailer,' Ched shouted.
'No it's alright, I need the exercise.

By this time, Jane had selected a particular tree and she called the others.

71

'Here, this one.' They went to her, 'Yes this one,' she stated again, 'I like the way the branches are reaching out, and its got character.'
'Ok,' said Millie, 'let's get started.' Jane thanked them and then walked away heading back to the upper decks. Ched mumbled that the tree had more character than Miles *ever* had!
'Ched, how could you? Millie turned on him angrily. 'Have some respect!'
'Sorry Millie.' He quickly got to work cutting away sods of grass and piled them to one side, ready to be re-laid later on top of the grave.

Amy and Albert had called at Greta's cabin to see how Jane was. They were also concerned about Greta because she was so heavily pregnant.
'Jane eventually cried herself to sleep in the early hours and didn't wake up until way past breakfast time,' Greta explained. 'Gunter had already left to help Millie and Ched. When Jane found out where he was going, she borrowed a pair of my trousers and a top, because obviously, she did not want to go back to her cabin. She left with bare feet to go to the orchard.'
Albert looked towards Amy and Greta.
'We'll have to prepare Miles' body for the burial. I'll call on Monty to help move him to one of the storerooms off the main deck. We've got to do it before Jane gets back. I don't want her to catch sight of Miles yet.'
'If you go now, Albert, I'll walk to Jane and intercept her on her way back.'
Amy went immediately, leaving Albert with Greta.

'I'm sorry, you must be really tired, but I'll need your help, Greta, to look after the children with Melanie while we move Miles. Could you possibly ask Patricia for her assistance to meet outside Jane's cabin as soon as possible? I'll go and get Monty and Marigold to help too.' She nodded to agree.

They set about the unpleasant task ahead of them. Monty and Marigold were still visibly shaken by the news of Miles' death. When Albert asked for their help, Monty responded immediately. Marigold was hesitant but Albert insisted that she came too.
'Just help us by leading the way to the storeroom, making sure fire doors are opened and closed so we carry Miles through quickly.'
'Yes, yes I'm coming.'

Off they went. Patricia was standing outside the cabin when they arrived. Albert had picked up a stretcher from the sickbay on the way. He opened

72

the door and asked the women to wait outside to allow him and Monty to dress Miles properly. Inside the cabin, they saw some of Miles' clothes were still on the floor near to where he lay. They unzipped the body bag and quickly pulled on the suit jacket he wore at the dinner celebration the previous evening, then the bow tie. Placing the closed bag onto the stretcher, they covered him with the bed sheet and called to Patricia to come in. Marigold remained outside the door. Albert asked if Patricia and Monty could take the head end of the stretcher and he would take the other. Patricia took it easily in her stride unlike Monty, who struggled with the weight. They were soon at the storeroom and laid him on a table.

'I'll prepare him ready for this afternoon. I know what to do.' Monty said.

'Thank you, that's much appreciated,' Albert replied. Monty and Marigold went off together while Albert and Patricia decided to go back to Jane's cabin to tidy it up for when Jane returned.

In the meantime, Amy found Jane sitting in the middle of one of the fields where wheat had been recently harvested. Amy sat down next to her and gently explained that Albert and the others were making preparations for Miles and that he would be buried at 1500 hrs that afternoon.

'Albert will speak a few words before he is covered. Is there anything you would like to say?' Tears trickled from Jane's eyes.

'Yes...I'll write something down for him to add.' Amy put her arm around Jane to comfort her and they sat there in silence. They were unaware of the seagulls' mournful cries, as the birds circled above the Ark. Twenty minutes or so passed as Amy and Jane stayed there, when they were disturbed by Albert approaching them. He had left Patricia to finish Jane's cabin, opening curtains and windows to freshen the place up. As Albert came closer, they both got up to greet him. He explained that Miles had been removed from the cabin and Monty was preparing him for the afternoon and that Jane's cabin was ready for her to return, if she so wished. Albert then left them to go to the orchard to see how the gravediggers were doing. When he arrived, they were about a metre in depth.

'How deep should we go Albert?' Millie asked.

'I should take it another half a metre; the soil seems well compacted, considering it's not been there all that long.'

'Yes,' said Millie, 'the sides are holding up well, but I don't like the look of those clouds heading this way. If we have any rain it will wash the excavation in.'

'Well we'll just have to keep our fingers crossed its 1200 hours now and we only have three hours to go before the burial. I shall be glad when it's all over and we're on our way south.'

Amy coaxed Jane back to her quarters. She entered the cabin where she had left Miles earlier. All evidence of what had happened had gone. The room was light, fresh and tidy.
'Thank you,' Jane said to Amy, 'I'm going to shower and dress for Miles and I want to be ready to say my goodbye to him.'

It was 1430 hours and everybody and everything was ready to take Miles to his resting place. Melanie had picked flowers: chrysanthemums, dahlias and gladioli, laying them neatly on Miles' body. Albert and Ched took the front of the stretcher, Gunter and Magnus took the other end. Lifting the four corners, they placed it onto a trolley and started the procession, with Miles at the head of the cortège. Jane walked behind Miles, alone. She was followed by Amy, Greta, Millie, Melanie, Monty and Marigold. Patricia had volunteered to look after the children. Slowly they made their way to the orchard, which took about thirty minutes. They laid him down on the ground at one side of the grave. Removing the covering of flowers, the bearers then slid lengths of webbing underneath Miles' body, before carefully lifting him off the stretcher and across the top of the opening in the ground. They slowly lowered him down, so that he lay neatly at the base of the grave. Ched and Gunter released the webbing at their end, while Albert and Magnus pulled the webbing from beneath Miles and up to the surface. The small gathering had lined one side of the grave with Albert and Jane on the other.

Albert started to speak.
'Please let us have one minute of silence before I say a few words for Miles.' There was silence, eerily, not even the sound of the gulls! That minute seemed one of the longest he had ever had to endure.
'This is a tragedy to us all in our newly formed community, especially to Jane who was looking forward to their long and happy future together. Miles was a very kind, generous person and the benefactor of our home here. May he rest in peace,' Albert bowed his head and took a few moments to think privately, how he had hoped that Miles and Jane would bring children to the Ark and what a sad loss that this was not to be. Albert took a sheet of paper from his pocket and continued, 'Jane has asked me to

say a few words on her behalf.' He cleared his throat and read aloud, 'Miles you were the kindest and most gentle person I knew. You are the only man in my heart. I will always love you and be near you. Goodbye my love, Jane.'

The spades were lifted. Jane put the first handful of soil on top of Miles. The men followed with spades of soil, quickly covering his body until it was out of sight. The women turned and walked away together, comforting Jane. Jane thanked Melanie for the flowers and arranging them on Miles.
'It was very kind and thoughtful of you. Thank you all for helping me so much.' They all walked slowly, returning to the canteen in the upper decks. The men stayed to complete the burial, leaving the flowers covering the newly laid sods of grass.

Later, everyone congregated in the canteen, where a small buffet had been prepared. Drinks were being dispensed and it became another, if somewhat sombre, social occasion. Patricia arrived with the three children. Stella and Vicky, now at four and a half and three years, started running wild as soon as they got to the canteen, leaving Patricia with Lucy in the buggy. They had no inkling of what had happened, being too young to understand it all. Soon Greta and Marigold took charge of their children and Millie tried to explain the gravity of the situation to Vicky. With everyone together, the gathering lasted for a couple of hours and then the various families gradually drifted away, leaving Jane with Amy and Albert. Jane had consumed a substantial amount of wine and her speech to Amy was slurred.
'Could you help me back to my cabin? Please stay with me for tonight Amy.'
'Of course I will.' Taking Jane's arm to steady her, Amy instructed Albert to collect her night things and bring them to Jane's. They all left for an early night for tomorrow was another big day.

ALBERT'S PRIVATE LOG – September 2016

The loss of Miles was a complete shock to us all, not having the full knowledge of the true cause of death, we can only assume that he suffered a massive heart attack and that is how it will be recorded. I don't think Jane will get over it easily. She had the opportunity to be put ashore, but insisted on staying close to Miles. I'm glad she didn't go; I don't want to delay the journey any longer.

With all of us being relative novices with this ship, the calmer the sea is as we get on our way, the better. I'm also glad that I didn't have any strong opposition to burying Miles on the Ark. It certainly gave a new meaning to *buried at sea*.

It's good to be ready to move south at last for the winter. It will be the beginning of spring when we arrive and if we stay until the season changes, it should work out so that we only see spring and summer seasons and miss the winters.

8. NOVICES AT SEA

The Ark came to life very early on the morning of their departure from just off the Welsh coast, to the southern hemisphere. It was a day later than planned and Jane could continue her mourning in transit. Albert did not want to chance being caught in any rough seas; it was renown in the northern hemisphere for weather changes at the back end of September and into October. He wanted to be underway as soon as possible. The ship was a hive of activity, the anchors were raised, and everybody was on the top deck looking towards the flickering lights in the distance that still shone in the dawning light, from the land that was just to go out of view. The turbines were running and the ship's propellers began to turn after their five months of being idle. A wake developed behind the Ark as it slowly moved south. Gunter had spent the last few days going over the course he would take to guide the ship on its several thousand miles to Tristan De Cunha; it would take them from Cardigan Bay into Saint George's Channel and out into the Atlantic Ocean. The name Atlantic is derived from Atlas, a Titan of Greek mythology and is the second largest of the world's five oceans and probably the busiest of all, Gunter thought.

On leaving British waters, the last sight of land was the Scilly Isles off the coast of Cornwall. Then they would pass east of the Azores, (the area that they planned to return to next spring) west of the Canary Islands, to the west of Cape Verde off the African coast, then towards Ascension Island and Saint Helena to the last leg of the journey to Tristan de Cunha. The wind and sea current would not be of help to them until they were well into the Atlantic, on the outskirts of the Bay of Biscay. There, the wind and currents move in a clockwise direction in the North Atlantic, from the Gulf stream around Bermuda eastwards to north of the Azores, before moving south to Madeira, the Canaries and then west, passing Cape Verde and forming the North Equatorial Current on its way back to Bermuda in the western part of the Atlantic. The part of the journey that should be good sailing for the Ark, and a real test of seamanship, would be from the Bay of Biscay to the Equator. The ship gradually gained speed and powered its way through Saint George's Channel in the south of the Irish Sea.

Gunter had set a course of 220°, and the Ark made good headway under the power of its gas turbines. The gas was from the original filling, when the ship was stocked, prior to their first journey. They had managed to store quite a lot of gas from the animal manure, but were going to need more if there was a lack of wind to put behind the sails, especially when they reached the Equator and the Doldrums. The top deck became empty of the Ark's on-looking inhabitants as they returned to their daily business. Albert took lookout, scanning the horizon for other vessels during daylight hours, but in between, refocusing his binoculars to watch Jane sitting at the side of Miles' grave, and occasionally on Millie tending the animals. Ched was at the ship's control with Gunter along side him, making sure they were on the right course. Magnus constantly listened to the engines, worried that they might let him down. He relaxed more as the day went on, and the engines purred away, pushing to fifteen knots by nightfall.

The Ark was heading out into the Atlantic. Gunter was concerned that he had been awake from the early hours of that morning, would need to do a shift of night watch, and fretted because Albert had not organised a proper shift rota. He decided to tackle Albert on the subject, but would discuss the problem with Ched first. It was obvious that Greta had a part in Gunter's slightly disgruntled mood. Normally he would be happy just to get on with the job he had been given.

'It is the pregnancy,' he explained to Ched. 'She is worried that I won't be there when she starts.'

'We'll have to think of a way to make it pan out then Gunter…Perhaps Magnus could take over your shift here? He'll probably be very happy to do so, because Patricia nags him and he'll be able to get out of her way. Monty is a waste of space; he can't even keep his eyes open when he's awake! Miles is dead and Jane is spending that much time at his graveside she might just as well join him.'

'Now, Ched, that's not fair to her. It's only been a short time since he was buried.'

'What I'm trying to say Gunter, who the fucking hell else is there?'

'Alright, alright Ched you've made your point. I'll go and see Albert anyway and see if he will let me do an early shift.' Ched looked at Gunter with a shrug of his shoulders as if he really couldn't care less.

Gunter reached Albert at the lookout point, when the sun had just disappeared over the western horizon, leaving the remaining cloud lit up with streaks of red and pink. The sky above them was clear, except for a three-quarter moon and the evening stars were starting to twinkle. Albert was staring into the night sky when he realised Gunter was there.

'You're early for the shift change? I suppose that's why you're here?'

'Yes, I want to finish my shift early. Greta needs me to be with her tonight. She is worried I won't be there when she starts with the baby, and the time is close.'

'Yeah, that's fine.' replied Albert, 'How long do you want to do?'

'Four hours, if that's ok?'

'No problem.' said Albert, 'I'll go and get my head down and I'll be back to relieve you.' Albert went away. Gunter was astonished by how easily the problem had been solved without a fuss.

It was 0600 hrs and the sun was showing itself over the east. Albert was hoping Gunter was going to change lookout shifts with him. He thought to himself that he'd give it fifteen minutes more before he contacting him. Perhaps he'd overslept. When he radioed Gunter a quarter of an hour later, he heard a young baby's cry in the background.

'Greta has given birth!'

'Congratulations Gunter! I'll get Magnus to put the radar on to give me a break and then Ched can watch the screen from the bridge.' Albert arranged for the radar to be switched on by Magnus, explaining that he needed a break now Gunter wouldn't be about.

'With the turbines on, powering the ship,' Magnus informed him, 'you could have had the radar on all night and I could have watched from the bridge. The radar would not have affected the energy resources.'

'Why the hell didn't you tell me last night?' shouted Albert.

'Because I thought you would have known and just liked looking at the bloody stars!' Albert knew he had made a mistake and could kick himself, but didn't want to show his bit of ignorance to Magnus. He thought he'd throw a shot back at him.

'Magnus are you in charge of energy systems and energy conservation?'

'Yes,' he timidly replied, realising very quickly where this was leading.

'Then could you please have ready for me, at 0900 hrs, a list of times when we are plentiful in the energy department to be able to use such bloody luxuries as the radar!'

'But I haven't had my breakfast yet. Patricia will be waiting.' Albert was building up with his retaliation and could see Magnus weakening; mentioning Patricia was the key to the final blow.

'Well, said Albert, 'the safe passage of the Ark is more important than your fried eggs. 0900 hours Magnus. Thank you.' and walked away trying to contain himself. Magnus was more worried about what Patricia would say to him for being late for breakfast than producing a timetable for Albert by 0900 hours.

Albert made his way to see Gunter and company to say hello to the little chap that he knew must have arrived that morning. When Albert turned the corner in the corridor to Gunter and Greta's, it was open house. The whole ship's company seemed to be there, except Jane and Magnus. Albert made his way through the crowded room to Greta, who was sitting up in bed, holding the child. He shook Gunter's hand, congratulated them on the arrival of the little feller, and asked what his name was.
'Venus.' replied Gunter.
'Venus... it's a girl then?'
'Yes!' he replied.
'Oh,' said Albert.
'Is that alright?'
Amy stepped in 'Of course it's alright. Go and get some sleep Albert. You must be very tired,' pushing him to the door.
'Yes I'll do that.' and he made his exit mumbling, 'the birth of Venus, I've heard that before somewhere.'

Albert was just getting off to sleep when there was a knock at his cabin door.
'Who the bloody hell is that?' he cursed, semi-conscious. On went his dressing gown and his feet automatically found his slippers. Another knock, then he heard a voice call out.
'It's Magnus here.' Albert blearily opened the door. 'Here's the rota you requested Albert, do you want me to explain it to you?'
'No, no I'll go and check it now, and if I have any problems I'll come back to you. Thank you Magnus.'
Albert closed the door and headed back to his bed.

Gunter and Greta were finding it difficult to get rid of the visitors; Greta kept gesticulating to Gunter to do something so that she could be left in peace to get some rest. Gunter went over to Amy and took her to one side.
'I don't want to upset the ladies by telling them to go. Please would you sort out the problem for us?' Amy, being the diplomatic type, soon ushered the visiting women and their children out, leaving them in peace. Gunter thanked her and took Stella to the nursery. Marigold and Melanie were taking charge while Greta was with her newborn. Gunter left Stella with

them and made a quick exit as Millie's Vicky threw a tantrum and Lucy screamed her head off. He decided to look on the bridge to check his course was being maintained. He was concerned the ship was rolling about more than it had been.

When he got to the bridge, Ched was at the control and keeping an eye on the radar screen, Gunter greeted him with a smile.
'Morning,' replied Ched, 'and congratulations!' shaking Gunter's hand.
'Sorry Gunter. I didn't get a chance earlier, with that lot in your bedroom. I've had to stop Millie going back to the bow again to tend to the animals this morning because the ship is making some big dips and quite a lot of spray is coming over the bow. All the animals are still in their pens and probably seasick now. We'll be getting butter instead of milk from them! We must be on the outskirts of the Bay of Biscay.'
'I've just come to plot our position,' replied Gunter. He studied the charts and marked out the ship's position, which was 046° latitude and 006° longitude. 'We should be at 047° latitude and 010° longitude. What course have you been steering Ched?'
'180 south.' he replied.
'How long have you been steering that?'
'It's the same course that Magnus had been steering. I assumed it was what you set before going off duty last night,' replied Ched.
'*Scheißer*! Well if we continue on this course, we will be on a beach in northern Spain in about five hour's time! Alter course immediately to 240° southwest. There should be plenty of wind to put some sails up in about two hours, after Albert and Magnus have rested. It will also be calmer seas when we are out of the Bay of Biscay.'
'Course being altered to 240° south west, Gunter. It will take about half an hour at the speed we are making now. How long do I hold that course?' Gunter rushed back to the charts to check.
'For the next twenty-four hours at least, do you realise we are over four hundred miles off course? Albert will go mad. Look, I must go back to see how Greta and Venus are doing. Radio me if you need me.' Gunter left the bridge, very upset.

When Albert and Magnus came back on duty, Ched explained to Albert about 'the little detour' the ship had taken in front of an embarrassed Magnus.

'What happened to the course Gunter told you to keep to, Magnus?' Albert asked.

'Gunter set the course to 190°; how it altered to 180, I don't know. I thought it was on autopilot. It was still going south.'

'Yes and heading for northern Spain if Gunter hadn't come back on duty. I know we're novices but we must pay attention to detail.'

'Sorry Albert. I'll make sure I stick to the course next time. I'll check the autopilot system.'

'Come on then Magnus,' Albert said, 'lets go and make use of this wind and try a couple of sails up to see if we can save some gas.' They both made their way to the forward part of the Ark and manoeuvred number one and two sails into position.

The sea had calmed, as Gunter had predicted, and it wasn't long before Millie was able to check the animals, mucking them out and making sure they had feed and water. When Albert had finished raising the sails, he thought he had better go and see how the animals were after the rough sea excursion through the Bay of Biscay. Millie was in the cowshed with Marina, trying to extract milk from her.

'Come on girl you can do better than that,' she urged.' Marina acknowledged with a groan rather than a moo. Millie didn't hear Albert approach and he startled her.

'Marina doesn't sound too clever does she?'

'No she doesn't. I think she is definitely seasick. She's well off her food. I'll need to get her to the field nearer the back of the ship and get her moving about. There's some good grass there and the ship doesn't roll and dip so much. Can you give me a hand to coax her there Albert?'

'Certainly'

Millie removed the milking equipment, put a makeshift harness on Marina's head and led her out of her pen. Albert went ahead holding and closing the gates as Millie brought Marina out to the orchard area. Then he followed up behind lightly resting his hand on the cow's rump as it waddled through the orchard. Albert looked towards Mile's grave expecting to see Jane knelt beside it, as she had done since leaving anchorage, but she wasn't there.

'No Jane today? Albert commented to Millie. 'Have you seen anything of her?'

82

'No. She wants to pull herself together, get stuck into doing some work, and give us all a hand. She's been too bloody spoilt if you ask me, and what's she going to do for a feller when she wakes up to the fact that Miles has gone, and he ain't coming back? She'd better not come sniffing round Ched, 'cause I'll feed her to the sharks!'
'Oh shit! Albert swore.
'What?'
'I said. Oh, shit! Marina's just had a piss and it's splashed all up my trouser leg!' Millie burst out laughing.
'It could have been worse Albert then you would have to collect it up and put it in the methane gas converter.' She continued laughing, while Albert muttered to himself.
'Just my luck, I can see its going to be yet another one of those shitty days.'

They finally arrived at the field to let Marina graze. She sniffed at the grass and started to tug at the green, lush blades.
'That's a relief Albert, thank you for your help. I'll need a hand to get her back at milking time. Can you come and bring a bucket and shovel with you? Better still send Jane.' Millie started laughing again. What a weird woman, getting pleasure from Marina pissing on me, Albert thought to himself as he walked away, holding his soaked trousers off his leg. He went straight to his cabin to shower and change and then to drop off his wet trousers at the laundry. As he entered the laundry room Patricia was busy doing some ironing.
'Could I leave these trousers with you to wash please Patricia?'
'Coo, they stink, what have you done Albert, pissed yourself?'
'No Patricia. I have not pissed myself, thank you; it was that bloody cow Marina.'

Albert left quickly and went to the bridge hoping to have a sensible conversation with someone. Ched was at the controls.
'How's it going, Ched?'
'Well we've missed northern Spain, just got to see what happens when we get near the Azores.'
'How long do we need to maintain this revised course?'
'Gunter said about twenty four hours, but I'm not sure. We have to get him back here soon to take a re-check on our position. I don't know why we strayed off course last night. It should have corrected itself and I'll feel happier when Magnus has tested the autopilot later on.'

83

'I want to see how Greta and the baby Venus are doing,' said Albert. 'Gunter will be there, I'll ask him to pop up to check the course. Venus, The Birth of Venus, I've heard of that before Ched. Have you?'
'Yes. It's a very famous painting by Botticelli.'
'How would you know that? I wouldn't have thought you knew much about art.'
'Well there you are Albert; I'm not just good looking. I was a budding artist at school. Then I left and became a piss artist!'
'You know Ched,' Albert laughed 'you're the only person I've spoken to today and got any sense out of.'

Gunter appeared on the bridge, as requested, to check the course.
'It's spot on Ched, but we've slowed right down. Albert will need to check the sail positions and see if we can put some more sail up. Mind you, looking at the weather front over to the west, it might not be a good idea to have *any* sail up.' Gunter radioed for Albert to come to the bridge. Albert was just on his way to help Millie with Marina back to her pen, bucket and shovel in hand. He sensed the urgency from Gunter, downed tools and went to the bridge. Gunter pointed out the evolving weather situation and how the Ark had slowed right down.
'We could have had more sail up earlier in the day, but now its looks like we need to drop the sails completely and revert back to engine power overnight, and see what tomorrow will bring us. I know we want to keep away from using radio for weather forecasts and be able to predict weather conditions ourselves. Well, that front does not look good to me, what do you think Albert?'
'Yes you're right. We'd better not take any chances; we've made enough boobs for one day. I'll get Magnus to help me with the sails. Revert back to engine power Ched!'
'Aye, Aye Captain.'
'Oh, shut up, replied Albert grumpily. He didn't like the formal Captain label and he was on a short fuse, mainly because he wasn't looking forward to his next job of helping escort Marina back to her cowshed. Magnus trailed behind on his way to the bow of the ship to help Albert drop the sails.

Albert caught up with Millie and Marina. Millie knew that once Marina got into a walking rhythm, the cow dung would start flowing and because of

84

the importance of getting it collected fresh for the methane producer, Albert would be busy. Grinning faces from the bridge chuckled with laughter as they watched Albert follow up behind Marina collecting shit, with Albert shaking his head and muttering to himself.
'I just knew it was going to be a shit day today.'

On arriving at the enclosure, Albert helped Millie get Marina settled for milking to end her productive day. He then went to assist Magnus in the lowering of the forward sails. Millie was pleased that Marina was over her little upset and even more pleased with the milk she had produced. She made her comfortable before meeting Albert and Magnus to return to the upper decks for the end of the day. Millie was smiling when she joined them for the walk back.
'I've had a lovely day. How's your day been Albert?' Albert turned and looked at Millie.
'It's been absolutely, bloody marvellous. And the first thing I'm going to do when I get back is to down a couple of pints.' He started smiling at the thought, which turned to chuckling and ignited them all into laughter. Albert and Magnus went straight to the canteen. It was teatime and as far as Albert was concerned, he had earned a pint of bitter or two.

'Come on Magnus, I'll buy,' said Albert.' Instinctively, Magnus, being a true Scot, accepted Albert's offer.
'Yes, thanks Albert.' But a fraction of a second later, he realised it was free anyway. 'Er... No... er I'd better go and see how Patricia is doing.' Albert thought to himself that there wasn't a lot of logic there. He was really pleased he had installed the auto-vac pump system for his beer. It meant he could pull through a fresh pint even if he hadn't had one for a couple of days.

Albert arrived at the canteen and could hardly wait for the beer. The canteen was dead, just prior to the evening meal sitting.
'Perfect!' he said to himself and quickly went behind the bar, lifted a glass from the shelf and pulled beer through the auto-vac until he thought it was ready to pull into his glass. He filled the glass, put it on the bar to let it settle, and looked at it. 'Hmm... it's a bit cloudy. Slurp,.., slurp... 'Oh shit, that's shite! That's not even drinkable,' and miserably poured himself some imported white wine instead. He was a disappointed man!

Still in a happy mood, Millie arrived at the nursery to collect Vicky. The poor child was in a state of apoplexy, not the normal way she would greet her mother. Millie went berserk and Marigold was first in line.

'What have you done to my child, you useless bitch!'

'Well you've been away a long time and I found it hard to occupy her. She's a difficult child. I'm only standing in for Greta. And please don't use that sort of language in front of the children!' Millie was about to leap at Marigold when Melanie came between them.

'I'm sorry Millie. We've had a very strange day, what with the birth of Venus and not having Greta in control of the nursery. I'm sorry but I thought I could manage with Marigold to help me.' Millie lifted the child into her arms and they both calmed down a little.

'Where's Stella, Melanie?' Millie demanded.

'Gunter took her a long time ago.'

'So, you've only had Lucy and my Vicky to look after for most of the day and this is the state she's in. How can I do my job looking after the farming, knowing Vicky isn't being cared for properly?'

'I said I'm sorry.'

'It's not good enough! I'm going to see Albert about this.'

Millie stormed out of the room and headed straight for Albert, knowing exactly where he would be. Sure enough, he was sitting at the bar, sipping a glass of wine, staring into a pint glass of what looked like dishwater, and frowning at it.

'Albert,' she shouted at him.

'Now what's gone wrong?'

'I've just collected Vicky from the nursery and she's in a right state. It's no good me leaving her with Melanie and Marigold if they can't look after her properly. Tomorrow I'll be looking after Vicky myself, so you'll have to find someone else to tend to the animals and don't forget the goats and Marina will want milking at six o'clock in the morning and again at teatime'. She said her piece and was off out the door like a shot, leaving Albert shell-shocked.

'Bloody hell! Why have I all these problems? It was easier dodging bullets in the Gulf!' He tipped his dodgy pint away down the sink, rinsed and dried the glass then put it away, muttering to himself that he needed Amy's help.

That evening, Albert discussed the major problem that had arisen, 'the nursery' with Amy. She said straight away, that she would help Melanie to look after the children until Greta wanted to resume her duties.

'But Albert,' she continued, 'you have to get Marigold to help with the farm because Millie is stressed out with having too much to do. And I don't want Marigold sitting on her backside watching me entertain the children.'

'Oh ok, I suppose you're right. I'll go and see Millie and tell her what you've suggested. I'm sure she'll be happier with you looking after Vicky, but not so sure about having Marigold as a farm assistant. We'll just have to see what happens.' Albert called on Millie and explained Amy's plan. As expected, she was not keen about having to nursemaid Marigold on the farm. But then, she thought to herself, hmm… this might be entertaining.

'Ok, Albert, get Marigold to knock my door at five thirty tomorrow morning, and I'll show her where the front of the ship is!'

'Albert grinned, 'I don't think those numbers are on her clock, but I'll make sure she is there.' Albert wanted to get everything sorted, so he walked to Monty and Marigold's quarters to tell her of the new arrangements and that he would personally call her at five twenty, to make sure Millie gets the help she needs. Just as he finished speaking and before she could protest, the canteen bell rang. With doors opening and closing, everybody made a beeline for the food. Albert thought to himself great, as soon as I've had something to eat I'm off to bed. They can use the radar tonight. I've had enough of today!

Things settled down to an almost normal routine the next few days. Since leaving the Bay of Biscay area and bad weather behind, the sails were constantly up, and the Ark made good progress in favourable Atlantic winds and currents. They had been in transit for just over a week and were crossing the Tropic of Cancer, five hundred miles north of the Cape Verde islands. Marigold had finally realised that the ship was not a cruise liner and was beginning to like working with the animals, even though Millie constantly took the mickey out of her, especially the combination of the long flowery skirts and wellington boots she wore.

Amy had been pestering Monty on a daily basis, asking when she would be able to have a sample of 'Maca' tablets to try out. He finally got around to producing them and told her they were ready for her to collect. Excitedly, she rushed around to Monty's laboratory to get them and thought that they should be crossing the Equator soon. I'll give Albert a little celebration when we cross it, she thought. She asked Monty if they would have any side effects or were likely to affect his heart.

'Has he got a heart condition?'

'No, not yet,'

'Well, that's alright then, but make sure you use some lubrication or you might have a problem.'

'Oh, right,' she replied.

A few days later, Amy cornered Albert.

'Albert,'

'Yes my love,'

'At what time will we cross the Equator?'

'Well, we've slowed down a lot but I would think about 2200 hours tonight.'

'Oh will we? Isn't it exciting.' she replied. But then she realised she forgot to ask Monty how long the tablets would take to work and it was almost time for the evening meal.

'Oh, I've just got to pop and see Monty about some herbs we are growing.' Off she dashed to see him to ask how long before to take them.

'It's not quite the same as Viagra; not 'a quick fix,' he replied. 'You need to take them on a daily basis for a while for the proper effect.'

'Oh Monty,' she replied, 'I'm disappointed. It won't be any good for tonight then?'

'Well, you could try! Get some into both of you before having your meal and you will just have to work hard on him tonight.' So off she rushed to the canteen before the dinner bell was due to ring. I might be in luck. I'll get him some orange juice and slip them in that, she thought.

Amy had accomplished her mission and after the meal she set about seducing Albert.

'Let's take the wine back to the cabin dear and finish it off while crossing the Equator.'

'Alright,' the unsuspecting Albert replied. They sauntered off, with Amy trying to contain her excitement.

'When will we know we are crossing the Equator?' she asked.

'I've arranged for Gunter to sound the meal bell several times when he knows we are over it, that's if he gets it right, of course!'

'There's no need for comments like that, I'm sure he'll do it correctly.'

They arrived back at their quarters.

'I'm going to take a shower Albert I just feel I need to freshen up a bit. I won't be long.'

'Would you mind if I join you?'

'Not at all, I'll let you scrub my back.'

'That's no problem, is there anywhere else that needs a scrub?' he asked suggestively.

'I think your own back may need some attention,'

'Oh yeah, that sounds good.' That's strange, Albert thought, she doesn't normally want me in there at the same time. I wonder if she's been reading a horny novel or something. I won't say no to some rampant sex in the shower though. It's ages since we had made love in there.

Amy was just finishing stripping off in front of the full-length mirror next to the shower. Albert was enjoying a view of her slender rear and a full frontal in the mirror. Hmm... she's looking fit. She bent down to pick up her knickers and placed them in the linen bin. As she reached down, Albert thought, bloody hell! It's winking at me! He immediately started removing his clothes, discarding them to the floor, leaving them where they fell. Amy was already in the shower, soaping the natural sponge that Ched had fished up out of the sea for her. She started to wash herself when Albert entered the cubicle.

'Here, I said I would do that for you my dear.'

'You must be after something.'

'I just thought you might like to be pampered,' he innocently replied.

'Oh yea?' she giggled. He was so predictable.

'Albert, oh, I'm so happy,' He took the sponge from her, re-soaped it, and started to wash her gently all over, leaving the best bits until last. Then, he dropped the sponge to continue with his hand.

'Oh, Albert, this isn't like you, are you feeling a little randy?'

'You just turned me on when you were undressing in front of the mirror. I could see all the back and the front at the same time. It was beautiful.' They embraced, starting by kissing and playing about in the good old-fashioned way. Her right hand was soon down holding his semi-hard penis and with all the years of practice she'd had with him, put the knowledge to good use to get the best for them both. She didn't want him finishing before she started!

She reached for the soap and applied it to his willing-to-do-anything cock. She stroked it gently with her soapy hands and then guided it into her, as they stood upright. They had tried this position a few times before, but it usually ended up in failure. But this time, she managed to get him into her, all the way home. At this point, she leapt up, with her arms clinging around his neck. Albert responded by helping her up to him by grasping her firm arse, as she clamped her legs around his now slimmer waist. Amy always knows when he's lost weight (probably due to his undrinkable bitter): she is able to wrap her legs completely around his waist, ankles crossed together. It certainly helped penetration. With her trimmer body, he thought, she isn't bad for a forty nine year old.

Next, Albert was having his head massaged between Amy's tits and he was not complaining.... the movement of her up and down, up and down on his excited erection, Albert felt like twenty one again! He went through the things in his mind that might be contributing to this renewed passion and how he had the energy to do it, at the same time enjoying the love and dedication of Amy expressing her joy on him. The good life, he thought, that's the answer. She reached her climax, the pulses taking over her body. Albert knew when she was there, because her eyes started to roll around with her lost in pleasure. Albert was still going strong, but not for long as Amy held on to him, wanting to feel the throb of him pumping what she always hoped could be future Alberts into her.

'Oh Albert, I love you. Are we on the Equator yet?'

'I don't know, but if we are, and that is what it does to you, I'll turn the Ark around and go over it again!'

'That sounds like a good idea.'

'I was only joking, my love.'

'No, she said, 'not turning the Ark Albert, doing it again.'

Come on then. Where's that soapy sponge?' he grinned.

9. MILES' PAST

After the death of Miles, Jane became a recluse. It was obvious that she felt alone and lost, trapped on the vessel and could not see a future. She stopped attending meals and, on the rare occasions that she was seen, looked thin and anaemic. All the crew were very anxious for her; some would call on her trying to help by suggesting what she should do and what would be good for her, but to no avail, she ended up by not answering the door. Albert and Amy kept a close watch on her and he tried to think of a way to make her snap out of it. He thought that if he could get her to talk about the real Miles and how he managed to get things done so easily, she may come round. She must have known some of his past. Albert told Amy of his plan and she agreed something had to be done. It was worth a try. Albert called on her. He knocked, thinking she might open the door.

'Who is it?' a quiet voice asked.

'It's Albert.'

'What do you want?'

'I need to ask you some questions about Miles to put in the ship's log.' There was a pause and then Jane unlocked the door. As she appeared, still in her dressing gown, she stared at the floor, not wanting to look him in the eye.

'This isn't the bonny girl of a couple of weeks back.' Albert thought to himself.

'Come in please,' she croaked.

'Thank you,' he replied.

Albert entered what was a combined living and dining room.

'Please sit down, Albert.' He sat at the dining table in front of some raspberry wine, from the first harvest, which had recently been bottled. It wasn't ready to drink for a few months yet. As he glanced around the room, he caught sight of other empty wine bottles, most of them raspberry.

'Would you like a drink Albert?'

'Just a small glass, please Jane. I'm sure it's not quite ready for drinking yet but I'll join you all the same.' She poured him a glass and topped up her own. Albert took a small sip.

'Hmm, it will be better in a few months.' He stood up and walked across to the chest of drawers at the side of the room, where a framed photograph of Miles was placed. He picked it up, brought it back to the dining table, and placed it in front of Jane.

'Yes,' said Jane, 'those were happy times, now they are all gone. As for the empty bottles you were glancing at, don't worry, they're not all today's, they were the last three days. This is my first drink this morning.'

'Please consider Jane, this is our first harvest of fruit, the plants are not established enough yet to get a full crop, at the rate you're going, there will be little left for the rest of the crew.'

'Sorry,' said Jane, 'but I need it at the moment. Well Albert what do you want to know?'

Albert produced a pen from his pocket and opened his A4 pad to take notes. 'Was Miles Overstrand his real name?'

'Not originally. He changed his name officially when he was in his early twenties. He was from a Russian family. His father was a diplomat in London. His name was Elo Mikovich. When his parents were called back to Moscow, Miles or should I say Elo, didn't want to go. He'd had five years of English education and made his friends and his life there. His parents couldn't persuade him to return with them. Miles was attending the London School of Economics and doing very well with his studies.' Jane paused for a drink; Albert joined her.

'Cheers! How did Miles end up running casinos?'

'I can only tell you what he told me during the short period that I lived with and loved him; now that's all gone.' Her voice became emotional.

'Take your time Jane, I'm sure you'll feel better talking about things, just take your time and try to relax.' Albert was about to say have another drink but thought better of it. She did take another sip, and then continued.

'When his parents left for Moscow, Miles had to fend for himself. They had arranged a monthly allowance for him to live on, whilst he finished his degree in economics. During his last year, the money wasn't enough, so he took a job in a casino, which meant working late into the night for six nights a week. He finished his degree. The casino manager offered him a full-time position to run the casinos in London. The company owned a number of casinos and gambling houses throughout the UK, with several in London. He accepted and was paid very highly, with bonuses when each establishment he ran, did well.'

'Did he ever marry before you knew him? Jane's answer was a definite 'no'. She was almost aggressive about it; obviously marriage was a subject for Albert to avoid.

'Anyway, he was always too busy with his work.'

'If he was doing so well, what changed him to want to start a fresh life, and how did he really make all that money?' Jane took a deep breath before replying to Albert.

'Well, I promised him I'd keep it a secret, but I suppose it doesn't matter now. This is what he told me. The business changed owners shortly after Miles had settled down to a good routine. With all the businesses he managed doing very well, some Russians suddenly turned up out of the blue, and told him that they were the new owners and that Miles was now working for them. From the onset, he was pressurised into rigging the tables to change the odds even more in favour of the establishment. Miles had control of all this, but they didn't pay him any more. Soon afterwards, he worked out a method of extracting cash sums from each operation and over five years the cash built up. The Russians never even suspected the missing money. It meant Miles had to be on top of the accounting, but that was what he was good at. They just trusted him more and more. Through his job he met all walks of life, a lot of business people, some genuine some seedy, the rich the famous and villains.'

'Is that how he was able to produce results very quickly when it came to getting goods and things done for the conversion of the oil tanker?'

'Yes, he used a lot of his contacts.'

'Was the Russian mafia involved with the casinos?'

'Yes, I believe so, but it was not evident at the beginning, Miles was always worried about that.'

'What if they were involved and they find out what Miles had done; is that possible?'

'I suppose it's a possibility, but again there was no indication of that.'

'How did you meet Miles?'

'Well, I was eighteen and needed a job. I fancied the nightlife, thinking if I worked in a nightclub or casino, I might meet somebody wealthy to date. Miles interviewed me for a job as a croupier. I got the job and it wasn't long before he asked me out. This was difficult because of his workload. I didn't like to refuse because he was my boss, which is always an awkward situation. At first, I went out with him as a duty, but I soon got to know him. He wasn't that good looking and he was older than me, but he was a true gentleman and treated me with so much kindness and he made me feel comfortable. I began to like him very much but it was a while before it got serious with him. I didn't want to look for anybody else I accepted that we were together. When I moved in with him, that's when he started to tell me

93

about the real situation and that he was looking for a way out. I was frightened, he realised this and sent me away to Paris. That was about the time he answered your advert.'

'I'm concerned that if the Russian mafia realise why he disappeared so quickly and start doing some sums, they're bound to start looking for him!' said Albert.
'How will they find us out here; besides Miles is dead?'
'Jane, don't be so naïve. If they wanted to find the Ark, they would use satellite photo tracking.'
'Oh no,' Jane whispered, getting upset again.
'Don't worry, at least I know what we are up against now and I think I understand Miles Overstrand, the man, a bit better. Now, about you, when are you coming back to help the rest of us, because we do need your help? Gunter has covered for you on lookout as much as he can. We need you back.'
'But I have no reason to be here now that Miles has gone.'
'Yes you have, this is your home and new way of life. What else would you do? Besides, you never know what's on the other side of the horizon.'
'I don't know Albert. Give me a bit more time. I'll be alright.'

Albert got up, finished the drop of wine left in the glass, and replaced it on the table.
'Thank you Jane.'
'I feel much better now. Thank *you* Albert.'
'I'm looking forward to you returning back to your new-found family.'
Albert smiled at her, gave her a hug and left her quarters.

Albert's first port of call was the newly stocked wine store to make sure it was locked. Next, he went to report to Amy, who was waiting patiently for the results of his quest. Albert explained all that had happened. They deliberated whether to tell the rest of them about the Miles' past situation, finally agreeing to keep quiet about the problems that may or may not occur. They thought it would be irresponsible to cause unnecessary worry.

Albert had already started to think of defence, asking himself, how could we defend the Ark if anybody tried to attack us? Would they come by sea or by air or both? Would they claim the ship for themselves if they knew their money had financed it? This was not even considered on the outset of the planning of the Ark. Then his brain began to fill with all sorts of scenarios. He had to stop thinking like this.

'It's all hypothetical, probably will never happen, but at least I'm on my guard.' he said out loud.

'Did you say something Albert?' asked Amy.

'Er no, Er, I'm just going to the bridge dear.' He made his exit rapidly and got to the bridge where Ched was looking at the charts of the South Atlantic and the Islands of Tristan De Cunha. Albert stood next to him to survey them too.

'I hope Gunter can understand what all these squiggly lines are for.'

'Isn't it about time you relieved Gunter on the top deck?'

'Ok boss!'

'And don't call me boss!' Ched went to the lookout post. Gunter was more concerned with the weather. He explained to Ched that the air seemed still.

'I want to check the barometer reading. It feels just like a storm brewing.' Ched took the binoculars from Gunter and continued to scan the horizon. Gunter went to the bridge to check the barometer and found Albert there, studying the charts.

'We are due for a storm Albert. It's dropped eight millibars since the last time I checked four hours ago.'

'I'll call Ched down to take over here at control. We'll need Magnus and Monty to help drop the sails.

Ched arrived at the bridge and got the turbines started and then radioed Millie for her and Marigold to secure the animals and get back to the upper decks. The four men set about lowering the five sails, starting at the fore deck through to the bow. Gunter was working with Monty and they were struggling with the last sail, which was the second sail from the bow. The clouds were increasing rapidly, especially the upper clouds, and the winds became gale force. The sea started to lift into huge waves and the sail that was still up moved back and forth, as the bow dipped and Albert and Magnus were unable to drop the sail down into its hold. They agreed there was nothing they could do at that moment to fix it, so they decided they would have to leave the sail as it was and steer into the storm. They returned exhausted to the shelter of the bridge, as quickly as they could.

The storm lasted for twenty four hours and then it petered out to a bright, clear and fresh weather system. It was time to get the sails back up, see if

95

the damaged sail could be repaired and return to the original course they were taking.

It was action stations when the crew woke up to a bright blustery day. Gunter was up on lookout (his favourite post). He could see a group of Blue Whales swimming parallel and moving slightly faster than the Ark. Some were spouting water fountains several metres into the air and occasionally a tail lifted out of the water. He could not believe it and radioed to the bridge to get everybody up there quickly to see the spectacle. Albert thought straight away of Jane, something to lift her spirits. He ran to Amy to ask her to drag Jane up on top to see this, no matter what. She did, without taking no for an answer, and in a very short time every man woman and child, was there to see the magnificent creatures put on a private show for them.

Amy pulled Jane along to see. The whales kept dipping under the waves, in and out of view. She pointed out to Jane where to look. Gunter told them that they can be up to thirty metres long, and might weigh in excess of one hundred tonnes each. Jane pushed back her unmanaged, straggling, greasy hair to see the streamlined, mottled bluish-grey whales perform. She came to life. It was as if those beautiful mammals were there for her, they moved something within her heart and made her appreciate with awe, the wonders of the natural world we live in. Undisturbed by the presence of the Ark, with the joy and amazement of everyone onboard, these graceful marine mammals disappeared into the distance, migrating to breed and feed.

Jane thanked Amy for forcing her on deck to see something so special. It must have been the first time Jane had smiled for over two weeks.
'Come on Jane.' Amy took her by the arm, 'Let's get you cleaned up and fed. We will be coming to our anchorage point soon. It's time to start a new chapter, don't you think so Jane?'

ALBERT'S PRIVATE LOG- October 2016

Amy's passion for sex on the trip down here was a bonus. It must be all this sea air and good food. I must make sure I can match up to it. She can only just cross her ankles when she wraps her legs around me, so I must try to keep my weight down.

It's a relief Greta is back in charge at the nursery school. I can understand how Millie felt, working hard all day and then coming back to a stressed child.

The Ark handled the storm very well. It was the poor animals that suffered. Repairing the stuck sail mechanism will have to wait till we get to anchor.

Let's hope that Jane will snap out of her depression and get back with the living soon. It was an uplifting sight for her to see the whales, such beautiful, graceful creatures so close, without us disturbing them.

I suppose I was a bit naïve about Miles' past. It's beginning to make more sense now: the way he was able to get things done through his network of connections. Makes me wonder how deep he was in with the Russian mafia. Will they bother to track us down? And what would they do if they did? Kill us all, no doubt!

10. WINTER OF CONTENT

The Ark was far into the South Atlantic and past The Tropic of Capricorn with only about five hundred miles to go before they were to start looking for a suitable anchorage. They knew it would be difficult, because of very deep waters there. Keeping a course of 160° southeast, they headed for an area east of the islands of Tristan De Cunha. The chart showed a ridge, Walvis Ridge, stretching fifteen hundred miles northeast to Walvis Bay on the west coast of Namibia, Africa. This area was the shallowest part of the region, but still with depths of a thousand metres, which would be too deep to drop an anchor. The ocean currents were very weak, so they did not think the Ark would drift far. The only option to keep their position was to raise some of the sails, and angle them to work against each other; so whichever way the wind blew, the worst that could happen would be to send them slowly in circles. A spot was chosen on top of the Walvis Ridge about thirty miles northeast of Tristan De Cunha, just outside the fishing exclusion zone.

They were coming to the end of a journey of just over six thousand miles, to float about in the ocean for the next six months, not interfering with anybody else, just living in peace and harmony together.
'We are now at 7.5° longitude and 36.6° latitude,' Gunter said. 'There isn't anywhere shallow enough to use the anchor, so let's try your method of keeping us in the same position with the sails instead, Albert.' All male hands made their way to the deck to set the sails for anchorage in the heave-to position. The area was well away from any shipping, not that there was much in the Southern Atlantic. If any, it would be the big factory fishing boats indiscriminately taking any creatures in their path. The sea was calm, as it normally stays, during the southern hemisphere's summer. It was about mid-day when they finally managed to pitch the sails at the best angle.
'That is amazing! We haven't moved a metre from our position in two hours,' Gunter said later. He checked the position with his GPS (Global Positioning System), which was against Albert's principles. He objected to too much reliance on mechanical devices, because traditional navigational skills, by calculations from charts could be lost over time. If the GPS itself was lost overboard, or failed, it would be very difficult to find their way if they depended on it solely.

It was time for everyone to relax to a slightly different daily routine than the past three weeks of non-stop sailing. With Amy's help, Jane came back to life and gradually resumed some of the duties she had started during the first six months. As the days passed, she wanted to be more involved in the running of the ship. She asked Amy where she could be most helpful on the Ark.

'What about health, nutrition and biology? We've all wondered why Miles died so young from the heart attack. We need to know how we can recognise signs of such illnesses, and be able to prevent that sort of thing happening to the rest of us.'

'Yes, I think I could get really interested in doing that, but where would I start?'

'If it was me, I'd look at the subject of food first.' Amy continued, 'I know that we all eat the best quality food we can and, considering the restricting factors limiting our resources, we do extremely well. But is our diet balanced enough? It's things like, well, you may have noticed, Albert's tendency to get a paunch and that's despite the fact that he is drinking less bitter.'

'Yes, mainly because his brewing is crap!' Jane added, laughing.

'Patricia is putting on weight again after doing so well at first, and, are the children healthy? Monty is alright for treating minor ailments but I'm concerned about all our general health.'

'Well that sounds like a task for me. I've seen the library and I'm sure there should be enough information there for me to get educated on the subject. Thank you.'

'No thank *you*, Jane.' Amy replied gratefully.

It was the middle of October 2016 and spring in that part of the world. Only three weeks ago, it was the beginning of the autumn in the northern hemisphere. In that three weeks journey to the south, the grass had grown so Millie let all the animals out to free range for a few days before cultivation of the land, for hopefully, a second season of crops. Ched was organising his fishing equipment ready for a few trips out to replenish the freezers. His main concern was what sort of fish was he likely to catch. He thought the water was too deep for lobster and crab pots but there should be some good tuna.

'I know; I'll have a look in the library later, see if there's any info there,' he told Millie at breakfast.

Normally the library was seldom used and on arrival, Ched was surprised to see Jane there.

'Hi Jane, It's nice to see you about again. What are you looking up, anything interesting?'

'No, no,' she replied not wanting to explain what she was doing. 'I'm surprised to see you in here Ched. I thought you knew everything.'

'Now, now, there's no need to be like that.'

'Sorry Ched, I was being facetious.'

'Face what? Never mind,' said Ched, 'You were right, it is a rare occasion to see me in here. I'm looking up fishing in the South Atlantic. I want to know what to catch. I just hope there's some information here for me.'

'Try looking over there.'

'How did you know that?'

'Well this is 'G' section so 'F' is just before it.'

'Oh yes, of course. What's that you're reading Gyna, what ology?'

'Ched, I'm trying to concentrate. Please leave me alone.'

'Sorry Jane. Right, fish... let's have a look here.'

Ched picked out a book, sat at the desk opposite Jane, who was trying to focus on her reading. He started thumbing through the pages, saying the titles aloud, which was too much for Jane. She slammed her book together and stood up.

'Hmm, I can see I won't get any peace and quiet in here,' she mumbled as she turned and strode out of the room. Ched was oblivious to what he'd done wrong.

'Strange woman,' he muttered to himself.

Not long after, he heard the meal bell. It was the first occasion for a long time that all onboard could, and actually did, sit together for a meal in the canteen: Greta, Gunter, Stella and now Venus, Monty, Marigold and Lucy, Ched, Millie and Vicky, Magnus, Patricia and Melanie, Jane, Amy and, of course, Albert. There was no watch to worry about, the navigation lights were on and the at-anchor ball was in place.

Amy and Jane had become very close, with Amy making sure that, where possible, Jane was always part of discussions and decisions. She proved she was not the stereotypical 'Miles' bimbo' as originally suggested by Ched, but an intelligent, extremely attractive, feisty female. Jane started on her quest, analysing each individual's weight in comparison to his or her

100

height, inherited physique and age. Then she studied their eating patterns and the amount of exercise they did or didn't take. This new project started to annoy certain residents of the Ark, especially Albert and Patricia, who were, relative to the rest, the two fattest people in their universe, so to speak. However, Jane was protected by Amy who encouraged her criticism of Albert's diet.

'You really should take notice of Jane's schedule of diet and exercise, Albert.' Jane continuously reminded him of his basic duty, to stay alive and always be compos mentis:

'Please take it seriously if you want to appreciate life more, and most of all, if you want to survive and keep the Ark as *Albert's* Ark. Think of the alternative. How would it be without you Albert?' He took the criticism from Jane, as well as an ageing man could do, from a very attractive and healthy young woman.

Jane was a little bit more diplomatic when it came to tackling Patricia on the subject, and would not approach her in the kitchen where weapons of mass destruction, such as meat cleavers and rolling pins were at hand. Gradually with Amy's help, the majority of people onboard were getting the message and taking note that it was for their own good. Jane wanted everybody to get regular exercise and consequently, the swimming pool had more use. The last time Patricia took a walk was to the orchard at the funeral. If she wanted any vegetables, she would ask Millie or Marigold. Now, under Jane's guidance, she had to go and get them out of the ground herself. The vegetable garden was situated next to the orchard so she had a good daily walk. Occasionally, Amy would assist if there was a lot of produce to carry back. Jane had even organised a woman's health check and a detailed log of every person onboard with age, ailments and any other relevant known history plus a basic family tree to avoid inter breeding in later years.

Crops had been planted and were showing through the ground. Marina was in calf but didn't know how it happened! It was Millie's first attempt at artificial insemination (A.I.). There was a litter of pigs on the way and the Billy goat had been busy. Chickens with their fluffy chicks were running all over the place. The only unsuccessful reproduction was the ewe. A.I. had not worked so Millie would have to try it again. Ched and Gunter went out in the fishing boat at least twice a week and were extremely productive with catches of tuna, mackerel, sea bream, hake, and menhaden of the herring family, which was good for oil, fish meal and fertilizer. Then there was always squid, octopus and various type of prawn. They very rarely failed to bring in a good catch and did not have to travel far.

Christmas was upon them, the first one together on the Ark. Albert and Amy were not that bothered about any celebrations.
'It's for the kids really,' they said, sadly regretting not having any children of their own. Everybody else was excited about it and some of the children were at the age when their parents could explain the myth of Santa Claus to them. A Christmas dinner was arranged, with roast pork and roast chicken on the menu. It was unlikely that they would ever see a turkey, under the scheme of things, but it was said that if any migrating geese wanted to take a rest on the Ark, they would be made use of. Albert was back on track, with Jane's help in the brewery and the raspberry wine was just about drinkable, although, they still had a stock of the original imported wines from when they stocked the ship.

Christmas Eve came and Gunter was on lookout. He spotted a fast-moving vessel heading towards them. He immediately reported to Albert, who thought the worst of course, but did not want to cause alarm. Albert went to the lookout to see for himself if he could make out any telltale sign of its origin. He took the binoculars from Gunter and studied the ship making its way towards them.
'It's a fast vessel but not at full speed, so they are not in that much of a hurry.' Albert noted. As it got closer, he could make out it was grey and the emblem was the blue Euro starred circle, with the Union Flag at one corner.
'It's a naval coastguard Gunter,' Albert said with a sigh of relief. 'When was the last time you checked our position?'
'Oh err..., about a week ago.'
'A week ago Gunter, that's a bit slack, we could have drifted fifty or sixty miles if we'd got caught in a sea current.'
'Well, we didn't seem to be moving since the time we got here, so I didn't bother checking it so much.'
'Can you go and check it now please, and have the position ready for me. If we have drifted, and we are some place we are not supposed to be, then get Ched and Magnus geared up to move on engine power, because these chappies will want to come onboard and will soon tell us if we are in the wrong. They will want to see our passports as well. I'll ask Amy to get the grab bag with all the documents out of the safe, and bring it to the bridge.'

102

The arrival of the vessel caused some excitement onboard, not having seen anybody else for nine months, especially Melanie, who thought there might be a young sailor or two, to look at. The vessel slowed right down and manoeuvred side on, to within fifty metres. A man in naval uniform raised a loud hailer and ordered to drop a ladder for a boarding party. Ched and Gunter immediately went to the access point at the foredeck and dropped the rope ladder and Albert joined them shortly after. An officer and two seamen carrying side arms were soon onto the ladder and sharply climbing up it.

'It looks like they've done that a few times before,' Ched commented. In minutes, they were onboard and Albert greeted the Officer, proudly introducing himself as Albert Crowther in charge of Albert's Ark.

'Albert Crowther,' repeated the officer as he took off his hat and shook hands. 'You don't mean Sergeant Albert Crowther of the Royal Marines?' Albert suddenly realised who he was.

'Bloody hell its *Package Pete,* Sergeant Peter Dunhill!' Ched and Gunter looked at each other, completely mystified.

'The last time I saw you was, now let me think… about 1991, when you dropped me and the squad off up the Euphrates inside Iraq,' said Albert.

'Well! What the fuck do you have here Albert?' the officer asked as he looked around and saw crops growing and farm animals in the distance.

'It's a long story,' replied Albert. Just then, Amy appeared with the other residents, including children, all curious about the visitors. Amy joined Albert to be introduced. The officer met the rest of the crew starting with Ched, Gunter then the remainder of the community.

Albert invited his old compadre and his ratings for a drink in the canteen to explain all about the Ark. He led the way, followed by the whole ship's company, even Millie and Marigold had come from the bow of the ship to see what was going on. They sat around a table and drinks were served with Melanie and Marigold smiling continuously at the two naval ratings. Albert told their story as briefly as he could and his old mate explained that the Ark had drifted into the fishing limits around Tristan De Cunha, and had to be investigated. They were on their guard because of problems with Chinese factory fishing ships disguised as cargo and other vessel types.

Albert apologised and said they would correct their position.

'Now that we know what you are all about, not to worry as long as you don't get too close to the islands. If you get stranded on rocks you'll be finished Albert!'
'We'll make sure of that, won't we Gunter?' Albert looked sternly at him. 'Yes Chief!'

After getting the business conversation out of the way, they exchanged life histories since the last time they'd met.
'How come you joined the Navy Pete? I would have thought you had enough of boats up and down the Euphrates every night during the war.'
'Oh, I got bored after the conflict died down. I wanted to see more of the world so I applied for a transfer to the Royal Navy, as it was then.' Pete leant over to Albert's ear and said softly so no one could hear, 'I was doing ok, then my package got me into trouble again with the Commanding Officer's wife. Her husband said that it was assault. I said *what with, a friendly weapon?* He didn't see the funny side of it.'
'Say no more. And that's why you're here at this little outpost. Well, you have done well for yourself!' said Albert sarcastically.
'Yes, I retire later this year and, looking around at these fine ladies, I might come and join you.' They both laughed.
'I suppose we'd better be getting back. They put me on duty all over Christmas and New Year. I might be out to see you again Albert. It depends how the rotas work out.'

'Just before you go might I have a private word?' Albert turned to the others.
'Please excuse us for a moment.'..... On reaching the bottom of the stair to the deck, they both walked together towards the fields.
'What is it Albert?'
'I think I may have a problem that I wasn't expecting at the start of our voyage. I might have a bit of a skirmish on my hands with the Russian mafia chasing us and we have no arsenal of armaments to protect ourselves.' Albert went on to explain the background to his predicament.
'How can I help, Albert?'
'Well, we will only be here until the end of March and then move to the north for summer. If you see anything unusual happening around, like odd visitors to the islands, I would appreciate knowing.'
'Yes. That's no problem, anything else?'
'There is something, yes, but I doubt if you could manage it.'

104

'Go on, Albert I know exactly what you are going to ask for.'
'You have firing practice with sidewinder guided missiles don't you? Couldn't you *lose* a couple for us?' asked Albert.
'Sidewinders! Good God! You'll get me shot! Even worse, I'll lose my pension… I'll see what I can do but I don't think it will be sidewinders. You don't bloody change do you Albert Crowther?'
'And neither do you, otherwise you wouldn't be here, Pete.' They both laughed as they walked to the top of the exit, shook hands warmly on parting and wished each other all the very best. Everyone stood at the side of the upper deck waving to the parting vessel.

'Why do you call him 'Package Pete?' was Ched's first question to Albert.
'Why don't you use your imagination, Ched?'
'Oh,' he replied, 'it's that then… Did you ever kill anybody when you were in the Gulf?' Albert paused.
'Yes, I did and I don't want to talk about it.' Albert walked away up to the bow. He didn't speak to anyone for a couple of hours.

Their first Christmas had arrived and all were excited about the main part of the day. The table was laid with the Christmas feast. Vicky and Stella were running around chasing each other with dolls in prams that Magnus and Patricia had made. 'Computerised toys are out of the question. Did they really need them anyway?' Magnus had asked when they had been racking their brains to think what presents to give. There was a general feeling of contentment, which made a delightful atmosphere. They were waiting for Albert to return from his walk. He had been out again today, the crew thought, to survey his created domain. They would not start the celebrations until he was present. Amy knew he was walking, but did not know the particular reason why he went for his quiet time. He did that when something was bothering him and wanted to reflect on things. He was surprised, when he finally arrived at the canteen, to be greeted with a round of applause from the entire Ark's community.

Gunter came forward to make a toast before the Christmas feast. Albert stood in amazement and, as he gazed around the room of happy faces, he thought, haven't we moved on? We are a thriving, established community and have room for growth. And, look at Jane! Only a few months ago when she lost the man in her life, she could have insisted that we took her to a coastal town in Wales. But she didn't, she stayed. Perhaps she was

105

mourning so bad, she didn't care what happened to her or she believed it was all a nightmare and Miles would just reappear somehow. The loss of someone very close can affect you that way. Melanie was a young woman all of a sudden and wanting to know if she would ever meet someone or was it her destiny to be trapped on this Ark with no one? There were Gunter and Greta with daughter Stella and now Venus, the first human born on the Ark. Ched and Millie and their daughter Vicky. Millie always busy on what she called 'her farm', her pride and joy. She never thought she would be in charge of such an organised, self-contained, prime-positioned piece of land, producing a good yield of crops, garden produce, dairy produce and every fruit, herb and so much more growing on this smallholding site in the Atlantic.

Then there were Magnus, Patricia and daughter Melanie, with Patricia thrown in at the deep end; Magnus did not even tell her where she was going. Yet she had become a big player and contributor to the people of the Ark's well being, undaunted by the job of, keeping the community fed and laundered (with the help and finesse of Amy of course). Magnus who is a mechanical genius, can work wizardry on machines, concentrates his knowledge one hundred percent into making sure that everything is working at its best. Next, he reflected on Monty, Marigold, and the little 'imp' Lucy. There hadn't been much call for his expertise yet, but Monty spent his time preparing herbs for his store and various sorts of medication. Marigold, yet to find her vocation in life, doesn't like doing anything much and has to be asked to help, usually with kitchen and laundry chores and occasionally in the nursery helping Greta. That just leaves Amy and me. It's a shame we have no children, but would have embraced it if it had been so, instead we have worked together to pull a bunch of misfits, in some cases, into a community that works (almost together) for no other gain than a happy existence. Such bliss!

Gunter proposed a toast.
'Please lift your glasses,' looking at Albert and then turning to Amy, 'thank you for making this all happen.' Albert and Amy were now arm in arm, Amy with a trickle of tears down her cheeks and Albert had a big lump in his throat. He rarely showed his emotions to others, but was so moved, he was unable to respond. Amy stepped forward.

'Cheers to you all, because without you, it would not have been possible, thank you.' They drank and they ate, the canteen was alive with excitement. Jane was enjoying being with them all; she even spoke to Ched!

One or two people had hangovers the next day, but nothing serious and gradually, normality returned until they heard the blast of a ship's hooter. It was the sound usually made when a naval vessel is entering its home port after a mission away. It was the coastguard ship of Albert's old friend Package Pete and crew. It was soon action stations in the Ark's kitchen for a near repeat of Christmas day. After a few drinks all round, Pete and Albert sat happily talking about their past together. Jane was approached and chatted up by one of Pete's company. She seemed very nervous but enjoyed the conversation and the male interest. Melanie meanwhile, was entertaining the other young rating in conversation.

'I've a little Christmas present for you,' Pete whispered to Albert and winked. How do you propose to get it onboard your ship, because I can't take it back?' Albert's eyes lit up.
'How is it crated? Is it marked?'
'No, just a plain wooden crate.' replied Pete.
'Right,' said Albert 'it's a spare outboard engine then?'
'Yes, it could well be.'
'Then just before you leave, I'll get Magnus to hoist it onboard and put it into the hold. Problem solved!' The time passed too quickly for those old comrades and duty was calling.
'We have a couple more visits to do before returning to base,' Pete confided, 'but not as enjoyable as this one, so we have to leave now.' The trio clambered back down to their vessel and manoeuvred it into a position to be underneath the hoist for the transfer of the crate. Magnus felt he had to say what was on his mind.
'Albert we don't need a spare outboard engine.'
'This is a special one, we might need this.'
'If you say so Albert,' he muttered as the crate was lifted into the air to the safety of the storage hold. The coastguards were on their way with the people of the Ark waving goodbye, with kisses blown from Melanie and Jane. Everybody returned to the canteen to finish off another fine day onboard the Ark.

Melanie went straight to Albert on his return to the canteen.

107

'When will they be coming again?' she asked excitedly.

'I don't know, I should think we may see them before we leave for the north in the spring, it will depend on Pete's rotas. He mainly does nights and bank holidays for some reason or other,' Albert informed her, not wanting to divulge the true reason for this: that Pete's anti social working hours were part of the punishment for his amorous misdemeanours.

'Oh!' she replied, and then went to her mother with an excited, hopeful smile on her face.

The Christmas celebrations were finally over and the daily routines got underway again. Because they enjoyed the special Christmas and Boxing Day meals, Patricia suggested that they should have each Sunday as a family day, where a similar, but not quite so grand, meal would be celebrated together. Everyone was for it, and this became the norm whenever they were at anchor.

On 31st December 2016, everybody congregated in the canteen for a celebration to see in the New Year. Gunter had the task of timing the exact moment of midnight, from their position in the Southern Atlantic. The children were in bed and watched over by Melanie and Greta, alternately, so that all the adults could be together at the stroke of midnight. During the build-up to this, the mood was very jolly with the ladies sitting down together, drinking mainly wine and having a good old chinwag. The men played darts whilst consuming large volumes of bitter. Initially no one could match Albert's skill at darts but it wasn't long before Gunter and Magnus were beating him on a regular basis.

Midnight came, with Gunter given the honour of doing the countdown. They all formed a circle, holding crossed hands to sing the traditional Auld Lang Syne.

****

In early March, just a couple of weeks before the move to the north for the summer, the gathering of the crops and other produce went at its usual pace. Everybody was at hand to help Millie with this heavy burden. There was always something about the months of March and April with Gunter, he felt the urge for sex more than he would do at other parts of the year, equivalent to the stag rutting season or 'full of the joys of spring' as a comparison. Greta knew this. She was scheming to make sure that she got maximum attention and response from him.

Greta was looking at ways to substitute getting Venus milk other than her own breasts. This meant working with Jane on how to best use the resources they had for this. The other reason was Greta had started to look at her body and realised it needed some trimming up to get back to her former shape. Although she had made an effort, she noted that the other women, with the exception of Patricia, were in a very fit state and the males would always turn their heads to look at the females when they passed by. She did not want to see Gunter turn his head to look at Jane, Melanie, Marigold, Millie, Amy or even Patricia. Although, if it was the latter that he turned his head at, she would be extremely worried. Reluctantly, she asked Jane for help on how she could substitute her milk that was drying up, for some of the cow or goat milk that was in abundance. Originally, Jane tried to persuade her to persevere with breast-feeding, because from her research, although it was a bind to the modern woman, she believed the breast to be the best natural way, and that was in line with the Ark's ethics. However, Greta insisted and Jane looked at a suitable combination and put it together. To Greta's amazement, after a few minor rejections from Venus, it was accepted, and it was appreciated. Greta respected Jane's efforts and advice!

Now Greta was off breast-feeding and she was concentrating on being a woman to turn a head, namely Gunter's. Jane's campaign to making sure everybody had a healthy diet, '*Diet or a Riot*', had mostly been a success. She had put the message across to everyone that a good balanced diet would keep the bad cholesterol levels in their bodies down and increase their energy. In return, they would be more alert, have better stamina and virility. Greta had taken this to heart and took the regime seriously, as most Germans would tend to do, if told it was good for them. Greta made sure that her man, children and herself were eating and exercising regimentally. She concentrated on her own body, looking in the mirror each day: checking her boobs, her waist and buttocks. She even noticed the hair growing under her armpits.

'*Scheißer!*' she said, 'Where's Gunter's razor? The other women have not this!' She gradually got her physique to a healthy and trim shape and now felt it was time to get something out of Gunter's body and entice him to do what the rest of the Ark were doing!

109

She had always had a different approach to sex, possibly a German thing; something a bit more out of the ordinary compared to the others on the Ark. She liked tools of the trade: leather garments and black silk sheets. The thing that really turned her on was her man in just lederhosen: short leather pants with braces and Greta had a special outfit too. It was Saturday evening and she knew Sunday would be a lazy day for them to rest after what she had planned. She got out his lederhosen and checked them over because they had not been used for some time. Then her outfit, she put it on as a dress rehearsal, to see if it still fitted, and looked in the mirror, bending and twisting about, to make sure nothing popped out prematurely. She was happy with it and began to get excited.

Next she collected a couple of bottles of wine from the store, choosing the imported rather than Albert's wine from the ship's produce, which wasn't quite ready by her standards. So, it was to be a Hock and a sparkling Asti Spumanti; these went straight in her fridge for later that evening. Now was the time to bathe, put on some make up, making herself attractive for her Gunter, before dinner in the canteen.

As with all the women, Greta wore hardly any makeup, partly because there didn't seem to be the need to paint their faces for the Ark's lifestyle, and also, they wanted to conserve their limited supply of cosmetics for as long as possible. Jane and Amy, with Monty's help, were experimenting with homemade beauty preparations but other projects tended to take precedence. It had been some years ago since Greta had used a serious amount of makeup. But, she decided to take her time and do things properly for this special occasion.

She started by plucking her eyebrows into neat arcs, and then smoothed moisturiser all over her face before applying a translucent foundation cream. Next, she pencilled and smudged in, dark brown eyeliner followed by brushing sultry green eye shadow on her lids and highlighter to shimmer just beneath her eyebrows. She coated her pale, thin lashes in black mascara to lengthen and thicken them. To complete the cover-girl look, she lightly defined her brows, brushed her cheeks with blusher to give a warm glow, and then swept a glossy dark red lipstick across her full lips. The whole process took about thirty minutes. She spent an equal amount of time to restyle her hair, then slipped on a revealing top and tight trousers, this

110

left very little to the imagination and stood back from the mirror to take a good view of her new look.

'Sehr gut!' she said to her reflection. 'I am ready for some action.'

Gunter was having his usual couple of pints of bitter with Albert and Ched before dinner, when in came Greta and the children. Gunter immediately went over to greet them and picked up Stella. He took one look at Greta.

'Wow!' he whispered under his breath. All the others' eyes were upon her. She had completely transformed herself from drab to stunningly attractive.

'You are looking wonderful my darling,' Gunter told her proudly, as they walked over to the bar. Lots more comments followed:

'You look superb!' said Albert.

'Fantastic Greta, looks like you'll be working hard tonight, Gunter,' from Ched.

'You're not working tonight!' snapped Greta.

'No, no, Greta,' Gunter replied, 'it's his little joke, forget it. Would you like a drink?'

'Yes please Gunter, what's the beer like?'

It's good, better than usual, Greta,' as he caught Albert's eye.

'I'll just have a small beer then,'

'Ok, if you sit down, I'll bring the drinks over, dinner will be ready soon.' Gunter soon returned back with his family, looking into his wife's eyes.

After dinner they concentrated on getting the children off to bed and fast asleep before settling down to a glass or two of wine.

'Are we celebrating something tonight Greta?'

'Yes we are, just being together and happy and I've a little surprise for you, so go and have a shower and put your lederhosen on. I will dress up for you *für ein bißchen Spielen.*'

'A little bit of playing, hey?' Gunter's eyes lit up. He quickly showered and by the time he had finished and entered the bedroom, Greta had her outfit on. He was getting an erection just looking at her. She was almost dressed in thigh length high-heeled boots, crotch-less pants, elbow length gloves and an 'over the shoulder boulder holder' with her nipples sticking out through holes, all in black leather. She stood with arms resting on her thighs and held a leather-bound stick with tassels at one end, in her right hand. Gunter thought she looked like somebody out of his favourite magazine and had better get his lederhosen on before his dick was too big to get into them. These were not ordinary lederhosen, (Morris dancers take

111

note) these had been modified with the crotch split and the cheeks of the arse cut away!

As soon as he had them on, she dusted his balls with the tassels and then his nipples, going back down to his semi-hard dick. He turned around, bent over slightly for her to whip his cheeks gently, and then back around again repeating the process, only harder each time. It stopped and she placed the stick to the back of his head guiding him to suck her nipples, each in turn, until it was back to the flailing of the buttocks, balls, nipples and dick. He was getting bigger and bigger with the excitement. The stick went behind his neck again, guiding him down to her. As he knelt to place his tongue on what he called her butterfly lips, she arched backwards resting on her hands, with arms at full length like an athlete. Her legs were well apart for Gunter to get his tongue into her at maximum length moving it in and out and up to her clit, making it expand. Now she was getting near to the peak of pleasure, it was time for him to enter and complete each others joy.
'*Schnell* Gunter. *schnell*!' she demanded. He got to his knees at the right height to slide into her well-lubricated vagina. As he entered, he helped support her and it only took a few stokes in and out with Gunter's massive penis and she was groaning with ecstasy. Collapsing onto her back, Gunter followed her down, still inside her to climax himself, letting his sperm pump. She clutched at him, holding him into her tightly as their muscles pulsed and throbbed. They were both puffing and panting side by side!
'Oh, Gunter that was fantastic! Let's have a drink then do it again. I'll open the *Asti*.'
'Yes, *Liebling*, you were fantastic too'…
'Prost Greta!'
'Prost!' she smiled.

ALBERT'S PRIVATE LOG- October 2016-March 2017

The sail repaired alright, when Magnus and Ched finally got round to it, just a bolt that had worked loose somewhere in the mechanism and we were able to get it back into its housing and operate it normally. Setting the fore and aft sails in the heave to position worked remarkably well although we drifted a few miles over three months. We just need to keep checking and correcting regularly.

112

I found it amazing how well the plants have adapted to the almost continuous growing season, giving us fresh produce all year round. Jane has done a really good job with the availability of good food produce for her to choose from: oily fish, fresh vegetables and salads, keeping us on a balanced diet, it could not be better.

Christmas was very enjoyable and fancy bumping into Package Pete all the way out here! It just goes to show you what a small world we live in. Not so easy to get off the planet after all! I hope I don't have to use Pete's present.

All in all, it's been a fantastic season here and a shame it has to end. Over the period, since last April, the first five month trial, the trees, shrubs and plants have done well. But we must prepare for the journey to the Azores, which will not take as long as the one from the UK. It's important we move before the bad weather starts. The transformation that has happened in just a year to all forms of life onboard has been amazing.

11. THE ASSAULT

It was the end of the first season in the southern hemisphere, which was a very successful one. The key to the Ark doing so well was due to plenty of rain and sun. The spot was perfect at the south west end of the Walvis Ridge, about thirty miles east of the islands of Tristan De Cunha, where the waters were shallower. A bumper harvest filled the storerooms and freezers. It was time to position the sails to catch the wind, and head for the Azores archipelago, a group of nine islands in the northern hemisphere, seven hundred and fifty miles west of Portugal and still in their control, although one island has an American air base that was used during the gulf war as a staging post; it is still there. Gunter set a course of 340°, which would take them almost parallel with the Atlantic Ridge until they reached the Gambia Basin just south west of the Cape Verde islands, off the west coast of Africa. Then the course would change to due north to the area of the Azores.

Magnus and Albert started at the bow, moving each sail to its new position, until all the sails were raised from their housings and angled to catch the maximum wind. Gradually, the Ark started moving, it took several hours for the ship to gain any sensible speed, but as the day went on, more wind came to help them onwards. They were reaching speeds of fifteen knots constantly twenty four hours a day.

They were ten days into the journey and about one hundred miles south west of the Cape Verde islands. Gunter was on lookout; visibility was good for fifty miles and a strong breeze was blowing. As Gunter scanned the horizon with the binoculars, he thought he could hear the distinctive thud of helicopter rotor blades. He immediately called Albert on the two way radio. 'Albert, I can hear a helicopter in the distance.' Albert was on the bridge with Ched.
'Well they're not crossing the Atlantic Gunter, so they must be looking for something or somebody and I guess it's us! I'll get back to you....Radio Millie, Ched. Tell her to stay at the bow with the animals and not to show herself because there is an emergency. Then go to the gun cabinet and get me the old AK47 that Miles got me. Make sure it has a full clip in and a spare, then meet me on the top deck near the water cannon.' Albert did not have time to get Package Pete's Christmas present, the grenade launcher, from the hold, because he did not want to startle the crew.

114

'We will just have to see how this turns out. I doubt if it's a social visit lads!'

Albert radioed to Jane to collect all female personnel to go to the lower decks, and stay there. He then radioed to Magnus.

'We have an emergency! Get up to the water cannon and prime it up ready for use with maximum power, as soon as you possibly can.'

'I can see it now, just coming over the horizon, it's a chopper alright.' Gunter called again, only more urgently. Ched returned with the machine gun. Albert instructed him to stay on the bridge, but out of sight. Then he left to join Gunter and Magnus on the top deck.

'Gunter, can you man the water cannon with it aimed at the helicopter. We may have to bring it down. Make sure you hit it straight off. Fire it, if I shout the order.' The sound of the helicopter got louder and louder and was now in full sight. Albert had the binoculars trained on the chopper. It looked like an old Westland Lynx and it was only a few miles away. As it got closer, it slowed down and turned, bringing the side of the helicopter to face the bridge on the starboard side of the Ark. The door was open and they could see a man in a harness leaning out, brandishing an automatic gun in one hand and a loud hailer in the other. The helicopter dropped to the same level as the bridge. Gunter and Magnus kept their heads down; the guy in the chopper did not know they were there and Albert had his AK47 concealed behind a vent. The man raised the loud hailer.

'We want Miles Overstrand,' he shouted. 'Bring him out and no one will get hurt!'

'There is nobody here of that name.' Albert shouted back as loud as he could against the noise of the helicopter. The man dropped the loud hailer and moved the automatic to his waist, firing indiscriminately at the bridge and to the top deck.

'Fire!' Albert shouted and returned fire himself. Before the pilot realised what was happening, Gunter had a direct shot with the water cannon, forcing the man in the harness to the other side of the helicopter, filling it with a huge volume of sea water. This put the pilot in an extremely difficult situation, and he stalled it. Hovering at such low revs, he hadn't expected a few tonnes of water as a load! Suddenly, the chopper was on its side and heading for the briny. It plummeted into the sea and sank quickly. The Ark was moving at about fifteen knots, leaving the wreckage floating behind.

Albert picked up the binoculars again and moved to the stern. He focused on the remains of the helicopter and looked for survivors. There were none. He was relieved; he didn't want to see a head bobbing in the water waving a hand at him. He thought to himself, bloody hell! You are a callous bastard Albert; but then on the other hand, we survived! As the wreckage disappeared, Albert lowered the binoculars and returned to the bridge, where all the other men involved were congratulating each other, asking questions about what had happened, but also praising themselves on their bravado.

When Albert entered the bridge, the crew bombarded him with questions. Ched was never one to mince words.

'What the fuck was that all about?'

'Well, Miles wasn't all he led us to believe.' Albert explained that when he questioned Jane about Miles' past, she had given him enough information to realise they may be in danger, and he was psyched up to deal with it, but had not wanted to worry the rest of them unduly, in case nothing happened.

'Unfortunately, and not his fault entirely, Miles ended up working for the Russian mafia. The company he was working for was taken over by them,' Albert continued. 'He was told to rig the tables of all the casinos and other gambling houses that he managed in London. He didn't want to run crooked establishments but if he had to, he thought he would make something for himself. Being such a brilliant, creative accountant, he was able to benefit from rigging the tables even more, and kept the accounts so that they hid the money he was taking for himself. Over five years he amassed a fortune, investing it shrewdly. It just got bigger and that became a problem. He had to disappear. That's where the advert that you all answered comes in. It's obvious from today's little episode he left a trail, and I'm sure they'll be back. They know where to look, so we have to be prepared. They will probably try again at some point, and we shall have to be extra vigilant.' The men were joined by the women including Millie who had rushed up from the bow. They immediately asked the same questions, except Jane, who knew what it was all about.

Suddenly, Albert realised that Monty was not there. He asked if anyone had seen him. Marigold said that he went to have a sleep by the swimming pool, earlier. Albert led the way to the front part of the top deck, to find him, closely followed by Jane and Marigold with the remainder behind them. As they got to the pool, they could see Monty in a sitting position at

116

the front of the pool on a sun bed. He still seemed to be asleep. One or two of them found it hard to believe he could sleep through the noise of the helicopter and the gunfire. But then they saw a pool of blood beneath the sun bed.

'Oh my god!' followed by a piercing scream from a frozen still Marigold. Jane overtook Albert and rushed to Monty. She lifted his eyelids as Albert checked for a pulse and confirmed, to everyone's relief, he was alive. He had a graze to the head and a bullet straight through his left shoulder and had lost a considerable amount of blood.

'At least he's stopped bleeding but he is still concussed. Ched and Gunter can you carry him to sickbay please and try not to disturb his shoulder?' Albert asked. In the meantime, Jane rushed on ahead to prepare, followed by Amy to assist. Marigold was being comforted by Patricia while Greta and Melanie took care of the children.

Albert led the way, making sure the access was clear. Monty was laid on the couch, still unconscious as Amy immediately started to clean the head wound, while Jane cut away his shirt sleeve to reveal the extent of the shoulder damage. The bullet had gone clean through and out the other side. 'With him being so skinny it didn't take much with it, so there seems to be very little damage, but he will be in a lot of pain when he comes to,' Jane pointed out to Albert. As Amy continued dabbing the head with cold water, Monty began to stir.

'Oh my head,' he groaned, 'what happened? I was fast asleep when all of a sudden all hell broke loose! Oh my head,' He was in agony. Jane prepared his shoulder for dressing and Amy put a bandage around his head.

'Amy, I need something for this pain in my head. I feel it's going to burst. I prepared some morphine from the poppies we grew.' Monty told her where to find the drug in his laboratory.

'Look in the cabinet above the desk and the key's in the drawer below.' To Monty it seemed ages waiting in chronic pain. Amy returned as quickly as she could with a plastic box with a hand written label 'Morphine' with the date he concocted the substance. She administered it as his instructions via a syringe into his left arm, once a place was found to put the needle. The drug had an almost immediate effect and Monty grew calmer as the pain eased.

Albert fetched Marigold as soon as Monty was conscious enough to cope with her. He poked his head around the door to check how he was doing, before entering the room with Marigold in tow.

'Will he be alright Amy?' asked Marigold.

'Yes, of course, he'll be up and about in no time at all.' Albert congratulated Jane and Amy on there roles as doctors and nurses.

'We'll have to get you two some nurses outfits made up,' he joked. Amy was not amused.

'Bugger off, Albert!' she replied. Marigold stayed with Monty and everybody else scattered. On his way back to the bridge, Albert felt pleased about Jane taking the role she had. Perhaps she felt guilty that the attack was partly her fault through Miles. He also smiled to himself on the way he handled the assault on his Ark, visualising the shock the gunman had when the water jet hit him forcing him across to the other side of the helicopter. But he was still concerned how it might be the next time... and knew he must have a conflab with the lads, to discuss the matter.

When he got back to the bridge, Ched was at the helm; Albert asked him where Gunter and Magnus were.

'Gunter is back on lookout and Magnus is checking for gunfire damage. I've spoken to Millie and everything's ok at the bow. The animals are fine.'

'Good. Sorry Ched, I had forgotten about Millie what with all that's happened.'

'That's understandable, Albert.'

'We need to have a little get together to discuss protection of the Ark. I'll go and find Magnus and Gunter to let them know, what about a meeting here at 0800 hours tomorrow?'

'That's ok by me.'

Albert found Magnus checking the water cannon, which received some bullet damage.

'How is it?'

'It's fine, just superficial.'

'Is there any other damage elsewhere?'

'Not really, only the contents of my under pants, I bloody well shit myself!'

'I'm sure they'll wash,' Albert replied with a dead pan expression. We need to discuss the protection of the Ark, so put your thinking cap on. I'm organising a meeting tomorrow on the bridge at 0800 hours. We also need to make sure the radar is paid special attention to at night, from now on.'

118

'Ok.'

Albert then went to the lookout post to see Gunter. As Albert approached, he could see him scanning the horizon. He sensed someone was nearing him and he lowered his binoculars to see it was Albert.
'Albert, I thought Jane would be here to take her shift.'
'I'll check that out, Gunter.'
'I want to thank you for your quick action and your accuracy with the water cannon. You certainly saved the day for us all. In the light of what happened to Monty, and he seems to be ok by the way, it was the right decision to bring down the chopper. It was a definite case of them or us. We are having a meeting on the bridge at 0800 hours tomorrow to discuss the protection of the Ark, please be there.' Albert radioed to ask Jane to relieve Gunter.

That night turned out to be quiet, each taking their shift on watch and keeping course. Next morning at 0700 hours, Gunter plotted a position of 32° latitude and 20° longitude as it was time to change course to due north. At 0800 hours Albert, Ched, Gunter and Magnus assembled on the bridge. Magnus asked Albert for a post mortem on why they had to fight off the helicopter, resulting in those men perishing in the sea.
'If we had let that man, and any others that may have accompanied him, onboard to search for Miles, even if we had explained that Miles was dead, I'm sure they would not have hesitated to kill us all, just for being associated with Miles. The firing of his automatic weapon was enough to convince me of his agenda. Miles and Jane thought they were free from the clutches of the Russian mafia once they were at sea.'
'Miles must have known that they would come looking for him and the consequences of what would happen to all of us, if by some chance they found him. In hindsight, he put all our lives at risk!' Gunter angrily replied.
'Yes,' said Albert. 'If I hadn't got the information out of Jane on Miles' past that certainly would have been the case and possibly all of us may have been killed. But that's enough of that we have to think of the future. Now I believe we will be under threat of another assault from the colleagues of our *friends* we met for a short period yesterday. We do have another weapon that we can use the next time. I've been keeping it away from you all, hoping my fears were false. You were told it was an outboard motor, it's not it is a grenade launcher. Package Pete got it for me at Christmas. But that won't be enough on its own, has anybody any useful

119

ideas on how we can defend ourselves against an attack from another sea-going vessel, probably a lot faster than us? Magnus you're the mechanical genius, what have you come up with?'

'What sort of weapon would they attack us with?'

'I don't know, it could be torpedoes, rocket launchers, guided missiles, heavy machine guns.'

'Oh, shit we're all finished!'

'Don't panic Magnus!' replied Albert, 'We'll have to keep further away from land than we normally do. I know they can track us by satellite, but they will have a long journey to get to us and we have size on our side. So back to the question, what has anybody come up with as a defence system?' It was silent then Magnus gave a grunt.

'Hmm... I could make some short range rockets if you could distil enough alcohol to power them, and use fused methane gas as a warhead. We have plenty of tubing for a launcher but we need to make some, and practice using them, to have a chance. We could also use methane in containers, as fire bombs.'

'Good Magnus, that's a start. I'll ask Monty, when he's a bit fitter, if we have enough ingredients onboard to make other explosive material, like gunpowder and in the meantime the distillery will be working overtime to make alcohol for rocket fuel. So let's get to work!' The meeting ended. Ched stayed at the helm, Magnus went to his workshop, Gunter went to relieve Jane on lookout and Albert was on his way to see how Monty was. Albert thought that if they had another attack, it would probably be at anchor, and they would just have to be extra vigilant. He decided to look at the charts after seeing Monty.

Ched radioed to Albert to tell him they were approaching the North Atlantic weather system and if they stayed on the set course, the Ark would come to a standstill, or worse, be forced backwards by the strong current. 'Ok,' Albert replied, 'I'll get Jane to relieve Gunter on lookout and he can plot a new course. Magnus and I will alter the sails accordingly once the course has changed.' Gunter altered the course to 320°. The ship almost came to a stop before the wind caught the sails and gradually, it was on its way again but only moving at four or five knots. Albert finally called in to see Monty. He was sitting up, with Marigold at his side and Lucy was running around screaming. Albert thought he'd better not stay long...

'How are we today Monty?'

'He's still in a lot of pain.' Marigold replied. 'He's been asking for more morphine.'

'Right,' said Albert, 'I'll get Amy to come down to see him.' He made a quick exit, mumbling to himself.

'I'm not surprised he's in pain with that noisy little urchin running about screaming!'

Amy was in the kitchen with Patricia, preparing food. Albert asked Amy to look in on Monty because he wanted more morphine.

'And could you ask Greta to look after the little monster to give Monty some peace?' Amy stopped what she was doing, gave Albert a glare and left. Albert looked at Patricia.

'What have I done wrong now Patricia?'

'Amy has only just got back from seeing to him, and Marigold is not much of a help with anything right now.'

'Oh I see.' said Albert.

Albert headed for the bridge, out of the way.

'Hi Ched, how are things?'

'Slow. We didn't move backwards, as I thought we would at one point, but we are picking up the clockwise weather system now and should be up to ten knots by the end of the day, maybe fifteen tomorrow. Albert, I've been thinking…'

'Bloody hell, isn't that dangerous?'

'Listen!' snapped Ched, 'What are we going to use as target practice, once Magnus has produced his rockets? We'll have to build a floating target. We have enough raw materials, and it just means more work to do, when we are all stretched to the limit.'

'Don't worry! I'm hoping it will be better when we are at anchor in a few days time.'

ALBERT'S PRIVATE LOG – April 2017

I've found another use for the water cannon besides putting out fires: taking helicopters down! It certainly saved the day. The pilot didn't expect that, the poor bastard! I know it's wrong to think it, but I'm

121

glad there were no survivors. At least the problem Miles left us is out in the open; they will probably try again at some stage.

Strange that no one questioned Jane on the matter, or showed any animosity towards her.

Monty will recover alright. He seems to be moving about ok but he was very lucky: another ten centimetres further over and he would have been killed. Amy's previous nursing experience came in very useful.

I wonder how successful Magnus' rockets will be. I suppose a lot will depend on how powerful I can make the alcohol. It's such a shame to use it as rocket fuel. That reminds me, I must take a look at that grenade launcher to see what condition it's in. Then, as Ched pointed out, we will need some target practice.

The first part of the journey went really well until the assault, not surprising it has given them all the jitters.

12. THE RESCUE

The final part of the journey to the northern hemisphere for the summer season anchoring was very slow, making only nine knots. The weather had been mostly moderate for the past week and now there was just a gentle breeze, with large wavelets and scattered white horses over the sea. The four thousand, five hundred mile journey from Tristan da Cunha to the area near the Azores was going to take them almost three weeks in total, at the speed they were travelling. They were approximately six hundred miles from their destination and four hundred miles west of the Canary Islands with about three days sailing left. The ship was relying on sail alone because of the small amount of methane gas left to power the turbines, which they were saving in case of an emergency.

Jane was on lookout and considered the job extremely boring. She was scanning the horizon with binoculars, looking for other vessels. Occasionally, she lowered the glasses to give a large yawn as the clear bright afternoon sun affected her. Jane suddenly called down to the bridge using the short wave radio hand set. She had spotted something that seemed to be drifting about four miles north east off the starboard bow, and wanted a second opinion. Albert, who was on the bridge with Ched, said he would go up to the lookout post. Jane passed the binoculars to Albert, pointing in the direction of the object. Albert studied the scene.
'Well it's a boat, my eyesight is not as good as it used to be but it looks like a yacht with a broken mast. I'll get Gunter to come up and put a bearing on it.' He quickly passed the binoculars back to Jane. 'Keep your eyes peeled on that boat. We must act quickly to check it out, without slowing the Ark down.' Albert picked up his radio. 'Gunter, get your arse up here, immediately if not sooner!' Gunter arrived in minutes. 'What do you mean by that request?' asked a confused Gunter.
'Oh it's Irish; never mind that, have a look at this.' Gunter took the binoculars from Albert who was pointing ahead.
'Can you give me a bearing on the position of the boat you see,' Gunter looked and checked his portable compass.
'030°, three miles and drifting south,'
'Thank you Gunter. I think we had better take a look.' Albert instructed Jane to remain at the lookout, keeping the binoculars on the boat and to let the bridge know if she saw any signs of life. Albert and Gunter headed for

the bridge. On the way back down Albert called for Magnus to join them, once all together, Albert decided on the action to take.

'Magnus get the inflatable from the hold and be ready to lower it over the side. Find a good tow rope and check the inflatable is full of gas.' Magnus disappeared.

'Ched, you and Gunter wait here until I come back then get yourselves into the inflatable. Be prepared to put the boat in tow.' A few minutes later, Albert returned with a pistol that he had taken from the gun cabinet and handed it to Ched. Ched was afraid when he put the pistol in his hand.

'Albert, shouldn't you be doing this; you're used to this sort of thing?'

'Ched, don't be such a fucking wimp and get on with it. Didn't they teach you anything in the Royal Navy? I won't be around forever you know.'

'Why do I need a gun?'

'It's just in case the yacht has been stolen and the occupants aren't very friendly. You know we need to be on our guard; just be careful. I'll take the helm we don't want to lose speed now, do we?' Ched was in unsure territory and not a willing participant.

'Do you want me to have the gun, Ched?'

'No! I'll take it but, you know Gunter, I'd rather tackle a fifty kilo tuna in my fishing boat than do this.'

'Come on Ched, let's get on with the job, there could be people in trouble out there!'

The inflatable was ready. Ched and Gunter climbed in and then Magnus operated the crane. Lowering the craft over the side while the Ark was making nine knots was precarious. The quick release shackle was pulled just a few feet from the water so the boat hit the sea with one hell of a thump, followed by a huge volume splash that drenched the pair.

'Shit!' shouted Ched, 'Why do I always get the crap jobs?' Just then, the inflatable banged against the side of the Ark's hull. Gunter moved quickly and started the engine. Ched and Gunter were soon bobbing across the choppy waves in the direction of the yacht. As they approached, they slowed down to within about three hundred yards. The sea was calm enough to enable them to keep a constant eye on the drifting vessel to see if there were any signs of life. As they were getting nearer, the picture was clearer: the yacht's mast was broken at the point where the boom was attached and the sail was strewn across the port side of the boat, dragging in the water. Now they were fifty yards away, approaching the stern on the starboard side. They prepared to board and Gunter stopped the engine.

124

'Hello, anybody home? Ched shouted.
'Hello, we are coming onboard.' No reply. Gunter grabbed a stanchion on the yacht and tied the inflatable to the nearest cleat. Ched had already climbed aboard and crept to the cabin access, which was open along with the sliding hatch. Gunter was soon there too.

Ched descended into the cabin, pistol in hand and shaking like a leaf, followed by Gunter. The galley was to the left, the chart table and radio to the right. Past the galley, lying lifeless on the settee berth was a young man. As Ched came near to him, he could see by his swollen and split lips, that he was dehydrated. He immediately harnessed the pistol in his belt then took the lad's left wrist to check the pulse. While doing so, he asked Gunter to check the forward cabin. He felt a pulse and lifted the lad's head slightly, supported it with a cushion and checked his airway to make sure there was no obstruction.
'There is another young man here.' Gunter shouted to Ched. He entered the forward cabin and repeated the action of pulse and airway check.
'He is in much the same way. We must get them back to the Ark as quickly as we can.' When Gunter checked the galley for drinking water, there was not a drop and he couldn't see any food either. He went up to the cockpit and tried to start the yacht's engine but the fuel tank was empty. Meanwhile, Ched looked on the chart table for information to show where they were from or heading.
'I'm going back to the inflatable to release it from the yacht and come along the starboard side to the bow. Can you pull the dangling sail onboard and make it fast?'

Ched handed him the towrope. After a few minutes, he was ready, waiting to make the rope fast to the bow of the yacht. When all was secure, Ched started the inflatable motor and slowly took up the slack in the rope. Gunter returned to the helm to steer the yacht behind. As the vessels drew closer to the Ark, Ched radioed ahead now that the short wave sets were in communication distance. He requested a human cradle to take the casualties off the yacht and asked Albert to slow the Ark down to enable this to happen safely.
'This is going to be a problem. It will take us over an hour to drop the sails. Is he brain dead or what?' Albert thought. Nevertheless, he instructed Magnus to get the women to help in the emergency and to help lower the

125

sails. All the crew were top side, even Marigold who had not been of any help anywhere for some time. They all assisted in lowering the Ark's sails. Magnus suggested starting the turbines to put them in reverse to slow the ship down and Albert did so.

Ched was heading to a position ahead of the Ark to meet it. The Ark would take about two miles to slow down, enough to make lifting out of the water possible. Ched and Gunter gradually pulled the yacht and inflatable closer and then tied them together. Gunter dropped the fenders over the side of the yacht to prevent it from damage through banging against the hull of the Ark. Ched then boarded the yacht to help Gunter with the first man out onto the sliding hatch. The two boats were now alongside the Ark and slowly edging their way to the point where the crane was situated. The cradle was already in position. Gunter grabbed it and pulled it to the side of the first casualty, where they rolled him in and quickly secured the straps. The signal was given to raise the cradle and he was soon on his way to sickbay shrouded by Jane, Marigold and Melanie.

Magnus lowered the cradle again to receive the second casualty. The operation was repeated, but they had to wait for the trolley to arrive back from sickbay with Amy, Greta and Patricia at hand. The unconscious young man was soon on his way, leaving Albert to operate the hoist to lift the inflatable from the water. The yacht was temporarily to be put in tow and the inflatable returned to the hold. Ched and Gunter started to climb the rope ladder that had been dropped for their return onboard. Ched went first, trailed by Gunter who had the tow rope, which was attached to the yacht. As Ched neared the top, he felt his strength waning, he was puffing and panting. Luckily, Albert was there to greet him, saw his distress and immediately helped him over the side.

'You sound like me when I've just had my rocks off and I'm nearly old enough to be your father!' Albert commented. 'I should get yourself back into a fit shape, I would have a word with Jane if I was you, or you'll end up alongside Miles.' Millie came from behind to greet Ched with Albert unaware of her presence. When she heard what Albert said, she turned on him to retaliate.

'If he has a word with Jane, he *will* end up alongside Miles. I'll see to that!' The comment did not go down well with Ched. He sat on a small capstan winch to get his breath back, mumbling to himself.

'Bloody hell, he's right, I am well out of shape!' and then turned to Albert, 'that mate of yours, Package Pete, he must be your age, he wasn't out of breath like this after climbing that ladder.' Millie was concerned about Ched's breathlessness but took a step back, now that Gunter was onboard.

Albert started to question Ched and Gunter on what they had found. As Ched handed back the pistol to Albert, Millie saw it and shrieked at him.
'Why have you got that thing in your hand?' Albert intervened.
'Millie, is Ched back here safe with you?'
'Yes, of course he is.'
'Well, if there had been a problem he had the upper edge by having some protection. That's why I gave him the pistol. Don't forget Millie, we all would have been goners if I hadn't taken to arms not so long back.' Millie quietened down.

Gunter told Albert what happened.
'It appears that they are from Italy. According to the charts, they have sailed from Salerno in the south west of the country to Cagliari in Sardinia and then on to Gibraltar. From there, to Lagos in Portugal and the last port of call was Tenerife, the port of Santa Cruz. The chart indicates they were heading for the Caribbean. They both seem to be about twenty years old. They must have encountered a heavy storm with the main sail still up, to break the mast like that. They left Santa Cruz about twenty days ago and they are lucky we found them, if they survive. They seem very young to have enough experience to cross the Atlantic. The yacht was out of fuel, water and food. That's all we know so far.'
'Is the yacht worth salvaging?'
'Yes' answered Ched, 'the mast can be repaired and it's a petrol engine, so it can be converted to gas.'
'Let's go and talk to Magnus to see how we can get this yacht onboard and into the hold.'

When Albert, Gunter and Ched reached Magnus, he was checking the inflatable, after its heroic first outing, and was pleased with its safe, unscathed return.
'What do you think the yacht weighs, Ched?'
'About ten tonne I'd say. What about lifting it Magnus?'
'The crane won't lift that weight. We'll have to use a main lifeboat hoist.'
The men set to work removing the lifeboat from its cradle and out of the

127

way, using the rotovator tractor to pull it along the deck. They winched the yacht to beneath the position of the lifeboat hoist. Ched cut away a section of the Ark's side rail, to allow the keel of the yacht onto the deck and Gunter volunteered to put the slings onto it. Steadily they lifted it out of the water. The yacht remained attached to the hoist, and secured to the deck. It was then all hands to the Ark's sails to raise them and get the ship back underway to their destination.

The men returned to the bridge with Ched taking the controls and Gunter correcting their course. Albert made his way to the sickbay to see how the guests were. He found Jane, Marigold and Melanie giving the young men their full attention. Monty had supplied an oral solution to administer to the patients, consisting of salt, sugar and cooled boiled water, for rehydration. Amy was busy with a leaf from the Aloe Vera plant scooping out the inner gel to treat their blistered lips. The girls were almost in conflict to who would hold the patients' heads while drip-feeding the fluid into their parched mouths. Albert looked at the two lads' faces; their eyes were rolling back and to, as they came in and out of consciousness. He wondered what was going through their minds. I bet they don't know whether they are in heaven or hell with all that female attention, he thought to himself. Albert called to Jane and she turned to scowl back at him, annoyed by his interruption. Before Albert could say another word, Jane jumped up in excitement.

'They are coming round,' she burst out. 'They'll be fine. You can see they are in good hands. They will survive! We'll make sure they survive. Please leave us alone now.' She turned back to her patients, scolding Melanie for giving fluid too fast.

'You'll choke him, for Gods sake!' Albert disappeared rapidly, considering himself in the way. However, he smiled at what he saw, thinking these lads were just what they needed as he slowly made his way back to the bridge. He was feeling exhausted after such a strenuous day.

Jane had organised a twenty four hour watch over the patients. When Albert called to see them the next morning, Jane was taking her shift. The two Italians were sleeping. Jane apologised to Albert for snapping at him.

'Sorry Albert, things were a little tense last night. The patients are breathing normally and we will try some food when they wake up.'

During the course of the next few days as the Ark was nearing its northern season destination, the crew settled down to their work again. The two Italian lads were speaking in Italian together, sitting up and taking normal foods, and quite capable of feeding themselves, although, the self-appointed nurses still insisted on feeding them. On one of his regular visits to see their progress, Albert approached them and shook there hands.

'Buongiorno! parli l'inglese?' Albert had found a phrase book.

'Non inglese,' they replied. That was the extent of Albert's Italian.

What about you Jane, how's your Italian?'

'I shall be teaching myself, as of today.' Albert and Jane smiled at each other, they both new the importance of the survival of these two men and what a potential gift to help the long term survival of the Ark, if they could get them to stay. Nevertheless, they both wondered how they were going to make them feel they wanted to stay. Albert decided to call a meeting of all the Ark's adults to discuss how to handle the situation. Prior to this, they needed to question the two men to find out more about them. Albert approached Greta to ask her about her languages. She said she did have some elementary Italian but was very rusty. So, Albert asked her to work with Jane on a basic questioning session in Italian, to find out more. In a very short time, Jane was able to understand some of the conversations the guests were having. She always made a point to greet them in Italian, in a formal manner.

The Ark had now reached its destination. They chose a position 33° 0' longitude and 37° 05' latitude about twenty five miles south west of the island of Flores. According to the chart, the area was less than three hundred metres deep so they were able to use the anchors. The anchors dropped to the sea bed to keep the Ark from drifting in the strong Azores current. It was now time for the residents to concentrate on replenishing the stores with everything they would need to produce and catch over the next six months.

The guests were soon out of bed and becoming inquisitive. It was obvious that they understood a certain amount of the English language, more than they cared to let on. But now they had become fit and well. They were still sleeping in their sickbay beds, pending a decision on where else to put them, but they had freedom of the Ark. They were well fed and naturally, received a lot of attention from the females.

129

Greta and Jane, at Albert's request, were ready to give the two Italians some questioning. The lads were summoned to attend a meeting in the canteen early one fine and bright morning. Greta and Jane had prepared a basic question sheet. Jane knew some of the answers, but wanted things to be formal and asked the first question to the eldest-looking and wrote down the answers:

QUESTIONNAIRE APRIL 14TH 2017

Che cosa è il vostra nomè ? (What is your name?)
Il mio nome è Antonio (My name is Antonio)

E che cosa è il vostro nome ? (And what is your name?)
Il mio nome è Marcello, il suo fratello (My name is Marcello, his   brother)

Antonio quanto vecchi siete? (Antonio how old are you?)
Sono 22 e Marcello 18 (I am 22 and Marcello 18)

Quale zona dell Italia provenite? (Which part of Italy are you from?)
Salerno in Italia del sud (Salermo in southern Italy)

Quante genta a bordo yacht? (How many people onboard the yacht?)
Tre. Marcello, nonno e me (3. Marcello, grandfather and me.)

Che cosa è accaduto? (What happened?)
Perso fuori bordo nel maltempo (Lost overboard in bad weather)

Á dove stavate navigando? (Where were you sailing to?)
Il mare caraibico (The Caribbean Sea)

Antonio and Marcello went on to explain that after the storm and the loss of their grandfather, without a mainsail they used the engine but did not know which way to head. Several days later, they were out of fuel and water. 'Grazie mille,' Jane thanked them as the questioning ended and Greta finished her notes.

The two men left the canteen to go to the swimming pool. During the short trip from the canteen to the pool, they were silent. After taking their shirts and trousers off, they both plunged into the pool. Then they started to converse rapidly in Italian.

'Antonio, what do you think, are we prisoners?'

'No I don't think so. I suppose it is more a practical problem of what to do with us. It is a very strange situation. They seem to have cut themselves off from the outside world. So if that is what they have done, it means that they probably do not want their existence known. We have put them in a predicament; they will not want to drop us off at the nearest port, because they do not go to ports. Also, the way the young women pay so much attention to us, there may be another problem! I think I might like it here, Marcello.'

'That is not for me, you know that.'

'Ha, Ha, Ha, perhaps Albert might fancy you?'

Don't be funny. It's not my fault that I'm ...'

Just at that point Marcello stopped. He had caught sight of Marigold at the side of the pool with very little on. Marcello turned away, immediately submersing himself and swimming as far away as possible. Antonio's eyes lit up and he swam closer to where Marigold was dangling her feet over the side of the pool and posing forward with her breasts provocatively in view. Antonio dived down and then leapt out of the water so his face was in line with her breasts. She couldn't resist, her arms were immediately around him and he pulled her into the water. She hung on to him as he buried his face between two of the most beautiful parts of the female form he had seen for a long time. Then Antonio's right hand found its way to an even more magnificent part of the female body. At that point, Marigold panicked and forced herself away and up to the surface. She swam to the exit ladder and, not wanting to lose face because she knew she had teased; she turned to Antonio and started laughing at him. He stopped, turned and swam away. Millie had watched Marigold's retreat and approached the two lads who were still in the pool.

'Right you two, out you come! We have work to do; there's plenty of the working day left and I need a hand!' I'll see you there in half an hour.' She pointed to the bow of the ship and made sure they understood.

As the day went on, Antonio proved to be very useful in tending to the stock and helping with other agricultural duties. Marcello had no interest at all and was nervous when near the animals. This was reported to Albert

later that day. When Millie approached Albert to discuss how they got on, he was busy with Amy preparing cabins for the two lads.
'I thought we had better make them feel at home and give them some privacy. Where are they at the moment?' asked Albert.
'They're in the swimming pool, where I found them this morning, only with three females instead of just Marigold.'
'Yes Millie, I'm concerned about Marigold.'
'I think she's lacking attention from Monty for some reason or another.'
'Well nature is working.' said Albert, 'Trouble is three into two don't usually go, but two into three goes sometimes, after all, it's what's in their trousers that counts!'
'Albert!' shouted Amy, 'Do you have to be so crude?'
'I'm only stating the facts, my dear.' Amy continued making up the bed for Antonio. This is Antonio's room. Do you like it Millie? I'm sure he will.'
'It would be far too small for me,' replied Millie.
'Right, how did you get on today with your new farm hands?' asked Albert.
'Antonio is fine, very helpful and interested in the work, but the other lad is a waste of space. You'll have to find him some other occupation otherwise he'll be unhappy, and there is nothing worse than a miserable teenager. Why not try him with Magnus?'
'Ok,' replied Albert, 'I'll have a word, thank you Millie.' Millie left the two to get on with the cabin preparations.

The cabins were ready for the lads by the time they had finished their evening meal. To get the best out of the produce and avoid waste, it was preferable for the majority of crew to eat together in the canteen at set times. Since the new arrivals, the menus had a definite Italian flavour, mainly through using more garlic, basil and tomato combinations, which became popular with everybody. Antonio and Marcello were delighted with their accommodation; the crew had gone out of their way to make them feel at home and comfortable.

Albert introduced Marcello to Magnus as his new assistant, and said he was in charge of the entire Ark systems, that is, Magnus was responsible for everything that moved mechanically. His new boss told Marcello he loved every part of his job and was proud of what he had achieved. He explained that for mechanical devices to work continuously they had to be maintained on a regular basis and this is what he would start Marcello on first: basic maintenance. Magnus believed this would make him understand how things

132

worked and if he didn't do his job properly, things would break down and he would be to blame. The new apprentice just kept nodding in agreement, trying to understand as much as he could. Magnus was thorough and did not let up on Marcello, making sure he was taking things in and not letting him get bored. Marcello took to his new occupation and steadily became more involved.

Within a couple of weeks, they were working well together and to a good routine. In fact, the whole Ark was working well; everybody had something to aim for and were all fully occupied. It was amazing, nobody had any bills to pay, no money to change hands, no taxes to pay, no rush hour to contend with and there were no fat cats. It was just great for them all to be away from those types of pressure.

ALBERT'S PRIVATE LOG- May 2017

Two more mouths to feed and it's a good job we have plenty to feed them with! They are both so lucky we rescued them. I wonder how they feel about staying on the Ark. We have also gained a yacht, something else for Magnus to look at, to make sure it's all up together. I'm certain it will come in useful.

The lads seem to be recovering very quickly, particularly the older one. He looks quite a fit healthy young man. Questioning them went well and I'm positive they understand and can speak more English than they are letting on. I suppose it's just easier for them not to, at this stage. Antonio is already useful to Millie, just the help she needs. On the other hand, Marcello is a bit of a wimp! We'll have to see what use Magnus can put him to on the maintenance side of things. I wonder how it's going to work out with these two young men with all the female attention they're getting. They are communicating more and more in English everyday; that does make things easier. The swimming pool has been getting a lot of use in the past few weeks. It is good that everyone likes the same food so we can all smell of garlic together. There's nothing worse than smelling garlic on someone, if you haven't eaten it yourself.

I'm very concerned about the situation between Marigold and Monty but I don't know the answer. I think I'll have a word with Amy to see if counselling them would do any good.

Millie having a go at me about using weapons upset me slightly. It's a woman thing. I suppose it's all about getting the balance right. No sensible person would want to use violence, but you have to protect your home and family the best way you can.

13. A PAIR OF RED KNICKERS

Jane had fancied Antonio for some time, he always looked her way and smiled, so she plucked up the courage and decided to make a move on him. She had seen the way Marigold had taunted him, always running away when he wanted something more. He had obviously become frustrated. Jane paid a visit to Antonio's cabin after everybody had a meal and the usual social gathering in the canteen. She knocked at his door and Antonio opened it.

'Oh hi Jane, What do you want?' Jane closed the door behind her and locked it.

'I've just popped in to give you a health check, to make sure you are fully fit.'

'Oh, that's alright. I'm fully fit thank you, you don't need to do that, I'm very good, thank you very much.'

'But yes, I do need to check you, now take off your shirt please and I'll listen to your breathing. I have my orders!' Jane told him as he backed away.

'No, No, it's ok. I'm fine.'

We'll see about that,' she said, as she lifted his shirt above his head and immediately put her ear to his chest.

'Now breathe in deeply... and then out again?' He did so, and again, in out, in out. This became too much for Jane. She fell to her knees grabbing hold of the waistband of his trousers.

'Now come, here you little Italian bastard!'

'I'm not little!' exclaimed Antonio.

'Well show me you're not!' Jane yanked down his trousers, bringing his underpants with them to his ankles.

'Jesus you're not, are you?' As soon as his penis appeared, Jane thrust her hands on it pulling back the foreskin to reveal the tip. Then she let it go to watch it hang down, with the foreskin pulled back. She lifted it, pulling it to her mouth. When it was at its full length, she put her tongue to the bulbous end, and licked it a few times.

'No, No, you must stop!' She moved back to watch it stiffen and rise, like an ostrich raising its head out of the sand to look at the sky. At the point of his full erection, Jane looked at it, looked at his face and back down again. She could not believe the situation she was in. Clasping his magnificent penis with both hands, she put her mouth straight down over it. Antonio cried out to her.

135

'Please, please, I'm not ready yet!'
'Oh yes you are,' replied Jane in between movements, 'and so am I.' She gasped as she stopped momentarily for breath, then, repeatedly moved her mouth up and down. She released the front of her blouse. In anticipation, she had not worn a bra. Antonio could not move. He had never experienced anything quite like this before. He started to groan with pleasure and weaken at the knees. She did not let go until she had swallowed every drop. His strength was drained for a while. Jane stood up, removed her blouse, slipped off her trousers and pushed him onto his bed. As he fell back, she pulled off his trousers and threw them aside.

They were both completely naked. As he lay flat out, Jane stood at his feet with her hands on her waist looking at him, waiting. He opened his eyes and with a glance up and down, and quickly again, to stare at a beautiful body with perfectly shaped breasts that were moving towards him and now over his face. He was like a lamb to the slaughter. He started sucking on her hard nipples going from one to the other, and sure enough, before long, his penis was moving in a perpendicular position between Jane's legs. She crouched to accept him as he slid gently into her naturally lubricated vagina. She moved her body up and down over his hardening penis, which changed to a full erection as Jane quickened the pace. She began to feel something she had not felt at this point before, a quiver, and then the fierce pulsing sensation before Antonio released his sperm into her receptive body. They both collapsed and fell asleep together, exhausted and at peace.

'Jane. Why are you smiling and humming tunes this morning?' asked Albert. 'That's not like you.'
'It's nothing really. It's just such a beautiful morning.'
'Jane, it's raining!'
'Oh is it? I hadn't noticed.' She walked off quickly. Millie was already attending to the animals and expecting Antonio to assist her. She had told him to be at the work place for no later than 0630 hours to start the day. It was 0700 hours. She was trying to be reasonable, thinking she would allow him a little time to adjust to his new role in life, but on the other hand, she needed his help. She used the radio to call Ched to see if he could find out where Antonio was.
'He may have overslept, could you go to his room and tell him to get his arse down here *rapido!*' Ched went to Antonio's new place of residence and knocked. There was no answer. He tried the door handle to find it

136

unlocked and went straight in to see Antonio still lying fast asleep on the bed. Ched reached over to shake him awake but as he leant down to pull at his shoulder, he spied a pair of female red knickers on the floor at the side of the bed. Before trying to wake him, he picked them up and stuffed them in his pocket, thinking, there's got to be a bit of fun in these. I wonder who's they are? He grabbed Antonio's shoulder and shook him awake.

'Come on sunshine. It's time to do a bit more work, only not on your back!'

'Yes, yes, I'm sorry, I'm coming, I'm sorry I sleep long, I'm coming.' Ched left the room with a smile on his face. Hmm, Marigold, Jane or Melanie, I wonder which one will bite?

Ched returned to the bridge and used the radio to tell Millie Antonio had overslept and was on his way. Meanwhile Melanie used every opportunity she could think of to make Marcello aware of her; by a warm smile, dressing revealingly and getting his food and drinks, asking him if there was anything else he would like. Marcello seemed to shy away from her advances, but nevertheless, she persevered, comforted by the thought that he was too young for Marigold and Jane but just right for her.

Marcello continued to do very well in his new line of work and looked forward each day to assisting Magnus in maintenance, and the engineering of the rockets that Albert had requested. Marcello did not understand why they were building these weapons and Magnus explained the best he could, that there was always a possibility that when they pass nearby some of the islands, they could be attacked by modern day pirates. This obviously concerned Marcello.

'Will we have to fight these men hand to hand?'

'Not if Albert spots them first.'

'I cannot fight. I'm not like my brother, he is always fighting.'...

Ched was waiting for the right moment to flash the pair of knickers in front of Marigold. He spotted her in the canteen on her own, having a drink of tea. He sneaked up quietly and sat down beside her, surprising her slightly.

'What's that you're drinking?' he asked.

'It's herb tea, peppermint. It's good for relieving indigestion. He took the knickers from his pocket and put them on the table.

'I found these on the floor and wondered if they belonged to you?'

'No, you pervert! Now leave me alone!'

137

'Alright, no need to be like that. I'm just trying to find their rightful owner. Perhaps Antonio knows. I'll ask him.' Knowing he had hit on a very sore point, he left the room rapidly.

'Well I don't think they are hers, now who is next? Melanie will be in the nursery, I'll try there. The kids won't know what I'm up to.' Ched made his way from the canteen, still with knickers in hand, and headed for the nursery. He had just turned the corner in the corridor, when Millie was coming the other way. She was too close for him to do anything and she immediately spotted the red lace.

'*Frederick Prestwick*! What's that in your hand?'

'Oh, this?' he replied, shaking. 'Er... I don't know.'

'What do you mean you don't fucking know? Whose are they and where did you get them?'

'No Millie you've got it wrong.' At that moment, with the knickers on display, Jane came around the corner and spotted her underwear.

'Where did you get those, you pervert! Have you been looking in my washing? You're disgusting.' Both women started slapping him on the head as he made a hasty retreat back down the corridor, around the other side, out of the way. The two women were left facing each other like a couple of angry cats with their hackles up, and Millie was on the attack.

'And where would he have got a pair of your knickers from?'

'I don't know, unless he's been in rooms he shouldn't have.' Jane knew very well where she left them. Millie's mind was racing, trying to think which room he'd been to, and it suddenly clicked.

'Antonio was late this morning.' she said, in a smug, sarcastic voice. 'Will you make sure he gets up on time tomorrow morning and that he's not so knackered,' Jane turned bright red.

'Well look at you! Your face matches your knickers now Jane!'

They both departed in opposite directions, Millie strolled to the canteen for her lunch, thinking with a smile I'll let that devious little bastard husband of mine suffer. I bet I know what he was up to; causing mischief as usual. Then her anger towards Ched turned. She planned to use the situation to have a bit of extra power over him. Just think I could get him to do anything I want, because he won't know that I know the truth. There's some mileage in this. No more 'wham bang, thank you mam' for a while. Ooh, I'm looking forward to this!

Meanwhile, Ched ran for his life, well that's how it seemed at the time. From the head pounding he got after being seen with a handful of knickers. He was running, looking for somewhere to hide, when he bumped into Marigold who had just returned from the canteen and was about to enter her cabin. Ched was thinking on his feet. He slowed down.

'Marigold, please let me apologise?'

'Oh ok then, you'd better come in.' Saved, he thought!

'Thank you.' She held the door open for him.

'No no after you.' She went in and he followed but had a quick look up and down the empty corridor before entering. He did not want to be seen.

They stood facing each other in her living room and she looked at him waiting for his apology and explanation. He paused and stammered like a naughty schoolboy.

'Yes, well er… um…, about the knickers. I've found who they belong to.'

'That's interesting,' but she looked more interested in him.

'They belong to Jane,' he spurted out quickly.

'Yes,' she replied, not seeming concerned about an apology at all.

'You see, I had to wake Antonio up this morning. He wouldn't stir. Anyway, his door was open and I noticed them on the floor by his bed.'

'What was on the floor?'

'The knickers Marigold,'

'Oh does he wear knickers?'

'Shit!' he thought, 'this is hard work.'

'And then, they wouldn't be mine now would they,' She bent down to lift her long multicoloured, hippie skirt up to reveal what she did *not* wear. Ched gulped and gawped!

'As you can see, I don't wear them.' Ched's eyes almost left their sockets as he stared at the neatly groomed triangle.

'Have a sniff if you want, you'll find it nice and fresh.'

'I just wanted to hide and be out of the way while things cooled down after Millie and Jane found me with knickers… He fell to his knees and buried his head between her legs. Then he raised his hands, placing his thumbs gently each side of the lips and opened them, to allow his tongue into her. He moved it up and down very gently, repeating it several times. She placed her hands on his smooth, bald head (also well groomed) pushing it into her harder. Soon she wanted a little more, and held his head to pull him away and make him stand up. The tail of his leather belt was dangling in

139

front of his trousers. She grabbed it and dragged him across towards a chair. Sitting, she looked up at him while releasing the belt.

'Let me see what's in here!' she whispered. 'I haven't seen Monty's for a long time. I've forgotten what one looks like. She unzipped his front, pulling his clothes down enough to let his dick flop out over his underpants. 'Oh, it's not very big, we will have to alter that,' as she took it in her right hand and soon she could see it was thinking about getting harder. Ched could not believe what he was doing a few minutes ago he was running from the wrath of Millie his wife and Jane, now he was with someone else, on a plate! And it was so nice, as she pulled back his foreskin very gently and then forward and back again repeating the movement several times before shrouding it with her mouth. Ched was taking extreme pleasure from this when he thought of Millie. She hasn't done this for a long time. I could enjoy more of this, now and again. She does, oh… do a nice job.

Marigold stopped, knowing that if she carried on she would exceed her quota of protein for the day! Still holding him, she stood up to lead him to the settee. Ched's trousers were around his ankles and he tried, unsuccessfully, to kick them off. She reached the settee and let go of him to take off her skirt and top to reveal her small, but beautifully formed tits, like two fried eggs, he thought. It was obvious what she wanted and he was hoping not to disappoint her. He shook off his trousers and slipped off his tee shirt. Marigold was lying down and Ched went straight to her with a kiss to her lips. That's unusual, she thought, most men go for the nipples first. This is nicer, as she put her arms around his neck, holding the kiss by entwining their tongues together. He wanted her so much now and let her place him, ready to slide gently into her.

'Oh, it's been ages.' she sighed.

As he stopped kissing her to take air, he was surprised how tight she was inside, yet it slid in so easily. He thought, Jesus! I'm not going to last long; I can feel every part of her. He started to move very slowly in and out, but she stopped him.

'You keep still!' she ordered, as she worked her muscles around him, contracting and then letting go, over and over again. They continued kissing as before, locked together. Ched knew he would come soon and gently moved in and out of her. He couldn't believe how long he had lasted with her in control of him, but no more, he came, releasing everything into her, collapsing with his full weight onto her thin body.

140

'Bloody hell, I don't remember ever lasting that long; I'm normally in and out, finished and half way to the pub by now, but this was fantastic.' She started manipulating her muscles again onto his now limp cock. Still kissing him with extreme passion, she gently rubbed his nipples. It aroused him making him slightly stiff, enough for him to move in and out of her again. When he increased speed as she tweaked his nipples harder, she pulled him up her torso so that the base of his penis was rubbing against the top of her bushy hair. Marigold moaned with pleasure at this but Ched had spent up, and had to stop.

'I'm sorry, I couldn't last any longer.'

'That's alright, I was getting so close though, maybe next time?' Ched panicked, Jesus I hope she don't mean now! They lay back together while Ched regained his strength. Marigold felt so proud to feel like a real woman again and started to smile. 'I'm fed up with being neglected and that's the first time I've felt being loved tenderly, instead of just being used.'

Ched began to feel guilty about what he had done, and decided to ask her about her and Monty.

'What's happened between you two?'

'He's found other ways to spend his leisure time and isn't interested in Lucy and me any more. It was like an arranged marriage anyway. I admit I was a bit naïve in accepting his proposal, but it's far better here on the Ark, than the situation I was in, in Todmordon. I was constantly pestered by drug pushers and pimps to work for them and chased by the social for not wanting to work. My benefits were cut all the time. I'd known Monty a while. He used to help me when I was down and he would sort me out with a bit of whacky backy for nothing in return, not like the other bastards. I respected him, and then all this, the Ark came out of the blue. He said if I wanted to get out of there and be in the sunshine all the time, on a large ship sailing the world, I would just have to be pregnant by him. It all seemed a bit clinical at the time but I thought he would really care for me. It turned out different, so here I am.' Ched got up and started putting his clothes back on.

'I'd better get back to work. I'm due on the bridge and, with a bit of luck, Millie will be back at the bow working. She should have calmed down some by tonight.'

'Ched, will you come and see me again, say once or twice a week? I'm only doing washing and ironing helping Patricia, so any time you can. I just

need a bit of *TLC*, you know: tender love and care. I won't demand too much and make trouble between you and Millie, I promise.'
'That sounds alright to me. I'll do my best, but we'll have to be careful and you won't want to get pregnant.'
'Don't worry. Monty taught me a few things on that subject.' He kissed her and asked her to put her head into the corridor to see if the coast was clear, then sauntered off.

Magnus and Marcello were having lunch. It had been on Magnus' mind to try to get out of Marcello, how he felt about his daughter and, with a bit of a language barrier, how to choose the right words.
'Marcello, what do you think of Melanie?'
'She is a very nice girl.'
'Don't you fancy her?' Magnus asked, as he inserted a sausage into his mouth.
'Oh no because, er… how do you say it, I'm gay.' Magnus choked on his sausage and was coughing and spluttering when Millie walked into the canteen. Seeing the difficulty Magnus was in, she rushed over and patted him on the back, to try to relieve the choking.
'Are you alright Magnus, did it go down the wrong way?'
On that, he started again, and now it really had gone down the wrong way. Magnus recovered after a couple of minutes, and managed to struggle on with his lunch. He was not one to leave food for any reason, but where he put it was a mystery because he was always as thin as a rake. He returned to his work but stayed very quiet, not saying much to Marcello for the rest of the day. His only thoughts were: what can I tell Melanie and what will Albert do? Probably feed him to the sharks!

Albert was on lookout duty. Since *The Assault*, it was agreed to have a round the clock lookout operation, and Albert was to be alerted, no matter what time of day or night, of any vessel that came within three miles. Magnus was plucking up courage to be the first to tell Albert about Marcello's disclosure. He just did not have the heart to tell his daughter. He couldn't even bring himself to tell Patricia, who, strangely for a woman, seemed to have very little understanding in the matter. He knew Albert would be on his own and well away from earshot of the others, so Magnus had a quiet word with him about Marcello.

14. THE MEETINGS

Off Magnus went to the lookout. Albert was busy scanning the horizon through the binoculars when he heard, and then saw Magnus approach.
'Hi, what brings you up here?'
'I wanted a private word with you if it's possible, please Albert?'
'Certainly, just let me have a good scan round and I'll be with you.' He studied the whole horizon, and lowered his binoculars.
'Now, what can I do for you?'
'Well, it's about Marcello.'
'Yes what about him?'... Magnus paused.
'Well, er, he's gay!' relieved that he had finally spat it out.
'He's what?'
'He's queer... you know?'
'Yes I bloody do know what a gay or queer is.' Albert was agitated. 'And how have you come to that conclusion?'
'He told me.'
'He just told you, just like that?'
'More or less,' said Magnus.
'Are you sure he's a shirt-lifter, an uphill gardener?' asked a visibly thrown Albert. 'What do you mean, Albert?'
'Oh for Christ's sake Magnus, you don't push shit up hill do you?' Albert was still somewhat taken aback by Magnus' revelation and curious as to how Marcello told him about this.
He really wanted to get to the bottom of it.

'What situation were you in for him to tell you?'
'Albert I hope you're being serious about this.' Albert just about managed to contain his laughter, which was bubbling up.
'Of course I am. Perhaps I phrased that wrongly.' (Knowing full well, he hadn't). Magnus was deadly serious.
'Well, you know Melanie is very sweet on him. She realises that Antonio has a choice between Jane and Marigold if he wants, and from what I've seen, he probably has both.' Albert didn't bat an eyelid. 'So Melanie, naturally, has been trying to get his attention...'
'Yes, go on...I'm listening.'
'I asked him if he liked Melanie. He said that she is a very nice girl. Then I asked if he fancied her. I even had to gesticulate with my hands and arms to make sure he knew exactly what I meant. You've no idea how difficult that

was for me to do, about my own daughter. Anyway, he just replied he was gay. I was eating at the time and my sausage very nearly went down the wrong way Albert!'... Albert let out a chuckle.
'If it wasn't for Millie coming into the canteen at the time, I would have choked!'

Albert soon got over the humour of Magnus' tale and became concerned at the potential problem it was going to cause in his tiny community. (Would Noah have approved of it?) Albert started his deliberation.
'What are we going to do with a homosexual onboard the Ark? The whole point of the project is to breed new life, so that all of the species onboard can continue. It all might be the norm, especially in big cities, where diseases like Aids are rife in the over-populated areas, but not in the extreme opposite, in a small, young community like ours. To allow that practice could have a devastating effect...' Albert stopped. His emotions and opinions were running away with him, and he knew it.
'Well Magnus, have you told Melanie yet?'
'Er, no, not yet,'
'When are you going to tell her?'
'Well Albert, I was wondering...'
'Oh no, not me,'
'She looks up to you. You always set her on the right track when she is down. She's too young, and in the wrong place for this type of rejection. I'm sorry Albert but if I tell her, she'll probably accuse me of making it up; you know what teenage girls are like. She will say that I don't like him because he's foreign, or something.'
'It won't be any different if I tell her.'
'No Albert, she has absolute respect for you, especially the way you've brought us through the recent difficulties we've encountered.'
'Ok Magnus, I'll tackle it as soon as I've finished this shift.'
'Thanks Albert... Oh, by the way, Marcello said something about his brother you might want to know. He said Antonio was always fighting and seemed to like it, whereas he didn't.'
'How did that come up?'
'He wanted to know why we are making weapons, and I tried to explain that we had been attacked by modern-day pirates, when passing some African islands. He seemed very worried by this, but he said his brother would not be, he was always fighting.'
'Well at least it's not double the problem.'

144

'What are we going to do about Marcello?'
'Leave it with me, Magnus. I think I'll have a word with Antonio first.'

Albert finished his shift and went to his cabin, desperate to go to bed and forget about his task with the soft, kind-natured Melanie. He explained it to Amy and she offered to talk to her, but he said that no, he had to do it himself, and it had to be done tonight, before someone else told her. Albert got on the short wave to Magnus to arrange to see Melanie in the canteen in about half an hour. This gave him enough time to talk with Antonio. He arrived at Antonio's cabin door and knocked. It opened and Antonio was there, all smartened up and smelling of lavender oil, which hit Albert straight up his nose.

'Hi Albert, I was not expecting you.'
'Are we off to a disco tonight or something Antonio?'
'A disco, is there a disco tonight? Jane did not tell me.' Albert immediately got the picture.
'So you're going to see Jane,'
'Si, yes, I thought it was her when the door knocked.'
'No, there is not a disco tonight, just me pulling your leg.' Antonio frowned, trying to understand.
'I called to have a little talk with you.'
'Please come in,' at that moment, Jane arrived looking extremely attractive.
'Evening Albert, is there a problem?'
'Evening Jane, you are looking fabulous, off out to a disco?'
'Don't be funny Albert.'
'Sorry Jane. I called to see Antonio about something, but now you're here, perhaps you would care to stay, while I ask him a question that cropped up today that I need Antonio to confirm for me.'

They entered the room, closing the door behind them, and sat around the table. Albert came straight out with it.
'Is your brother gay, Antonio?' The question did not seem out of the ordinary to him.
'Yes, he has always been different that way since I can remember, but in Italy it is um, how do you say...?'
'Common.' Jane chipped in.
'Yes it is very common for young boys to be this way. Many change, to be straight, later and some stay that way.'
'Did you know Jane?'

145

'I had my suspicions, but never said anything to anybody. Come on Albert, it's not a big deal these days, it's accepted.'
'Yes Jane, I'm well aware of that and this isn't a witch hunt on homosexuals. The problem I have got is Melanie. You must have noticed she is very sweet on Marcello, especially him being the only eligible male suitable for her. Marcello told Magnus he was gay and could not think of Melanie in any other way but being a nice girl. Now I have the task of explaining this to Melanie and deciding what to do with him. I suppose, not a lot.'
'Albert you have just got to accept him into the community, as anybody else who we bump into would be accepted. Let's face it, it's going to be bad enough for him being alone that way,' Jane emphasised.
'You're right I'm afraid I am a bit out of date with my thinking sometimes. I'd better go and see Melanie and try to explain to her about him. Thank you for your time and wisdom. Enjoy yourselves!'
'Don't worry Albert, we will.'

Albert headed for the canteen where Melanie was waiting. She was curious why Albert wanted to see her, as she knew she had done nothing wrong. Her father told her Albert just wanted a chat about something.
'Hi Albert, Dad said you wanted to see me, so here I am. What's it all about?'
'Thanks for coming. Would you like a drink of anything?'
'A glass of that raspberry wine please. I know I'm not supposed to, but if I'm old enough to have babies, I think a glass of wine is alright.'
'Yes,' he replied, 'that's not a problem.' He poured her drink and one for himself and they sat down at one of the tables.
'Come on Albert, what is it?'
'I found out something today that I think you ought to know, before you get hurt. I have been told that he admits to it, and I've had it confirmed from his brother, that Marcello is gay.'
'Yes, I guessed that a couple of days ago Albert. It's not his fault he's like that. But he is a very nice lad and I still like him and want to be his friend. Maybe in time, he may like me.'
'Melanie, you are a shining star and a credit to us all!' They both stood up and Albert embraced and thanked her. They said goodnight to each other and Melanie left for her cabin.
'I think I deserve a drink.' Albert thought.

The time had come to make a decision on the future of the two young Italian lads. What should they do with them? Was there any possibility, other than keeping them as guests on the Ark, blending them into the community as part of the family and accepting Marcello without prejudice? A meeting was called. Albert wanted to organise it so that Antonio and Marcello did not know what was happening. Antonio was already working on the farm, so Jane decided to send Marcello to the bow of the ship to tend to the animals with his brother. Jane told them that Millie was not so well that morning. Marcello said he wanted to work with Magnus, but Jane persuaded him that Millie needed him to help Antonio, until she felt better. He left with a disappointed shrug and slowly strolled up to join Antonio at the bow with the animals. Everybody else gathered in the canteen.

Parents had to bring their children where they could keep an eye on them. They knew the importance of these rare meetings and took them very seriously. They had all come a long way on their journey and were passionate about the well-being of the Ark, even more so than before. Albert chaired the meeting with everybody sitting in silence, waiting for him to commence.

'Right people, I'll begin. It's a waste of time going through all the background to why we are here, so I'll get to the point. What do we do with Antonio and Marcello? I would add one thing that has come to light about Marcello, and I know you would accept him anyway, he is… he admits to being gay.'
'Albert, you've changed your tune! Ched burst out straight away. It's not so long ago you were saying there was no place on the Ark for queers!'
'That's true, but after talking to Melanie, Amy, Jane and Antonio I know I have to accept him, just as any other human being. You may have some reservations but I have the feeling that the majority of you feel the same: we would like the lads to stay of there own free will. Knowing of our own situation, for the future of the Ark, I want to hear from each of you, your true full view, no matter how draconian it may seem. We will start with the women. Right Amy, what do you think we should do with the two lads?'
'It's no good asking me Albert, you already know my point of view and you always make the decisions at the end of the day.'
'Oh shit, it's going to be one of those days. Could someone get me a drink please?' Melanie obliged Albert with a glass of water. Albert looked at it in disgust. Then Amy glared at him and he decided to accept the water.

147

'Greta, could we have your view please?'

'Well I have already spoken to most of the adult women about the situation and I can speak for all of them, we must encourage them to stay on the Ark and be part of the driving force that keeps our ideals alive.'

'You bloody well haven't spoken for me Greta!' a rattled Jane piped up.

'Sorry Jane, you were busy. But what if they do not want to stay with us Albert?'

'If that's the case, now is the opportunity to get them off to one of the Azores islands in the fishing boat,' Albert replied. 'They still have their passports. It would be a shame; we could do it, but I would be very reluctant. So Jane is your point of view different by any chance?'

'No, I just like to speak for myself.'

'We cannot force them to stay and do not have to give them the means to leave either,' Albert continued. 'We have their yacht, which we could repair, and supply them with some of our limited rations, but they are not sailors. Their grandfather did the sailing and navigation, so that would send them back to where they were before we saved them. The other point I would like to make is that we took on this way of living on the Ark and isolated ourselves from the outside world, because of the oppression and crooked politicians of our governments. We are free from that and I believe you all want to stay that way.'

'YES, YES, YES!' came the unanimous reply.

'So we don't really want the Italian lads back on the mainland telling the rest of the world our business, do we?' Albert sat down for a few minutes while the others muttered between themselves. Albert rose to his feet again, hoping to conclude matters quickly.

'Right then, I think we have come to a decision, there is no point in asking the men their point of view, now is there?'

'That's not very democratic, is it?' Ched shouted as he stood up.

'Do you want to be heard as well?' asked Albert.

'No.' replied Ched and sat down again.

'The women have an overpowering mandate, which is the Ark's future survival. In our present situation, we need more males to ensure that. So I will leave it to Jane and Melanie, how can I put it? ... to coerce, these lucky young men to feel at home here and to become part of our community.

'What about me?' Marigold shouted out, 'I'm eligible too. Monty isn't bothered about me. I'm young. I have needs. Why can't I be included in this 'coerce' thing you are on about?' Ched looked a bit peeved with Marigold's outburst and Albert scanned through the faces and was relieved that Monty had drifted off somewhere.

'Oh shit, can I have a proper drink this time please someone?' Melanie got up and looked at Amy. She gave Melanie one wink and Melanie delivered half a beer shandy. Albert frowned and thought to himself, there's a bloody conspiracy going on here.

'I know you and Monty are not too close at the moment,' he replied to Marigold, 'but I think Jane is with Antonio now, and you heard the situation with Marcello, so why not concentrate on your Monty. By the way where is Monty?'

'Um... I don't know,' she replied. Suddenly, Marigold felt very shaky. Albert sensed a problem and quickly summed up the meeting.

'I take it that all the sound thinking adults, at this moment in time, agree to accept these two young survivors and take them into the bosoms of the Ark's destiny, and make them part of us all.' The women nodded. Albert told everyone there that he would ask the two lads what they thought about spending the rest of their lives in the community of the Ark.

'Meeting ended!' declared Albert.

As most people made for the canteen's exit, Albert made it to the bar, followed by Ched until a shout from Millie pierced the air. Ched turned tail and went to her. As Albert was just about to pour himself a beer, the quality of which he was now very proud, he heard the voice of his loving wife.

'ALBERRRT' Albert obeyed the order.

Millie returned to the farm at the bow of the Ark telling Antonio and Marcello that she felt a lot better now and could they go to the bridge, Albert would like to see them, so off they went to find him. Albert was on the bridge with Ched discussing the meeting when the Italian lads turned up.

'Millie sent us.' Ched looked at Albert.

'I'll just pop up and see how Gunter is doing on lookout.' Ched winked and made a speedy exit.

'Right you two, you are both fully fit now and settling in well with us. It would be very difficult for us to drop you off on an island somewhere, because we do not want anything to do with the outside world. All the

149

people on the Ark have had a meeting and we have decided we would like you to stay with us.' Antonio looked at his brother and then to Albert.
'I love Jane and I will stay here. You saved my life.' Albert looked at Marcello.
'I don't know. I miss my home, friends and family but I will try my best to be one of you.' That's that settled then, Albert thought.

The next day Albert decided to put a watch on Monty because of his presence being vacant and the vacancy in his presence when he did see him! It was obvious that he was up to something and Albert took the view that he had found a means to chill out a bit too far. Albert talked to Amy about the herbs and medicinal plants they were growing that might be used for purposes other than the norm. The two plants that came to mind were hemp, and the poppy, from which the morphine originated, for the dreadful pain Monty was in after he was shot. Amy explained to Albert why they were cultivating these plants and how they could be used.

He decided to make a visit to Monty, finally tracking him down in the rarely used area next to the engine room, where the desalination plant was set up. As Albert got closer, the stench was horrendous! He had heard the name skunk before to describe what he could smell. Monty, unaware of Albert, was busy sorting out his whacky backy ready to roll it into a piece of paper that was attached to the end of his tongue by saliva, hanging down ready to receive the substance. From this it was obvious what Monty had been cultivating, and not only for medical purposes. Albert decided not to approach him, his number one reason being that Monty was in a different world, and number two, he couldn't stand the smell. He left as quietly as he could and went to find Ched, Gunter and Magnus, in person, rather than use the short wave communication, just in case Monty had his set switched on. Albert asked them to meet in the canteen at a said time. He explained what he had found; the others were not surprised.
'Did any of you know what he was doing?' Albert asked. They looked at each other and Gunter spoke first.
'Well, we had an idea that he was smoking because of his glazed eyes and his bad smell.'
'Why wasn't I told sooner?'
'We didn't want to make a fuss Albert. He was out of the way, not bothering anybody.'

'What if we had a problem and we needed his skills to help one of us, when he was too spaced out to even help himself? You've seen them on the streets, in the towns you called home. That's one of the reasons you decided to be here, to be rid of that sort of shit!' Albert was on a crescendo, they could see the pressure building, it just needed someone to pull the string and he would blow his top like an old steam train entering a tunnel. Normally he would ask someone to get him a drink, but the thought did not enter his head. The others were silent, more for the fact that what Albert said was true and they were embarrassed for letting him, and themselves, down.

'Marigold must have known for some time.' Magnus spurted out. 'Why didn't she inform you?'

'How well would Patricia cover up for you, if you had a habit like that? Bloody good, I should imagine? Look, this isn't getting us anywhere,' said Albert, 'we have to sort him out him one way or another. We haven't the EHS (Euro Health Service) to continue feeding him the habit because it's easier and more cost effective to the taxpayer! I think we will have to go back in time with him for a while, and then bring him more up to date and put him on garden leave, and that doesn't mean digging up potatoes.'

'Please explain.' Gunter asked.

'In days gone by, on the high seas, as we are now, the rule of law was the Captain, supported by his Officers. Between them, they would decide on the punishment for the crime and the Captain would order the punishment to be carried out. In most cases, so many days in the brig with just being fed bread and water would do it. It just so happens, that we have such a secure room that has better facilities than a brig in days gone by.

'What will our partners think, and Marigold?' Ched nervously spoke out.

'They haven't missed him for the past couple of weeks,' Albert replied, 'a few more weeks won't make any difference. They'll find out, but they will have to come up with a bloody good alternative that will work. I'll explain to Marigold what's happening.'

'Garden leave, what does that mean?' Gunter asked.

'Normally it means you get paid to stay at home. In Monty's case, he will be confined to a secure room, fed and watched. We will give him cold turkey for a few weeks, see how he gets on and decide how we can help him get back to normal.'

'Don't you mean chicken we do not have any turkeys?' Gunter asked. Ched briefly explained the meaning of the term to Gunter.

151

'We will have to have another full meeting later, to discuss how to help Monty from then on.' Gunter, Ched and Magnus started conferring together. It was obvious they were worried about Albert's harsh methods, but could not think of an alternative. They all finally agreed it had to be done and Albert set the plan in motion.

'We have to act straight away. Magnus, you know the room with the grid over the window on the lower deck at the stern, could you prepare it for him. He'll need just a mattress, soap, hand towel and toilet paper, and leave the ventilation port open. Ched and Gunter, come with me. You'll need to hold your breath when you get there, because he stinks to high heaven. We'll have to drag him between us.'

Off they went to collect Monty.

'Oh my god, that's disgusting!' Ched was appalled at the state he was in. The stench coming from the room alone was bad enough, but when they got near him, it made them feel physically sick.

'Come on Ched,' said Gunter, let's get this over and done with quickly.' They lifted him between them, while Albert cleared the way. Fortunately, they only had to go up two flights of stairs. When they arrived, Magnus was opening the window to finish off the room and he too, was surprised at what he saw and smelt.

'Jesus! What a bloody state he's in!' They lay him on the mattress and Albert checked to make sure he had no substances on him. The door slammed shut and Monty was secure.

'Who's going to wash and feed him?' Magnus asked, as they walked away.

'By rights, Marigold should, but I doubt if she has the stomach for it,' said Albert. Ched started scratching his head.

'The thought of him is making me itch!' he complained. 'The first thing I'm going to do is have a shower.'

'Me too.' agreed Gunter. 'Millie's pigs smell better than him!'

'I'll have a word with Amy and get things explained to Marigold.' Albert was a worried man.

He went straight to see his wife who was helping Patricia prepare food in the kitchen.

'Amy, my dear...,'

'Albert,' she interrupted, 'whenever you say, *my dear*, it means you want something.'

152

'Can we go for a little walk?' he asked. She knew from this, it must be important and left what she was doing dried her hands and told Patricia she wouldn't be long. They went down the stairs from the upper decks to the fields, before Albert explained what had happened to Monty and the problems they were going to have getting him washed and fed.

'I hope you're not thinking I should do it?'

'No, no, if you will let me finish, it's Marigold who should be doing it, but I can't see her wanting to go anywhere near him. You know how they've drifted apart and this situation has made it worse. I really don't know what to do for the best. All I can think of to help now is to have words with Marigold and see if she's going to help the father of her child. At least, that's a start. You know, I have killed people, I've saved people, but I am struggling with this. I suppose if all else fails I will have to wash and scrub him myself. Could you sort out some nice smelling herbs to put in his room?'

'Yes, that won't be a problem.'

Magnus spilt the beans to Patricia.

'Oh, the poor wee thing,' she responded and immediately asked who was going to look after him.

'That's the big problem. With the situation between him and Marigold, we are at a loss to know what to do.'

'I'll sort him.' she said. 'I'm not having that man fester in some cell you've locked him in.'

'Me locked him in? I was obeying orders.'

'Well you were there, weren't you?'

'Yes but…'

'There'll be no buts about it!' She stopped what she was doing and was off.

'Where are you going?' Magnus cried out feebly.

'To see Albert,'

'Oh shit!'

Albert and Amy were just entering the canteen to have a cold drink to cool them down after their walk and talk in the fields. It had become very warm and humidity was high.

'I'll have this drink then I had better check the barometer reading; it feels like a storm is brewing.' Patricia burst in from the kitchen.

'Albert!' she shouted.

'I predicted a change in pressure Amy. What is it Patricia?'

153

'Amy, I'm glad you're here too. Magnus has told me about poor...' she lowered her voice, 'poor Monty,' then raised it again. 'I'm not having that man locked up like some criminal. He has to be looked after.'
'And how do you propose we do that?' responded Albert sharply.
'I've seen hundreds of these people in the streets back home.'
'Yes but that doesn't answer the question.' Albert was getting annoyed and fired back at her, 'I repeat, how will you possibly look after him? Will you physically tend to his personal hygiene, washing and scrubbing him, making sure he has clean underclothes? I wouldn't be surprised if he isn't full of lice already.'
'Albert, please,' Amy exclaimed.
'Well you haven't seen the state of him.'
'Yes, I'll do it' replied Patricia.
'Bloody hell!' said Albert. 'Are you sure?'
'Yes I am positive,' she confirmed.
'And I'll help you Patricia.' Amy added.

Albert was rather taken aback by their offer and thought afterwards, that he may have goaded Patricia into a corner and Amy joined in, in sympathy. However, the two women seemed determined and set off, followed by Albert, to assess Monty's state. Monty was still out cold. Patricia and Amy were shocked and started blaming themselves for not noticing sooner.
'We'll get him some clean clothes Amy and strip wash him to start with. Then we will fill the room with lavender. That should help the smell,' Patricia said, taking control. Albert insisted that Monty was to stay locked in the room, at all times, for the next three weeks.
'Well if it was left to me, he told them, I wouldn't strip wash him, I'd hoist him over the side in a net and he'd get ducked in the sea to wash him on a daily basis.'
'Albert you wouldn't?'
'Actually, it's not a bad idea!' Albert taunted them, 'Would you rather I do that to start with anyway?'
'No, definitely not! Don't be ridiculous!' they both chided together.

Albert locked the door behind them as they began their mission, with Albert chuckling to himself as quietly as he could. Ched and Gunter were on the bridge, unaware of the latest developments with Monty. Gunter raised the subject.
'Ched, I wonder how Albert will sort out Monty?'

Feeding him won't be a problem. We can give him pizzas and pitta bread.'
'Will that help?'
'Not much, but that's all we can get under the door!' It took Gunter about ten seconds to get the joke. Then he ignored Ched and checked the barometer.

'We are in for a storm, Ched. The barometer reading has dropped sharply.' Ched immediately radioed to Millie to get the animals secure and told her and Antonio to get back to the upper decks as soon as possible. They soon responded.
'Its good to have a storm now and then,' said Millie to Antonio. We get to finish a little earlier and put our feet up for a change.'

15. THE MEDIA

Three weeks of virtually solitary confinement and Albert was under pressure from the women to let Monty out of his cell and get him back into the working community again, but under better surveillance. Albert agreed on a trial and Amy volunteered to be his minder. Some suggested that the hemp and poppies, the providers of his problem, should be destroyed. Then the questions followed on what they would do if one of them desperately needed morphine for excessive pain relief. In addition, hemp was used in a variety of products such as soap and textiles and would be missed. If someone became terminally ill or chronically sick, cannabis could be produced to help that person through. There was a lot of humming and haring about the for and the against, so a vote was set up and it was a compulsory 'yes' to keep and 'no' not to keep the plants. Melanie was the one somewhat confused about the benefits of keeping them, because all she could associate them with, was the misery drugs caused the young kids on the streets of Glasgow. She was glad to be away from that, and as for illness, like many young people, she tended not to worry about things that did not directly threaten her. The result was in favour of keeping the plants for medicine, cloth, soap and so on.

Monty had gained some strength by eating normally. He tried to get back into a daily routine by tending to the herb garden with Amy, making compounds and drying herbs for future use. After his three weeks of cold turkey, when not supervised, Monty was locked in the secure room for a number of weeks more. Albert could never be sure that Monty might have a stash of cannabis hidden somewhere and all the hard work by everybody, would have been wasted. Eventually, he earned a little trust, but not without a private word warning from Albert of a daily ducking in the sea without clothes and a piece of meat tied to him to attract some company. Monty didn't know whether Albert would carry out his threat or not, but decided to give him the benefit of the doubt.

The Ark got used to fishing boats and leisure craft, either from the islands or from elsewhere, making visits to them. They never bothered them or got too close to investigate or have a better look, as one would expect on seeing a ship with trees growing out of the forward part and the noise of sheep bleating across the sea. Until one day, a light aircraft kept circling so close you could see a man taking photographs of all angles of the Ark. This began to annoy Albert. He wondered if it was *our friends from Russia* planning another visit, but discounted that idea, for they would be a bit stupid, with all the boating activity there and the Portuguese Eurocoastguard passing by every other day. After the plane had been around several times, it left, with nothing sinister happening. The crew put it down to someone being nosy, really hoping it was just that, and nothing else. Settling back to their daily routines, the aeroplane subject in conversations exhausted itself.

Several days later, a helicopter approached the Ark. It looked brand new, gleaming in the sunshine. Albert had the binoculars focused on it and was deciding what to do. There were no signs of armaments and the doors were closed, but as it got closer, he could make out writing on the side, in very large letters, saying 'PRESS'.

'Oh shit! That's all we need!' Albert shouted as the helicopter flew above the Ark and hovered over the field nearest to the upper deck. Millie and Antonio were running as fast as they could from the bow where the animals were in the fields. They shouted angrily and waved their arms in protest, because the aircraft was frightening the animals. Albert came down to the deck to try and stop the helicopter landing, by which time Millie and Antonio arrived, soon backed up by Gunter with the rest of the Ark's population following. They all stood in the way of the helicopter wherever it moved, to prevent it from setting down. Then a window opened and a man with a loud hailer appeared.

'We want to land,' he shouted out. We will buy your story. Just name your price!' This infuriated Albert who rushed to the chopper as close as he could get and shouted at the top of his voice.

'Fuck off and leave us alone. You are frightening our animals. If you don't move it, the water cannon will be fired at you.' They seemed to get Albert's message and the helicopter started to lift. As it was doing so, the spokesperson withdrew and threw out a parcel before lifting up and away out of sight. Albert went over to retrieve the package and ripped it open on his way to show the others.

'Look they've sent us some toilet paper!'

It was a well-known German magazine and on the front page, was an aerial photograph of the Ark showing the crops, orchard, gardens, greenhouse and livestock. Underneath, the caption read, '*SEA HIPPIES*', with just a small reference to what the photographers had spotted. Worst of all it detailed

156

where the Ark was located. Everybody gathered round and, as the magazine was passed from one to another, their faces turned to sadness as they realised the consequences of what the media had done to them.

'We will be overrun by anybody with a boat. There will be boats charted to bring sightseers, thinking they could just come onboard to see *strange people and their alternative lifestyle*. Well that's it, my friends. We can't stay here,' Albert sadly declared. 'I'm sorry, but we have no alternative but to go elsewhere. We're only halfway through the season and won't have enough gas yet to go south, besides which, the weather is still unkind there.' Jane was the first to ask the question on everyone's lips.

'Then where can we go?'

'I don't know at the moment, I'm still furious about the invasion of our privacy by people who think money can buy anything at the right price.'

Albert asked Gunter to join him on the bridge to look at the charts to try to find a suitable destination in the northern hemisphere until September far enough away from the clutches of the media and all that went with it. They got the chart of the area between the Azores and the Cape Verde Islands and because of their recent challenge not far away from Cape Verde, they decided those islands were best avoided. Gunter spotted a place called the Great Meteor Bank, which is quite shallow in places. It was about nine hundred miles north of Cape Verde and seven hundred miles from their present position and they should get there in three days. Albert decided to try it, leaving at first light, so everybody had a busy job preparing for the relatively short journey.

Thinking it would be a couple of days before being pestered again, they were surprised late that afternoon by the sound of another helicopter coming towards them. Albert peered through the binoculars and saw that it was a very small Bell type two-seater craft carrying two people. Everybody onboard, who now had a drill for this, congregated on the deck where the last helicopter tried to land. As the helicopter got near to the Ark, a rope ladder was thrown out and the passenger climbed onto it and descended quickly. The person was dressed in a black jumpsuit and balaclava, carrying a rucksack and the scene looked just like the old advert to drop off a box of chocolates! The Ark's crew couldn't prevent the intruder from jumping down the last few feet to the deck. Albert went into a rage, the likes of which not even Amy had seen before. He headed straight for the

157

person, who was of a small and slight build and now landed on Albert's Ark!

Ched and Gunter could see Albert's anger soar. They both looked at each and realised that if he got hold of the trespasser in his present state, there would be an even bigger problem. They both rushed to Albert, one at each side to restrain him, just before he reached the person who was about to take off the balaclava. Then off it came, to release long, blonde flowing hair, shaken loose like some film star advertising anti-dandruff shampoo, who didn't have it in the first place. Albert stopped dead in his tracks.
'It's a bloody female!' He shook his fist at the helicopter pilot, shouting, 'Come back here you cowardly bastard, there's enough women on this ship!'
'Mr Crowther, can we talk please?' the woman asked politely.
'No!... Throw her over the side!' he ordered Ched and Gunter, who just stood there, eyes glued onto the attractive female.
'You can't Albert!' Ched replied.
'Can't I? Just you watch!'

In no time at all, the woman was across Albert's shoulder, her legs kicking in the air and thumping Albert's back.
'Let me go! Let me go, you beast!' she screamed. He ran like mad, heading for the side of the ship, with everybody chasing him and struggling to keep up. He reached the side, but was too out of breath to lift her above his head and over the gate access to the waves below. The woman was in a state of shock, thinking she was going overboard. If Albert had been the fit man he was when serving in the Marines, she would have been very wet by now! Albert put her down on the deck, by which time all the crew were surrounding them. The next words he heard were from Amy.
'ALBERRRT Control yourself'
'Alright, alright, you can bloody well sort it out!' Albert pushed his way through the circle of onlookers and walked off to the upper decks.

Amy approached the woman and helped her to her feet.
'You know it's against the law now, for the media to invade one's privacy, no matter where in the world, don't you?'
'Yes I do Madam,' the woman replied 'but I am not from the media.'
'Then what do you want with us?' Amy asked.
'My name is Holly Hansen and I work for the Salvation Army.'

158

'Fucking hell,' Ched said, 'they must be desperate I haven't read a copy of War Cry for ages.' Holly overheard him.
'No, no, it's not that side of it I do.'
'Oh,' replied Amy, 'what do you do then?'
'We locate missing persons throughout the world and try to reunite them with their loved ones.'
'And who are you looking for?'
'Well,' she replied, 'according to our satellite survey records for last April, at the time a yacht went missing in a storm, on its way from Tenerife to the Caribbean with three Italian men onboard. It was about five hundred miles west of the Canary Islands and the only vessel nearby was this tanker.'

Marcello moved forward and spoke up.
'I was one of the crew.' Antonio stayed back, out of sight, holding his arm around Jane. He looked at her and Jane put her arm around Antonio tightly, realising he wanted to stay with her on the Ark. Marcello didn't look at his brother but coolly continued speaking to Holly. 'There were no other survivors and I want to go home!'

Holly took a mobile phone from her pocket and called her contact.
'Please send a chopper to collect me and one survivor. I repeat, just one survivor.' Then she explained there would be a helicopter there in about an hour from Sao Miguel, to take them away. Millie tugged at Antonio, being careful not to give away his name. She knew the difficult choice the brothers had made and was near to tears.
'Come on, let's get the animals into the pens, so that they won't be frightened by the noise of the helicopter when it comes.'

Amy invited Holly to the canteen to have some refreshments while waiting for her transport.
'I can only apologise for Albert, my husband, for his actions. It's because of being pestered by the media recently in a very intrusive way that he thought you would be after the same thing, and we have been attacked by some pirate type people, using a helicopter and with arms, that Albert and the crew managed to fight off.'

Now that the excitement was over, the rest of the crew continued with the preparations for the next day's move. Amy entered the canteen with Holly and Jane to find, which was no big surprise, Albert at the bar quaffing a

159

pint of bitter. He looked at Amy as she entered with the others and wondered what was going on. Amy walked straight over to Albert, who had just taken a large sip of his ale.

'Let me introduce you to Holly Hanson of the Salvation Army.' With his mouth full of his brew, he couldn't swallow and sprayed it over the bar.

'Excuse me.' He wiped his mouth with the back of his hand. 'Did you say Salvation Army?'

'Yes.' replied Amy.

'Are you taking the piss?'

'Albert, how many pints have you had?'

'Not enough, my dear,' he replied.

'Albert this is serious. Holly has been trying to locate any survivors from a yacht that went missing and we happened to pick up *just Marcello* from the sea at the time. Albert realised the deliberate mistake she had made and clicked on to *just one survivor*.

He apologised profusely to Holly for his behaviour.

'It's alright Albert. Your wife has explained the problems you have been having from the outside world.'

'Would you like a drink?' Albert asked.

'Yes please, I don't normally, but I think I would after that little episode. Have you any whiskey or other type of spirit?'

'Yes. We certainly have and I'm sure you'll like it.' He went to the clear bottle on the optics, poured a large measure into a glass then offered it to her.

'Thank you.' She placed it down on the bar and waited for the others to get their drinks so that she could make a toast to them for picking Marcello from the sea.

'Amy my dear, would you like a drink?'

'Yes. I'll try one of those, the same, whatever it is. I didn't know you had any spirits. Is it one of yours?'

'Yes, my own creation.'

They all raised glasses and chinked them together. Holly thanked them for saving the young man's life. Albert couldn't wait for them to put this drink down there necks. They sniffed at it and made no comment, then they both took the full measure, straight down the hatch as Albert sipped his beer, watching the expressions on there faces.

160

'Argh,' and 'Wow, that's potent.' The two women both went week at the knees at the same time, clinging to the bar. Holly tried to ask what it was called.

'*Flas,.*'

'Yes, I can see why. Do you have you any lemonade?'

'Would you like ice with it?' Holly and Amy nodded.

'Yes, two lemonades coming up.'

Do you mind if I sit down, my legs are a little tired?' Holly asked. Albert tried to contain himself from laughing knowing the effect the drink would have on them.

Meanwhile Marcello had gone to the Ark's bow to see Antonio and Millie to say goodbye. He greeted Antonio, who was expecting him.

'Thank you for not giving me away. Please keep the secret that I'm lost at sea, which is really the truth.'

'I shall, my brother, and I hope you have many little Antonio's.' They embraced each other and then Marcello kissed Millie on each cheek and held her hands.

'Look after my brother.'

'I will Marcello. You take care here isn't the place for you.'

'Yes, I know.' Marcello turned and walked away knowing that probably he would never see his brother again.

By the time Marcello had said goodbye to everyone, the distant sound of a helicopter could be heard. The Ark's community were on top deck, ready to wave goodbye. Amy and Albert walked with Holly, Marcello and Melanie to meet the helicopter. It landed, the door opened and steps automatically dropped to the ground from within. Marcello kissed Melanie on the cheek.

'I think you understand,' he whispered in her ear. Then he and Holly quickly climbed onboard. They lifted off the ground making a partial turn as they rose from the deck. With rotor speed increased further, the helicopter ascended quickly and away. The waves and shouts of goodbye from the Ark died down as it went out of sight.

Ched, Gunter and Albert met in the bar for a pre-dinner drink.

'You managed to get rid of the gay boy, then Albert?' Ched quipped.

'Yes,' he replied dryly, 'but I very near cocked it up by trying to throw that girl overboard.'

161

'We had quite a laugh watching you with her over your shoulder, her kicking and screaming and us trying to keep up with you.'

'Tell me Albert,' asked Gunter, 'Would you really have thrown her over the side?' 'Yes! And that's enough of that. Let's have a beer and forget it. 'Cheers!

'Cheers!'

'Cheers!'... But I still have the problem with Melanie. Albert reminded them. How are we going to bump into another opportunity like that, with two young men of perfect age?' Gunter gave Albert his point of view. 'We need another two, not one. The way Marigold is with Antonio, that's causing problems between her and Jane.'

'What do you mean?' Ched butted in. Gunter carried on regardless.

'I think Antonio has settled on Jane, but I would not put it past Antonio to play away from home, he's a true Italian. It was a shame about Marcello; Melanie would have been quite happy trying to change him, and let's face it, if his homosexual tendencies were denied over a period of time, he may well have settled to a normal male/female relationship. Plus he was a great help to Magnus.'

'Gunter you're so polite.' commented Ched.

'Are you being sarcastic again?' asked Gunter.

'Yes!' said Ched.

'Stop it you two,' Albert interrupted, 'you're like a couple of silly schoolgirls!' They finished their beers and headed for their cabins to get cleaned up for dinner.

It was a fine, bright July morning, when they were forced to leave the fruitful area they had chosen, a particularly beautiful spot, south west of Flores, an island of the Azores with a perfect summer climate. There was a very gentle breeze, not enough to be any significant force behind the sails, but they hoped it would increase as the day went on. They were looking for another suitable place to spend the remaining summer months in the northern hemisphere, before moving south again. Magnus and Albert went to the bow of the ship to raise the anchors and start pulling up the sails. Ched had the turbines underway, and was waiting for clearance from Albert to go slow ahead, once the anchors were up from the depth and secure. Gunter set the course of 160° south and marked the position they were going to of 30° latitude and 29°05' longitude. The Ark gradually gathered speed with the combination of its sails and turbines, until they felt they were moving fast enough to cut the engines. It would take about three days

162

to get to the Great Meteor Bank and hopefully, far enough away from the media, and anybody else that had an interest in them.

The crew had become more experienced with the handling of the ship, especially the sails and now Antonio could use his strength and energy to help getting sails up and down, taking note of the angle at which they gave their best performance with the wind direction indicator. By the end of the day, the Ark was making reasonable progress at about twelve knots, which is what was expected. The watch and control rotas were organised and now easier with Antonio and Jane in full working mode. Albert was at the helm, watching the sun go down rapidly over the western horizon, as he had done so many times since setting off on this adventure, when he was joined by Melanie. Straight away Albert thought, I'm on my own. Melanie comes to see me, can only mean one thing, its talk time.
'Hi, Albert,'
'Hi, Melanie, what can I do for you?'
'It's the same, basically, as the last time, only probably worse.'
'Why is that then, Melanie?'
'With Marcello gone now, I don't even have someone to try for. What am I going to do Albert? I don't want to be left on the shelf. Perhaps I should have got onto that helicopter with Marcello?' Melanie bursts into tears. Oh shit! Albert thought to himself. How am I going to get out of this one?

'Remember the last time you came to me about this situation? It was the night Miles died and that's something else nobody knew would happen. My answer is the same as then.'
'You never know what's over the horizon,' she remembered. 'Like, we didn't expect the Ark to be attacked by a gang of criminals.'
'And, Melanie, we didn't expect to save two young lads from certain death at the hands of the elements either.'
'No. That's true.'
'Well does that not say something to you?'
'Yes Albert it does, you never know what's over the horizon.'
'Yes, Melanie and have I been right so far?'
'Yes Albert, you have.' At that point, she kissed him on the cheek, saying thank you and good night. Albert was relieved that she accepted his explanation, but couldn't help thinking, perhaps she should have gone with him. But then you can't opt out of something just because it seems an easy

answer at the time. Seeing things through, will make her a better person, I'm sure I am right, he thought.

The second day of their short trip, Millie was up early as usual, to milk and feed the animals. Antonio had been on a night lookout watch and did not finish until the early hours of the morning. By the time he had slept, it meant he didn't make his way to help Millie with the farming until late in the morning. Millie was going about her duties with the normal dedication she put into it. She let the chickens out into the orchard and was scattering corn about for them from a bucket. She suddenly felt extremely colicky in her stomach and rushed towards the toilet, which was at the very front of the bow. She made it to the edge of the orchard and could not hold herself any longer. In desperation, she quickly slipped off the top part of her boiler suit and crouched down. As she stood up, she raised the boiler suit back up, to pull over her shoulders, and then it hit her!
'Oh shit, you stupid cow.' She had only relieved herself into the back flap of her boiler suit and then deposited it onto the back of her neck!
'Thank Christ Antonio's not here, how embarrassing!'

She decided to go to the animal pens to strip off and use the water hose to rinse herself down and clean up her clothes, not having a change of work wear nearby. She hosed herself, before starting on her overalls. She was stark naked when, unseen and unheard by her through the noise of the pressure hose, Antonio came up from behind her and stood there to admire the view. She sensed he was there and turned to reveal her full frontal to Antonio. She stood still, totally startled and he was amazed at her beautiful body. She immediately pointed the nozzle and showered him with water. He rushed to her to try to stop her completely soaking him, and they struggled for control of the water. He started laughing, and so did she, as they grappled for power of the hose. In no time at all, the hose was discarded and they were groping at each other. Next, he lifted her up and carried her to the hay stack, where he laid her upon her back while he undid his shirt and removed his trousers and pants to reveal his stiffening cock. Millie took one look at it and immediately put her index finger to herself, rubbing the upper part of the opening between her legs. He climbed over her and she held his fully erect penis and guided it in. He moved it further into her. She gasped as she felt him fill her. He kissed her passionately as he moved up and down inside her. She clasped her hands on his buttocks encouraging him to go faster, until he collapsed onto her with delight as he

164

released himself inside her. She clung onto him, holding him into her as far and as long as she could. They lay quietly together for a few minutes, realising what they had done, and then, considering the possible consequences of their passion. They had both acted on impulse, pure animal instinct!

Millie spoke first.
'Antonio, this must not go further than here. No one must know. Ched will kill you if he ever finds out and Jane will cut off your balls!'
'Will we do this again?' Antonio replied.
'No! ... I don't know.' They got up and he put on his wet clothes as Millie checked to see if she had removed all the mess from her boiler suit before putting it back on.
'I'll go and work in the fields to dry off.' She said. 'Can you let the pigs out into the orchard for a while?' They both went about their work as if nothing had happened, except for an occasional, remembering smile.

The sails were lowered, now that they were nearing their temporary destination. It was late at night when they arrived at the chosen place, and they were all very tired by the time they had the sails down and the anchors dropped. All the crew wanted to do was go to bed and sleep, but somebody had to do a watch. Albert decided to put the radar on and do four hours from the bridge and then it was Ched's turn to relieve him.

ALBERT'S PRIVATE LOG   May – July 2017

This past few months have flown by, I haven't kept up my notes on what has happened and, as usual, if you don't make notes of things at the time, you forget the detail. It has been an eventful time since taking in the Italian lads: from being the subject of the world media; to the Salvation Army looking for the lost boys; the collection of Marcello and the cock up, I made, wrongly assuming the reason Holly Hanson was boarding the Ark. I wouldn't have thrown her over the side, but it certainly shocked the others. Then Antonio staying, and hitting it off with Jane.

165

I must be getting soft in my old age; I had conditioned myself to accept young Marcello into the community, knowing full well he was gay and would not have thought him to be a physical contribution to the Ark's breeding programme. People do change, especially when in their teens.

Monty! What a dickhead! Has he no respect for the people around him? No, he's just bent on satisfying his own selfish needs, letting down and deceiving us all. Men like that can never be trusted. I have only myself to blame for taking a chance on him joining the community in the first place.

The meetings were interesting, strange how most of the women are the domineering type and that's not a bad thing, because they do seem to keep their houses in order.

Now we are here at The Great Meteor Bank as a temporary refuge. We need to be away from the eyes of the paparazzi parasites who can only think of financial gain, exploiting people's misfortune or intruding into the lives of those who have become celebrities by hard work. As far as the Media is concerned, anyone is fair game.

16. HURRICANE

After almost eighteen months at sea, at the beginning of September 2017, everything was ready for the trip to Tristan De Cunha, their winter retreat. They only spent two months at the temporary site on The Great Meteor Bank, but it had been excellent, other than a little too hot at times, but well worth a visit in the future. The media left the Ark alone, and daily life got back to the comfortable routines. Tensions had settled down to a reasonable level. Marigold had Ched as an occasional friend, when she wanted. Jane and Antonio were well suited and Melanie was still hopeful and looking forward to the move, spurred on by the thought that the coastguard may visit them on a regular basis, when they anchored for the winter. Millie and Ched had long forgotten the case of the red knickers. Monty preferred to stay in the secure room where he set up home, rather than with his young partner and child. Albert was not happy with that, so organised an alternative room, which was almost finished for Monty to move into, leaving the secure room vacant. Albert and Amy had become very sexually active, now that Amy had found out how to prepare the *Maca* tablets herself. Albert still did not realise why their libido had increased, and when he asked, Amy had a plausible explanation ready for him.
'It must be the diet that Jane worked out for you. Haven't you noticed you've lost that belly you had? And I must say, you have a lot more energy,' smiling at him.

Gunter and Greta both plodded on, completely for one another, and doting over their children, everything they did was for the family first, unbelievably dedicated to each other and worked the system to maximise time together. Patricia had lost a lot of weight and was more agile. So trips to the orchard and garden became the norm, which in turn made her feel better and being out in the sunshine more, improved her complexion. She started to think that Magnus might fancy her more.
'This is the new me!' she told everybody. Her and Magnus became very lovey dovey, and often left the canteen after the evening meal, hand in hand, to the embarrassment of Melanie. It all added to the pleasant ambiance of the Ark and a general contentedness.

Magnus had finished the weapons, but was not happy for them to be used in a live situation, without some practice first. They never got around to that, with Albert saying they would take potluck, reminding Magnus they still had the grenade launcher that Package Pete gave them.

The anchors were lifted once again and the sails were in position. They had a good breeze and decided it was not necessary to use the turbines to get them moving as they normally did, all sails were raised. It was not long before the Ark was at fifteen knots and heading towards the Cape Verde where the helicopter assault took place, about six months before. The course was set to 185° south that would take them within fifty miles of the islands. Albert, Ched and Gunter agreed to take a chance and pass the islands closer, to be in earshot and sight of any authorities that should be patrolling the area. They would use the turbines to give them full speed to get past the islands and out of any possible danger from attack. All the men were briefed on what to do if they found themselves in this situation. Magnus had set up his rocket launcher on the top deck; the water cannon was ready and Albert had an ancient grenade launcher with a case of grenades, courtesy of Her Majesty's Government, before it went Euro.

It was going to take the Ark two days to reach the vicinity of the islands, at the speed they were travelling. The weather was good, about a force six with a strong breeze. Large waves formed with white foamed crests just showering a light spray of sea over the bow. It was getting a bit rough there for Millie. She and Antonio had settled the animals down and decided to head back to the decks. On the way back she had to stop, feeling a little sick. Antonio noticed.
'Are you ok Millie?'
'No, I just feel sick.'
'Yes it is a bit rough, more than we are used to.'
'Stay with me Antonio, don't go on ahead.'
'Sure Millie. Come here.' He put his arm around her and helped her back to the upper decks. On the way back she realised she has missed a period and started thinking, Oh shit no, I can't be! Her mind in a whirl, she worked out how long ago it was when she had that experience with Antonio, the first time. And was Ched active then? Yes he was, she thought, but a bit pathetic compared to stud muffin here. Her brain started working overtime. What if it comes out with dark hair, a suntan and chewing spaghetti? That will take some explaining! Thoughts and questions were going round and round her head, exhausting her, so she went to her cabin to lie down for ten minutes, before going to see Monty to fix her up with something for her sickness.

She told him it was probably due to the fact she might be pregnant and not the rough sea conditions, which didn't normally bother her.

'Not to worry,' he said, 'it's not your first so you know the ropes, eat plenty of snacks and I'll give you some ginger, to make tea. Have a couple of cups a day, it will certainly help you.' Strange, she thought. The last time I had morning sickness, the doctor prescribed strips of pink tablets. I wonder if Monty's simple remedy works, well there's only one way to find out.

On her way back to her cabin she decided to pay Ched a visit on the bridge to tell him about the news, because she was positive it could only be pregnancy. When Millie arrived, Ched was at the control and Albert and Gunter were debating whether to drop some of the sails slightly, because the weather was turning to more of a gale. They agreed and set about lowering the sails from the upper decks to the bow, leaving the two forward sails up. With the help of Antonio and Magnus, the operation went quickly.

'Ched I think I'm pregnant!'

'Fantastic!' he grinned as he embraced her. 'When did you know?'

'Well, I realised today. I'm just about seven weeks.' She knew he couldn't think back more than seven days, let alone seven weeks. Ched started counting forward on his fingers.

'April, next April, we should be back to the north by then.' He was genuinely delighted. 'Albert will be pleased and everybody else. You had better go and lie down and take it easy. I'll be with you as soon as I've finished my shift here.' She left him and went back to her cabin, still wondering if the baby was Antonio's.

Over the next thirty six hours, the heavy seas continued. They rated it at about gale force seven or eight, nevertheless, they were making good ground track, according to Gunter, and were getting to a point where they had to be extra vigilant looking at the radar, because the visibility outside was only a few hundred metres. The weather was on their side. Any vessel or aircraft trying anything on, in those conditions, would be a bit unwise, to say the least. The constantly heavy seas started to affect some of the women and children and Monty! His ginger tea was not working for everybody. Patricia came to the bridge to see if it could be turned down or something, and Albert told her he would do his best. They made the decision to drop the rest of the sails and Antonio and Ched volunteered for the task and were soon at the bow dropping the forward ones. Antonio looked in on the animals while he was there and he could see that Marina

169

the cow was distressed. He tried to comfort her. Antonio thrived on adventure, nothing seemed to faze him, and all the other activities were a bonus.

They were distancing themselves from the Cape Verde Islands, but the wild weather was relentless. They hadn't experienced such a long period of heavy seas before. Then, over a matter of hours, the winds ceased with the sun bursting through the remaining clouds, which quickly dispersed, and the sea went calm to everyone's relief, but not so for Albert and Gunter. Gunter took a particular interest in weather conditions, and Albert had experience, years ago, of something similar in the desert.

'It's called a *Gibli*, Gunter, which is one hell of a storm. The conditions were the same as they are now: high winds and then suddenly the sea went dead calm, no wind at all, and then all hell let loose'

'The barometer has dropped rapidly Albert; means trouble, don't you think?'

'Yes, deep shit! Looks like a hurricane's on its way!'

For the first time since setting sail, they wanted to use the radio weather forecast stations, to see which way the hurricane was coming and if they would be able to avoid it. Albert, a little panicky, finally worked out how to tune the radio in, found the right channel and wrote down the information given. Gunter knew, just by listening to the broadcast, that they were heading into the mouth of the storm and had very little chance of avoiding it. The thing they had on their side was the size of the Ark and the power of its engines, if required, and in Gunter's and Ched's experience at sea.

'We must make sure the bow is pointing towards the waves and thrust of the storm,' Gunter explained to Albert. All onboard were told they were heading into a bigger storm, but it should not last as long as the one they'd just been through. During the calm period, they used the time to check that everything was battened down and secured the best they could. Millie was even more concerned about the animals, especially since Antonio came back from Marina. Both Millie and Antonio pleaded with Albert, to allow them to bring the cow down to a hold at mid-ships or the stern, where the ship is not thrown about so much. Albert paused to think.

'Millie, Antonio, I always try to be logical, I think the animals would have more stress moving them to a different, strange environment than to leave them where they are, to ride out the storm like the rest of us.' They both thought about it, and realised he was right, but it took a few minutes to sink

170

in. They both were worried, more about the animals than anything else that they were facing. Albert said it was time to go, and asked them to tell everyone to stay in their cabins. He also asked Antonio to warn Jane to give up on lookout, and get to her cabin too. Antonio went up to see her first. The air was freshening when he got to Jane, who had just spotted a fast moving vessel heading towards them travelling from the Cape Verde Islands.

'Jane, Albert said to stop now, because of a storm coming.' Ignoring Antonio, she radioed to Albert about her sighting. Both Albert and Gunter moved quickly to the lookout post.

'Yes,' Albert said, seems as if they mean business,' as he passed the binoculars to Gunter.

'It's making twenty knots travelling direct from the south east and the sea is swelling fast; they are going to be in trouble.' As Gunter spoke, he looked to the western sky. He could see blackness moving very fast towards them. Ched had already turned the Ark in that direction, on hearing the forecast. Albert radioed to Ched.

'Give it some power Ched, there's some fool in a boat after us!'

Ched gave the turbines maximum power. It took a relatively long time for the Ark to respond to the thrust that the propellers were generating, in which time, the powerboat was gaining rapidly on them. Albert kept the binoculars on the speedboat to see if it had any identification. He couldn't see an emblem, but what he did see, more clearly by the second, was a manned, heavy calibre machine gun on top of the cockpit, and a rocket launcher to the port side on the deck. Magnus was told earlier, to be ready with his version of a rocket launcher and Antonio had the grenade launcher ready for Albert to operate.

The sea was making a big swell and the powerboat started to dip up and down. They launched a rocket at the Ark! Albert shouted to Magnus to fire his first rocket above the powerboat. The missile shot up into the air in a twirl and Magnus thought it was going to be useless, until the timed igniting device kicked in, and the rocket changed into a ball of flames in front of the powerboat, with droplets of fire landing on the deck, but not enough to do any serious damage.

Albert thought, these guys are brain dead or they *will* be dead if they don't get to us first to complete their mission! As the boat gained on them, it took

171

to the starboard side of the Ark to try and machine gun the bridge, but the boat was getting into deeper troughs of waves. Albert ordered Magnus to fire another rocket at the vessel, which again burst into flames above the boat. This time, the droplets of ignited methane gas caught the machine gun operator, who jumped into the cockpit to douse his clothes. Albert gave the order to slow the engines right down, to leave enough power to challenge the oncoming waves, which were some twenty feet high and increasing. He could see the speedboat must turn around soon, or, if left much longer, it would be tipped on its side if it tried to change direction. With the machine gun unmanned, Albert told Magnus to fire another rocket at the boat, which had slowed right down by now, with the waves almost covering it. At times, its propellers screamed to high revs, when they appeared out of the water. The rocket ignited again, and this time, a lot more of the target was covered by flames. Still, the speedboat battled onwards, probably in fear of turning suddenly and capsizing.

With the engines on the Ark shut down to steady ahead, the force of the waves with their increasing height hitting the bow, made the Ark slow down quicker.

'They're in Shit Street now, lads!' Albert shouted, against the roar of the wind and sea. The powerboat had to ride the storm, hitting each wave with a thud, dropping from the top of one, to the bottom of another, and totally helpless. The machine gun and any other weapons would not help them now, and they knew it. They would be lucky to survive the ferocity of the hurricane. The boat gradually overtook the Ark, battling its way through the waves. The Ark was taking a pounding at its bow, but its sheer size held it in good shape as long as it faced the waves. Eventually, the hurricane passed on, to cause havoc elsewhere.

The Ark got steadier and in a couple of hours, the seas were back to about a force five with moderate waves having long lengths of white foam rolling at the top of them. Albert was still at the lookout post with his binoculars pinned on the sea, to see if there were any signs of would-be assailants, when Gunter joined him. He passed the binoculars.

'My eyes are straining, could you take over from me.' But before he had raised them, Gunter pointed to floating debris.

'I don't need glasses to see that!'

'I didn't think they'd get very far,' Albert said. 'I knew they couldn't turn around, they were knackered whatever they did.'

172

Gunter raised the binoculars to scan the area.

'There's someone lying face down. He looks dead, no movement at all!' As the waves rolled by the Ark, different parts from the boat came into sight and were gradually left behind, until another body in a life jacket, and still moving, appeared.

'He's obviously sighted the Ark, Albert. Listen, he's blowing the whistle attached to his jacket, the poor sod!'

'Oh shit! That's all we need, a survivor! That means we have to pick the bastard up before I hang him!'

'Albert, you wouldn't get away with that, and you know it,' warned Gunter.

'Yes Gunter, just thinking aloud. Come on let's get him out of the water.' The Ark was passing the survivor by, so Ched and Antonio volunteered to be dropped in the inflatable to retrieve him. Gunter kept his binoculars trained on the man in the water to guide the rescue party. The squad moved as quickly as they could, fetching the inflatable from the hold, and then lowering it over the side on the hoist. Gradually, the man in the water was dropping from Gunter's sight, but they still kept looking and took a bearing of the last sighting. Ched and Antonio were soon bobbing across the waves in the direction given by Gunter, via the short wave radio. Ten minutes passed.

'I can see him, I can see him!'Antonio shouted. They sped up to him, circling three times and reporting back to Albert,

'He's either a black guy, or he has a burnt face.' Ched passed the radio to Antonio telling him to speak to Albert, reporting every move. Ched had taken it upon himself this time, to pack a sidearm, complete with holster. As they came in closer, Ched, with pistol in hand, pointed at the man in the water.

'Don't shoot me boss! Don't shoot me! I'm not one of them. Don't shoot me!' Ched passed the pistol to Antonio.

'I'll pull him out. If he makes any wrong moves while I check him over, shoot the bastard!'

'No problem Ched. Maybe I shoot him anyway and save us all a problem.'

'No! Don't shoot me! Don't shoot me!' The terrified voice came from the water. Ched grabbed him and pulled him half over the side of the boat and thumped him on the back of the neck.

'Uuugh!' he went as Ched frisked him while he was dazed and desperate to survive; then they dragged him into the boat. Ched rolled him over to take a better look. The man was shaking with cold and fear.

'Watch him like a hawk Antonio!' Ched took control of the outboard and headed back to the Ark.

'You can resume back to our original course for Tristan De Cunha,' Ched said to Albert. 'Get Magnus ready to lift us all up back to our home please.' Albert smiled at Ched's remark, *our home*, and he repeated it to himself.

Since the hurricane had abated, Millie left to go to the animals, to see how they had fared. She was worried about her two men out there on the sea. One is a dickhead, but lovely, she thought, and the other has a lovely dick! Marina was also in a state, and needed calming. Millie stayed with her and talked to her, while rubbing her head and neck, she knew she would respond. Then she fed her a little and when she started nibbling, she knew that she was alright. She put her arms around Marina.

'I hope my two men are back safe and sound soon,' she whispered into her ear.

Magnus had dropped the hoist and the inflatable was moving steadily alongside the Ark.

'I bet that old bastard won't slow down for us,' Ched thought. He was right, he didn't! Ched kept at the controls, while Antonio grabbed the shackle from the hoist and connected it to the eye on the sling on the inflatable. Magnus was hoisting them up before Ched realised the engine was still going. They were back onboard with an audience to greet them, clapping and relieved with their safe return. Millie had made it back in time to grasp Ched. Marigold stood back, cheering with excitement. Jane was squeezing Antonio till he was blue as Millie looked on at him. Albert and Gunter dragged the survivor from the inflatable, stretching him out on the deck, removing his lifejacket and making sure he had nothing concealed. Melanie looked on, wondering why this man would want to attack them. He certainly didn't look Russian. Gunter made him stand up and everyone gathered around him, just staring at him. He turned and looked at Millie and then to Greta, to Ched, to Jane. He kept going round the faces and ended up in total fear, collapsing to the deck.

'Better get him off to Monty's ex residence,' Albert suggested. Ched and Gunter, the usual combination, pulled him up and frogmarched him away. Monty and Jane were asked to check him out, in case he had any injuries.

174

They only requested dry clothes for him, which were thrown into his new abode. Locking the door behind them, they left, not even asking his name.

Ched went back to control, Gunter had worked out the new position they had ended up in. The wind direction was favourable, which some sails could take up. All hands were there to operate the hoists, as the Ark made a new course of 160° south. Once this was achieved and the Ark was back on its way, Ched succumbed to autopilot, with Albert's permission; lookout duty was postponed; everybody was in the canteen celebrating the heroes of the Ark, *themselves*, all of them. A substantial amount of drink was consumed and a relaxed mood soon set in. Ched and Antonio were bragging to their women, exaggerating the danger in getting the villain out of the water. Even Magnus, was feted, dodging rockets and bullets to defend the Ark and the triumph when he got a direct hit. Amy was just glad it was over. She had spent too much time in the past wondering if her man would return home and in one piece. Albert said he would be surprised if they had any more threats from these people after losing a helicopter, a boat and a number of men. He was now broadening his horizons though, starting to look at the bigger world map to speculate where else would be suitable to move to each season.

ALBERT'S PRIVATE LOG – September 2017

That was an interesting episode; this Ark can really move when the turbines are at maximum power. Those chaps must have been complete dickheads heading out when it was obvious a major storm was brewing. Well, they paid the price for their stupidity with their lives and that black lad is a lucky man to be picked out of the water without a scratch. What are we going to do with him? I suppose we could put him in the fishing boat with Gunter and Ched when we pass near the Ascension Islands or one of the Cape Verde Islands and throw him over the side, near the shore and let him swim for it and sort himself out. We can't dump him on Tristan de Cunha because they will just bring him back to us. In the meantime we will have to keep him onboard and that means he will have to work.

Millie's pregnant. That's good news. Antonio came in the nick of time to help on the farm while she's expecting.

The animals struggled in stormy seas, especially Marina and co. But they soon settled down and found their sea legs.

Ched seems more positive about things lately. I noticed he packed a sidearm without being prompted, when he went to rescue the survivor.

17. A PRISONER

The Ark had about ten days sailing before they would be setting themselves up for anchorage near where they were the last winter. Albert did not have too much to drink during the celebrations, because he was at the helm watching the radar screen that night so that everybody else could rest properly. It was a long shift and he stayed at the controls and watched from 2200 hours until 0600 hours. Ched was first on the bridge to relieve Albert and Gunter followed shortly after.

'What are we to do with our friend below?' Ched asked. 'Do we feed him? Ask questions?'

'No,' replied Albert, 'just give him some water and make sure there are two of you there. Don't let the women anywhere near him. He needs to be very hungry before we even think about talking to him. Make it three days without a crumb.' Ched and Gunter looked at each other.

'The women won't like it Albert,' Gunter said.

'Just remind them that he was one of those men that tried to kill us all, and he will be fed and looked after, but not yet. Those are my strict orders. I'm going to get my head down. Please try and give me six hours of peace. See you both later.'

The Ark had to make changes to the course on the way to Tristan, to catch some better winds. They were all eager to get to the anchorage. It was now three days since the hurricane saved the day in destroying the attackers. The order not to feed the rescued man went without question, and now he was a prisoner of the Ark.

'It's time to have a little chat with our friend,' Albert said to the others. 'I think the bridge is the best place to bring him to get fresh air and to stretch his legs. And I still don't want any interference from the women.' He sent Ched and Antonio and told them not to be gentle with him, to give the captive psychological fear. Albert had a lot of experience in enemy interrogation. The current situation was mild compared with back then.

The man was marched to the bridge and made to stand facing Albert. Without being prompted, he bowed his head and then looked at him with deep brown eyes on pure white backgrounds. His dark chocolate skin shone on his smooth, young face underneath a crop of tightly curled jet black hair. He had large lips that almost met his nose and chin. He wasn't skinny, but quite muscular, medium built and, at a guess, in his early twenties.

177

'Good grief!' Ched blabbed out,' with lips like that, if he got too close to a shop window, he'd stick like a limpet!'
'Shut up, Ched!' snapped Albert and began the interrogation.

'Do you understand English?'
'Yes sir.'
'What's your name?'
'Zimbo sir,'
'Where are you from?'
'Santiago, Cape Verde Islands'
'Who do you work for?'
'Me sir,'
'Why did you attack our ship?'
'I did not sir. I was hired with my boat, to deliver two wooden crates and two men to your ship. When we were out at sea, they pulled a pistol on me while they set up weapons that were in the crates, and told me to get them to the ship as fast as the boat would travel.'
'Where were the men from?'
'They were white sir, and spoke English.'
'Did they speak any other language to each other?'
'No sir, just English.'
'Why did you head out, when a hurricane was forecast?'
'They paid me one hundred thousand euros, in cash, to catch up with you, I took the risk. You went faster than I thought.'
Albert looked at Ched and Antonio and requested.
'Take him to the canteen and feed him one small meal, then back to his room and lock him in,' the pair escorted the prisoner away.
'Do you believe him?' Gunter asked Albert.
'Well it sounds feasible, but that was a fancy, powerful boat! Where did he get the money for that? I don't know yet, Gunter. But he speaks good English, seems intelligent, and was obviously well educated somewhere. We need to have a get together about it, just you, Ched and me, to work out a couple of tests on him. To lie to someone, you have to have a very good memory. We'll see. There's no hurry, is there?'
'True.' replied Gunter.

They had finally reached their destination for the winter and set the sails in a heave to position, in the same way as they did when last they were in the area. This time, Gunter took a daily plot of their position to check that they didn't drift too far, with not being able to drop anchor, because of the sea depth.

Zimbo was locked up, and just fed and exercised, during the journey to Tristan. Albert had given a lot of thought about what to do with him, and was annoyed that he had to be fed, with nothing in return. He was fit and able; it was logical to put him to work. Albert knew the man was intelligent enough to realise the only way to escape was to swim the fifty miles or so to the nearest land, in shark infested waters, and that would save Albert a lot of trouble. He was brought up to the bridge to be told that he was to work on the farm, to help Millie, who was pregnant, and Antonio would be in charge of him. This would be until April next, when they passed the Cape Verde Islands. The plan was, to drop him off to the authorities there. When Zimbo heard this, he was horrified.

'Oh no, you cannot send me back. I will be shot!' Albert immediately thought that there was more to his story and started questioning him again, with the threat of sending him back and handing him over.

'Why would you be shot?'

'Because I stole the boat sir.'

'Aaah, so you told me a lie when you said, '*my boat*' implying you owned it?'

'Yes sir. I didn't think it mattered where the boat came from at the time sir.'

'That is not the point. The fact is you lied to me.'

'I'm sorry sir. I won't do it again sir,' Zimbo replied quickly.

'But what else have you lied about?'

'Nothing sir,' Albert got close to him, with anger in his voice, and then backed off because of the stench from Zimbo's body.

'Good God! When did you last have a wash?'

'Ten days ago, when I was pulled from the water sir,'

'That smells about right.' Albert turned to Ched.

'Surely there are towels and soap in his room?'

'He's got everything there. He's just a dirty, little bastard!'

Albert asked Ched and Gunter to take him to his room and give him time to shower before taking him to Antonio to help clean out the pigs. Gunter asked if getting Zimbo cleaned up first was a waste of time.

'No we don't want him smelling worse than the pigs and upsetting them, do we? Oh and when he finishes work get Antonio to make sure he showers and is clean to join everybody else at the normal mealtime.'

179

'Do you think that will be acceptable to all the others,' Gunter asked.
'I don't know,' replied Albert. 'We'll have to cross that bridge when we come to it. I just don't want somebody having to run up and down to his room with food on a tray at meal times any more.'

Off they went with Gunter still fretting about Zimbo eating with them in the canteen.
'I know Greta and Antonio won't want to eat a meal with him at the table and probably some of the others will feel the same. What do you think, Ched?'
'Yes, I think Albert's a bit premature in allowing that. I'll have a word with him when I get back to the bridge. You know Gunter, I'm looking forward to getting out on the fishing boat and catching some tuna. What about it, shall we go tomorrow?'
'That's a good idea. It will be a change from being on lookout all the time.'
Zimbo heard the words *'fishing'* and *'boat'*.
'I'm a good fisherman. I can help you.'
'You don't have a chance of being anywhere near the fishing boat,' Gunter replied, 'so don't even mention it again.' Ched was surprised at this strong reply and sensed Gunter's intense dislike for Zimbo. They both marched him to his room, waited outside while he cleaned himself up, and then continued on to the farm area. Ched explained to Millie and Antonio what Albert wanted him to do. Millie thought it was ok, but Antonio said that his pigs were fussy. Antonio openly showed his dislike of Zimbo and roughly pushed him to the pigpen to start work. Ched thought trouble was brewing and decided to stay for the rest of the day.
'Gunter, you go back and explain to Albert that I'll stay here to keep an eye on things. If he needs me, he can call on the short wave.'

Gunter headed back to the bridge and made up his mind to approach Albert on the subject of Zimbo, before Ched got to him....
'Don't you think it's a little too soon to be having him eat with the rest of us? Can you not give a bit more time and get the others point of view?'
'I suppose you're right Gunter. Perhaps I was a bit hasty, what do you think about bringing him up to eat in the evening after everybody else have finished, still under supervision of course.' Gunter was surprised at Albert's immediate change of mind.
'Yes, that sounds better,' he replied, 'but what about other meals and lunchtimes when Millie and Antonio come back to the canteen?'

180

'Well, at the moment, he's only having one meal a day and it's staying that way until we find out more of the truth from him. As for lunch, they can march him straight to his room and lock him up while they have their meals in peace. We can try it, see how things go and then take another view on it later.' Albert suggested.

'Ok Albert. I'll go and see everyone and explain what's happening, so it's not too much of a shock to them.'

Antonio was extremely arrogant, shouting and balling at Zimbo, making him work very hard and he laughed heartlessly, when the sow knocked him over onto his back to roll in the pig shit.

'There's going to be trouble there, I can see,' Millie commented to Ched.

'That's why I stayed to keep an eye on things.'

'Oh, I thought it was to be with me for a change.' Ched froze.

'What do you mean?'

'Well you always seem to be on the bridge or on lookout these days, there's more to the Ark than that.'

'Oh,' Ched went on, relieved she hadn't found out about his TLC sessions with Marigold. 'Well the trip down was full of different things as you are aware, and now that we are at anchor, I'll be able get over here to see you more often.'

'That's good,' she replied, 'because by the end of this season, you will have your hands full with our new baby. Gunter always helps Greta with Venus. He puts his family first.'

'I always look after Vicky, when required, and when you're too busy down here.'

'Ched, do you realise what it takes to keep this farm producing two seasons a year? I don't know what I would have done if Antonio had decided to leave with his brother. He has been absolutely fantastic in everything he does here. He looks after things really well,' she stopped, thinking she was going a bit too far. Ched decided to get a word in, but felt guilty about his exploits with Marigold.

'I'll help you more, I promise. Just tell me what you want, and when you want me to do anything.' Bloody hell, he thought to himself, I wish I hadn't volunteered for this job, I should have left Gunter here, oh, but then Zimbo would not have stood a chance with both him and Antonio disliking him.

Ched was getting bored with wandering about, following Millie in whatever she was doing, and having to listen to her, trying to keep an eye

181

on Antonio and Zimbo at the same time. He needed to do something else, otherwise he would find somewhere to sit down and then probably end up falling asleep. He thought better of it, and he started to help Millie with the feeding of Marina.

'Here, let me help you carry that.' Millie was surprised at his involvement.

'Just look at Marina, she's just like me!'

'What, a cow?' Ched's reply flew out of his mouth.

'No you pillock, *pregnant!*'

Zimbo had finished cleaning out the pigs and ended up with even more shit on him. Antonio pulled out the pressure hose and started to sluice down Zimbo at maximum power. After getting him clean, Antonio thought he'd have some fun and pointed the hose at his crotch. The force really hurt Zimbo and he turned and stumbled away in pain. Antonio was angry.

'Stay there, you black bastard!' Reluctantly, Zimbo turned and faced him. Again, he pointed the hose but this time Zimbo managed to shield himself with his hands, so Antonio pointed the hose at his face. This was repeated up and down, over and over with Antonio laughing pitilessly. Ched had taken his eye off things. As he made conversation with his wife, he heard Antonio's cruel laughter and Zimbo's pleas to stop. He ran over to investigate, saw what was happening and turned off the hose.

'Ched,' Antonio shouted, 'I was having fun.' As soon as the hose was off, Zimbo flew over to Antonio, at full pelt and they went hell for leather at each other.

'Oh shit!' said Ched as Millie rushed over to them, screaming at the top of her voice.

'Stop, stop! Antonio, stop this!' Ched tried to stop Millie intervening.

'Leave them for a few minutes they obviously have too much energy.' But Millie was thinking of her *other man.*

'Zimbo might hurt Antonio.'

'I'm sure Antonio can look after himself.'

'Ched, stop them now!' Ched thought he had better do what he was told and pulled Zimbo away, because he was coming off worse.

'Millie you control Antonio, talk sense into him, if you can?' She went straight to him and commanded Antonio to stop. He took one look at her and walked away. She immediately followed and asked what got into him.

'Zimbo, come on you! I'll take you back with me.' They made their way back to the upper deck. Meanwhile, Millie was trying to get an explanation from Antonio. He headed for the hay store as she chased him, shouting and pleading.

'You must promise me that won't happen again, Antonio. Promise me, or I won't...'

'You won't what?' he asked as he turned to face her.

'I won't...' and he began undoing the front of her boiler suit to reveal her breasts. Pulling the suit over her shoulders and holding it tight around her arms, trapping them, he buried his head into her breasts. He looked up at her.

'You were going to say, you won't let me have you?' He pulled down the boiler suit completely, lifted her from it and put her down. Then he slipped off her pants, undid his belt, releasing his trousers enough for his stiffening cock to spring out, and entered her without even caressing her. She let out a small cry, as he got very hard on entry. In a perverse way, and despite her pregnancy, she enjoyed this rough sex with him and, once in, wanted him to last forever, but his ejaculation was in record time. Just five strokes of movement and he was finished.

'That didn't take long!' she said, as he lay on top of her.

'I got so excited when you were angry with me, I had to have you and I couldn't stop myself.' Ched wasn't even halfway back to the upper deck, with Zimbo dragging his feet behind him, when Millie pulled her boiler suit back on and Antonio his trousers up. Millie was not elated by Antonio's action, because he was so quick, but certainly enjoyed the spontaneity and the thrill.

Ched went straight up to Albert, who was in the brewery with Jane making preparations for a batch of *Ark's Bitter*.

'It's about time we had some more beer. That last lot didn't take long to shift, after the binge we had on the way down here.'

'No Ched it didn't.' replied Albert, 'The sad thing was, I only had two pints, because it was my shift at control and radar lookout. So what brings you here? I thought you had him on pig duty?'

'He was, but Antonio wanted to hose him down afterwards and decided he wasn't clean enough and they ended up fighting. Zimbo here, didn't come off too well, as you can see.' Jane looked at Zimbo.

'My Antonio did that?' Zimbo's eye had become swollen, with the lids closing together. 'Wait 'til I see him tonight!' Jane went on, voicing her disapproval.

183

'That boy is very handy with his fists Albert. It's a pity we didn't have a match for him, it would be a good fight!' Ched remarked.

'You men disgust me!' Jane objected. She stopped what she was doing and left the room.

'What's up with her?' asked Ched.

'You've upset her and now I've got to finish this brew on my own. Let's take a look at him...Oh well he'll just have to work with one eye. Go and see Monty to fix him up with something. That'll give me some time to think how to make better use of his time.'

Ched was beginning to feel like mother goose, trailing around with a lost soul in tow. He finally tracked Monty down, fast asleep in his cabin.

'Come on Monty wake up!'

'I bet I don't find any red knickers at the side of his bed!' Ched said as he shook him.

'What did you say?' Monty stirred. 'What knickers?'

'Oh, nothing, you must have been dreaming.'

'What do you want?' asked Monty, annoyed.

'Albert said to fix his eye with something.' Monty rubbed his own eyes to clear his vision and took a look at Zimbo's.

'Take him to the canteen, cut up a raw potato and rub it gently, it will stop the swelling.'

'Is that all?'

'Yes, that's all we've got and it works better than a beef steak.'

'Beef steak, he's not worth a beef steak, even if we had one!' Ched exclaimed.

The pair arrived at the canteen.

'Anybody home,' Ched shouted into the kitchen. Patricia emerged, in her white chef's smock and hair bundled into a net beneath a white hat, clutching a meat cleaver in her right hand. Then she looked at Zimbo.

'We haven't come to rob you, so be careful with that knife.'

'Yes Ched, what do you want? Oh, you poor wee thing!' she gasped as she saw Zimbo's bulging eye.

'Looks like you've found a friend at last, my lad.' said Ched. 'Monty said to cut a raw potato and dab it onto the swollen skin.' Patricia waddled quickly into the kitchen to return with a sliced raw potato and immediately applied the remedy. Zimbo winced as it stung.

'Seems to be working already.' said Ched. 'Here give me that!' and Ched took the potato and handed it to Zimbo. 'He can do it himself, thank you Patricia.'

'Thank you Mam, said Zimbo.'

'Come on; let's see what Albert has come up with for you.'

Albert was still working in the brewery, only Magnus was there too discussing maintenance that was required, to do with greasing the sail mechanisms. Magnus was worried about them not being used for the next six months and they needed protecting, but it was too much of a task for him to tackle by himself.

'Here's your man.' said Albert, as Ched and Zimbo entered the room.

'Zimbo you have a new occupation: helping Magnus.'

The security on Zimbo became more relaxed as he worked with Magnus. Zimbo got more respect from everybody and they were impressed by his impeccable manners. Patricia was making sure *the poor wee thing* was fed three meals a day, without Albert knowing. His physical condition improved over the next few weeks, having being fed properly, and Patricia making sure his personal hygiene was up to scratch.

Ched and Gunter went out fishing on a regular basis and always returned with more fish than they could eat or store in the freezers. So, Albert came up with a solution for some of the excess: to cut it into fillets and use salt from the desalination plant as a coating to preserve them. Ched made some steel frames with netting across. These were positioned on deck with another net over the top to keep seagulls off. The fish were then placed across the netting and left to air-dry in the sun. Albert had seen similar methods used in many countries, especially where refrigeration was not possible. When it came to use them, the fillets were boiled to remove the salt and then cooked in numerous ways. One of the favourite Ark recipes was to mix the boiled soft fish with mashed or chopped potato and onion, similar to the Portuguese *bacchalau*.

Albert had not finished questioning Zimbo on his true part in the hurricane attack; he just kept putting it off. During those weeks, you would hardly know that Zimbo was there, let alone a prisoner. With Magnus taking charge of him, the reports coming back to Albert were full of praise. He was Magnus' brown-eyed boy! Through Patricia and Magnus' kindness

185

and concern for Zimbo's well-being, the lad, he was only twenty, and younger than Albert had thought, had gradually become more accepted by most of the community, especially being so young. There was still uneasiness from Antonio and Gunter. Aware of this, Zimbo gave them a wide berth and, with Albert and Ched softening their feelings towards him, he felt more accepted himself. Zimbo was so grateful for being alive, well fed, clothed and strangely enough, protected, more so than he was when trying to scratch a living, back in Santiago, Cape Verde.

Melanie would talk to him briefly, at first. He was very courteous to her and always smiled. It was not long before they spent a little longer in conversation together. She asked the questions, mainly about his home life. Magnus was always about while this was happening, usually whilst having a meal, but then Melanie would pop in to see her father and Zimbo wherever they were working on the ship. The security risk became less and less with Zimbo, and occasionally, he could be seen on his own, running an errand for Magnus. Later, Melanie persuaded Albert to let Zimbo use the swimming pool and, whenever he had spare time, they would spend it in the pool together, usually racing each other, or throwing a ball about. There would nearly always be someone else there, usually Marigold sunbathing, and sometimes, she joined in the swimming activities. She had no interest in other males now that Ched saw her regularly, to give her some tender loving care. Greta would quite often be there at the pool, teaching the children to swim as part of their education programme. When Jane and Antonio used the pool, there was no more animosity as Zimbo was gradually being included.

It was the beginning of December and becoming very warm as the middle of summer approached in the southern hemisphere. Millie was resting more, now that her bump had increased in size, and she was still wondering which of her two loves, was the father. Antonio had settled down and moved into the posh suite with Jane, as they had become a settled couple. Magnus and Zimbo were working on the methane gas plant at the bow of the Ark. Millie was having a rest period and Antonio was in the fields nearest the upper decks when he was approached by Greta with all the children. She wanted to take them to see the animals at the bow and asked if it would be ok. Antonio told her he thought it was a great idea and, as soon as he had finished what he was doing, he would join them to explain about the animals. He could tell them what they ate, what they were used for, and so on. He also mentioned that Magnus was working on the methane plant up there.

Greta led the way then the two older children, Stella and Vicky, ran further on ahead. She was pushing baby Venus in a buggy and holding Lucy's hand, when the toddler wanted to walk and then carrying her when she wanted to be picked up. Greta was forever calling the older girls not to go on too far and made slow progress with the two younger ones. Eventually, they all made it to the orchard, with Stella and Vicky chasing each other around the trees and when they could hear the animals, they were off to see them. Greta shouted for them to come back, but they took no notice. Vicky stopped chasing, went straight to the pens, and climbed on the railings to look at the pigs. Stella showed little interest in the animals and went exploring on her own. She climbed up the steel side to look over the bow of the Ark and, in no time at all, she was balanced on the top, which was almost two metres from the deck and about fifteen metres to the sea below. Greta had not seen her, and thought she was with Vicky looking at the pigs.
'Where is Stella?' Greta asked when she caught up with Vicky.
'She went over to there,' and Vicky pointed to the side. Greta started to panic.
'Let's go and find Stella, Vicky.'
'No,' she whined, 'I want to stay here.' Greta desperately shouted for Magnus to help. He soon arrived with Zimbo at his heels.
'What is it Greta?'
'It's Stella. She ran off somewhere and Vicky did not want to come with me to look for her.'
'I'll stay with the girls here. You and Zimbo go and find her.' They started to run over to the direction Vicky had pointed, and could see Stella on the skyline, balanced, looking out to sea. Panicking again, Greta shouted at her and startled Stella. She wobbled, and quickly disappeared over the side of the ship. Greta screamed at the same time as Stella's screech ended in a splash. Zimbo raced to the spot where she fell, clambered up and looked to where she was thrashing about in the water. He threw off his shoes and dived as close to her as possible.

Antonio had just come through the orchard in time to see Zimbo about to dive over the side, and Greta running to that spot. Antonio was soon there.
'What's happened Greta?' Greta was hysterical.

187

'It's Stella, she is over the side!' Antonio immediately ran to the nearest safety buoy, released it, and climbed up the side to throw them the ring that was attached to a rope. By this time, Zimbo had reached Stella and was treading water, clinging under her armpits. He saw the buoy splash nearby and swam on his back to it. No way could Antonio pull the two of them out together, so Zimbo slipped Stella into the ring and told her to hold tight and not let go. He signalled to Antonio to lift her up, which he did, pulling as carefully as he could so as not to jerk the rope. Zimbo swam beneath, watching her rise the forty feet or so up to Antonio. As soon as she was near, he grabbed her to safety and lowered her down to a tearful, grateful Greta. Magnus had managed to get the other children over to the scene and Antonio asked him to help lift Zimbo out of the water.

Magnus stood below Antonio, to help pull the rope. Antonio then threw the buoy to Zimbo, who quickly put it around himself. Antonio started to pull. Magnus was trying his best, but not being a Mr Universe, was struggling. Greta saw the problem and put Stella down firmly, telling her not to move, then went to assist them. It made the difference! Gradually, Zimbo cleared the water and slowly rose up to the side, and finally landed back on the deck.

'You're too heavy!' Antonio complained to Zimbo. 'Loose some weight if you want pulling from the water again!' He was smiling at him as he said this, and they both laughed and shook hands. Greta rushed to them both, clasping her arms around Zimbo, first kissing him on his cheeks and repeating the same for Antonio.

'Thank you! Thank you so much!' Magnus was looking on in line, waiting for his kiss, but was disappointed. Greta realised that she had learnt a painful lesson. She promised herself to ensure Melanie or Marigold accompanied her the next time.

The children still wanted to see the farm. Greta asked Antonio to explain about the animals, as they had previously intended.

'I'm all wet!' Stella moaned.

'It's a nice, warm day. You will soon be dry and you will now behave yourself!' Magnus and Zimbo returned to the gas plant, as if nothing had happened.

Not long afterwards, Greta returned with the children to the nursery, with the dreaded task of seeing Gunter to explain the near loss of Stella. She was

188

worried about his reaction to how Stella had managed to be out of her sight for enough time to scale the side and fall overboard. She felt so guilty and the terrible vision of Stella drowning kept flashing through her mind. When it came to explaining to him, he was more relieved that she was safe and wanted to thank Zimbo and Antonio. When Gunter told Albert about the incident, he thought it was about time questioning Zimbo about the attack was put to bed.

'Is he friend or foe?' he asked Gunter.

Later, Albert went to see Zimbo's best friend, Melanie, to ask her if he had mentioned anything about his part in the attack. She replied that nothing had been said and that she would have told him if he had disclosed any information. She then asked why there was all the sudden interest in Zimbo again. Albert explained the day's events and that he would like to find out, if he was friend or foe, or just a victim of circumstances, who had become a friend. He said he needed to question him for a final decision.

'Well I want to be present when you do question him,' said Melanie.

'Sure no problem I'll arrange it on the bridge before dinner tonight.' Albert contacted Magnus on the short wave and told him what he wanted to do. Magnus agreed that it was a good idea, to get it out of the way.

Albert and Gunter were waiting for them to arrive, Melanie turned up before Zimbo, proudly seating herself in the Captains Chair, smiling.

When Zimbo arrived he was surprised to see Melanie swirling around in the big leather chair.

'Yes Mr Albert, sir, Mr Magnus said you wanted to see me.' As he looked at Melanie, he seemed nervous, wondering why she was there and thinking he had done something wrong.'

'Relax!' said Albert, 'Gunter has something to say to you.' Gunter thanked him for saving his daughter that day and shook his hand.

'Oh, is that all, Mr Albert? Can I go now sir?'

'No, not just yet,' he replied, 'we want to know the truth about your part in the attack.'

'Oh, that sir,'

'Yes, that.' replied Albert.

'I'm just a fisherman. I worked my father's boat. Once, my father had many boats and was doing very well. He sent me to school. I can read and write,' he said excitedly.

'Yes, yes go on.' Albert chivvied him.

189

'And then the bigger boats came and flooded the market with cheaper fish and we could not compete. In the end, my father had only one boat left, and he lost a lot of money. He had to sell the other boats for very little and we became very poor. Then one day, two men arrived in the village, looking for someone to drive a boat for them. I heard about these men, and I went to them. I said I would drive a boat for money, and I knew the area. They said that I would have to steal a fast boat and I said no, sir. I did Mr Albert; I said no.'

'Yes, yes, so what happened?'

'They showed me one hundred thousand euros in cash. It was the most money I had ever seen in my life. I thought this could help my father.

There were many fancy boats tied up in the harbour, belonging to very rich people. So, I chose the most powerful one that had been tied up for some time with nobody using it, and I broke in and hot-wired it, to start it. It was easy. A truck arrived and we loaded the two wooden crates onboard, and the rest is as I told you before; they pulled a gun on me as soon as we were out to sea. That's true Mr Albert sir.' Zimbo looked at Melanie when he said the words *'that's true'*.

'How were you going to get the boat back without being seen?'

'I was just going to beach it, *Mr Albert* sir, just run it aground on a remote beach that I know, and make a run for it to hide with the money. I know a place to hide nearby, to get away from the men.'

'So the money was on the boat?'

'Yes, Mr Albert, sir. It's gone with the boat sir. And if you send me back there, they will shoot me for stealing the boat, Mr Albert sir.'

'Albert you can't send him back,' cried Melanie. 'He can stay here. I'll look after him.'

'What do you think Gunter?' Albert asked.

'I think he is telling the truth, Mr Albert, sir!'

'Stop that Gunter, and you Zimbo, from now on, it's just Albert.'

Melanie rushed up to Albert putting her arms around his neck, kissing him over and over again.

'You're wonderful Albert,' she said and then grabbed Zimbo's hand. 'Come on Zimbo. Let's tell Mum and Dad.'

'What do you mean Melanie? Can I stay on the Ark?'

'Yes of course you can. Hurry up! I can't wait to tell them.'

The dinner bell went and the queue for Patricia's dish of the day was getting longer now that Zimbo was there with everybody else. And he was welcomed with smiles all round.

ALBERT'S PRIVATE LOG - Oct - Dec 2017

He's a strange lad that Zimbo, although quite likeable. He's certainly caught Melanie's eye and has been very useful about the place. I think they call it a 'victim of circumstances', although he did steal a boat. It took Stella to almost get herself drowned to make people, including me, think he's not as bad as we thought. To dive forty feet into waters where we know there are sharks, was a brave thing to do.

I must have a walk round the Ark with Magnus and Ched to see if there are any other areas where children could climb up onto the side. Now they are older, they will be all over the place so we must put some sort of guards or barriers up. That's a nice little job for Ched and his welding kit.

Marina's due to calf again soon; that should help a bit with the methane gas supply. Millie's bump is getting bigger. She must be nearly five months now. That will make it difficult for Ched to get his end away. Makes me wonder how we would have managed the farm without Antonio throughout Millie's pregnancy.

It won't be long and Christmas will be upon us again. Perhaps we will get a visit from the new coastguard this time. It wouldn't surprise me. I bet Pete's back in the UK now. I don't think he will ever settle down. It will have to be a strong woman to keep him in tow!

18. CHRISTMAS SURPRISES

It was almost two years since the Ark formed a community onboard. This was expanding: with the birth of Venus now aged fourteen months; Antonio, who decided to take up residency with Jane, and Zimbo who seemed to be more and more like a permanent resident as the days went by. Millie was about six months pregnant, with the baby due in early April, to the joy of everyone.

The children were growing up rapidly, with Vicky four, Stella five and Lucy nearly two. Melanie, almost seventeen, has become very friendly with Zimbo, although not fully kissing yet. They were all looking forward to Christmas which was almost upon them again and the excitement was even more so this year, because the children were that much older and wanting to know what Christmas was for, and who Father Christmas was. Greta had touched on the religious side slightly, more for general knowledge for them, than pressing religion into their minds at such an early age. They certainly liked the idea of Father Christmas and receiving presents. Vicky and Stella were looking forward to Christmas day, with toys in mind. They remembered getting the dolls and prams the previous year, but understood less of what it was all about then. Magnus and Patricia were going to be busy again, and the biggest problem was what to make them, with their limited resources.

Ched was due to go fishing with Gunter, hoping to catch a big tuna for the Christmas dinner, but Gunter was suffering with stomach cramps and said he'd give it a miss.
'You need to see Monty. He'll soon sort you out, Gunter, even though his remedy for everything is herbal tea!' Ched was a bit disappointed. Knowing Antonio would be too busy on the farm, he thought he'd ask Albert if it would be ok to take Zimbo, who seemed perfect for the job. Albert didn't have a problem with him going. When Ched found Zimbo to tell him, he was with Magnus as usual. Magnus was quite happy for him to go, and Zimbo was ecstatic.
'I must tell Melanie,' he said. 'I'll meet you at the hold to help get the boat out.' He went off to find Melanie who was with Greta in the nursery.
'Melanie, I'm going fishing with Ched!' he beamed. 'They are letting me go fishing.' Melanie's thoughts were only for his safety, and she seemed worried for him. 'You take care, and make sure you come back to me!'

Then she gave him his first passionate kiss, straight on the lips, and held him to her. She stood back from him and he was grinning from ear to ear.
'You bet I'll be back! See you later.'
'Bye, please be careful.' Zimbo was soon down to the hold where Magnus and Ched were lifting out the fishing boat ready for the trip. They were quickly aboard and lowered down to the sea within ten minutes; this had become a well-practised operation.

Ched was heading to an area nearer to the coast of Tristan De Cunha. Their time there last year, had been improved, because of Package Pete, who had arranged for them to fish closer to the island in the shallow waters, which enabled them to put down lobster pots. He promised he would make it an official permit and record it for their future visits, so even when Pete was not about, there should not be a problem. Ched and Gunter had been to the area a few days earlier to put down pots and Ched wanted to go there first, to pick them up. It was quite a way from the Ark and would take them at least an hour.
'I'm very happy *Mr Ched*,' said Zimbo.
'Stop calling everybody Mr before their name; it's not necessary.'
'Ok, *Mr Ched*, I mean Ched, right?'
'Why are you so happy? We are only going fishing.'
'Yes, I know but, but…'
'But what man? Spit it out?' Zimbo was obviously embarrassed.
'Melanie kissed me!' he finally spurted out.
'She what,'
'She kissed me. I'm so happy.'
'Cor! You are doing well.' Ched was thinking, bloody hell, this trip's going to be fun, the poor bastard's in love. Mind you, he's a lucky bastard!

Zimbo asked questions about the Ark. Ched explained how it all began, and why they were always moving from place to place. He went on to give the reason they had been attacked twice, with the possibility of another.
'Mr Albert, he is a very good man.' Zimbo said.
'Yes he is, but Zimbo, you are bloody well annoying me! How many times do we have to tell you? It is just Albert, *just Albert* and the sooner you remember that, the better for everyone. Let me tell you something else, if you always go around thinking you are the underdog, then people will treat you with less respect, but if you speak to people on their level, with politeness and always use that smile of yours, then people will respect you

193

more. You are lucky to be here, because they are all the best people on this planet.'

They got to the first pots and lifted them. They had rocks inside.
'Well that's a bit obvious Zimbo, looks like we're not wanted around here!' They collected all the pots and threw the rocks back in the sea, moving on to do some net fishing away from the coast. They went round in several circles, pulled in the net and it was disappointing: a few squid and menhaden, so they dropped the lines for tuna but nothing was biting. They tried the net again, going round and round, pulling it in, with nothing worth having.
'Right,' said Ched, 'this is the last time.' Ched thought to himself that the place was where he and Gunter had been many times and never failed to get a good catch, maybe Zimbo was a jinx bringing bad luck and then immediately contradicted his thought, no, that's old fisherman's talk.

'We'll put the line out for tuna, and if we don't get a bite, then it's back to the Ark in disgrace Zimbo.' Out went the line once more and they slowly pulled it along, keeping minimum engine sound but with the line taught. Then, there was a sharp tug, enough to make the engine groan, and slow the boat down. Ched was excited.
'We've got one Zimbo! I'll increase the revs so we don't stall the engine, then we'll give the tuna a little fight. The boat's speed increased and Ched winched the line in. The fish was pulling harder and Ched increased the power again, to compensate its pull.
'Oh ho ho, Zimbo, I think this is going to be a big tuna for Christmas.' Whatever it was, it was slowing the boat down even more, Ched just kept winching in the line and Zimbo was perched at the stern, looking to see the fish emerge from the water.
'Ched cut the line! It's a shark, a big one! Cut the line quick!' Ched had not faced a shark before. He ignored Zimbo's shouting, and went to see, but had left the winch pulling it into the boat. Then Ched saw it, picked up the axe and cut the line at the cable runner. With the pull of the shark gone, the boat shot forward with a leap, throwing Zimbo, who was balanced on the stern, into the water. Ched moved to the controls at full pelt, putting the accelerator to tick over, which automatically put the boat out of gear.

'Holy shit, that fucking thing will have the poor bastard!' Ched was panicking to see where Zimbo was, before he could throw the man-

194

overboard marker buoy and line to him. Away it went, as hard as Ched could hurl it. Rather than go around in a circle and lose sight of him, he went into reverse at a very slow pace. Zimbo moved as if he was swimming for the Olympics. Ched couldn't see any signs of the shark but was sure it could smell Zimbo. He had managed to get hold of the buoy and Ched put the rope around the fishing net capstan to pull him to the boat. As Zimbo was holding to it for dear life, Ched knocked the accelerator lever into tickover again, while he went to help Zimbo back onboard. Zimbo had just taken hold of the rope on the side rails when Ched's right hand grabbed his trousers and hoicked him out of the water, and his legs followed. A crash of the sharks chin whacked the stern, the pair of them moved to the front of the boat without knowing how, as if they had coiled springs in their shoes. They now knew the colour of adrenaline! They came to their senses.

'What did you do that for?' Ched shouted at Zimbo. 'I thought you were a hardened fisherman. They don't fall in the water!'

'You didn't listen to me when I said it was a big shark. If you had listened to me, I wouldn't have had that thing snapping at my heels!' Zimbo angrily retaliated.

Ched realised he was wrong, and sat down without saying a thing, his hands on his head, looking at the deck boards, and thinking of the consequences if that shark had got hold of Zimbo. It would have ripped him apart, and if he had gone back without him, Melanie would have cut him into tiny pieces. He stood up and faced Zimbo.

'I'm sorry. I'm so glad you are back here in one piece. He put an arm on Zimbo's shoulder and again, almost in tears said, 'I'm so sorry. Let's start again.'

'No problem Mr Ched, oh, I mean, Ched. We need to fish a long way from here; the fish know when the sharks are about and that's why we haven't had much luck.'

Ched pushed the accelerator lever forward and the boat rapidly picked up speed, distancing them far from that dangerous area. They headed to a place Ched had not tried before. He had seen it on the chart, back on the Ark's bridge and according to Gunter's GPS gadget he borrowed, the spot was 38°5, latitude and 9°9, longitude, where the depth showed a mountainous peak at eight hundred metres. It looked a likely fish habitat. Zimbo picked up the severed fishing line Ched had cut, and repaired it ready for another attempt to catch some tuna. They noted that the shark was still near them for a while, but then disappeared. Ched was worried it would be like a film he saw once, when a massive shark cut a boat in half with its jaws. He had the jitters just thinking about it. It all ran through his mind, how poor Zimbo always seemed to get the worst end of things, from the attack in the hurricane, then diving to save Stella and now being fancied by a shark! Wait 'til Albert hears about this!

They had travelled about five more miles, put out the line and just dragged it about steadily. Ten minutes later, they had a bite and pulled in two small tuna. The line went out again, and no sooner was it fully extended, when they felt a big jar on the boat again. Ched was dreading an action replay of the shark episode, and rushed to the rear of the boat where Zimbo looked to see what the catch was. This time he asked Zimbo.
'It's ok; it's tuna and a big one!' Ched was relieved. He started the capstan winch to pull in the tuna and, as it got closer to the boat, it gave a good fight. They got it onboard between them and then Zimbo dealt with it so quickly, Ched didn't get a look in.
'Well that's the biggest I've caught,' Ched said proudly. Their eyes met, 'That *we* have caught,' he corrected and they both smiled.
'This will give your future mother in law a shock Zimbo.'
'My mother in law, am I going to be married to Melanie?' Ched panicked. He only meant it as a joke.
'No. No. Zimbo I was just joking.' Ched was backtracking as fast as he could, thinking to himself, oh shit now what have I done?
'It doesn't mean anything Zimbo; it's just an old English saying.'
'Oh,' said Zimbo, visibly disappointed 'I would like to marry Melanie. Do you think she would marry me, Ched?'
'I don't know. It's up to you to ask her anyway.' A confused Zimbo sat down next to the tuna. Ched looked at the two of them, Zimbo and the dead fish, and had a job to decide which looked the saddest. Then he cursed himself, and wondered why he doesn't keep his own big mouth shut.

They moved on, and then put out the nets, as they headed towards the Ark, not expecting to catch much. They weren't that bothered, but they pulled a mixture of fish, some suitable to eat, the rest for oil and fertiliser. They had had enough for one day and were looking forward to being back on the Ark, their home. When they got back onboard, they had to carry the tuna between them, it was so heavy. Magnus returned the boat to the hold for his

inspection, to note any maintenance required before the next trip. Ched and Zimbo walked proudly into the kitchen with the huge tuna aloft.
'That's no good. It won't fit into the oven!' Patricia said.
'Don't worry. I'll sort it out into steaks for you to charcoal grill. Albert enlightened her. 'And well done lads!' It was the biggest tuna they had ever seen onboard. Zimbo's clothes had dried in the heat of the sun and did not show any signs of his ordeal. He did not want to go on about it to Melanie, thinking that if he did explain the peril he'd been in, she would persuade Albert not to let him go fishing again, the thing he really loved doing. But, typically, the fisherman's tale was already out, and the shark got bigger after every pint of bitter Ched consumed, and ended up nearer the film version than reality. Zimbo's explanation to Melanie was that it was a baby one, more frightened of him. But she was so pleased to see him back and she showed it, and made full use of his lips. He was amazed by her affection. They became almost inseparable: apart from work and sleep, they were always together. When it came to goodnight, it was a kiss, 'goodnight', and no hanky panky, the way it should be for virgins at this stage of their relationship, according to Melanie.

With a few days left until Christmas, it was an exciting time for them, getting the best of all they had produced together, ready for Christmas day. The coastguard was in sight again. Albert said they were probably calling to book their Christmas or Boxing Day dinner, but decided it would be better to keep Zimbo out of sight, because he had no documents, and the less questions asked, the better. Ched remembered about the rocks in the lobster pots and explained to Albert, asking if he could get them to do something about it, in return for the hospitality.
'I'll have a go, but it won't be Package Pete this time. He will have retired by now.' Just then, the coastguard's siren went off:
'Whoop! whoop!'
'Well at least it sounds friendly.' Albert said as he, Ched and Gunter set off to the deck access gate, to welcome them aboard. The boarding steps were lowered down the side of the Ark for the visitors to climb. The first up was the Captain, quickly followed by his two ratings, all had side arms.

'Welcome to the Ark, Captain.' Albert shook the man's hand and introduced himself, Ched and Gunter.
'Captain Matthew Nutter; pleased to meet you.' He did not acknowledge the ratings, which Albert thought was arrogant and who does he think he

197

is? He's only a coast guard, for goodness sake. The officer stood tall but he was quite thin with a very pale complexion and on removing his hat showed short, dark hair. His age would be about thirty five. Albert immediately asked after his old friend Peter Dunhill. The officer confirmed that he had retired and was back in the UK. He then handed Albert a letter.

'This was left in the postal out tray, with a note attached to deliver it to the Ark the next time she visited. We have been meaning to come to see you before, but we have a problem on the west side of the islands with illegal fishing that keeps us very busy.' Albert thanked him for the letter, folded it and put it in his pocket to read later. He offered him and his company some refreshments.

'That would be very decent of you, but my men would like to have a look around the ship.'

'No problem. They can carry on. I'll get Ched and Gunter to go with them.'

'Oh, there's no need.'

'But I insist, for their own safety, the billygoat doesn't like strangers and the bees are a little temperamental this time of year.' Ched and Gunter tried to keep a straight face as Albert delivered this codswallop. The ratings seemed glad to be accompanied by their bodyguards and left the scene. Albert escorted the Captain to the canteen.

'Were you looking for anything in particular on the Ark?' This threw Captain Nutter.

'Oh, I just need to confirm that all is as reported by Captain Peter Dunhill, my predecessor.' Albert reflected that perhaps Nutter thought Pete bent the rules because he was a mate, but this red neck wouldn't have a clue about all the shit we'd been through together Albert thought, and managed to contain himself.

They entered the canteen and Amy and Patricia were waiting in anticipation. Albert introduced them to the Captain before asking what he would like to drink.

'Have you any spirits?'

'Yes, but it's our own blend of Irish moonshine, poteen.'

'That sounds interesting. I'll have a glass, if I may. I'm of Irish extraction myself, you know.' Albert, who was in a very crabby mood, thought, not in your piddling brain you are not, time for some fun, lets see what this tosser is made of. He showed the man to a seat and went to the bar to get the drinks, asking his wife for two glasses of *Flash*, winking at her and saying very quietly, to dilute his own with half water. He returned to his guest, glasses in hand, passed one to the Captain and immediately made a toast. 'Here's to your health and hope you visit us many times in the future to enjoy our hospitality.'

'Cheers.' the Captain replied. The *Flash* had the usual effect on its victim. 'Jesus!' slipped out, as the Captain felt the burning sensation as it trickled down his throat. 'Whoa!' He finished the remainder of his glass with one gulp. Then, to Albert's amazement, Matthew Nutter seemed impressed.

'Ah, that's some good stuff. I'll have another if you please. Do you mind?'

'Not at all, have as many as you like!' Albert asked Amy for the same again. Amy looked at Albert with a disconcerted frown, refilled the glasses and returned to the table to repeat the process.

'Sorry Albert, for the inspection my men are carrying out at the moment,' the Captain apologised as he sipped his new drink slowly. Albert realised the drink was working as they had got to first name terms.

'But I have a report to do on every ship in the area, even outside the fishing limit,' Matthew explained. 'I looked at last year's report, and found it hard to believe that anything like this could exist. How long have you been at sea?'

'Let me see now, it will be two years next April, and that's when we leave here to go north to spend the summer there.' The Captain continued to sip his drink with Albert and asked about the ecosystems that the Ark relied on. Albert began to explain about some of the devices for collecting energy. As the Captain finished his drink, he started to nod off.

Albert looked across at Amy and put a finger to his lips for hush. Both of them disappeared to the kitchen, out of the way. They looked in on Nutter after a few minutes.

'He's giving it some serious Z's, Amy, with his head on the table.' Albert was well aware of the situation, and just let it happen, not wanting to disturb him. He sat there for the next twenty minutes or more, listening to his guest snore his head off.

Albert could hear voices outside the canteen and thought he ought to wake the Captain before an embarrassment occurred, thinking the inspection hadn't taken long. Albert woke the Captain before the ratings entered the room. They looked at him and stood to attention, awaiting his orders.

'Everything seems in order, Albert. Thank you for the drink.' He tried to stand but his legs were frozen. His men saw his predicament and went to his aid, helping him to his feet.

'Oh dear, I seem to have sat down too long and got stiff in my legs.' No more was said as he was helped out of the canteen and down to the deck, to make the exit from the Ark, to their ship. As they came to the gate, the Captain turned to Albert thanking him for the drink again and said that it would be good if a visit could be made in an unofficial capacity. Albert decided to invite them.

'You are most welcome on Boxing day, if you can fit it into your busy schedule. There will be a buffet and we'll make sure there will be plenty of drink ready for you all.' Albert thought that was probably a bit facetious because he didn't really want them there.

'Thank you Albert. We would be delighted, hey chaps?' he slurred.

'Yes sir,' was their straight-faced reply. The Captain made his way steadily down the ladder with a rating before him and another very close behind.

'Oh look Albert,' said Ched 'he's sandwiched between two ratings!'

The coastguard vessel was heading back and out of sight as Albert and the lads turned and walked back to the canteen.

'What happened there, he looked out for the count. You haven't been giving him a drop of *Flash* have you?' Ched asked.

'Of course, just a couple of glasses,'

'Two!' repeated Ched in amazement, 'No wonder he couldn't get up and struggled to get to the exit gate!'

'At least I had a peaceful twenty minutes or so. How did you two get on?'

'No problem at all, was it Gunter? All they asked was about the women onboard and was there any spare? We told them that they were all married or with partners. But I did mention that we had a bit of a do for the coastguards last Boxing Day and that everyone enjoyed it. As for the Ark, they didn't seem interested in anything much at all. I even offered to introduce them to the billygoat but they said they weren't into goats!' Albert chuckled.

'What was the Captain like?' Gunter asked.

'I don't really know, he was asleep most of the time!'

'Did you mention about the lobster pots?' asked Ched.

'No, it will be better to save it for when, and if, they turn up on Boxing Day.'

They finally arrived back at the canteen and Albert informed Patricia and Amy of the high chance of Boxing Day guests. Then, taking advantage of time on his own, he sat down at a table, where he pulled the envelope from his pocket and opened it. The letter read:

Dear Albert,

Just thought I would drop you a line because I know you will be back safe and sound, you are one of life's great survivors and I admire what you have achieved in the 'Ark'. I hope you didn't have to use the little present I managed to get for you but it's nice to know it's there if required. I'll be back in the UK by the time you get this, where I'm looking for a young woman that will put up with me and then I'm going to find you, so please make up another room because I will find you, I cannot see me settling down in Civvy Street, so goodbye for now.
All the best. Pete.

* * * * *

The quality of Albert and Jane's brewing and winemaking had improved even more, mainly because Jane took the trouble to study the subject and look up the problems they were having, using the comprehensive library that Albert and Amy had put together, when stocking the ship. The Christmas meal was organised for a full sit down banquet, and would be ready for 1500 hours. Prior to that, a drink and wine tasting from the various produce grown on the Ark, would take place. There was the favourite light, quaffing raspberry wine, a red grape, a white grape, apple wine, a cherry liqueur, a plum wine and Albert's bitter. Soft drinks were real lemonade, fresh orange juice and a mixed fruit milkshake, which the children loved. With everybody in the canteen and the wine tasting just about to begin, Jane wanted to make an announcement. Holding Antonio's hand, she called for hush.

'I'm pregnant everybody!' she shouted out, with a big smile across her face. The news was welcomed by a round of applause. Millie thought to herself, *that bastard Antonio!*

Once the clapping had finished, it was the start of the drink tasting. Millie and Jane refrained from alcohol, because of their condition, hoping to give the best chance to the children developing inside them. Greta went for the cherry liqueur; Gunter stuck to the bitter saying it was the best he had tasted in two years and Ched drank the same. Magnus decided on a beer shandy, persuaded by a look from Patricia. Monty preferred soft drinks, saying alcohol could damage his liver! That statement raised a few eyebrows considering the other abuse he did to his body! Marigold, Patricia and Amy liked the raspberry wine, Albert and Antonio thought the red grape was palatable. Melanie preferred the white wine mixed with lemonade. Zimbo tried his first pint of bitter, under the watchful eye of Melanie. Like mother, like daughter! Albert thought. Patricia asked everyone to be seated, ready for their second Christmas dinner on the Ark. Amy and Melanie assisted in the dishing up.

No one touched the food until the last plate was in place, which was Zimbo's, served by Melanie. It was almost like a pecking order, and even Stella and Vicky had the manners to wait. *The old man*, as Ched had started to call him, was urged to give a toast. Albert stood up quickly and gave a brief message.
'Here is to us all, long may we continue to enjoy our lives together. Merry Christmas everyone,'
'Merry Christmas!' was returned to Albert and to one another. The feast was very soon in full flow. Initially, all that was heard was the clashing of knives and forks on the plates as the community gorged in the fruits of their toil. How mellow the meal made everyone feel, knowing that they had at last become self-sufficient. They ate, drank, talked and laughed. Melanie played some classical guitar, followed by Greta on the piano which resembled marching music. Not a cross word or upset between them. In addition, no secrets were divulged and a few could have easily slipped out!

Anticipation of the next day came into conversation and it was agreed that it would be a very diplomatic occasion, purely to maintain a good relationship with the coastguard. With the ratings comments about 'spare women' in mind, the females were asked to play down the socialising, so as not to give the slightest impression of any promiscuity.

'Not that any of you would dream of doing that sort of thing,' Albert assured them, 'but with alcohol in those brains, just a look could give the wrong idea'. Albert made a mental note to water down the *Flash* spirit, rather than refuse the consumption of it.

'To be truthful,' he continued, 'entertaining these outsiders goes against the grain of the independent lifestyle our Ark community is trying to follow. We want to return to this area each year and live a peaceful existence without external interference, so we just have to be diplomatic to the dipstick coastguard and concede to his authority. The only alternative would be to move further away, but then we may encounter other problems, which could be worse.' Others nodded in agreement.

The Christmas banquet was at its end and the tables were cleared.
'I don't know about you Albert, but I'm absolutely pogged!' Ched blurted out.
'Pogged?' repeated Albert, 'what sort of language is that?'
'Oh, it's Yorkshire. Haven't you heard that expression before?' He looked to his fellow Yorkshire-woman Marigold.
'Yes, there are some strange words in Yorkshire, another one is, *druffen*. Albert laughed, and asked Marigold what it meant.
'It means drunk.'
'*Ee I wi druffen lest neet*', she continued in a broad Yorkshire accent They all joined in and laughed at the colloquial words and phrases. More drinks were consumed and then the families said their goodnights and finally it was just Albert and Amy left.
'What a wonderful day,' said Amy.
'Yes Albert replied, I wonder how many years it will go on. As long as the Ark's hull lasts, I suppose.'
'Come on lets go to bed Albert.'

The coastguard vessel arrived at 1300 hours the next day and the guests were soon onboard and heading for the canteen. On their way there, the Captain explained to Albert that they could only stay for a couple of hours, because there had been a lot of activity on the west side of the islands and they needed to be in that area, on watch, which was a relief to Albert.
'Oh, that's a shame. I hope you lads will be able to get through the mountain of food we have prepared for you'.

203

'I see what you mean,' said the Captain as they entered the canteen. 'Yes it certainly is a shame, come on lads. Let's get stuck in!' Ched asked the men what they would like to drink, 'Bitter' came the replies. Typical, thought Albert, now that he'd watered down the *Flash*. Ched delivered the drinks on a tray for them, they were soon guzzled down and the order was repeated. The women discreetly joined in the party. The children were allowed to be as disruptive as they liked, being told it was a *'free from being good day'*. Stella and Vicky soon put it to the test. Some of the guests' drinks found their way to the floor and Ched was very slow to replace them. After the meal, they decided to stand at the bar away from the children. They managed another couple of pints and the Captain prepared to leave.

'Unfortunately time has come for us to go Albert.' Albert decided to raise the subject of the lobster pots. To Albert's surprise, he was very obliging and said he would deal with the matter and that if it happened again, to let him know on his next visit. Then Captain Nutter addressed the community.

'Thank you all for your hospitality, we have enjoyed it immensely, haven't we lads?' 'Yes sir,' was the reply. The guests and the community slowly ambled from the canteen to the exit gate to board their vessel. They said goodbye and thanked everyone again as they left the Ark.

ALBERT'S PRIVATE LOG- Dec 2017 – Jan 2018

What wonderful news to hear Jane is pregnant! Lucky Antonio! I'm sure he will be a good father and look after them.

In a way, I'm glad the Christmas celebrations are over. All that food and drink, it's just too much! It takes days to work off the excess, especially for an *old git* like me!

I hope the Captain will stick to his word and sort out the lobster pot problem with the local fishermen. We'll probably be back here next year. I wonder if Nutter will still be on duty.

From what Ched has been saying, Zimbo was lucky to survive a shark snapping at his heels. I can't be sure how big it was; the size varied depending on who told the story. Zimbo seems to have settled into things. Perhaps it was like he said that if he did go back to face the music, I don't imagine the law would be very kind to him there.

Magnus and Patricia have been real gems when it came to providing Christmas toys for the children. We now have a pet sheep that trails behind Vicky on wheels and a pig on wheels for Stella. (Greta didn't look particularly impressed, but had the grace to keep her mouth shut). Lucy had a doll and pram, so that sorted that for another year.

19. MONTY'S MUSHROOMS

It was January 2018, half way through the summer in the southern hemisphere and the rain had been continuous for over two weeks, which was good for the grass and the crops; they had never been so lush. Then it stopped and changed to constant daily sunshine with azure blue skies and occasional feathery, fair weather clouds, which gave everything on the Ark a boost.

Monty was in the herb garden, doing his usual pottering about: sorting out various bits from the herbs to make mainly everyday things, like teas, compounds and so on. He thought he would take a wander to look in the orchard, knowing that the ground was warm and moist, ideal conditions for mushroom growing, which had not been achieved so far, for some reason. Mushroom spores were left off the seed list when the stocking of the ship took place, but now, with the animals occasionally grazing there, and the present conditions, there was a good chance for mushrooms to grow. He was spot on with this assumption, and found, not just one variety but several. Some were growing from the stump of a diseased tree that had to be cut down. Monty was excited, and decided to go back to his laboratory to check up on the different types he had discovered in his reference library.

He noticed that one sort was very similar to those he dabbled with in his younger days. It had a brightly coloured orange cap, with white scaly warts on it and stood up like those ornamental toadstools with a figure of a gnome next to them. He used to find them in open woods in the early summer, knick-named the *magic* mushroom, which could make you hallucinate, and even seriously freak out. He was thinking it was about time he had a relaxation session, seeing that Albert has starved him of his other pleasures. He got back to his books as fast as he could to check out his find, and sure enough, the variety that he was excited about was the Fly Agaric. The others were Chanterelles, the Pore and Cep mushroom, all edible and the kitchen staff should be delighted. Monty hot-footed it back to the orchard. He thought this was energetic: the length of the ship four times in one day, but considered the ultimate reward should be worth it. He had to act quickly, before Millie anybody else spotted the fungi, also there was a chance of insects getting in, spoiling his find. Off he went, with labelled paper bags from his stationery store, to keep the crop separate from each other. He picked all the mushrooms he could find, it was quite a weight, and he struggled carrying them back to his cabin where he dropped off his secret prize. Then, on to the kitchen, to give the others to Patricia and Amy, who were delighted and thanked Monty for his thoughtfulness.

'This will give the cooking a different dimension.' said Amy, 'It's ages since I've eaten fresh mushrooms. We'll put these on the menu tonight.' Amy asked Monty why had they not appeared before and what type they were. Monty explained that the spores were probably dormant in the soil and the conditions had not been good enough. With the animals making use of the orchard, the recent rain and then the heat, the conditions were perfect for mushrooms, pointing out the Chanterelles and the nutty taste they had. 'Oh you are clever knowing all these things!' said Patricia. He made a quick exit to his cabin, to wash and dry out all but one large mushroom to store them for future use, thinking that he would try the other that night, in his cabin. Long may they continue to grow, he hoped.

At a very late hour, he took the mushroom, sliced and diced it and fried it gently in a drop of olive oil on his small two ring electric hob. A few minutes later, he dished up the delicacy and started to eat, mopping up the juices with some bread. After cleaning the dish, he went to lie down to wait for his cocktail to work. Within minutes, he dozed off and started to dream...

He could hear the roar as they waited for him to appear on stage, with all the spotlights beaming down into a massive stadium.

'We want Freddy, we want Freddy!' The crowd were chanting. This continued, until every stage light went out for a few seconds and then back on, as the band struck up the music, with the lead guitarist's well-known opening melody. And he was there, Freddy Mercury. The late, great Freddy Mercury! Wait a minute it's me! I'm him, on stage, it's me, and the crowd are screaming for me, they think I'm Freddy. Brian is looking at me, waiting for me to start singing. I start, my voice is his, my clothes are his, it's me, and I'm Freddy! I'll show them. He sang the same beautiful, perfect pitch of notes, as Freddy used to. I don't believe this, I'm strutting the stage just like Freddy, the crowd is going mad with excitement just like I did in the eighties when I went to see the band live; perhaps its reincarnation? I've brought him back to life. Look at the crowds. They are going mad with excitement. I must be him! I've finished the first song, the audience is fantastic, and they are applauding me.

Brian's given me a nod to begin the next song, the crowd are ecstatic, I can't believe it; I'm singing his notes perfectly. I must be dreaming, I'll pinch myself to check. Ouch! Yes, it's me. I'm not dreaming and the crowd didn't notice me pinching myself, so it must be true. I'm him. I'm blessed. And it's all so vivid, the colours, and the faces of the audience. It's real, I'm him, one of my heroes; I always knew I would be famous. Freddy lives on in me. It's the way life should be. Good, famous people should never die. The show must go on. Oh, that's my next song, Brian's looking at me again, the show must go on, the show must go on............

Some hours later, Monty was gazing at the ceiling above his bed believing he had made a real connection with Freddy, that he lived on in him. He lay there, just thinking about the gig he did last night. It was me. I've made a breakthrough, it must be the power of the Ark creating the correct circumstances that makes things right. I've noticed how everything is easy to grow. Millie doesn't have to do much, and it all just pops out of the ground. Well I've got a secret about something else that just pops out of the ground. Again, the dream filled his head. I was Freddy last night, I know it's true. I was there.

In eating the magical meal, Monty believed he had found his niche, to become the famous singer and the thoughts continued in his head: It's altered me. It's my metamorphosis. It's so different than I've ever felt. I don't feel sick or have any other side effects like when I tried them out in my Uni days. Then, I always felt sick afterwards and the hallucinations were mild in comparison but they would give a pleasant cannabis effect of relaxation. I know, today, I'll try to be like all the rest and go and have breakfast. Then I'll go up to see if any more of my precious little beauties have arrived in the orchard.

Monty was off to the canteen for breakfast; not something he normally did. There were lots of acknowledgements, "good morning Monty", as everybody there was so surprised to see him. Ched greeted him with one of his usual wisecracks.

'Morning Monty, it's about time you had something to eat, might see you again in two years time, then?'

'Good morning Monty, nice to see you at meal times, perhaps you would have the time to join us for dinner this evening?' Albert added sarcastically. Then, Patricia greeted him.

'Good morning Monty, would you like some bacon and eggs? The bacon isn't fatty at all. That Antonio is doing a fantastic job with the animals. He seems to be good at whatever he puts his hand to.' Millie overheard and smiled. 'And just look at these eggs, you couldn't buy eggs like these. And thank you for those mushrooms yesterday. They were fantastic, weren't they Ched?' who was still waiting in line.

'Mushrooms,' said Ched 'did you find them Monty?'

'Um yes,'

'Any *special* ones Monty?' Ched asked, always suspecting Monty was up to no good.

'No, you wouldn't find that sort of thing out here.'

'What do you mean *special ones*?' Patricia cut in innocently, 'the ones we had last night were very special, they were the first we have grown on the Ark, weren't they Monty?'

'Err, yes… Can I have a cheese roll and some orange juice and I'll be off? I need to get up to the mushrooms early to get them fresh. If there are any, I'll bring them down to you straight away, Patricia.'

'Well, hopefully there will be enough to make some nice cream of mushroom soup,' Amy added.

Ched walked away, smiling to himself thinking, the crafty old devil! He's found something special, alright. Meanwhile, Monty was panicking and mumbling under his breath.

'Ched's sussed me, Damn it! I know he has.' Monty drank his orange juice and walked out, cheese roll in hand.

'That bloke is a waste of space!' Ched, in his usual mode of ignorance, said to no one in particular. As Monty left, Marigold and Lucy were on their way into the canteen to have breakfast and Monty didn't even acknowledge them. He was more concerned in getting to his mushrooms before anybody else did. Ched noticed this, as Marigold turned her head to look at Monty and he saw the lack of response. She went over to Ched, who was tucking into his bacon and eggs.

'Did you see that!' she said to him. 'He totally ignored both of us. Can you just hold Lucy, while I get our breakfast please?'

'Hello Uncle Ched!' Little Lucy got up onto his lap. A red-faced Ched looked around to see who was watching: everyone! He concentrated on holding Lucy.

'Hello Lucy, and how old are you now?' She was a very quick and bright child.

'I'm two,' and put up two fingers to show him.

'Yes, well, mummy won't be long... I hope!' and looked hungrily at his rapidly congealing breakfast, wanting to get stuck in. Marigold was soon back with their food and retrieved Lucy from the thankful Ched. He polished off his plateful as quickly as he could and got up to leave.

'I'm out fishing today, with Zimbo. I'll see you *later*.' She looked at him, and winked as a signal, that it really would be ok for him to see her later.

'See you all later' he said to the rest in the canteen, and off he went, planning just a short fishing trip, to get back to Marigold in time whilst Lucy was still in nursery.

Monty had just arrived at the orchard and was looking about to see if Millie or Antonio were there. Millie only visited the animals in the mornings since she was getting so big with the baby and finding it difficult to work as many long hours. The coast was clear, so he started to hunt for *his* mushrooms first, and there were a few more, but not as many as the previous day's find. He quickly put them in a bag, and walked for about twenty yards and remembered he ought to look for some of the others for the kitchen. So, he went back, and there were dozens of them. He got busy, picked as many as he could carry and made his way back to his cabin and then to the kitchen, as he had done the previous day.

That night, when all was quiet, he thought he would have another session at being Freddy. Instead of just one big one, he sliced and diced up several mushrooms, fried them in olive oil, and ate them on their own because he forgot to get some bread from Patricia. He finished the lot and went to lie down again afterwards to let the power of the fungi change him into Freddy again. He slowly drifted off into a deep sleep, and then the vivid dream started, only he wasn't Freddy this time. He was sitting at a desk in the newspaper office of *The Daily Planet* and he was dressed like Clark Kent. I'm Clark Kent. That means I'm Superman!

Well, Freddy was soon forgotten. There must be some trouble somewhere and they need me to save somebody. Yes, I can hear somebody shouting for help. I'll use my X-ray vision to see where they are. It's a young girl trapped on top of a burning building! I must fly to save her. He rises from his desk and tells his curvy assistant, that he's just got to pop out and shan't be long. He quickly exits the room, runs along the corridor to the outside door then to the edge of the building, removing his clothes on the way. In his red and blue tunic, he climbs the parapet wall, stands on the top and he leaps into the air flying off to save the poor girl from the burning building....... He's gone.

The next morning at breakfast, Patricia was waiting for Monty to come in, so that she could ask him if he was going collect any more mushrooms.
'No sign of Monty yet,' she said to Amy, in earshot of Ched.
'That cheese roll he had yesterday, will last him a month. I don't know how he manages to survive on what he eats!' he commented. Everybody had their breakfast, but still no sign of Monty.
'I'm going up to the orchard to see where he's been getting the mushrooms from,' Amy told Patricia, 'because if there are any more to pick, they want collecting early. Monty must have slept in. I'll pick some herbs as well, while I'm up there.' Amy found her trug, and set off. Antonio was just about to let the pigs out into the orchard and she asked him to wait a few minutes, while she looked for mushrooms.
'That's ok Amy; I'll give you a hand.' They wandered about gradually filling her trug. Amy came across an orange-capped one, and went to pick it.
'Not that type Amy,' Antonio warned her. 'It's very bad for you. I used to go with my father picking mushrooms back home, and he told me all about how to recognise the right ones to pick, and I know that one is very bad for you.'
'Oh, that's why Monty never picked them for us. He must have known.'
They finished and Amy left the orchard for the pigs to forage about, thanking Antonio for his help.
'See you later.'
'Sure Amy, bye.'

Amy walked back to the herb garden for a few kitchen herbs. Soon after, she asked Patricia if Monty had shown his face, but there had still been no sign of him. Amy looked at the clock and because it was so late, knocked on his cabin door.

'Monty are you up? ... Monty,' she called out. Still no answer, so she went in; the door was ajar anyway. As she looked around, she thought to herself, what a tip it was with his clothes strewn on the floor and unwashed cooking utensils and plates on the table. She looked in the bedroom and shower. He was nowhere to be seen and then on the hob in his small kitchenette, she spied a frying pan and by its side a paper bag, the type he collected the mushrooms in. There in the bag was the same type of mushroom, as the ones that Antonio said not to pick. Realising there was a problem she rushed to find Albert who was in the brewery with Jane.

'Albert, I think we've got trouble with Monty again. He's nowhere to be seen and he's been cooking some strange mushrooms in his room.' Albert immediately stopped what he was doing.

'We'd better find him,' he said. 'I'll call everyone to go and seek him out.'

They all looked and called for him, but to no avail. This continued for the remainder of the day, until they were exhausted. Everyone met later in the canteen and discussed where each person had checked, to make sure everywhere was covered. Ched was first to voice what was on one or two other minds.

'If those are the type of mushrooms I think they are, he would have been hallucinating, so he could even be in the sea, and if the sharks are in the area he won't have a chance!' At that point, they dispersed, looking very glum and thinking the worst.... Monty was never seen again.

ALBERT'S LOG – January – March 2018

Monty's disappearance was a big shock to me. From the evidence he left behind it was obvious he had been consuming a type of mushroom or toadstool that had hallucinatory effects, and he must have somehow ended up over the side of the Ark. He was nowhere to be found, not even any remains to bury in the orchard to help the apple trees on. Perhaps I was a bit naive in thinking that a lifelong hippie would change. At least we tried to help him. What a waste of a life. Why couldn't he just make something good from his knowledge of herbal remedies? I mustn't forget he did make some positive contribution to the wellbeing of the community, after all. It was strange that no one, not even Marigold, requested any words to be said for his loss, not even a minute's silence, in respect. I just hope between Jane and Amy, they will be able to pick up the necessary know how, to continue being able to provide some sort of help when illness or an accident happens.

What's next on the calendar? I thought getting out of the rat-race would slow the pace of life but time seems to pass too quickly down here. It won't be long and we move north again. We should have had Millie's arrival before then, the baby is due at the beginning of April; that will give Ched something to do other than fishing, that's the only time he does some work! Goodness knows how he spends the rest of his time. Before we move the Ark, there's some painting to do. I'll check with Magnus, I'm sure there are some blisters forming on the sails. That will keep Ched busy!

We have been growing cotton for two seasons now, picking the crop and storing it for the future. We must do an inventory of our paper stock, mainly toilet paper, also the ladies' sanitary towels; hopefully the cotton will be a satisfactory substitute. I only hope we can grow enough for when we have to rely on it fully. After all, the nomads in the deserts of the world manage; so will we!

20. MILLIE'S PISSED OFF

They had only two more weeks left down in the south Atlantic, before leaving to go north for the summer. It was still undecided where to go, somewhere they would not be intruded upon. Albert had been on a walk to survey the estate; he did this quite often of late. He was like a gentleman farmer with his walking stick, poking at things in the ground as he went up through the fields, round the orchard, inspecting the animals and back down again. He thought to himself on his way back, that he should have introduced a couple of rabbits to the land, and imagined how he would have quite enjoyed bagging a few with a shotgun, on a Sunday morning. As he got nearer the upper decks, his next thought was a couple of pints before dinner. A call on the short wave jolted him from his daydreaming.

'Millie's gone into labour and Ched isn't answering his short wave radio. She keeps asking for him,' Jane bleated out, in a stressed, staccato voice.

'Right,' replied Albert, 'I'll see if I can find him and I'll be there as quickly as I can.' Albert hurried through the corridors and up the many steel staircases to the living quarters of the vessel. As he climbed the final stair, his footsteps echoing around him, he opened the door to the canteen expecting to see Ched at the bar with his head in a glass of beer. There was no sign of him. Albert thought it strange, because he was usually there at that time of day. He was not prepared to chase around the ship looking for him for too long. If he wasn't responding to his radio, it meant he did not want to be disturbed. And in Albert's experience, it was best not to pry.

Oblivious to everything else, Ched was stuck between Marigold's legs in her cosy bed, and she didn't want to let him go. Meanwhile, Albert was out of breath as he completed the final strides to Ched and Millie's cabin, which was at the rear of the ship's living quarters. He opened the heavy fire door and as it opened wider, he could hear the pained screams of Millie, deeply in labour, about to produce her second child, her first onboard the Ark. Albert entered through the open living room door to the bedroom. Jane, who was reluctantly acting as midwife, was crouched over Millie, mopping the sweat from Millie's forehead.

'Come on, Millie, hang on in there. It must be soon,' Jane reassured her. Amy was at hand. She had prepared everything much earlier on, feeling that better too early and safe, than scrabbling about in a panic for things too late. Jane acknowledged Albert as he came closer to the scene, by a pissed-off glare and grunt. Amy took over from her at Millie's bedside, ordered Albert to scrub his hands, and Jane went over to him.

'Why was I picked for this job?' growled Jane.

'You weren't picked, if you remember, you more or less inflicted it on yourself, because you took an interest in biology and the wellbeing of all of us onboard,' replied Albert.

'Well I didn't expect this shit!'

'Look on the bright side Jane, it will be you laying there in a few months and you will be dishing out the orders to whoever is playing midwife at the time. What stage is she?'

'Millie's waters, or amniotic fluid, as my self-taught biology lessons showed me,' Jane was being sarcastic now, 'burst some time ago. The contractions have been strengthening at a rapid pace.'

'Ched, Ched, *CH-E-E-E-ED*. Oh my god, where the fucking hell is that bastard?' Millie cried out.

'Come on Millie, Push! Push, you slack cow!' Jane wanted the ordeal to end. Her tone and comments angered Millie even more and she flew back at Jane.

'Don't you talk to me about being slack, what do you bloody-well know about it?' she spat out through gritted teeth. This had the effect of making Millie push even harder.

'She's been shouting for Ched and swearing like I've not heard from her before.' Jane told Albert.

'I've looked for him in the usual places and he wasn't there. He must be getting his head down somewhere, because he's not answering the radio. (Little did Albert know how near the truth it was) Don't worry she'll forget it all when it's over.'

'I fucking well won't!' shouted Millie. 'Where is that bastard, I'll pull his fucking balls off!'

'That's probably why he's not here!' exclaimed Albert.

'Aagh, Aagh, Aagh….Aagh, Aagh, Aagh'

'That's it Millie. Push… push… push!'

'I can see the head! Look, the head!' Albert was getting excited.

'You're not supposed to be looking, turn your head away at once!' Amy said to Albert.

'I want to see what it is,' he replied.

'We'll tell you when it arrives. Just let us get on with it!' Disappointed, Albert turned away.

215

The baby's head was coated in a glossy substance, making its dark hair look as if was plastered with too much Brylcream. Its eyelids were squeezed together within the wrinkly skin of its face. As the head cleared, Jane took hold of the baby to assist in its delivery into the world. The final stage of the birth was taking place. Albert couldn't resist having a peep. He was not normally squeamish, but he felt queasy. He took a deep breath and looked at the scene again.

'It's not breathing!' Jane shouted to Albert. 'What shall I do?'

'Give it here; you sort the umbilical cord out,' Albert commanded calmly, in his soft, low toned, mature voice. Amy was concentrating on Millie, mopping her brow, trying to bring her round as she had passed out. Albert lifted the baby quickly by the ankles, still covered in slime; he raised it in one hand and slapped its buttocks gently, with the other.

'Wha-aa-a!' the newborn cried, and Amy wiped its mouth and nose and draped a small white cloth around it. Albert lifted the baby up, to cradle in his arms and mumbled to himself.

'Another split-arse,' He had desperately wanted it to be a boy to help even up the numbers for the Ark's future generation.

Millie came round slowly. Jane and Amy helped her sit up and offered a glass of water to her lips. As she came to, she beckoned to them to let her hold her child. Albert passed the baby to Millie. She was still out of breath through the sheer exhaustion of the birth and still fretting Ched's absence.

'I'll go and find Ched,' said Albert, as he headed to the bathroom to wash his hands and arms. 'I think I know where he might be.' He called into his own quarters on the way, to change his shirt, which was soiled at the birth. Albert made his way to the canteen bar, where he was sure Ched would be, he was always there by that time. Sure enough, Ched was leaning against the bar, with his head down over his glass. Albert crossed to the bar's gate access, took a pint glass, poured himself a bitter and placed it next to Ched's.

'Your glass is empty,' Albert said. 'What would you like to drink?'

'I don't want any more of that shite!'

'What do you mean? This is the best you'll get around here, anyway, you've got a new daughter, and this is to celebrate the birth.'

'Oh no, not another female,'

'Yes, and that's what I thought, when I was doing what you should have been doing, not 15 minutes ago. You didn't answer the short wave radio. I looked for you earlier, thinking you might be here. You must have found some hole to crawl into instead of being at Millie's side.'

'You could say that, sorry Albert but I haven't the guts for that sort of thing.'

'That's ok, it's done now and they are both fine. Have a quick drink before you see them. So what will you have?'

'I'd better have a large *Flash*.'

'You be careful, you know how that stuff affects you.' No sooner had the glass been placed on the bar, Ched picked it up and threw it straight down his neck. He gulped.

'Argh!' he gasped as he felt the fierce sensation of the ship's distilled spirit burning the sides of his throat, then the heat, as it swirled around his stomach. 'Boy that stuff works fast!'

'Steady,' warned Albert, you know why that drink is called *'Flash'*.' And, in a flash, Ched was clinging to the bar and taking deep breaths to try to alleviate the feeling of light-headedness. 'Too late... I was going to say, you'll be in no fit state to see your newly born daughter,' mumbled Albert, as Ched released himself from the bar, and with a slight stagger, headed to the exit.

Albert looked at the clock and it was 16.35 hours. I'm glad it's Friday, he thought. Good, I can stay and have a couple more pints before the dinner bell goes. He hadn't even noticed the first one he sank but, after pulling his second drink, he moved to the opposite side of the bar, drew up a stool and sat down to relax, and enjoy the ale that he was so proud of.

'Bloody hell, this is shit!' he swore. He made a mental note to take another look at this brew and thought, oh what the hell it's just about drinkable and has the desired effect.

Within a few minutes, he was relaxed and started to ponder on the situation at hand. The problem was how to overcome the imbalance of females versus males being born. Albert wondered what Jane would have in a few months' time. Then he thought Melanie was coming to breeding age, and would have bet a bottle of *Flash*, that Zimbo's already had his hand inside her knickers, and best of luck to them. Albert continued with his musing: what about Marigold? She's still young enough, now Monty's gone, the silly sod that he was! We will have to find some shipwrecked sailor to mate with her, although she doesn't seem bothered too much with men, unless there is something going on that I don't know about. He then started to go

217

through the people that had joined the venture, and the offspring they had produced. He thought of Miles: who would ever think that he would stop living at such a young age, especially as he had just begun to relax and enjoy his time on the Ark? Obviously he and Jane had their privileges, but they soon started to *muck in*, so to say. Well they couldn't stay in their cabin and shag all day long, could they?

Albert's mind rambled on: then there's Ched, who I'm a bit disappointed with at the moment; he's not showing to be the master of things, as I expected him to be. He's a bit weak, compared with his better half, Millie. I know as soon as she's fit and the child can be taken care of, she will be back to what she likes best, the animals and the land. That's her priority, but the thing is, what about now? Antonio can do her job if anything happens to her. Her knowledge is being passed on to him, and he has been fantastic in all he's done. Gunter, well he's doing alright. He seems to be at ease with everything, he's always on duty, he's probably hen pecked.
'Oh Albert stop being so cynical! Now I *am* talking to myself.'

Ched had finally mustered the courage to go and see Millie and *their* newborn child. Millie was fully compos mentis when he got to the cabin.
'*Frederick Preswick*! Where the fucking hell have you been?' Jane and Amy decided to make a quiet exit, sensing that someone was in trouble. Millie continued her tirade.
'You were supposed to be here with me, and help me through this. I expect you've been drinking instead.' Ched was shuddering at the barrage of Millie's words, like lumps of wood hitting him on the head, one at a time. He fought his way through this, and made it to the bundle that was snuggled in Millie's arms. He went to pull back the cloth covering the child's hair, and a few more *lumps of wood* hit him.
'Don't you dare breathe alcoholic fumes on a newborn child, what are you thinking about?' He managed to get to the poor baby, who must have felt some splinters in her ears too! Then he saw her for the first time.
'Bloody hell, it's got a sun tan already Millie!' Millie glared at him. She was very relieved that Ched had not been at the birth when the baby first showed its thick black hair, followed by that lovely Mediterranean complexion, before she had time to concoct an explanation!
'She looks like my Spanish grandmother. Isn't it nice that Vicky looks like you Ched, and the new baby takes after my side of the family?'
'I suppose so.'

'What do you mean, you suppose so? It's true, how else do you think it is?'
Ched thought Millie was becoming riled again and sensed it was time to go.
'I'd better be off. I'm sorry I wasn't here for the birth, but I fell asleep and
a very deep sleep. I have been very tired lately.'
'Tired?' Millie was on a roll with him, and knew she'd got the upper hand.
'You should be up there, helping poor Antonio with the farm duties.'
'That's alright, Zimbo is with him and now I'll be helping you with our
daughter. What are we going to call her?'
'Rose?' Millie immediately suggested.
'That's a lovely name, that's fine with me.'

Over the next few weeks, Millie became as grumpy as hell and she made
Ched's life a misery. Very occasionally, he would escape and have a short
time with Marigold, who soothed him, and gave him strength for another
day.

There were a number of factors, which contributed to Millie feeling so
down. The main one was the obvious one of post baby blues. Then, she was
angry and, in hindsight, embarrassed with herself, for falling for a baby
through pure lust, for she felt certain that Rose was Antonio's baby. She
still remembered clearly, the day she was conceived, and the many times
they had spent together since. It also preyed on her conscience that Antonio
and Jane were living together as a permanent couple, and she was now
bearing a child from him. Millie thought it unlikely that her lusty affair
with Antonio would spark off again, and perhaps to let it die would
probably be for the best, she decided. Time would tell.

It wasn't long before she was leaving baby Rose with either Ched or Greta,
whenever possible, to get back to her love (the farm, that is) just doing a
couple of hours a day and then back to feed the baby. It was nothing
unusual, to be seen with breast out and uncovered, feeding Rose in the
canteen, whilst Millie tucked into her meal. Gunter was scolded by Greta,
on several such occasions, for staring at them. Millie was never big in that
area, but having Rose certainly made a temporary enlargement, and it
suited her. She looked better with a little bit of weight on, but Millie would
soon lose it, once working back on the farm. As the weeks went by she
became less pissed off and no more was said about Rose's complexion
other than it being, just rosy.

It's been good here again, always a relaxed atmosphere in the south. Jane and Antonio seem to have settled down as a couple. He is quite a handy lad and enjoys his work and Jane has certainly blossomed. What a change in her, compared with when she first arrived with Miles. He's well forgotten. His name is barely mentioned these days.

It didn't take Millie long to give birth to Rose, thank heaven! Ched was a waste of space. When it came to it, he should have been there. It was a good job I was nearby to get the poor little sod breathing. I've never seen Millie as mad as that time and I wonder where Ched is getting his head down? He's found somewhere, out of the way. He's getting a bit elusive, like Monty was.

Well a few more days, and we will be on our travels again. What's in store for us on the next trip? Another birth is coming up in June. Let's see if Jane can produce the Ark's first baby boy! All the children seem very healthy so far, and I hope it will continue.

I must make a check on our defence equipment, make sure it's ready and in position. If they try again, it must mean that the contract on Miles is still running, for revenge. We will have to see if we can give the Cape Verde Islands a wide berth this time.

I must ask Magnus if it would be possible to make some balloons and place them about the Ark on long wires, so that the balloons suspend the wires for a hundred feet or so to deter any air craft from getting near us, just like they had in use in the Second World War.

21. SARGASSO SEA FOR A CHANGE

The hot climate they considered the norm on the Ark had started to change to slightly cooler weather at the end of March 2018. Now it was April and they knew it was time to move north, as migrating birds would do, to find a warmer climate for the winter. Albert had been pondering for some time about trying somewhere else for a change, after last year's problems. He had been studying the charts with Gunter to discuss the seasonal move. They could risk going around Cape Horn and into the Pacific to head up to the Californian coast. That would probably take them several weeks on sail. There was no chance of going through the Panama Canal because the Ark was too wide and they couldn't pay the fee for it anyway. So they looked at the Sargasso Sea and around Bermuda, not as far north in latitude as the Azores but worth a try, and if it was not right for them, they could move onto the Azores or return to the temporary spot on the Great Meteor Bank as they did last year, when they were pestered by the media. They decided that Bermuda was the best option. They had just agreed that when Magnus burst into the bridge and they could see he was very excited.

'We've done it Albert.'

'Done what?'

'We have full gas tanks at last and all the produce of shit!'

'How have you managed that, stuck a pipe up all the animals' arses?'

'No, but that's a good idea though, but we haven't enough pipe for that.'

'Anyway, well done, that means if we wanted to get ourselves around the Horn, we could do, and still have spare fuel.'

'Yes,' said Magnus proudly.

All was prepared for a trip to the Sargasso Sea, the majority of the community did not know where on the planet it was. The Bermuda triangle was not mentioned in case they worried about the infamous history that shrouded it with tales of mysterious disappearances of ships and planes. The usual able bodies were out putting the sails in position to move the Ark in a direction, instead of the continuous turning about it had been doing of late. The ship was soon underway and, as normal for the time of year, there was a good wind to help them along Gunter's course, set at 340° north. They were up to fifteen knots within a few hours which seemed to be the maximum speed they could achieve and, as they sailed away, they all looked forward to returning the next season. Ideally, they wished they could stay there all the time but the weather was unsuitable in the southern winter; the Ark would get a continual battering. They estimated it would be about sixteen days sailing: seven days to get to the equator and then another nine days to put them about three hundred miles southeast of the island of Bermuda.

Millie had recovered from the delivery of Rose and was soon getting back to some sort of routine, she stuck rigidly to her story that the baby's dark hair and Mediterranean complexion were from her Spanish Grandmother, but unspoken speculation was rife: that Millie had had a big Italian inside her, and Jane was very suspicious. Antonio just shrugged it off. No one said anything because of possible repercussions and Ched was very cool about it, probably a little guilty over his affair with Marigold. He thought perhaps if, the child wasn't his, it evened things up in a way. The thought had only touched his mind, he discarded it as fast as he thought it. Besides, he reasoned, we all need a bit of loving and excitement occasionally.

Zimbo was excited with the thought of travelling to a different part of the world, having spent all of his life, bar the past six months, in and around the Cape Verde Islands. Now he was fully committed to the Ark, like the rest of the community. Moving about the world, constantly in a warm climate, with the best of food to eat, apart from the elements and the trials and tribulations they had faced, so far they were doing alright. They felt they were the richest people on the globe, and the Ark gave them security. Zimbo had the same privileges as the other inmates. He would go fishing with Ched and was courting a very lovely young girl and they spent their free time with each other. Being together for four months on the Ark had a certain inductive progression. Because there was no real choice of other partners, they developed what opportunities arose. During the transit to the next destination, they had even more free time and the two young lovers, hand in hand, made the most of it. It was easy in the evenings walking out in the moonlight, surveying the stars, stopping for a kiss and a hand up Melanie's jumper; and they would stop for at least ten minutes because Melanie was exceedingly well developed in that area. Zimbo had small hands so a grope would turn to a massage. Now they had time together in daylight and had to find somewhere where they could be private. Off they would go looking for a special place. They checked out the bow, where the hay was stored, and found Millie and Antonio busy tending the animals.

222

Hay stores, hay stacks and barns; they must have been the refuge of millions of young lovers over the centuries.

They were walking by one of the lifeboats that were positioned about the Ark, port and starboard, on the foredeck. As soon as they saw it, Melanie sniggered and Zimbo smiled. A couple of minutes later, they were under the tarpaulin cover and very soon exploring each other bodies. Melanie's top was pushed up to reveal her works of art. As the nipples got bigger, it affected something between Zimbo's legs. Melanie felt the swelling against her leg and said, 'What's happening down there Zimbo?'
'Whenever I touch your tits, it does that. You just excite me so much and turn me on.'
'Would you like me to touch it?' Melanie whispered.
'Yes! I feel it just wants to burst out in joy.'

There wasn't much light under the tarpaulin, but her eyes lit up as he unbuttoned his trousers and as gravity has its way it flopped out, unravelling itself. She looked at it. 'Is that a big one, because I don't know? I've never been this close to one before.'
'I was the biggest in my class at school!' They both giggled and then she put her hand on it and stroked it gently. It soon became as stiff as a rake. Not knowing what to do with it next, she just caressed it lovingly thinking, this is mine now. They kissed and kissed.
'Oh Melanie, I want you. Let me put this inside where it belongs.'
'Zimbo, you'll have to marry me first,' she insisted as she unwittingly brought him to a climax.
'Oh yes... oh yes!'
'Zimbo, Zimbo, I love you. I'll ask Albert to marry us. Oh, what's all that stuff, it's sticky? Is that your sperm?' Zimbo was still rolling his eyes after his ejaculation. Melanie was so excited she was up and heading out of the lifeboat. Meanwhile, he was coiling up his deflated penis to put back in his trousers, and then trying to button up his flies in the right sequence. He staggered out of the boat following Melanie who was going straight to find Albert.
'Melanie wait!' Running after her, he called, 'Wait!' He caught up with her. 'Please wait a minute.'
'What for Zimbo? You said yes and there's no time like the present. If you love me and want me and you aren't going anywhere else in your life, then we'll get married. I'm sure Albert will do it. He is as good as a Captain and

223

then we can be together at night. Just think you'll be able to put that thing inside me as much as you like!'

Zimbo went quiet for a couple of minutes, obviously weighing up the pros and cons of the situation: It's not a bad life here, better than back home and you never know there will be plenty of opportunities to escape if married life gets too bad, he thought.

'When do you think Albert will marry us Melanie?'

'As soon as preparations are in place for our living quarters and a celebration is organised. It should be as simple as that, about a week I would say.'

'Ok,' he said, 'that's soon enough. You will just have to stroke me until then. Melanie can I ask you a personal question?'

'Yes, what is it?'

'Have you had a man inside you before?'

'Do you mean, am I a virgin? Yes, I definitely am, what sort of a girl do you think I am?'

'Oh that will be nice; I'm going to marry a virgin. My father would be so proud of me that I've found a virgin,' he beamed.

They discovered Albert up on lookout. Melanie was shouting for him as soon as he came into view. He turned to see her dragging Zimbo by the hand.

'Please will you marry us?'

'What, now?'

'Not right at this moment, but as soon as you can.'

'Well it's going to be a couple of weeks before we are at anchor. It would be unwise to do it while we are in transit, because we would all want to celebrate together. The Ark may end up going around in circles and be a danger to other shipping. What have your mother and father said?'

'Oh they'll be fine, but I haven't asked them yet.'

'Don't you think it would be a good idea to speak to them first, before saying anything to anybody else?'

'Yes Albert, I'd better get to them sharp. Come on Zimbo, let's go.'

She grabbed his hand and tugged him away. Albert thought, the poor sod I can see who will be the boss there. Melanie headed for the canteen with Zimbo trailing, to where she knew her mother would be.

'Mum, can I ask you something in private? And Dad, do you know where Dad is?'
'I don't know exactly, he'll be somewhere on the ship, I hope.'
'Is there a short wave here?'
'Yes, it's in the kitchen, I'll get it.'... Melanie grabbed the radio from her mother, 'Dad, can you come to the canteen quick, it's important?' Patricia was thinking, well she's pleased about something. She's probably pregnant and is excited about telling us we're going to be grandparents. It took Magnus about five minutes to get to them from her call, wondering what it was all this about.
'You're not pregnant are you?'
'No Dad, how could you think that?'
'Yes Magnus, how could you think that of our wee bairn?'
'Sorry hen, but they have been together a lot lately.'
We want to get hitched as soon as we anchor.'
'That's alright, isn't it hen?'
'Oh yes, a wedding on a ship, that's really nice. Now who can we invite?' Magnus looked at her in exasperation.
'Who do you think, you stupid woman. Everyone aboard would come of course!'
'Oh, I was forgetting where I was.'
'I'm getting worried about you hen. You need to get out and look where ye are. You spend too much time in the kitchen lass. Jane will have you back in shape when she's had her bairn.'

Work started on getting the living accommodation prepared. It wasn't the biggest of cabins, but it had a living room with a small kitchenette. It was previously Monty's when he had wanted to be on his own and not bother with the canteen after his cold turkey stint, and his downfall. The bedroom had a single bed and now Magnus had to change it for a double from the stores. Finally, there was a shower and toilet cubicle. The place was just right for a couple starting out with no rent or other bills to pay, and it would certainly do until any children came along.

The Ark was approaching the equator and now they had rigged up an alarm that would sound one hour before the line and then five minutes before crossing the line, no matter what time of day or night. Some of the couples had developed a fetish about this occasion, Amy especially. She geared herself up for the moment and Albert had begun to look forward to crossing the line too, knowing it did things to Amy that made her very randy. He still put it all down to the good life and had no inkling of her Maca secret. He thought it was far better than being in Kingsbourne Tarrant. Sex wasn't like this there!

They expected to cross the equator at about 2330 hours that night and Ched was on lookout duty. It was a very clear evening and the Ark was moving well under its own sail. Marigold had asked Melanie to babysit for her for a while. She said she wanted to go on deck to look out for the line when they crossed it, because she hadn't seen it yet! Melanie agreed to listen out for Lucy, thinking that would mean an hour on the couch in private with Zimbo. Then she thought again, the silly cow. There's no line, I know. I've looked, and Albert showed me it's just on charts and all that complicated stuff. Oh well, whatever turns her on. Melanie asked if it was alright for Zimbo to be with her while babysitting.
'Yes of course,' Marigold replied, 'but don't make a mess on the sofa.' Melanie went quiet and bright red.

The two young lovers arrived to babysit.
'Lucy is fast asleep,' Marigold said. 'I won't be long. It should only take a moment or two to cross the line. I'll knock and give you time to get dressed when I come back.' 'Oh, that's alright, we will behave, won't we Zimbo?'
'Yes, Miss Marigold, I promise I won't make a mess.'
'Zimbo shut up, you're embarrassing me!' Marigold giggled to herself as she left them to it and made her way to the lookout post on the top deck where an unsuspecting man on duty was about to have a surprise.

She kept very quiet and slowly approached him as he was busy looking out at the horizon with his binoculars. She kept at bay, just studying how intensely he was concentrating. She had a few minutes before the alarm was due to sound the crossing of the equator. Marigold crept up behind him at a low level in the moonlight, reached his trousers and touched his leg. He nearly jumped out of his skin.
'Aaargh!' he shouted. He looked down and saw Marigold at his knees. She hadn't expected a response like that.
'Shut up Ched, it's me!' The shiver that ran down his back settled but the hairs returned to a raised position as she unbuttoned his flies.
'What are you doing?'

'I'm not nicking your trousers, if that's what you think! Sorry Ched, I came here to cross the line with you, to give you something special.'

'That's nice of you.'

'I'll carry on then.' She finally unfastened his front and put her hand inside. She rummaged about for a while.

'Well, where the fucking hell is it?' she hissed. He put his binoculars to one side.

'What do you expect for Christ's sake? You've just frightened me to death it will need encouraging now.'

'If I could find it I would fucking well encourage it!' She eventually found it and showed it to the atmosphere by pulling at it roughly.

'Ow! Steady on, it's not a hose pipe!'

'I should be so lucky!'

Marigold started to talk to it, as Ched stuck to his duty looking out over the horizon, knowing there could be the odd cruise ship about.

'Oh you poor thing, come to Momma.' She kissed its head and moved the skin back and forth until it responded. She was happily getting the attention of the cock of the man who was kind and loving to her, with no questions asked between them. A relationship that suited them both at present, and the cock was paying attention to its Momma, growing by the second! She licked the point and Ched shuddered with delight at the wonderful surge of feeling. He thought, bloody hell; she hasn't done that to me before. He calmed down after his fright and as he relaxed, he got bigger and bigger. She now had his full attention, moving it in and out of her mouth. Ched looked at his watch thinking at this rate, I won't make it, and he started to pulse. As he shot his load, his knees went slightly weak, but she still held on to him as his juice pumped into her mouth. When the stiffness left his cock, so did she. The alarm sounded as she wiped her cheek and crept away leaving Ched to button up his flies. Bloody hell, that was nice he smiled to himself, fastening his trousers, and happily resumed his duties.

As the equator bell rang, Antonio was getting a hand job from Jane, due to current circumstances. Millie was fast asleep as were Magnus and Patricia. Zimbo was being stroked again, with Melanie carefully holding a towel. Greta was chasing Gunter around the bedroom with her tasselled stick, both of them in leathers. Albert and Amy were just having a conventional shag.

For the last two days of the journey, the Ark was becalmed and had to resort to the turbines for propulsion to get them the rest of the way to their anchorage. They picked the shallowest spot of 2000 metres and again it was too deep to put down the anchors. The sea was very calm and the air was dry. Albert commented to Ched and Gunter that it was strange to think it was only just April, yet the weather was like the middle of August. They were all relieved to be at anchor and soon got back into the normal routines, just the way they liked it.

For the first time in the short history of the Ark, a marriage was being planned. It was arranged for the first Saturday at anchor. They were all digging deep into their stores for something special to wear for the occasion. The clothes they had been wearing on a daily basis for the past two and half years had been washed and changed several times a week and were well worn and drab. Because everybody's attire was in the same state, they had got used to it. It wasn't until fresh clothes were pulled from storage that they realised how scruffy they looked in comparison. They busied themselves trying on things that hadn't been seen since boarding the Ark. The men required some of the waistbands taking in because of weight loss. The women, with the exception of Jane for obvious reasons, all found suitable new items to wear and Jane eventually managed to alter a kaftan to cover her bump. Patricia just looked like a sack of spuds whatever she had on. The dress rehearsal showed an amazing transformation. It was like finding an old master that had been in the attic for a hundred years or so and had been cleaned and refurbished to its former glory. Ched was about the same build as Zimbo and lent him a lightweight suit and a shirt he had. Melanie had changed so much that nothing she had to wear was suitable so Jane gave her something from her well stocked wardrobe that just needed a few major alterations because of her large bust.

The accommodation was completely redecorated and cleaned after the mess that Monty had left it in. Melanie gave it those personalised, womanly finishing touches: hanging pictures she had painted; arranging colourful cushions on the sofa and placing vases of freshly picked flowers. That just left the food and drink to be organised and the kitchen crew were seasoned masters at this. Albert had his work cut out composing some words to bond the couple together. He dug out what he had written for Mile's funeral and thought if he altered parting for joining, it would be similar, and then thought better of it. They were bound to suss him out. He resorted to the library to see if there was something standard that he could adapt for a wedding.

The day arrived and Melanie woke with excitement. She had already asked Albert for a time of midday for the ceremony. The whole community assembled in the canteen waiting for Melanie, who arrived on her father's arm. All eyes lit up when she entered. She had transformed herself by using make up, which was seldom used by the women and never on the men for that matter, and a lovely, tight-fitting dress showing her full figure to its best. Zimbo's eyes opened widely in amazement, revealing the enlarged pure whites, which looked as if they would pop out on springs, like a cartoon character. Magnus brought his daughter to Zimbo's side to face Albert and then the others gathered around them and formed a circle. Zimbo was holding a ring that Jane had given to him. It had belonged to Miles, it was one of many he had had. Albert waited for silence then began his ceremony speech.

'We bring this man and woman before you today to ask the permission from the community to make a contract of marriage, for the purpose of founding and maintaining a family. This marriage is a necessity for their future children to undergo a long period of sound development, before attaining maturity. This responsibility is gained by uniting this man and woman. I ask you all now that if there is anybody in this community that opposes this marriage of Zimbo and Melanie, please step forward now or forever be silent... Zimbo please place the ring on Melanie's finger... I now pronounce you man and wife. Can you all raise your glasses please?' Everyone scrambled for a glass of wine from the tray. 'Here is a toast to this young couple wishing them a life of happiness together. To Melanie and Zimbo.'

They had just finished the toast when Jane called over to Albert.

'Antonio and I have discussed getting married for a while now and were going to wait until the baby was born, but after listening to your words for Melanie and Zimbo we would like you to marry us now. It seems fitting to do it today.'

'I'll announce it now... Ladies and Gentlemen, oh, and the well behaved children, I have an announcement to make. Jane and Antonio would like to get married here and now. Unfortunately it means listening to me again and before I start, can we have the wine glasses refilled please, these are thirsty occasions...

We bring this man and woman before you today to ask the permission from the community to make a contract of marriage, for the purpose of founding and maintaining a family. This marriage is a necessity for their future children to undergo a long period of development before attaining maturity. This responsibility is gained by uniting this man and woman. I ask you all now, that if there is anybody in this community who opposes this marriage of Jane and Antonio, please step forward now or forever be silent... Antonio the ring please.' Jane slipped off a gold ring she was wearing on her right hand and gave it to Antonio. He placed it on the wedding finger on her left hand. 'I now pronounce you man and wife. Can you all raise your glasses please?' Another scramble to the tray of wine followed. 'Here is a toast to this young couple wishing them a life of happiness together of which they have experienced some already.' Jane started laughing at that remark and put her arms around Albert as he finished the toast, 'To Jane and Antonio.'

Melanie was soon at the other side of Albert kissing him on one cheek as Jane was on the other. It was a very happy occasion for them all. The celebration continued until the early evening when the young couples left to go to their respective quarters. The sight of them leaving, knowing what they would be doing, inspired most of the rest to get to bed too.

ALBERT'S PRIVATE LOG – April – June 2018

The trip up here went reasonably well apart from the last two days when we had to use the turbines, which takes our stock of methane gas, but at least we can go in a straight line using the propulsion. It's a shame the animals couldn't shit enough to enable us to use the engines all the time, instead of having to move the sails each time the wind changes.

Two weddings in one hit, that's not bad going. My ceremony speech was good, even if I do say so myself. I hope they all make it work and stay fit, devoted and happy. Melanie will have to watch it or she will end up as fat as her mother was, heaven forbid! That reminds me, I wonder how Amy's mother's doing. That was a big decision of Amy to leave her,

230

knowing that it was very unlikely ever to see her again. It wasn't too hard for me though.

I don't like this area of sea much, it sounds glamorous, Bermuda, but it just seems so dead. I don't think the rest are too keen either, especially Millie with her animals. I'm sure the pigs are getting a sun tan. She will have to be careful with them or the crackling will be done too soon!

I enjoyed crossing the Equator again, I wonder if anybody else did anything special for the occasion. I'd like to be a fly on the wall in some of the cabins. I bet there's a thing or two going on. We will have to start looking at the accommodation situation soon. At our rate of expansion, if we run into anybody else who wants to get off the planet, we will have to commission the other level of accommodation and use furniture from the storage bays. At least we can produce plenty of food now, and the fishing helps, although there's not much around here, not even for the sharks.

22. ALBERT'S JOY

Rose was nearly three months old and Millie had started leaving her in the nursery with Greta and Melanie for longer periods of the day so she could help Antonio on the farm. Greta and Melanie had their hands full looking after the children and since the day Stella went over the side of the Ark, the discipline was far stricter, especially from Greta. Stella and Vicky had so much energy and Lucy copied every naughty thing the older girls did. They certainly had their work cut out in the childcare department. Jane was almost due to have her baby. Albert wanted to move the Ark, either to the Azores or The Great Meteor Bank, because they were not getting any rain at all and fishing was very poor. But he did not want to move until Jane had delivered her child. The usual preparations were in place. Patricia was on standby with Amy as back up. Jane moved about as much as she could, but usually stayed close to her cabin. Antonio had the short wave radio and he would be informed as soon as anything started.

For some strange reason, everyone was on tenterhooks. They all wanted this child to be a boy, but nothing could be said. It came from within. It was that psychological thing, if you comment that it must be a boy and it turns out to be a girl, the bearer of the child feels she has disappointed everyone. But if you say nothing and just wish in your private thoughts, at least you can say I just knew it was going to be boy or girl, whatever it turns out to be. When Millie had Rose, it all happened so quickly. Millie had worked on the farm for as long as she could manage and when she wasn't working, she was resting and out of sight of people. Perhaps it was because everyone was more relaxed in the Southern Atlantic, their favourite place to be. The atmosphere in the Sargasso Sea did not feel the same, for some reason. The third of June, another hot dry day with temperatures reaching between 35°C and 40°C. Normally when they experienced such periods of constantly dry, still air, they would think a storm was on its way, knowing that when it was over, the air would be fresh and they would have had some rain, but no, not there. The animals were kept inside in their pens away from the scorching sun but the problem was how to keep them clean. Antonio was working as hard as he could. He asked for some help and Zimbo was there without question, making a joke of 'you can hose me down after work and I'll hose you down too'. All the animosity had gone between them and they worked to keep the animals in reasonable conditions with the minimum amount of stress as they could.

The poor animals were becoming infested with flies, the worst affected were the sheep where the insects would lay their eggs upon the cleanly shaven skin, turning to maggots eating away their flesh as they moved. Antonio took some advice from Albert, who was not a farmer only the son of one. He remembered back to when he worked for the contractor on Ramsey Island off the coast of Wales. There were many sheep farmed by a caretaker farmer. During the evening walks Albert took after his day's work, he saw an abundance of rabbits, which he would bring back for dinner quite easily. Ramsey had never seen myxomatosis so he would almost trip over them. He would also be amongst the sheep and noticed the irritation of a number of them. On closer inspection he saw the sheep were being eaten by maggots. Because of the cliffy terrain, quite often the irritation would lead to a sheep falling into the sea. Young Albert reported the tragedy and a reluctant farmer would be lead by Albert to a sheep, trying to keep itself afloat. Albert used to put his life in the farmer's hands as he scampered down rocky cliffs with just a rope around his waist to collect the sheep from the perilous waves. This process was repeated over the months that he worked on the island and the recoveries were not always successful. What he noticed on his walks was the maggot-infested sheep that had been in the sea, were healing. He passed this information on to Antonio who made a cage and put the Ark's affected sheep in and doused them in the sea. It worked and even Millie was amazed at the success with just a natural solution not other chemicals!

Jane was on a walkabout and decided to go to the bridge. She wanted simply to look to the bow of the Ark to see her man, the father of her child at work on the farm. All was forgotten of Miles now. It felt like a movie she was playing a part in had finished, making her redundant, unemployed, and unwanted. But being a strong-willed, talented person, she found another part to play and this role seemed to have more meaning and job satisfaction. She wondered what will her and Antonio's child be like? Will it be a boy or a girl? Will it be healthy strong and intelligent? If the movie had been three years ago, on the so-called terra firma, she would know the sex of the child, if it had any deformities, any hereditary problems and so on. And, if all were to the satisfaction of the parents, its name would be down for a well-known private prep. school and there would be ample funds planted in a savings account in its name, a privileged start into the modern world. Her present part seemed to be the best role she had played so far and she hoped she continued through it with success.

'Jane what on the Ark's earth are you doing up here? You have climbed those steps on your own. You must be mad. You might have fallen. Here let me help you.' Albert took her arm and with his other arm around her for extra support, he carefully led her to the captain's chair and helped her onto the comfortable leather seat. She sank into it gratefully, with sweat pouring from her moistening her huge homemade maternity dress.

'I just wanted to look out from here over the Ark and see Antonio at work.'

'You probably won't see much of him because they will be working inside, looking after the animals.'

'Oh, well, I know he's there. He is a fine man Albert, isn't he?'

'Yes, he certainly is. It's nice to be in a warm climate Jane, but this is too hot for us. We've decided that as soon as you've delivered the precious goods, we are moving on to a better climate.'

'Albert don't wait for me. I'll be ok. Let's get out of here and move on; anything to cool us down.'

'You know she's right Albert,' Gunter said. 'Sitting here is not doing any of us any good. It's making tensions. Let's sail! We have Zimbo reasonably trained for lookout, why not Albert?' Albert thought about it.

'Are you sure Jane?'

'Yes Albert, I want the Ark to move.' Those few words stirred Albert into action.

Magnus was soon checking the engine room and everyone was quickly told of the plan. Within an hour, the Ark was breaking through the calm sea. The turbines had started and were vibrating through the stern of the Ark, leaving a wake with their powerful thrust.

'Have you made up your mind yet on where we are heading?' Gunter asked Albert.

'The "Great Meteor Bank," that will put us nearer our winter destination. What do you think?'

'Sounds alright to me,'

'What do you think captain?' Albert asked as he looked at Jane sitting in the captain's chair, smiling as the light breeze came through the windows from the speed of the ship.

'That's fine by me. Carry on boys!'

Gunter gave Albert a course to steer of 090° east.

'090° east it is,' Albert confirmed. They were only one hour into the journey and Jane was still in the captain's seat, when her waters suddenly broke.

'Albert, please get Antonio now,' she begged. He calmly picked up the short wave radio.

'Antonio, get your arse to the bridge immediately, if not sooner!' Antonio stopped what he was doing and told Zimbo he was going to Jane as she had started with the baby. Magnus had rigged up a shower for them near the animal pens so they didn't smell too much and were reasonably clean when they got to the upper decks. Antonio quickly showered with his clothes on and then ran to the bridge to Jane. Albert had called Patricia who was in the kitchen. Amy got there a couple of minutes ahead of her, being able to run that bit faster. Now it was panic time! Amy asked Albert if the chair reclined because it was too late to move her. As Albert adjusted the chair, Gunter made a hasty exit.

'Oh, bloody hell! That means I have to stay here at control. Jane saw Albert's awkward situation and tried to reassure him between pants of breath.

'Don't worry Albert I know this won't take long. I've been drinking raspberry juice and leaf tea for some time. It appears to be helping. I'm sorry about the mess on your chair.'

Patricia went off to get a bowl of hot water and towels. Amy was counting and timing contractions, which were increasing in both frequency and severity, making Jane, shudder with pain each time. This went on for a few hours. Jane thought it should have been over long ago. All the time she clutched on very tightly to Antonio, who braved out the time with her. Then it started. Albert thought, thank Christ for that! I thought I'd never get off this shift! As Jane lay back in the chair with her knees up in the air and legs wide apart, the dark black hair of the baby pressed on with its journey into the world. Amy and Patricia encouraged Jane to push harder. Jane looked around for Antonio.

'Where's Antonio?' she screamed. Albert picked him up off the floor. He had fainted! He propped him up against the control desk, slapped his cheeks, and then took him to an open window and poked his head out to breathe some fresh air. After a few sips of water, he was soon ok to resume his station at Jane's side, holding her hands as she gripped him to her. The baby's head was clear and the body followed very quickly to reveal its sex.

235

'It's got a willy!' shouted out Patricia.

'What?' Albert couldn't resist turning to see after all this time looking away.

'It's a boy, it's a boy!' He jumped up and down with joy as he went over to kiss Antonio.

'What's his name? Have you thought of one yet?' Jane and Antonio looked at each other.

'Yes we have,' an exhausted Jane said, 'Albert...it's Alberto.' Albert was dumbstruck for a few seconds.

'You've named the boy after me?'

'Yes Albert, we had already decided and if it had been a girl it would have been Amelia.' They looked at Amy and smiled.

It was congratulations all round. By the time Patricia had tied the umbilical cord and cleaned the baby to hand back to a very proud mother and father, the word had got around the Ark very fast, that Jane had given birth to a boy and had named him Alberto. Everyone was delighted, even Millie who had been through what was thought to be a short period of post-natal depression. She seemed very happy with her lot. When she walked to the bow through the fields that she controlled, she could look and think everything she saw in front of her, she owned, as could everyone in the community.

They all realised it had been a mistake to move to the area near Bermuda, but knew that was all very well in hindsight, in a world that was becoming so small. The Ark had managed to do what it was created to do: to build a community away from the pressures of living under different government regimes and the bitterness of religious hatred throughout the world. They had overcome intolerances between diverse types of people and even Albert had learnt a thing or two. They had managed to sail through the elements now the only real pressures they had to face was a revenge attack from the crooks and intrusion by the media.

ALBERT'S PRIVATE LOG - June - 2018

I'm very glad to be away from the Sargasso Sea, I made a right balls-up of choosing there! We should have left sooner. I know it's my fault.

Well, at least everyone is relieved to be away from there. We should be at the Great Meteor Bank in a couple of days.

I wish it had been mine and Amy's child being born. We can still but hope, although our biological clocks are ticking away... When that was all happening on the bridge, it was amazing - a boy at last and naming it after me, well almost. Ah, what does an 'o' on the end matter? Jane and Antonio are extremely proud. It certainly looked like Rose when it was born though. Did Antonio slip Millie something when he first started working on the farm? All the women had eyes on him at the time, and it was about nine months before. That will upset Jane's community tree of who has fathered whom and might be a problem in later years, especially if Alberto fancies Rose and wants her knickers off, because it makes them half-brother and sister. Could be awkward, how am I going to find out and protect their future? I might have to make some laws on who's allowed to shag who.

I wonder how long it will take Melanie to get pregnant. I hope he's got plenty of good fertile sperm to scramble her eggs. We will certainly know who the father is if anybody else has a coloured child other than Melanie, so he had better point his dick in the right direction!

Bloody Hell! I wonder what will face us next. Will we see our *Russian friends* again? I haven't used my grenade launcher yet. I had better make some more alcohol for Magnus's rocket launcher, he was pretty handy with that. It wasn't fit for drinking after all.

It's amazing to think that it is June 2018. Just over three years ago, the Ark was only an idea and now look at it! All in all, we haven't done too badly, who knows what will happen to us next. I'm sure we will find our utopia or perhaps we are in it already.

Everyone is happy; there must be a lot of shagging going on! I've never had so much myself. Amy's still a fit woman after all these years. I wonder if it's the Ark's Bitter that's making me randy all the time, you never know. Well there's only Marigold to find a partner, though she doesn't seem that bothered. She smiles a lot more now and seems happier with Monty gone. Somebody is putting a smile on her face. It can't be Antonio; between the farm and Jane he's a busy lad. Gunter would have his balls cut off and dished up to him as bratwurst! Zimbo's having problems getting out of bed these days. Magnus doesn't even come into the equation and I wouldn't have thought Ched had it in him. Well, strange things happen at sea.

23. REVELATIONS

At fifty seven years, Albert started to wonder how long his good health would last. He was considering the responsibility he had. Being the only one with military experience and active service, he thought he ought to start training the Ark's younger element to defend themselves and the ship. This was something he had not entered into the equation when he came up with his original pipe dream of the Ark. In hindsight, he realised he should have acted sooner in initiating some sort of defence training after the initial assault. Of the two attacks, the first was unexpected and the outcome almost incredible. The second was very naive of the hunters and, as Albert put it, total stupidity, obviously a desperate act of aggression.

Now that they were a successful, growing community and solid unit, with the men feeling naturally very strongly about the safety of their families, Albert put his military mind into gear to do something serious for the Ark's protection. He considered that perhaps the enemy would take a different approach to the situation after the previous attempts. His thinking was that Antonio and Zimbo were at the right age and both extremely physically fit. With an adventurous spirit, they would take to combat training, as he did when he was taught by the best in the world, the Royal Marines, as it was then. There seemed no better time than now, while they were on their way to the Great Meteor Bank, prior to the journey past the Cape Verde Islands where the Russians might take the opportunity to strike again. Albert wondered how long they would keep trying to take them, and would their motive for attacking the Ark be confirmed, if they struck again?

With all this fresh in his mind, Albert called Ched, Gunter and Magnus, the quartet considered now as *the elders*, to discuss his concerns and explain the action he would like to take to help protect the Ark. They met on the foredeck by the big greenhouse biome, agreeing that the ship could handle itself for half an hour. Albert was pacing around the first field when the men caught up with him. He said nothing until they were in front of him, with Ched a number of paces behind.

'We have come this far and have been successful, better than expected,' Albert stated. 'When we started out, our only threat was moving this vessel north to south and growing enough food to sustain us. But we have inherited a problem that does not seem to want to go away. From our experiences of the attacks on us, there is reason to believe it will happen again by our Russian friends or some other assailant. We have to protect ourselves. I will not be fit enough and here forever so we need to train, get wizened up and organised in methods of combat and defence.'

'I've no stomach for physical fighting,' Magnus immediately responded. 'I can aim and pull a trigger when my eyes are shut, but the combat stuff is not for me.'

'Nor me' said Ched.

'I would like to know how to defend myself if it came to it,' Gunter replied, more positively.

'Ok,' Albert went on, 'the way I see it is, Magnus, you can indulge yourself, with Ched's help, to set up an early warning alarm system. Also, you can concentrate on making more missiles and we can work together on maximising the positioning of the armaments and munitions we already have. I will start to train Gunter, Antonio and Zimbo in the methods of armed and unarmed combat.'

'What will the women think of this, won't they be worried?' Ched asked.

'Well, we will have to convince them that it's necessary and for the best, and that it will help to protect us and our way of life. They are well aware of the threat we are under. As for unarmed combat, it is good, physical education and I'm sure some of our ladies would like to take part.'

'Now you're talking.' Ched grinned, with a glint in his eye. 'Perhaps I might need some unarmed combat training after all.'

'Didn't they teach you any of that when you were in the Royal Navy Ched?'

'Er… yes, but I wasn't any good at it.'

'So when I mentioned getting the women involved, you're interested now.' Ched realised his big mouth had embarrassed him once more.

'I was only joking Albert.'

'Hmm,' Albert replied, unimpressed. He then asked if anyone had any objections to the training. They each looked at one another, nodding and agreeing to the defence plans. 'Right, I'll explain the plans to Antonio and Zimbo. I don't think there'll be a problem in getting their participation. If you all can explain the situation to your respective partners, I will tackle Jane, Marigold and Melanie.'

The response from all the females was positive although, abhorring violence, they understood the need to be protected and could see the merits in Albert's defence strategy. Melanie and Marigold took a keen interest in unarmed combat lessons.

On reaching the Great Meteor Bank, there was a feeling of relief. The air was fresher and there were clouds in the sky, unlike the Sargasso Sea which became unpleasant to be under the relentless sun, raising thoughts of wanting air conditioning, which would have been a nightmare for poor Magnus and his energy resources. Within a couple of days, Albert was giving physical training basics to limber up the team ready for the serious art of unarmed combat that followed. He tried to instil mind conditioning of 'kill or be killed', which he addressed at moments when the trainees had adrenaline running at its highest. Magnus had set to work on his side of the defence system with Ched helping, when he wasn't ogling at the busty Melanie and the scantily clad Marigold during training sessions. Magnus had designed and manufactured an improved rocket and launcher. He described it as a 'cow's revenge', obviously in reference to Marina and Co.'s contribution of methane to ignite the missile.

The next task for Albert was weapon training and he knew this would be difficult because of the lack of expendable ammunitions. He decided to limit this type of instruction, thinking the AK47 would be better off in his hands, for the foreseeable future. Training became a normal part of the Ark's routine and the participants took it seriously but also enjoyed learning the expert knowledge Albert was passing on to them. He just hoped that his team would never have to be put to the test.

Albert would call to see Jane and baby Alberto on a daily basis and was soon criticised by Amy for not doing the same for Rose and the other children. She told him to get more involved with *all* the children to explain things to them about the Ark.
'It just cannot be left solely to Greta to educate them,' Amy pointed out. 'She is limited in her teaching skills. What will happen if we have to resort to going back to the mainland? The children will be at a total disadvantage in *Euro-land*.' She was quite harsh in her criticism that made Albert think, she's bloody right!

They had been at anchor for two weeks and things had settled down with everybody doing what was important to them, making a comfortable existence. Lookout duties were on a rota as usual and Gunter was on duty.

241

It was just about dusk and he spotted a vessel about five miles away. He studied it for a few minutes and made it out to be a large, luxury motor yacht, moving at a steady cruising pace of approximately ten knots, but it was heading towards them. He called for Albert who responded immediately and was by his side in minutes. Gunter passed his binoculars to him and Albert watched the ship for a while.

'It's slowing down,' he said to Gunter, passing back the binoculars and apologising for not bringing his own pair. Gunter focused on the yacht.

'Yes it's coming to a standstill some three miles off Albert.'

'Keep your eyes peeled and I'll go and warn the others to be prepared for the worst.'

He rushed off to alert the crew, as an amber alert, then, he returned to lookout with his own binoculars, to study this vessel further. By now, dusk had turned into darkness and all that could be seen were navigation and one or two cabin lights. There was an eerie quietness over the calm sea with not a sound from the yacht, even though the breeze was blowing from it towards the Ark. You can normally hear people talk at that distance in such conditions, but it was dead. Albert took over the next lookout shift, relieving Gunter, who was reluctant to leave, returning twice during Albert's duty.

Dawn arrived with the sun rising rapidly from behind the horizon with rays peeping through the clouds and soon dispersing them. Antonio was on the next shift. He was keen to be away from his crying baby who had kept him awake for most of the night. Albert asked if there was a problem.

'No he is just so hungry; Jane can hardly keep up with him.' This made Albert smile.

The yacht stayed at its position for three days without any sign of life onboard and then, at the end of Albert's shift on the fourth morning, its engines started and it headed south east towards the African coast. This worried him and made him think that it was a reconnaissance exercise. If it had been anything else, people being what they are, inquisitive, they would have made contact to find out what this oil tanker was doing growing trees out of its bow, with cows and sheep making their farmyard noises in the middle of the ocean. Albert now had a dilemma, would they be back, or was it when will they be back? He settled in his mind that they *would* be back and again the question of the link with Miles gnawed away at him. It

242

was quite obvious that Miles was very important to the Russians, but was there more to it than he knew already? Albert surmised that they still didn't know that he was dead, and they probably didn't know why their previous attempts to get him had failed. But they had not moved in guns blazing and their yacht was a very expensive piece of kit. He started to think back to when Miles and Jane joined the ship and remembered the large number of trunks that were delivered by fork lift truck and craned onboard. At the time, he just accepted that they held an excessive amount of clothes and other personal effects you would expect a rich young couple to have. He knew some were still in the store, but where were the others now? Perhaps they held some paperwork which would help unravel the connection? He did not want to upset Jane who was only just recovering from Alberto's birth, but he had to find the trunks to look for clues.

Antonio was due to relieve Albert on lookout, so he decided to stay with Antonio a few minutes and question him about the trunks' whereabouts. The young man strolled up and they both watched the yacht fade into the distance.

'When Miles and Jane arrived on the Ark, some metal trunks came with them. Are they still in your quarters?'

'There are some in the spare room, off the bedroom. They will have to be moved soon because we want to use it for Alberto.'

'Have you seen what's in them?'

'No, Jane said it was Miles' personal belongings and she did not want to open them and be reminded of the past.'

'Well Antonio, I want to look inside them to see if we can find any link with that yacht and there is no time like the present. I'll call Ched to take this watch and Magnus to assist us with bolt croppers.'

'Jane will be in the canteen having breakfast holding Alberto at the moment so it will be an ideal time.' Antonio added.

Ched arrived wondering why the change in shifts, when the yacht had gone and he was enjoying being in bed, which did not go down well with Albert.

'Wake up you slack bastard and keep your eyes on the horizon! It's not over yet.'

'No need to be like that Albert. I'm looking, I'm looking.'

They met Magnus at Jane and Antonio's quarters and followed Antonio in, through to the side room where the trunks were stored, four in total.

Magnus used the bolt croppers and sheared off the first lock. The three looked eagerly on as Albert lifted the lid to reveal the contents.

'Bloody hell,' Six, bulging eyes stared at bundles of used euro banknotes. They continued to open the other trunks; all had similar contents: two in US dollars and the other in high denomination euros. Just then, Antonio heard the same sound that had been keeping him awake at night. Jane and Alberto were soon in the room and she demanded an explanation, before seeing what had been discovered.

'Oh my god!' she screamed. 'Miles the bastard, I swear I knew nothing of this, I promise. They were Miles' personal property. I don't know where the keys are and I never bothered with them, especially after he died. I didn't want to look inside and bring old memories up again.' Antonio reached to hold Alberto as the baby sensed Jane's shock, increasing the extent of its lungs. Antonio comforted the child and the noise soon died down.

'It's alright Jane,' said Albert, 'but I would like to know when Miles intended to tell you about this. What was he going to do with all this cash? It explains why our *friends* are so persistent and the biggest problem we have is what to do with this money without giving ourselves up to them.' They turned and stared at the trunks in silence, some of their minds racing in thoughts of how they could spend it if they were free of the Ark. Jane broke the silence.

'I don't want anything to do with it; you can throw it over the side for all I care. I want none of it.'

'Well that's one alternative, but it wouldn't stop the Russians from looking for us and they would still want to silence us all.' Albert picked up some of the euro notes and studied them, checking for telltale counterfeit signs.

'These look genuine, and at a guess, are laundered, so I expect the stash was ready for use somewhere. This amount of money could fund a revolution; you could buy a lot of arms and people in some African countries, for instance. This sort of thing has been going on for many years. I know only too well. But with no knowledge of world news for the past two years, I couldn't guess where and if I'm correct in my assumption, this money floating about with us for all that time has held things up for them. The Russian gang may have entered a new phase in increasing their power, and someone is under pressure.'

Magnus was still stunned by what he was looking at.

'What can we do Albert?' Antonio asked.

'Well first of all, with your permission Jane and Antonio, I want every adult to see this obscene amount of money and think about what it represents. One of the main reasons we bonded together to live the way we do, was to do without it and all it stands for!'

'Yes Albert.' Jane immediately responded not even looking at Antonio. 'Get them all in now and then get rid of it.' Bloody hell, thought Albert, Jane can be quite domineering, but was she like that with Miles?

'Magnus, MAGNUS.'

'Oh, sorry Albert, did you say something?'

'Please could you take your eyes off the filthy lucre for a minute and go and ask everyone, including the children, to meet us here, whatever they are doing, as it is an urgent matter of the Ark's survival. Do *not* tell them what you have seen.'

'Yes Albert, straight away Albert.' Magnus started to move towards the door but kept stopping and turning his head to look at the cash.

'MOVE MAGNUS,' Albert commanded.

'You see what I mean Jane. That's why I want them all to see it so I can gauge their true feelings. It's going to be interesting but I could do without this problem. It is something we inherited from Miles and it's got to be sorted.'

'I'm sorry Albert I had no idea how deep Miles was into this and now it's obvious a lot deeper than he told me.'

'Don't blame yourself. It was my decision to choose Miles and his money, even against worries from Amy, but then, if it wasn't for him, you would not be here with Antonio and now little Alberto, so don't blame yourself and try to undo things. What happens in life happens. You cannot stop the life clock and wind it back. Even if you could, how could you be sure that if you changed your mind on what you did, would the outcome be any better?'

Antonio was still holding the now sleeping baby in his arms. He smiled at Albert as his interpretation of events began to sink in. Jane clasped her arms around Albert.

'You are becoming a wise old man with great respect from everyone and especially from us three. I hope we all stay together a long, long time.' Albert was moved by her sincerity. He returned the embrace and a rare tear came to his eye. He broke away as they heard people approaching. Jane stood with Antonio and started to think what the others would assume about the extent of her involvement in this. Would they think the stash belonged to her now Miles had gone, and focus the blame for all the trouble on to her?

They filed into the small room to see what all the fuss was about. Albert told them they were welcome to come around again for a second or third viewing. Magnus had already been round several times. Albert studied each of their eyes as they filtered through.

'We're all bloody rich!' Ched burst out. 'We can buy anything we want now!' Albert shook his head thinking, sad bastard. He then asked if they could all convene in the canteen to discuss this latest development. The interest in the cash was very moving in the fact they were all sitting in the canteen within minutes, waiting for Albert, although Jane and Antonio moved at the same speed as Albert, not looking forward to the others' response. As Albert confronted the community, Ched was the first to fire a question at Albert.

'Did she,' pointing at Jane, 'know about this all along and their plans went wrong when Miles popped his clogs?'

'Clogs, did he wear clogs? I thought he was Russian not Hollander,' Gunter asked. Albert's hand went to his forehead, slapping it in exasperation.

'Oh shit!'

'Albert, language please; not in front of the children,' Amy chastised him.

'Right Ched, I can assure you that Jane had limited knowledge of Miles' doings and take it that the information that was given to all of you after the first attempt to attack us, by the helicopter, was all she knew. We are not here now to discuss Jane. We are here to find out how strong you are to make this community survive after over two years of a mainly blissful life together. Now we've run into this money dilemma, when all this time, we've been trying to get away from everything associated with it.'

'Well can't we go to the Caribbean, anchor up and just spend the money a bit at a time? We wouldn't have to bother working for a few years and my wife would get a break from farming.' Ched suggested.

'Are you brain dead?' shouted out Millie. 'I know you wanted to get off the planet, but you've left your brain behind!' Albert slapped his forehead again. He wanted to get on with the meeting instead of listening to their domestic sparring and was also disappointed that Ched could consider changing their way of life back to a material world.

'Oh Damn.'

'That's better Albert.'

'Can we get to the point of the present predicament, please?' He looked around, eyeing everyone, until he got a nod of approval to continue.

'Right it's been suggested by Jane, to tip the whole lot over the side of the Ark as she doesn't want the money, or any part of it.' (Ched and Magnus looked horrified) 'Jane is content living this life with Antonio and Alberto.' He paused. 'The question is now what do we do with that cash, because whether we have it onboard or not, we are faced with extermination just knowing about it,' that made them all look at each other, with some couples conferring. Greta cleared her throat to speak.

'Albert you have brought us through safely to where we are and as far as Gunter and I are concerned we will support what you think is best. We know you do not want the money.' Patricia was next.

'I agree, don't we Magnus?'

'Yes dear.' He looked at her with henpecked resignation. Melanie followed her mother in agreeing, as Zimbo pleaded with her to think about it.

'Zimbo, shut up! You have no say in this.' He was silenced. Millie and Marigold rose at the same time, each interrupting and then apologising to each other. Then Millie got in first.

'Albert what does Amy think about all this?' He paused.

'Let's ask her.' Amy stood up to reply.

'I spent many years waiting for Albert to come home. Knowing the type of work he did, it was often, *if* he would come home or if he did, what physical state would he be in? Would he have two legs and two arms? Would his face be intact? Would his brain be all there? One of the reasons I was glad to come on this project was I new I had a good chance of seeing him every day, and as Greta said earlier, he's brought us through safely this far, I, and we can only trust in his judgement.'

'Thank you for that Amy; it makes me feel stronger that there is solidarity amongst the women,' Millie said and then she caught sight of flapping arms in the air at the back of the group. 'Oh, Marigold, sorry, I got ahead of you. Would you like to speak now?'

'Thank you Millie. I've always felt like an outsider: that I don't really fit in with the rest of you. With Monty being the loner he was, it was difficult from the start for me to be part of this community. The only thing missing for me now, is a man to share my life with.' (Ched looked away.) 'What gives me hope, is Albert's strength and wisdom and, as Antonio has turned

247

up for Jane, and Zimbo for Melanie, I'm sure someone will turn up for me and as far as the money is concerned, it's dirty money and can only be bad.' There were loud applause and Albert soon had a beer in front of him, pulled by Melanie, at ten o'clock in the morning, which was totally against the rules!

Ched decided to have another go at Albert.
'Right, Mr Commander. What are you going to do with the money to get us out of this mess?' All eyes descended upon him, even the mild easygoing Marigold scowled at her part-time lover.
'We are going to put you to work for a change,' Albert retaliated. They all laughed. 'What do you mean? I work very hard.'
'Would you like that to go to a vote while we are altogether?' Ched looked around and thought perhaps it was not a good idea.
'So what am I going to do then?'
'Can you remember the yacht that we pulled out of the water when we rescued Antonio and his brother?'
'Yes, of course I do.'
'Well, I want it put in full working order and painted the darkest colour we have in our stores, including the sails. And I want the engine running like you cannot hear it. You are lucky to have Magnus' expertise to help you.' Patricia thumped Magnus on the arm to make him pay attention.
'Why do you want to go sailing about in a totally black yacht, are you kinky or something?' Ched quipped. Millie looked at her husband in despair; she could see Albert had a serious plan and was fed up with Ched's ridiculing.
'Ched! Just shut up and take note. And stop floating about in the middle of the ocean on four trunks of used bank notes that you can't spend!' she snapped.
'Yes Millie,' he mumbled.

'What have you in mind Albert?' asked Jane.
'I know *our friends* will be back but they don't know Miles is dead. I'm sure they suspect the money is here and will want to board us and take the cash, rather than try to sink us. Besides that, sinking an oil tanker is not an easy option for them, and they don't know if we know about the money. So I want to use Antonio's yacht as a silent spying vessel to get close to them at night, when they arrive near us, and survey them. If we can remain

undetected, we may be able to see if they have any heavy armaments onboard.'

'It is obvious Albert that you personally intend to carry out this reconnaissance, but you cannot possibly handle that yacht and carry out all that on your own, surely?'

'Well if I have to, I will, but it would be nice to have a volunteer to help me.'

'I will.' said an eager Antonio.

'You must be totally mad, Albert,' Ched scoffed.

'Yes Ched, I probably am but I'm still here and so are you.' On that note the meeting ended without another word, just some glum faces from a few females, worried by the continuing threat.

In only ten days, the adapted yacht was having sea trials with Albert and Antonio putting them to the test in brushing up their sailing skills. They soon got the hang of tacking to change direction and making use of changing winds. Then they started sailing at night with Gunter looking out on the Ark to see how visible they were. They realised that, as usual, the weather was the most important factor to help them: they relied on good cloud cover and a reasonable wind.

The stay on the Great Meteor Bank was coming to an end and it was time to make preparations for their third visit to the area around Tristan De Cunha. They had recovered reasonably well from the loss of produce damaged by the period in the Sargasso Sea and were confident that, once further south for the winter (summer there), things would be even better. It was only three days to their planned departure when lookout reported a vessel on the horizon heading towards them. Just as before, it slowed and stayed at a distance of about two miles. Albert stopped all practising with the covert yacht and lifted it out of the water, strapping it to the side, hoping the Ark would not turn in the next three days to expose it to the visitors. The constant watch on the Ark went on and when the Ark slipped its anchor, so did the visitors, and for the next two days the Ark was stalked with no let up.

As Albert took his night watch, he gave the situation some more thought. He already had a plan to take a closer look at *our friends* if they returned and now they had done. Weather conditions were on the change, with less moonlight and a lot of cloud cover. Albert thought the sea was getting rougher, but there was no better time to take a really good look at the enemy. Antonio came to relieve Albert.

'Antonio, as soon as you have finished your shift, get some sleep; eat high protein foods, not stuff that makes you fart, and make sure you are fully toileted by 2200 hours tonight. We are going to a disco, and I don't mean in the canteen! Don't say anything to anyone, not even Jane. She will only spend the day worrying.'

'Yes I understand.' He left him to his shift and Albert went to bed and, as Amy was getting up, he climbed into the warm sheets she had just left.

'Hmm that smells nice,' he murmured. In seconds, he was asleep.

He was up and about at 1300 hours after his normal six hours sleep. He felt good and at peace with himself, other than being very hungry. He showered, dressed and went speedily to the canteen. Patricia and Amy were busy serving meals and the majority of the inhabitants were eating. Albert was offered the best of the dregs.

'Oh right, I'll have what's left of that chicken, some potatoes and some baked beans please.' Patricia started filling the plate.

'Oh no Patricia, forget the baked beans.'

'Why Albert, they are not the tinned type, these are our own produce.'

'They make me break wind.'

'What do you mean?'

'FART!' Albert had raised his voice with Amy in earshot.

'Albert, manners'

'Sorry Patricia, just chicken and potatoes will do,' and he carried his plate to the farthest corner of the canteen.

Later that afternoon, Albert started his preparations for the night-time operation. Firstly, he made sure Antonio was getting some sound sleep by visiting Jane to explain that they were going out that night, just for a trial reconnaissance.

'Try not to worry; we've practiced it time and time again.'

'Please make sure both of you come back safely to us.' She kissed him on his cheek, leaving Albert to ponder over his responsibility, once again. I think I'll take some backup kit with me, he decided, just in case I need to do some damage!

The black yacht, as Albert called it now, was hung by one of the lifeboat hoists, dangling but secure, to the port side of the Ark, ready to put to sea in a minimum amount of time.

The stalker was trailing on the starboard side, on the west. As far as Albert was concerned he was delighted because the sun sinks down in the west, so the darkness would come from the east, covering the black yacht.

Albert went to Amy to tell her he was out tonight with Antonio and would like some provisions, just in case the wind was unfavourable to get back directly. She looked into his eyes and at Albert's telltale grin. It was the grin he had when he was holding something back, told Amy he was up to something.
'I'll sort out some food for you both and make sure it's nothing that's likely to go off for a while.'
'Don't worry, I'll be back soon.'
'Albert you are not as young as you were, think seriously about what you're doing.'
'I'm pretty fit! You can still get you legs around my waist.'
'Only just,' she chuckled. 'Take care; I don't want to see you again until you are back, I'll only get upset.'

He arranged to meet up with Ched, Gunter, Magnus and Zimbo on the bridge. It was 1800 hours when they met. Albert briefed them on what he wanted to happen.
'We are under sail at present with a favourable breeze and making twelve knots. We are going to alter the pitch of the sails to slow us down to four knots. I don't want to draw too much attention and drop any sail completely, because they know we have no reason to, but altering the pitch, they won't know the difference. We will lower the black yacht at 2200 hours with Antonio and me onboard. I want to be able to catch up with you within the next forty eight hours. So, if there is no sign of us and that stalker is still with you, just go full steam ahead and forget about us, because you will be on your own anyway. Gunter if that happens you take command. We will all go out now to alter the pitch of the sails.'

On the way, Albert made a detour with Magnus.
'We have another little task to do, I'll explain as we go.' They headed back up to the top deck where Magnus had positioned the present from Package Pete.
'What are you going to do with this Albert?'
'I need it for defence Magnus, for our little sortie tonight.'
'Will you use it?'

251

'Only if I have to'
'You're mad'
'Maybe'
'Come on. Let's get this grenade launcher into the yacht.'

The black yacht was ready. Albert had planted his AK47 onboard earlier. He blacked up Antonio and himself.
'Right Zimbo, let's go!'
'I'm not Zimbo.'
'Sorry, just my little joke,'
'You English are very strange people. How do you say it? Fucking mad,'
'First Ched, then Magnus and now you, I'm getting a complex about my sanity now.' They both smiled at each other; Albert knew the lad's adrenaline must be running high but Antonio showed no sign of nervousness.

2200 hours, and the black yacht was lowered into the water. No sail was hoisted; they just relied on steering it towards the stalker, following west of the Ark's wake. Albert worried that if the moon appeared and showed their silhouette, the stalker would know something was up. They edged closer and closer, drifting dangerously near. Albert could almost make out what was on the deck. He looked at the motor yacht's identification written on the bow and jotted it in his notebook. Revelation II was a good name for a boat, Albert thought. He returned his focus to the bow and the foredeck to see if there was any solid evidence of heavy weaponry. He could see the outline of machinery under covers, but nothing positive.

Then they were spotted and it was action stations on both sides! Albert had caught them napping and whereas he was calm, the opposition were panicking. Small arms fired indiscriminately at the silhouette. This is all I need, Albert thought, as he picked up the grenade launcher, aiming to the stern deck and fired. It landed right in the middle of his target. There was a flash followed by an explosion, a fraction of a second later, which sent debris into the air and lit up the area. The black yacht's sails were raised quickly to catch any favourable wind to take them away from the mayhem on the *ex* luxury motor yacht as panic ripped through its crew. They heard shouts and screams as they sped away from the scene and Albert could make out the dark outline of figures, jumping over the side. Antonio took the helm whilst Albert trimmed the sail before returning to the cockpit to join him.

'Wow that was a surprise for them.'

'Yes Antonio that's what it's all about; you hit them hard when they least expect it.'

'But what now Albert, we're going in the opposite direction to the Ark.'

'Put yourself in their shoes. If any of the Revelation crew is left onboard they are in deep shit and sailing nowhere. We have food, water, fuel, sails and I've nicked Gunter's GPS, he doesn't need it at the moment, but don't you tell him.' Their laughter brought a feeling of relief.

As they sped away they looked back at the diminishing flames on the motor yacht and Albert was concerned that he hadn't done enough damage.

'Antonio start the engine we're going back to take another look. I'll drop the sails,'

'But Magnus said we haven't much fuel.'

'Don't worry about it; let's finish the job we started, tonight.'

'But what about the noise of our engine now,'

'If there's anybody left on that boat, they're going to be more worried about us.'

Albert quickly dropped the sails while Antonio turned the black yacht around and put her under engine power. As they approached the stationary vessel, Albert donned his AK47 and wondered why Miles had agreed so easily to get him this piece of kit, but it was all speculation so he put all other thoughts aside and refocused. At the moment, I'm here, I'm armed with it and I will use it if I have to, he thought.

Suddenly, Antonio spotted sharks splashing about as if they were feeding… He whispered to Albert, pointing. Albert acknowledged them, thinking the cavalry had arrived to finish the job! He now had more confidence to board the vessel. Approaching the yacht from the stern, he went to the bow of the black yacht and was poised ready to board the smouldering stern deck. Albert took a rope to secure his exit and jumped to the rear bathing platform. Antonio had cut the engine and listened. He could hear movement in the water, splashes but no screams. His mind started to work overtime as Albert disappeared through the smoke that bellowed from the stern of the yacht. Albert, as always, stuck to his training when investigating, remembering the work he and his squad had done years before. Caution

253

was paramount, never think you have finished the job without checking; if you don't think that way, the job will finish you. Steadily he made his way to the bridge, ready to fire at anything that moved, going from side to side with his AK47. Then he crept to below decks as silently as he could. It was empty. It seemed as though they had all panicked and went overboard. This is too easy, he thought; there's something wrong. He continued to search below, through the cabins and then, as he opened the final door to the stern he came to a room which must have caught the down force of the blast. With the ceiling in tatters, lights and wires were dangling, but all around were rows of desks and computer stations and above them, each had a wall map of the world with operational information.

'Shit, I have upset things!' he said aloud. He turned and headed back, clambering onto the yacht where Antonio was eager for information.

'Well what did you find?'

'A major operation centre for some big organisation. I just hope it's the Russians and not the CIA! Come on let's get out of here.' They were soon away moving where the best breeze would take them. Albert plotted the route back to the Ark using the GPS and with the wind being in the direction it was, he realised they would have to do ten miles to travel five with a lot of tacking, changing the sail position to catch the wind to take them in a zigzag across their point of direction.

Albert hoped that when Gunter saw the firework display on the stalker, he had the sense to slow the Ark to a standstill. It wasn't long before they could see the navigation lights and the Ark's outline. It *had* slowed and was waiting for them. Dawn was showing its head over the horizon, when Jane, who should not have been, was on lookout, started jumping up and down, as she spotted the black yacht.

'I can see them! I can see them,' she shouted down the two way radio. They're coming back!'

Nobody had managed to get much sleep so far that night but it wasn't long before the lookout post was crowded. The black yacht was about two miles away from their home.

'Let's give it some power.' Albert said. 'I'm tired of all this tacking.' The engine was fired up and Albert lowered the sails as they steered a straight course home. As daylight became brighter and the yacht was getting close, the congregation moved to the lifeboat hoist that was used to lift the yacht in and out of the water. Magnus was at the controls, ready and waiting to snatch them from the sea. Jane waited with Alberto in her arms. Amy just wanted to see her man in one piece and she smiled when she could see he was. As they climbed from the yacht, once the lifting operation was complete, it was a joyous moment of hugs and kisses, then questions. They had all seen and heard the explosion and knew it was the stalker that was hit.

'What happened to the people on the boat?' Gunter asked.
'We were spotted and fired upon, so I launched a grenade into the rear of the boat, they all must have panicked and dived overboard. That's the last we heard of anything other than sharks splashing... I went onboard and searched the boat. There was no sign of life and the damage was minimal. We need to turn around and put the stalker in tow, strip what we want from it then sink it quickly.'

They all went to the canteen as the night raiders were hungry and Albert ordered a full English breakfast.
'Would you like any beans Albert? Or are you worried about the repercussions?' asked Patricia.
'I could tell you a story about the consequences of a battalion of men who had baked beans for breakfast before they went into battle, but my meal would be cold by the time I finished it, so, yes I will have baked beans today please Patricia.' She looked bemused.

It was an arduous task for the Ark to reach where the stricken vessel lay, to strip it, before sinking it. First, they wanted the computers and any other potentially useful arms and equipment, and to drain fuel from the tanks. The biggest problem was the need to keep stationary, to enable goods to be transferred to the Ark safely. Magnus worked extremely hard, logging everything and marking connections. Even Ched, as Albert commented, had pulled his finger out, but Ched was more worried about who might come looking for them next because, while they had this thing in tow, he considered himself a target. Albert was ecstatic when they transferred the arsenal. It was top technology, though some of it was way over Albert's head. He started to work out how to use items of this high tech stuff and realised that it was all computerised from a central unit. To use them he would somehow have to recreate the computer room he saw when searching the Revelation.

'Shit!' he said aloud, looking to see if he was heard and thought, I've been a fool in some ways not wanting anything to do with new technology, but no matter how you try to get away from it, it just follows you around, and I suppose I have been selfish as the Ark's younger generation will probably want to know about it, whereas I've wanted to be away from it.

Zimbo was helping move computer equipment to an area that Magnus had designated in one of the storage holds.
'I expect you're an expert at working one of those?' Albert asked facetiously.
'Yes of course, any fool can!' Albert then sought out Jane and asked her what computer skills she had.
'Extensive,' she replied. 'You don't work anywhere in the city, not even if you are a toilet attendant, if you're not computer literate.'
'I can do the basics but I'm no whiz kid at it,' replied Albert.
'Looking at all that kit coming onboard, if you plan to make any sense of it, you will need Melanie, Zimbo, Antonio and me to operate the computers once Magnus has set them up. They must have had one hell of a communication setup that's suddenly gone dead for them, so what will they be sending next, Albert?'
'Yes that's one thing I've thought about a lot today, and that's why we have to sink it, to get it out of sight, once we've taken what we want'

They were only a few days from their winter retreat and now the motor yacht's contents had been salvaged, it was down to Albert to sink it. He was undecided which way to tackle the task, because he now had a wide range of methods, like a child with new toys. He chose the tried and tested, old fashioned way: semtex, detonator and timer. It didn't take much to put the stalker to the bottom and, at the depth it was going, to almost four kilometres, Albert felt sure nobody would think about looking for it there. He knew it would take an extremely well organised unit to challenge them to recover the cash. Albert told the rest that time was on their side: the longer it takes, the less the cash is worth; as he expected that, as in other decades, world inflation was rising rapidly.

It took most of that day to turn around using engine power, before they could finally get under way to their winter home. The Ark slowly came to a standstill as Gunter guided them to the spot they had been twice before.

Gathering on the upper deck, the community looked around and all they could see was sea.

Melanie grabbed one of Albert's arms and Amy grabbed the other.
'You know you always told me Albert, that you never know what's over the horizon, well how about this?' Melanie winked at Amy.
'We're both pregnant!'